A Collecti

J. C. Martin, III

Dear Chris,

Thank you for the many enjoyable conversations we have enjoyed during the last few months - I appreciate the helpful commentary. Best wishes to all your successes!

Sincerely,

J. C. Martin III

Table of Contents

◆

Prologue

Hello, companion. Thank you for sharing the following text with me; I hope you find the stories entertaining. I am including a prologue with my first collection of tales. I am excited to present this set of stories as my first book. These are mostly bedtime stories that I have shared with others for a few years, now.

Ideas for stories are always endless; I like these stories for various personal reasons. A few ideas I came up with were from the past; those are purely fictional, too. The stories praise the notion of a short story - one can summarize a book-long tale and still entertain an audience with vividly portrayed characters, intriguing plots, and a usual climax.

I have endured an amazing amount of fun learning and recalling proper grammar for use with the following pages. I use mostly the active voice even when speaking of the past, and rarely do I permit colloquial phrases. I leave some of these notions out of dialogue so characters seem more realistic.

I hope you enjoy these stories - I have read them all many times. I include more information about the tales in the epilogue. Have a happy time reading!

♦

A Chess Game in the Park

Once upon a time, there was a young boy named Waldon. He enjoyed playing chess. His grandfather taught him how. They were playing chess in the park one day. Waldon's grandfather, Harold Grimsbury, said, "Your mother tells me you have been reading chess books from the school library and playing solitaire chess." "Yes sir," said young Waldon to his beloved grandfather. "It is nice today," said Harold, as he opened his box of chess pieces and lay out a chess board. "Yes sir," said Waldon again, as he helped his grandfather set up the chess board.

"So have the books advanced your understanding of the game of chess?" asked Harold. "Yes sir," said Waldon, "I have been studying various openings, mid-game tactics, end-game procedures, and sacrificial positioning strategies. One book that I am reading a second time includes moves called *gambits*. It was written by a world renowned chess master." "Wow," said Harold, "I hope these activities have not been distracting you from school." "They have not," said Waldon, honestly; he usually made decently competitive grades.

"I have found in my readings that most of the openings in famous games I have reviewed are very similar, and I imagine that gambits can be tricky," said Waldon. "Gambits?" asked Harold. "A 'gambit' is an opening strategy that uses the sacrifice of a piece in order to gain position. The tactic is named after a very famous chess player," said Waldon. "Wow," said Harold, "Have you come across the famous Russian player named Gary Kasparov?" "Yes sir," said Waldon, "I have even played out some of his recorded games." "Wow," said the boy's grandfather.

The two had finished setting up the chessboard, and Waldon asked, "May I have the white pieces, this game?" "Sure," said Harold, "I imagine you want them in order to try an opening?" "Yes sir," said Waldon, "I am working on a four-pawn gambit technique that just is not ever really that easy to do. It depends on the moves of the opponent." Seldom had Waldon won in a game of chess with his grandfather. Usually, Waldon only won after a long and drawn out battle involving winning back his queen. Waldon moved a pawn two spaces forward and the game was on. Harold Grimsbury tried not to gaze, as his own blood sat before him, in a ferocious and contemplative state of mind. Mr. Grimsbury thought of how quickly his life had occurred thus far - time had sure flown by.

The two chess players were not the only people in the small park. Various others, including old men playing dominoes, people walking their dogs, and a park attendant, where also there. About two dozen people were there, total. The day was beautiful. The sun bright, the sky was clear. The small park was half-circumvented by an intersection of two neighborhood roads. As the two chess players where making preliminary moves, the screeching tires of a four-door black sedan with darkly tinted windows came from a block away. The car was heading swiftly toward the park in such an alarming manner that it caught the attention of everyone there.

As the speeding vehicle came up adjacent to the park, the pedestrians began to get to the ground. Bullets rang out. Waldon managed to lie flat on the pavement below the table as he heard the rapid fire of automatic weaponry. Harold was not able to get to the ground before getting shot twice in the back and once in the side. There were others that were fatally wounded, as well. Waldon watched as the black sedan sped away. He was unable to make out the vehicle's license plate number. Harold had taken three bullets. Waldon picked up his grandfather, slightly, as the old man was losing blood. The man's body went pale, and Waldon closed his grandfather's eyes as tears ran down his cheeks. Paramedics would be on their way, but even the young boy could tell that his grandfather was no longer alive. What else could he do but cry?

Waldon looked up to see the others in the park. They were frantic; some had screamed at the sight of their injured loved ones. Others were on their phones calling for help. As Waldon had guessed, an ambulance came within minutes. Four lives were saved, and three were not. Waldon's grandfather died that day. Waldon's mother took him home from the park in melancholy. The random act of violence was on the news that evening. None of the pedestrians in the park were able to properly identify the black sedan or anyone in the vehicle. All that they where able to tell the authorities was that the guns were firing rapidly, and that the car was speeding.

The story was on the news the next day, as Waldon and his mother, Janice, ate breakfast together. In tears, Waldon apprehensively asked his mother, "So do you think grandpa Grimsbury is in heaven?" "Of course, honey," said Waldon's mother, crying slightly, "He is there because he was a devout Christian. If there is a heaven, and I believe that there is, I am sure he is there." "Thank you, mom," said Waldon. He was happily reassured to hear her comforting answer. Waldon himself did not really understand how upset he was, but he would soon be presented with a dilemma, none of the less. She then said, "The funeral is tomorrow, are you going to be okay at school, today?" "I will be fine," said young Waldon maturely, "Fridays are fun, and I think we are playing dodge ball in gym class." "That sounds like fun," said Janice, and they finished their breakfast.

School was fun that day for Waldon, even though he had a few things on his mind. He would always remember his grandfather for the times they had together and the things they shared. If nothing else, his grandfather had taught him the basics of chess, and even a few lessons on life. Waldon's father was an incredibly busy man, and Waldon sometimes learned more from his grandfather. Waldon's teacher and his friends in school where polite and considerate of his loss. They mourned together for a short time that morning. They prayed together for the victims in the park.

Waldon had fun during dodge ball that day. It was Friday, and he was released from school the same time as always. Before his mother returned from work on Fridays, he usually was home for an hour. His father, who also left for work very early in the morning, returned even later. They survived happily together.

Waldon rode his bike home that day, as always, yet he decided to swing by the park. Waldon did not intentionally hunt down the gangsters, he just wanted to scope out the area better. He rode around the park and saw nothing abnormal - no real indication of where the shiny black sedan may have sped off to. Waldon then decided to take the long way home. He still had a good half of an hour before his mother would be there. Not even four blocks from the park, much to his surprise, he saw the black sedan! Waldon flushed pale as he stopped his bike on the side walk. He was far enough away to be hidden mostly from view of the vehicle, and Waldon watched as it drove into a garage. The door open and closed automatically, like something Waldon had only seen in the movies. "The gangsters must have a lockup," thought Waldon, "And now I have found it."

Waldon continued to watch as he biked towards home. He then turned adjacent to their building's lockup to see four men in suits crossing the street on foot to a city transit station. There was no doubt in Waldon's mind. The car was the same car he saw while in the park with his grandfather, and those four men were responsible for the death of his grandfather and others. He biked home with his mind racing. What was he going to do? He made it back in plenty of time to bathe and await the return of his parents. The family slept well that night and attended Harold Grimsbury's funeral the next day.

The funeral was sad; many people mourned the loss of Waldon's grandfather. That night, Waldon went to bed on time as usual and in an appropriate manner. He set his watch alarm for 11 PM, though, because he had some things to figure out. Waldon's parents usually went off to bed around ten thirty, and he arose to check out his electronics. With a dimly lit nightlight, Waldon designed multiple devices. He knew he was not in a sane state of mind. He remembered a legal discussion between two adults concerning the two week holding period for guns. As he recalled, a statement on a human's mind was made dealing with legal insanity and how it can be considered to be a temporary thing. Waldon decided to wait for two weeks, starting three days after the drive by, before acting upon any form of a decision or plan, whatsoever.

For these reasons, Waldon decided to hold off on his construction of an explosive device of some sort. He spent most of the night trying to figure out what to do with the gangsters. He could tell adults, but that would possibly cause harm to innocent people. Waldon decided to wait two weeks, and then determine whether or not to notify the authorities. He supposed the authorities were already onto the bad guys, and the problem would be solved in no-time. Waldon went to sleep in a decent amount of time, knowing that he would need to have plenty of rest to keep an appropriate secret of sorts. He fell asleep with thoughts of the value of human life.

Waldon's two week time period seemed to fly by. He continued to do well in school. Waldon watched the news daily, either with his mother in the morning or with his father at 10 PM. Waldon made the dangerous decision to bike to a block away from the clandestine lockup two Fridays in a row. The four men where seen both times at precisely 2:30 PM. Waldon thought about it over the weekend, and decided to tell the authorities, somehow. After all, two weeks had gone by, and the gangsters where still at large.

Waldon jotted down a short note giving the address of the lockup and an accurate description of the black sedan. He kept the note and waited until Friday to deliver it to the authorities, anonymously. Waldon simply put the note in an envelope obtained from a gas station with lunch money, and taped it to an unattended police car at the local police station.

A few days went by, and nothing happened to the gangsters. Waldon was somewhat surprised. He would have to decide to let the guys go, or take matters into his own hands, somehow. A prodigy with a beginner's knowledge of small electrical devices, he could only think of one temptation - to go and see the veteran down the road from his parents.

The old man had retired from the military decades ago. He was a pyrotechnics expert who had made a living recently by blasting away pathways in hills and mountains for the highway department. The veteran's name was Howard Whirley. Howard was an acquaintance of Waldon's father.

After school, one day, Waldon asked and received permission to travel the neighborhood in search of a yard to mow. As he was allowed to do so,

Waldon went to speak with Mr. Whirley. Howard said he would be more than

happy to help Waldon out. Howard would pay Waldon for mowing the yard.

Waldon agreed to a payment and had an in-depth conversation with Howard

about explosives. Howard even allowed Waldon to read through some of his

journals on plastic explosives. Waldon asked to see Howard's side shop, and

Howard showed him various devices used for highway blasting. The current

method for these actions utilized a miniature form of c-4 that was a more

modern form of plastic technology. The small yellow sticks resembled yellow

highlighters. They were far more powerful than traditional c-4. Waldon

planned to activate the explosives with a special fuse-like wire. It would be all

the young man could justify.

That Saturday, Waldon went early and mowed Mr. Whirley's yard.

Howard was impressed with the yard and attempted to pay Waldon. Waldon

refused and asked for a very special and secret favor, instead. The risky

request was, of course, a dangerous move for Waldon, because Mr. Whirley

could have easily told Waldon's parents of his mischievous request. Waldon

would have had less chance of blowing up the gangsters, and he would sure

have been in a heap of trouble for a gargantuan electrical fire cracker. Howard

agreed to a big secret fire cracker, however, as Waldon promised to be very

careful with his experimental item.

Waldon obtained four small yellow sticks of plastic explosives. He then rode his bike home with the explosives in his backpack. For the next few days, Waldon spent time at night piecing together a remote with a button and a receiving device. The device incorporated an ignition fuse, so the explosives could be detonated remotely. Every Friday, on the way home from school, Waldon had seen the gangsters from a block away. This week, he had a dangerous and risky plan.

Waldon tested an explosive-free fuse with the remote on that Thursday afternoon, and it worked properly. Friday morning came, finally, and Waldon had slept well the night before. He reluctantly brought the explosives and his remote to school, keeping them safely in the bottom of his backpack. School went fine that day, and he biked swiftly toward the lockup. He would have a small amount of time to plant the yellow sticks, and he would have to do so in broad daylight. The task was easier than he thought it might be - no one was really watching as he approached the door of the lock-up.

His decision had been made the night before - these gangsters were *dead-men*. How was he going to do it? His only hope was to break into the lockup's automatic door. The task was not too difficult. He biked directly to the door and quickly pulled on the bottom. The door opened enough for Waldon to pull his bike in, and he closed the door behind him. He secured the sticks to the door, opened the door again, and pulled his bike outside. Waldon closed the door and biked away in silence. Across the street, he sat on a bench behind a sidewalk tree. Only one pedestrian was in sight. She was an older woman walking away from him two blocks away. Waldon checked his watch and it said two thirty three. He then checked the remote in his pocket and it was fine.

Suddenly, as suspected, the black sedan rounded the corner and the automatic door opened as it drove inside. Waldon watched the door close and pushed the button as he biked away. The explosion was very loud and blew out a portion of the building that the garage was housed in.

Waldon biked home and dismantled his remote. He smashed the remote with a hammer on street's pavement; he then went inside and broke the tiny pieces into smaller pieces with a pair of pliers; and, finally, Waldon flushed the small pieces down the toilet. He took a shower and relaxed, as his mother would be home any minute.

Waldon acted normal and awaited the evening news while doing his homework. As he thought it might be, the explosion was on the news. Waldon told his mom that the remains of the burning black sedan that could be seen on television highly resembled the black car he saw with his grandfather the tragic day he was playing chess with him in the park. Waldon's mother said the possible criminals probably had a problem with the gas tank in their car. The news reporter said that the explosion had caused four fatalities, and no one else was harmed. Waldon and his parents lived happily ever after.

◆

A Girl Named Nightingale

Once upon a time, long before currently known and recorded history, there was a beautiful girl named Nightingale. She was born from a hardworking farmer named Stron and his beautiful wife Maurine. The two fled their home village as adolescents due to a terrible winter storm and rumored town upheaval.

Stron and Maurine traveled east for nearly a year living off the land. They found a huge rock in the side of a mountain and built a log cabin into it. It was their first home. Their home's foundation was mounted aside a rocky mountain. Because of the large rock the house was built into, Stron and Maurine where able to delve out a small basement into the side of the mountain. They used their basement for preserving foods. They survived their first winter there. Years went by, and Stron proved to be a rather successful hunter and farmer. Maurine and Stron had their first baby. It was a boy. They named him Thor. It was not for a few years later that they had their baby girl previously mentioned. They named their new miracle Nightingale.

The family of four worked hard. They watched the seasons come and go like the continuous mornings of a week. They learned to make clothes and fashioned fine handmade musical instruments. They never really knew it, however they were vampires. They did not drink the blood of scared people. They commonly used the blood of their game to make a nice dressing for their vegetables, however. These practices kept them alive.

The vampires farmed vegetables on the east side of their mountain cabin. While they were still in their early years, Maurine became pregnant again. This, being her third baby, would be her last. Having engineered a nice rock bath from natural warm spring water on the west side of their mountain did not save her. As she was giving birth to her third child, the child died, and so did she. Their spirits where released as ghosts. They slept and woke for decades in various locals around the mountain, the cabin, and eventually the stone house. They spent their favorite times listening to Nightingale's poems she often whispered during nocturnal hours in their garden.

Their tragedy of passing was terribly sad for the other three in their family. What were the three sad vampires to do? They mourned heavily in black dress for three long days, and kept them in their memory. They spoke of all of the wonderful times that they had spent together as a family. Stron taught his son, Thor to hunt. Thor learned a great many techniques, and surprised his father by bringing back more animals than even Stron had, before. Thor became closer to nature, and he learned how to release his prey into the world of magical praise. The two strong men built an even larger house, with stone and mortar.

They turned the nearby stream into a source of running water for the new abode, and Nightingale never ceased to amaze them with her poetic verse and precious song. Now with less stress to survive and added time, the three where able to do some landscaping. They dug out a wonderfully huge mountainside garden with stone paths, carved sculptures, and polished stone benches.

Nightingale enjoyed singing to the men gently before they turned in at night. She adapted her gardening skills to many herbs of beauty and medicine, while continuing to grow the vegetables her mother had shown her to be good for healthy food. The three survived for years, having to work and hunt less and less, times were still rough and rigid, though easier.

For some time, the small family enjoyed happy times. Stron hardly went hunting, because Thor liked snapping the necks of anything inhuman - mainly elk and large bears. Thor had become quite the young and accomplished monster. The den in their large stone house contained a display of their most memorable trophy game. They kept the largest heads of the animals they killed. They also kept rare animals' heads. Stron and Thor used traps and fishing lines, however their preferred method of hunting was the throwing of properly sharpened spears. Taxidermy was their way of celebrating the hunt.

One morning, Stron woke long before the sun arose, with a natural desire to go hunting. He prepared for the hunt, took a favorite spear of his own making, and departed. Not too long after the sun arose, Stron spotted a young fleeing buck on a nearby mountain. He hiked long and hard to get to the buck. The nicely sized deer was having trouble getting away due to the thickness of the brush in the lower parts of the mountainside. Stron saw the perfect opportunity to come down on this buck and end him. Spear upright with perfect balance, Stron slid down the pebbly side of the mountain.

Little did he see, however, that there was a nine-foot tall cliff right below. The morning was foggy. The small cliff was a corner to a much larger, very high cliff, with the ground an unknown distance below. Stron fell airborne until he encountered a small broken tree trunk, about six inches in diameter, which impaled his right thigh. It might as well have been a four-foot tall fang with tightened roots. The buck escaped, and Stron hung upside down on the side of the mountain. He hung only by his leg. The sharp stump of an old tree pierced through it.

"Help!" hollered Stron, but he was miles away from home, and no soul was near. Stron was in great pain and losing blood. As his blood poured from the side of the mountain, he figured he could twist his leg off the stump and risk both the pain and a long cliff fall, well over hundreds of feet, to save his life. He now saw the rest of the cliff, with nothing but clouds and fog below. He tried to free himself and gave in due to the immense pain. Stron gathered the strength to try once more, and came only inches away from freeing his body, yet he collapsed due to loss of blood. He died only moments later.

During the same day, some time had passed. Thor had been hunting all morning, thinking Stron had been doing the same. During a lengthy return to the stone house, Thor found his deceased father hung on the cliff. Stron really was not too far from their large stone house, yet Thor was still surprised he found him. Thor figured his father had gone hunting. He found Stron lifeless on the side of the mountain, his favorite throwing spear lodged below him in the cliff. Thor and Nightingale gave their father a formal burial and cremation ceremony, as Stron had taught them these things in the passing of their mother, Maurine.

Distraught by his father's death, Thor decided to hunt even more. He did so. He brought home many kinds of fish and animals from various terrains nearby and far away for years. Nightingale had quite a collection of poetry, songs, and books by then. She composed many kinds of cooking recipes, stories, and poetry. She made her ink by mixing the blood of Thor's slayings and the boiled acids of selected vegetables. Most of her inks were black. She wrote and drew rarely with many other colors of ink, too.

Years went by and the two where getting along fine. They normally slept in separate rooms. They became very close. Thor and Nightingale became too close, eventually, and she ended up giving birth to twins. She named her precious babies Stron and Maurine, because one was a baby boy and the other a baby girl. "I miss mom and dad," thought Nightingale, "I will give these people the names they had."

The family slept soundly at night and continued to live life as the sun continued to rise. Thor was having a harder and harder time with his hunting, and he and Nightingale discovered methods of salting meat. This helped keep their happy family from starving, however times turned rougher quicker. Thor had to travel further and further for game, and he even found the old village. The village, over the course of time, had turned into a fully functioning town with a local economy and people of multiple occupations.

Thor remembered his bedtime stories Stron had told him regarding the village long ago. Stron had spoken of the older nomadic people. He told his children how they had settled into a village. Stron and Maurine had to leave because of a great big storm and social reasons. Thor did not know any of the townspeople.

The small town had a tavern. The tavern usually closed a few hours after midnight. One night, Thor realized that he had not brought home an animal for over five days. His family was hungry due to a diminishing supply of vegetables and fruit, and he had no choice known to him. He embarked on a completely new kind of venture.

Thor made his way to the tavern. Nightingale slept away peacefully under the pale full moon of the night, while Thor cloaked himself in black and traveled to the village. He quietly made his way to the tavern, unseen, and saw the last patron stumble out as the owner locked the front door.

Thor was upon his victim in no time, snapping his neck and carrying him back into the darker side of the dark night's woods. The night was lit well for him by the moon. Highly skilled in taking the life of any animal, the victim was of no challenge for Thor. He brought the sot back to the stone house, and processed him as he would any normal animal. They cleaned their animals for meat. They used the remains for cremation and other purposes.

Though Thor saw his actions as necessary for survival, his family could never know - they would not understand. He processed his man in such a manner that all that was left resembled elk sausage. He worked quickly and was through long before daylight. He returned to bed and slept soundly until the morning. "I dare say to you, Thor, what sausage is this?" asked Nightingale as the sun was rising and Thor was sleeping. She happily shook the foot long sausage above Thor's squinting eyes. Thor said, "It was a spotted elk. I found it in the night. I am currently tracking a heard of them." He then slept a few more hours as Nightingale cooked a nice breakfast. She would never know his secret, and their hungry souls would not suffer the fear of starvation for some time.

Time went by, and the population of the town increased. Thor and Nightingale raised Stron and Maurine with strict principles and learned skills including magic and survival. The twins, Stron and Maurine, could speak every other word of a sentence they were speaking together, taking turns so that their sentences were understandable. The twins always kept secrets secret. The family of four stayed away from the village for good. Nightingale sang her precious words on the whispers of the wind in the night, as she loved their mountain's garden of stones and luscious delights. Thor hunted mostly

animals, mostly, and the vampires, humans, and animals all lived happily ever
after.

♦

A Night on the Floor

Once upon a time, a young boy's family moved to a new neighborhood. He did not have too many companions, so his mother took a walk around the neighborhood with him to meet other children. They met many people, and he befriended a boy about his same age a couple of blocks down the street.

One weekend, the young boy and his new friend decided to spend the night together. Their parents let them, and they decided to stay in the new friend's house. They played in the backyard and caught dragonflies for fun. Of course, they let the shiny little creatures back into freedom, and time had flown by. Night was falling, and the new friend's mother called them in for dinner. Upon having dinner and conversation, the boy learned from his new friend's mom that she had a twin sister and was afraid of heights. He also learned that the father was a rather thrifty man.

Once everyone was through with dinner, the mother instructed the boys to shower and to go off to bed. Once clean, the boys tucked their selves in. The new friend lay in his normal bed, and the boy lay down in a comfortable sleeping bag on the floor. His new friend and the parents fell fast asleep. The boy closed his eyes, concluded a prayer, saying "Amen" in his mind, and awaited sleep.

No sleep came for the boy. Because he could not sleep, the boy opened his eyes and gazed through the crack in the door. The door only let in a faint amount of light, so the boy opened it gently attempting to prevent any noise. Gently as he opened it, the door still made a scary creaking noise. The noise was rather loud in the dead silence of the night. No one woke or stirred, so he opened the door enough to peer into the hallway. The door creaked and popped until it was half open. It was then silent. He gazed into the hallway to see tall shadows cast from the hallway light, with no light whatsoever coming from outside of the house.

There was nothing to do; the boy could not sleep. The faint ticking sounds of the grandfather clock in the living room clicked and rung like a symphony of bones. The faint ticking sound occurred in rhythmic clarity. "Obviously," thought the boy as he decided what the ticking sound was, "That is a grandfather clock." The minutes went by and the innocent boy tried as he could to sleep. The clock rang a chime. The chime echoed deep in the hallway, like the bellowing sound of Father Time edging his way into the silence of the dark, dead night. "Ah," thought the boy, "Maybe now I can get some sleep..." He rolled over and closed his eyes. He awaited sleep, again. The sound of the clock continued on, like a relentless metronome. He opened his eyes; the shadows stood tall in the hallway, and the ticking did not cease. Instead of letting the time pass to the repetitive ticking and chiming of the clock, the boy allowed the sounds to drive him partially insane- what torture! After some time, the clock rang once more. The boy decided to go and see how much time had gone by, wondering if the chime was hourly.

Making as little noise as possible, he silently crept through the house. The doorway was little problem, for he had opened it earlier. He passed right through. He would certainly be in trouble if anyone were to wake up. He silently made his way toward the sounds of the clock, passing through the shadows, the hallway light, and into the even darker, dimly existing den. The only light in the entire structure of the house came from the hall light in the epicenter of the structure.

He found the clock in close to absolute darkness, however he could make out the various forms of artwork on the clock, and wondered about the various chains and weights on the inside of the clock, able to be seen through the glass door. Considering his usual bedtime to be slightly before nine, he could tell that the clock rung on the quarter hour. He looked over his shoulder, sensing some form of paranormal activity.

"No big deal," he thought. The curious boy really had no reason to be afraid of ghosts - he thought he might have seen them before. So as he peered over his shoulder, he could not decide if what he saw was something other than a faint glimpse of his own imagination or not. At any rate, he watched as shining spirits in faint hues of pastel color went from the kitchen to the dinner table and back, exchanging small items and remaining in loving conversation while passing through the shadows. Where they ghosts? Were they figments of his imagination? Who knew?

"Dong!" went the clock all of the sudden. The boy having no idea what it was at first, figured another quarter hour had passed, so he decided to make it back to bed. He walked back to the room, step by step, in silent success. As the ticking sounds and chimes of the clock passed the time, the boy lay on the floor staring at the wall in boredom-induced terror. Midnight being the most musical, the boy noticed the hourly chimes rung in a number consistent with the hour they were ringing for. The shadows did not move, and the boy never slept - not that he could notice.

Tossing and turning, the boy endured the ticking and chimes of the grandfather clock. He stretched and relaxed. The boy noticed a bobcat on the window seal behind him. The cat had been there the whole while. Gaining insomnia induced curiosity, the curious young boy decided to go and explore the various parts of the house. He was, by then, scared out of his mind. He rose from the floor, went through the doorway again, and began to explore various parts of the house. The front den did not seem to be to overly interesting, yet still full of shadows. The kitchen and back den seemed to be spooky, too, yet he decided to walk past the large and well-made grandfather clock towards the room of the parents. He could hear the father snoring softly through the door. "Maybe my new friend's mother is awake and reading," thought the boy. "Maybe she will read me off to bed," he thought.

He gently grasped and turned the doorknob to open the door just enough to peer inside. As he guessed, the father figure was sleeping, deeply. The mother, however, seemed to be overly quite. He walked to the other side of the room. Even the clock seemed to be overly quite, now. She was lying peacefully on her back, with her eyes closed.

"Well," he thought, "She certainly is not reading a book." He then left the room in silence, successfully closing the door without making a noise, and returned to the sleeping bag on the floor. Gazing through the doorway, again, the shadows had not moved, and the clock continued with its various ticks and musical chimes. Time was going by, chime after chime. The boy remembered that the clock's hourly chime rung a number consistent with the hour. Three four and five o'clock had rung by now, and he eventually heard the clock chime six times.

He lay resting in the dark dead night, staring at the wall from the floor. As the clock rang the second quarterly chime for the hour, the boy noticed a slight gradual change in the hue of the shadows. It was a faint and dim shade of sky blue. The boy arose to go check the back window, or rather, the large glass doorway to the backyard. The sun was rising - its distant light glistening and sparkling shined through the new-fallen dew atop the various flower beds and parts of the lawn in the backyard.

As the boy was appreciating the esthetic value of the yard just before dawn, he forgot he was not in the room he belonged in for the evening. "Bethel," the boy heard coming from behind a closed door down the hallway. Scared, the boy realized the sound was coming from the parents' room! He scurried quickly and quietly back to the proper room, trying not to make any noise as he ran. He made it through the doorway and quickly got into the sleeping bag while pulling the door to. He acted as though he were sleeping.

"Bethel," the father figure said again behind the well-closed door across the hall, with seriousness and a deeper tone. "She must be sleeping rather soundly," thought the boy, as he calmed his pants and took a deep, relaxing breath. He was relieved to have not been caught walking around in the shadows of the night.

"Bethel?" the man's voice asked again, in surprised curiosity, yet there was no answer. The boy heard the man pick up the phone and call for help. The paramedics came and went through their normal procedure of attempting to revive or save a human's life. The young boy was silently hoping behind the door that she was alive or could be resuscitated.

Never having left the room during this time, the boy watched the floor as the shadows were changing a great deal. Someone or something else was coming, someone much more quiet than a group of paramedics. The boy continued to watch as he saw large, shiny black shoes passing the doorway. He then heard the voice of the tall figure casting the long shadows say, "I am sorry. She has passed."

♦

Beautiful Amy

Once upon a Christmastime, there was a happy Christmas Eve's after-party. A seemingly pleasant group of evening party goers stayed up later than usual to play cards together. Of course, various youngsters were acting up and asked to go off to bed. Only attending adults with known ability to control their alcohol were drinking. They consumed their own beer, wine, and liquor.

A beautiful woman named Amy and her significant other, Samuel Stone, were drinking lightly. Everyone had a ball. It was a fun time, and the treasured memory of the get together will remain in the minds of the attendees as long as they can keep it.

The next Christmas came, and the same get together did not occur, and neither would it, in all probability, ever occur again. During the year, one of the card players of the after party asked her grandmother if her uncle's friend Amy and her significant other where okay. Many thought Amy and her husband to be a lovely couple. The grandmother said, "No, sweetheart. Amy has cancer. When her man found out, he left her." "Really?" asked the after party attendee, named Misty, "Is Amy really terminally ill?" "Yes," said the wise woman, "The doctors say she has about three years to live."

Upon hearing this, Misty was confused. Her grandmother recently told her that this grown man, fully competent in the working world and seemingly honest, left his wife due to her being terminally ill. "Is not that the one time to stay with your wife?" thought Misty. "It is," she decided. "I am going find him," thought Misty.

She thought long and hard about it. This did not call for some elaborate plan. No, this called for a swift lesson. Months went by and Misty remained deep in thought, as she carried out her casual and normal everyday tasks and duties. "I know where he works," Misty thought, "I know what city, and I know his name. How will I find him?" she wondered.

Misty had some time one weekend, so she went to check out the corporate office of the man's company in a city in her neighboring state. "All I need is some information," she thought, "I hope things do not get too bad or surprising. I would prefer not to have to risk doing this deed by hand."

The day was a Saturday. Misty walked in the front doors of the huge corporate building. It housed lots of people and documents. The sky scraper was known as Corporate Tower. In the foyer area she noticed the shiny buffed floors. The elevator music playing played a song titled "Crystal Sensation" softly in the background. To her right was a desk attendant. The attendant was turning the pages of a fashion magazine, as she spoke on a phone mounted on her right ear.

Misty found a board on the wall with interesting pictures of corporate overachievers and various facts on events and information about the company of the Amy's husband for all to see. Misty's soon to be victim was a shining star! His picture was already in bronze and framed. "Well that is nice," thought Misty.

Suddenly, Misty smelled a smell she just preferred not to smell from time to time - alcohol. Without forgetting how much could happen, she turned gently to find the person responsible. It was a woman, looking at the board. "Are you alright?" Misty asked. "I am fine," said the women. The well dressed women and Misty engaged in conversation without too much wonder on the intoxicated woman's part as to why Misty was even there.

The woman was Mr. Stone's secretary. Misty asked the secretary about the man nonchalantly. Due to the secretary's inebriation, she was not too difficult to converse with. The secretary said that he was going to the corporate Christmas party this year without question. He would be attending a promotion celebration.

Misty's egress went unknown by the lady reading a periodical, and her travel home that day was safe and full of calming and peaceful thought. Christmas was in a month or two. During this time, Misty obtained all she needed, information wise, from a public access computer off the internet.

The party was on the top floor of an old electric company's building. There was a web address for the party. Having no problem doing so and being surprised that she could, Misty even went inside of this building and scoped out the floor and the various means of escape. "It almost looks too easy," she thought, as she returned home for a good nights sleep that day.

Christmas Eve came. Misty made her departure with a full tank of gas, a mask, and a murder weapon - the neighbors' machete. She left in plenty

of time. Misty even left in order to arrive during the highlight of the party.

She timed her arrival nicely. Misty thought to herself, "I will park on the

darker side of the tower, three blocks away. I will take the stairs up and down

with the mask on; my hair covers most of it. I will not take long; I do not have

too much to lose. Amy deserved more for these last few years - more than

some man without the cohunes to at least stay by her side."

Misty parked well. Mask in tact and machete hidden in hilt properly

under her business dress, she took her time in walking to the tower's side

entrance. Nothing was locked. Misty found the stairs with ease, and walked

all the way up to the forty-second floor. Ready for anything, she was so

energized that she could barely see. Misty kept moving towards the door to the

party. By the time she was closer to the closed door, she was jogging. There

were no people by the door. All Misty saw was a small sign which included

party information. She opened the door in her calculating state of mind while

jogging.

Misty immediately identified Samuel. He was laughing as he poured

himself a spiked glass of fruit punch from a large bowl. She took half a dozen

steps towards him as people in the room began to notice her. Misty increased

her speed. He had the time to look her way, but this did nothing but line his

head up just right. She drew her shining machete and brought it down with

enough force to completely slice his neck, and his erstwhile head fell into the large punch bowl like a volleyball in a public pool.

Misty's bloody act of violence and been performed, and she kept in motion. Misty ran to the door on the other side of the room. Just as she planned, she was out of the party-room before people could really react and chase her down. Misty went to floor forty-one by the stairs. To be safe, she crossed the floor to get to the other side of the tower. Misty then fled down the adjacent stairway.

She left the building in a dead sprint and slowed to a casual jog for a block or two to get into her vehicle. Misty's path of travel bending with every curve, she drove swiftly. One right angle turn after another led to busier and wider roads, until Misty found herself keeping her speed with a pack of traffic on the interstate highway. Misty drove home, cleaned and returned the neighbors' machete, and went off to bed. She lived a long and healthy life. Misty died four days before she turned 87, no one ever knew that she had taken life.

◆

Chemorphosis

One time, there was a young woman named Mary Lowery. She slept. She arose. By the age of twenty-four, she knew more about science than most people ever really figure. Her life was already exciting, even before her peculiar incidental occurrences. Mary grew up in the middle class of America. Upon being graduated from high school, she was not really sure what she wanted to study in life. She also did not really know if she would be successful in the sciences. Mary decided to apply for acceptance into a two-year degree program to learn about business.

The program accepted her, and she graduated with A's and B's. Upon completion of her studies, she could have stayed in school to attain a bachelor's degree or she could have tried to go to work. What she thought she may have really wanted to do was to study chemistry more, yet she found a job while searching and learning of various degree programs around the country. She accepted the job of secretary's assistant at a contracting laboratory that designed and researched various pharmaceuticals for the top five big name pill companies in America. Mary's idea was to work there for a while, as she decided on whether or not to pursue the arduous, time consuming, and sacrificial path of a pre-med student.

Our story unfolds as we enjoy conversation between Mary and the chief operator and sole proprietor of her laboratory on a beautiful Saturday morning. "Thank you for coming in this morning, Mary," said Dr. John Griswald, a man with a p. h. d. in Chemistry. "No problem," said Mary, "You know how excited I always am to help you out in the laboratory. I also enjoy answering the phone and helping with business in the office."

Mary rarely ventured into the actual laboratory of the private facility. She may have gone in there a dozen times during that last year. Dr. Griswald had retired from a pharmaceuticals company about four years ago. Since retirement, he had enjoyed various new experiments. He had even employed a slew of young scientists for research purposes. His team consisted of brilliant candidates from around the country. They each had various degrees and were considered by the academic community to have been brilliant scholars.

Dr. Griswald always required Mary to wear full body protection when in the laboratory. This was because of the humorous idea that her name sounded like the infamous Madam Curry. Ms. Curry was a woman who walked out of a laboratory glowing green after discovering a new element not found on the periodic table. There was also a legitimate reason for Mary to wear her p. p. e. (proper protective equipment) - *bio-chem* studies.

"I know you are working on something exciting," said Mary. "In just these past few months, alone, I have seen you develop new and unique pharmaceuticals. You increased our sales by over 200% on an international level with your various marketing techniques and patents. We are in league with the top five pharmaceutical companies in the world, and you normally handle your various successes as if they were nothing other than common achievements. To see you excited, and if I may say so, to see you *obsessed* with something, is intriguing indeed."

The patient doctor was waiting for young Mary to finish, as he recalled admitting to giving her the job of his chemical marketing company's secretary, in part, due to her high scores in her applied chemistry and sciences classes. She was also able to easily discuss various topics without much preparation for their interview. "I know you know I have enjoyed helping you with cleaning flasks and solving stoichiometric equations from time to time," continued Mary, "You have even told me that some of my solutions and deductions were impressive ~~from time to time~~. I have thought of these things as thought provocative puzzles," said Mary.

"Mary," said Dr. Griswald, "You are a rarity in the world of genius. I just wanted you to hear me say so." "Well," said Mary, "Thank you, Dr. Griswald." "So," she said, trying to get to the point without peeing in her pants, even though she did not necessarily need to go to the restroom during the time, "Are we here today to further your biological matter change experiments? I remember you saying that with no conclusive evidence, you would have at least proven some of your theories as inconclusive or, rather, impossible." "Yes, Mary," said the Dr., wondering of the unknown ethical drawbacks that could only be on the horizon in theory, "That is precisely why you are here with me today. My team of research scientists have been on this project for weeks now, due to various findings that we have proven. Humans consist of water and various things besides that, and there exists in this world male and female creatures."

"Right!" exclaimed Mary, "I remember you saying that a few weeks ago. You were considering the ethics behind a possible sex change project. Is that what all of this 'side study' has been for? Have you found any evidence to support those possibilities?" "Yes," said Dr. Griswald, "We have labeled and documented just enough data proving that, with a single tiny pill of pressed starch and designed pharmaceuticals, we can successfully add a cocktail of various acids and growth hormones that, when taken, depending on which side of the bilateral experiment the pill comes from, will change the sex of an adult, physically. With no pain, in the amount of time it takes for the average human's hair to grow only a fraction of a centimeter, this person would have a new gender."

"So we will, in theory, be able to change a person's gender with a pill in about two weeks?" asked Mary. "Precisely," said the doctor, "My team and

I have our research summarized in these binders, and on this computer. We have proven reactions and data," informed the doctor. "We have not yet solved this enigma. It is nothing more than a large pile of children's building blocks, waiting for assembly into a miniature toy mansion."

"Splendid," said Mary, perfectly happy to help. She agreed to help her company with close to no regard to her own ethical considerations. "You mean I have full access to these findings?" "Not only that," said Dr. Griswald, "I have also doubled your income for the next year, as I know you are still considering furthering your education. You will only be required to work a minimum of thirty hours a week, here." "Amazing," said Mary, "Thank you, Dr. Griswald."

Mary then inquired, "So, if I complete both sides of this experiment successfully... " "Of course," interjected the doctor, only partially knowing what Mary was about to ask, "Are you inquiring about counseling?" "Yes," answered Mary. "Yes, we will require counseling," began the doctor, "Any company that makes these prescriptions available will require extensive patient consultation. Upon taking the medication, patients will also be monitored for weeks by a team of randomly selected doctors and nurses from all over America. A new team for every patient will be required. Various checkups will also be highly recommended, as the pills will be new on the market, no matter how much testing we conduct."

"These statements must all be preliminary dreams," said Mary, as she waited for any indication of the doctor's opinion on the matter. "That is accurate," said Dr. Griswald, "We, in a sense, do not want to count our chickens before our eggs hatch. I do believe, however, that we have a great many *eggs* here in our findings. This means that it is worth our time to satisfy these certain curious notions." "I am impressed. We will make history," said Mary. "Yes," said the doctor, "We will make history in a whole new way." "May I begin now?" asked Mary. "Of course," said the doctor, "Our findings and the entire laboratory are yours to play with."

With that, young Mary dove into their notebooks. She referenced the various indexes throughout the day, mixing chemicals and documenting which chemical reactions canceled chemicals out and which reactions caused flesh and other biological chemicals to occur from existing sources. She made amazing progress, adding her findings to the computer as she went along. Most of the work for this project was complete, already, and the information was on the computer. She worked well into the night. In a matter of hours, she had two final test tubes full of liquid. One would change a man into a woman, and the other would do the exact opposite.

Because Mary had documented procedures and findings, she also wrote out a simple procedure for mixing chemicals and performing reactions. There was no reason to keep the actual final product, as it was in liquid form.

Mary had solved a bilateral puzzle that may have taken the chemistry team months to complete, though they were near its completion. Mary was exhausted. She meant to dispose of the test tubes and return home before sunrise. She had been drinking water from a beaker most of the night as she was working. She poured both test tubes into a beaker and put away the notebooks, including her new journals, and tidied up the laboratory. She then poured her beaker of drinking water out into a sink, thinking that she had disposed of the final product of her experiment. Finally, she drank down the experiment, thinking it was her drinking water! She returned home safely for slumber, without realizing her crazy action of consumption.

Mary slept in soundly that Sunday, as she dreamt of her findings. The pills would be able to change the sex of a person in a matter of an hour or so - not in two weeks of time. She thought of this while in deep slumber.

Mary awoke in the afternoon. She went to freshen up in the bathroom. She was about to call Dr. Griswald and let him know that the puzzle was already solved. Upon getting out of bed, she noticed that she was sporting the package of a man! Mary went to her phone and saw that there was a message on the machine. It was a quick message from Dr. Griswald asking her to come to the lab to help process the liquid success story into pill form. He congratulated her on her historical achievement. Mary called Dr. Griswald with the touch of a speed dial button. Before the doctor could speak, she said,

"Dr. Griswald, we have a problem."

"A problem?" asked the doctor. "Yes," said Mary, not noticing that her voice was deeper than normal. "I woke up just now with the genitalia of a man," she continued, "I mixed the two final test tubes in a beaker similar to the one I was drinking water from. I must have accidentally consumed the experiment; I thought I disposed of it properly. I must have poured out my drinking water. The experiment would have tasted similar." "Come to the lab immediately," said the doctor, "I am going to assemble a secret emergency team of colleagues." Mary trusted the doctor. She gave herself one last self-examination and went to see him.

Various doctors and nurses welcomed Mary upon her arrival. The medical team gave Mary a complete examination. She was perfectly healthy, at least physically. "We have agreed not to let this incident go public," advised Dr. Griswald, wondering if Mary would have anything to say. "No problem," said Mary. "Will I still be able to work for you this year?" she asked. "Of course," said Dr. Griswald. "Our grunt work with these pills can wait until the morning. Go and get some more rest," he said happily, almost shocked that she was completely okay. Both individuals considered her to be a woman, no matter what her body was made of.

Mary went home and went to bed. She did not really want to let herself know that she was a man, not yet. She would get counseling for that as needed. She slept soundly, possibly without even a single memorable dream. As it often does, the sun came up, again. Mary actually woke up excited, thinking that she was going to play around with her genitalia in full morning fruition. Upon checking herself out, however, she found that she was again a woman, just as before. "Maybe it was just a dream," she thought. "I am not even going to call the doctor," said Mary, and she drove to work.

Upon walking in early, she sat at her desk. She organized some paperwork and buzzed Dr. Griswald on the desk phone. "Dr. Griswald," began Mary, and the doctor said, "Mary!" "More news," said Mary, "I am completely back to normal... I am, again, a woman." The doctor rushed into her office in pure surprised curiosity. You are back to normal?" inquired the doctor. "Yes, Dr. Griswald," replied Mary. "My voice, my genitalia, and even what excuse I have had before known as breasts are all back to normal. I am also perfectly alright." "Maybe we should go through the physical exams, again," said the doctor, as he thought aloud. "If it is okay with you, let us just wait until I have a legitimate reason before we do more testing," said Mary.

The doctor actually agreed to that, as he trusted Mary's intelligible thought. It was a sort of end to certain conversations on Mary's gender. They both agreed to keep these occurrences secret from the knowledge of the medical community and the public. Mary went to bed that night, thinking that these crazy biological reactions would not happen anymore.

The sun came up again, however, and upon checking under the covers, Mary found that she was a man! Poor Mary did not know what to think. "I am not even going to tell the doctor," she thought to herself, though she knew he would hear her voice. She went into work that day, and she told Dr. Griswald the truth. They worked out a plan. If this were to continue to occur every day, she would simply work in the lab on the days that she was a man. She would help develop easier and less psychologically dangerous pharmaceuticals such as vitamins and other dietary supplements. As a woman, Mary would answer the phone and help with the business side of the company.

The two got along just fine. Mary had a newly changed body every morning. They successfully released their sex change pills within the completion of the same year. Dr. Griswald and Mary fell in love. They got married on one the days in which she was a female, and they lived happily ever after.

◆

Catfish Lake

Once upon a time, in the northwestern part of Texas, there existed a
happy and successful American family known as the Sugarcanes. They ran a
sugarcane farm and had done so for many generations. In this family there was
a seven-year-old girl named Callahn. *Callahn* is similar to the name of a
common white and yellow lily. She lived in a large farmhouse with many
people. These people were her mother and her father, her father's parents, her
aunt's family, and her uncle's family.

Together, the Sugarcane family ran their farm on a vast amount of
property. Within their property existed a very prodigious natural lake. An old
river fed into and out of part of the perimeter of the lake, allowing it to be a
habitat for many monstrous catfish. Biologists and geologists from universities
had come to the lake from time to time for scientific study.

They ascertained that the lake had existed for well over two hundred
years, so the fish and wildlife had many years to develop into their matured
ecosystem. Large catfish were common in the lake, so the Sugarcane family
named their lake Catfish Lake. They caught catfish in their lake all the time;
some of the catfish where well over two hundred pounds!

One morning, well before sunrise, Callahn woke up to go fishing with
her father. She hurried into his room to wake him. "Daddy," said Callahn
softly as she shook him gently, "Are we not going fishing, today?" Walter

Sugarcane rolled over to look at his clock and said, "Yes, sweetheart. We are

going fishing today. Go and get ready, and I will make us both some

breakfast." Walter woke up and cooked them bacon-egg-and-cheese biscuits.

As the sun would be up in half an hour, the two anglers departed hand in hand.

   The day was going to be a beautiful day. Callahn loved her father for

good reason. Walter was a part of a hard working Christian family. Farming

large plots of sugarcane and maintaining livestock was not always easy.

"Daddy?" asked Callahn as they were walking. "Yes, Callahn?" asked Walter.

"Is it true that the sun always rises in the east?" she asked. "Yes, sweetheart,"

said Walter, in absolute admiration of his daughter, "We are headed due east,

now. Judging by the shadows glowing in the morning dew, we will reach the

canoe just as the sun's brim is peeping over Catfish Lake." "Wow," said

Callahn, "How far out into the lake are we going?"

   "Well, sweetheart, we usually fish the moss beds in more active

current close to the river. Today, however, we are going to the shallow beds on

the north side of Catfish Lake to see what we can find there. I have been

deciding upon a good place to fish all week. We are going to try and catch a

big one today." "Yay!" exclaimed Callahn enthusiastically, "We are going to

catch ourselves a big ol' catfish!"

   They walked quickly for twenty minutes or so with their fishing

equipment. The two found their old canoe. The canoe was handcrafted from

wood for two adult passengers, equipped with side handles and very sturdy, indeed. As they entered the canoe, the sun rose above the horizon. The sky showed various beautiful hues of purple and gray, as rays of brilliant and golden yellow-orange colors shown through. Walter and Callahn had timed the sunrise precisely. Daybreak was usually the best time for fishing.

They paddled for nearly an hour to get to the moss beds Walter had in mind. A prodigious natural lake, many parts of the lake were deep. The area Walter and Callahn had found was only about waste deep to Walter. Walter was above average in height for most men. As the canoe slowed down, Callahn noticed activity on the surface of the water about thirty yards away. "Daddy look!" whispered Callahn, as she pointed out the activity with excitement. There was activity surrounding a large old tree that had fallen down into the lake.

"I will get us closer," whispered Walter, as he paddled the canoe up to the old tree. The tree must have fallen long ago in a big storm. Its huge hollow trunk barely broke the surface of the water and provided a natural habitat for a dark green form of algae. As they approached the tree in an effort to promote absolute silence, they both saw a six-foot long catfish swim inside of it.

Callahn was speechless, but she knew what to do. She was no beginner. She quickly tied a small fish to a string with a weight and sunk the bait down to the center of the mouth of the trunk of the big tree. Walter and Callahn waited in silence. Good fisherman, they had concluded before, made little to no noise.

Only a few moments later, the monster catfish swam over and swallowed the small fish on Callahn's line. She pulled the rope back tight, and Walter dove in and grabbed the massive catfish. He was careful not to let the beast's colossal dorsal fin injure him. A catfish's dorsal fin of this size could certainly wound a man. The spikes in the fin where longer than Walter's feet. He blocked a spiky jest from the monster with his forearm, and muscled the fish into the canoe. "We caught him!" exclaimed Walter, and Callahn helped him tie down the enormous catfish to the rails of the canoe. "Wow daddy!" said Callahn, "That is the biggest catfish that I have ever seen!" "Me, too," said Walter, and they finished hog-tying the gigantic catfish.

As they began to paddle back, Callahn said, "This is a channel cat, too, right Daddy?" "Yes," said Walter, "Everyone will be amazed back home. You can tell that it is a channel cat due to his darkened blue back and white belly. As I have said before, these fish taste much better than the yellow-back or mud-cat catfish we catch more commonly." Callahn watched in amazement as the big fish shook the canoe trying unsuccessfully to free itself. "You said, before, that the blue-cat catfish taste better because of their diet. Is that true?" asked Callahn. "Yes, sweetheart," said Walter, "From what I gather, the channel cats, like this one, live off of small fish and berries. The yellow-belly or mud cats live off of algae in the muddy water they swallow off of the lake bottom."

Walter and Callahn paddled back to the shore of the lake. By then, the sun was shining bright in the middle of the morning. "Daddy, how are we going to get this monster back to the house?" asked Callahn. She had been trying to figure that out since they began paddling back and finally decided to ask him. "Very carefully," said Walter, "I will grab him behind his head, carrying most of the weight, and you can carry his tail." The fish had ceased to struggle as much, so they did not have too much of a problem carrying him that way.

The fish was big and heavy, but the two managed to carry him all the way to the porch. Callahn saw her grandmother and said, "Grandma Sugarcane, look at this big channel cat we just wrestled!" The family in the house had been up for some time. Callahn's grandmother hollered to the rest of the family saying, "You all come out and see this big catfish Walter and Callahn just caught!" Everyone came outside, and they all agreed that the colossal fish was amazing, indeed.

"Now what?" asked Callahn, as she wondered how they were going to clean the huge fish. Walter said, "Go to the tool shed, and get my machete. Tank and I will meet you at the oak stump." Callahn left to attain the sharp machete. The rest of her family, short Tank and her father, went back inside. Tank was her father's brother. Walter and Tank carried the huge channel cat to an old oak stump on the side of the Sugarcane family's large farmhouse. They commonly used the huge stump as a chopping block and for playing "outside games." They watched the fish breathe on top of the stump, as they waited for Callahn to join them. She finally did, saying, "Daddy, Grandpa and I could not find your machete, so he gave me this to bring to you." Callahn handed him her grandfather's old Katana. It was a long Japanese sword that Grandpa Sugarcane had brought back from overseas during his time in the military.

Tank held the fish down on the stump, right behind its gills, and Callahn held fast his tail. At this time, Walter drew the sword, gripped the weapon with both of his hands, and came down upon the colossal monster, decapitating him in one powerful stroke.

Callahn and tank handled the catfish's body as it wiggled and eventually ceased to move. They then filleted the fish and cooked it over a fire for the family to eat that evening. Grandpa Sugarcane, as Callahn called him, froze the beast's head to bring to show his confidants he knew at a barbershop in town. He was proud of its catch.

Weeks went by, and operations continued as normal around the Sugarcane family's property. "The meteorologist said a very large and dangerous storm with possible tornadoes is headed our way," said Grandma Sugarcane to Callahn one morning. She and Callahn enjoyed waking up early to cook breakfast. "How bad of a storm is it, really?" asked Callahn. "Well," said her grandmother, "It must be pretty bad, because your grandfather said we are boarding up the house, today. I will have to get out the candles in case the power goes out."

The Sugarcane family boarded up their windows that day. They knew to do so, but they did not know how bad the storm was going to be. The big storm terrorized their property. Only one tornado touched down, but it was so huge that it completely sucked all of the water out of their prodigious natural lake. Only dead catfish lie in the dried-up lake. Debris was scattered, everywhere. People in the house were safe. The Sugarcane family was only without electrical power for about four days or so.

Once the storm had passed, Walter, Tank, and Grandpa Sugarcane went and assessed the property damage. Upon their return, young Callahn was full of curiosity and met them on the porch. "Well?" asked Callahn, "How bad is it?" "It is pretty bad," said Tank. "Our entire sugarcane crop was destroyed, and the lake was completely drained dry by the big tornado," said Walter. "Yes," said Grandpa Sugarcane, "No big deal, though. We are going to plant a crop twice the normal size by using part of the land the storm cleared for us." "What about the lake?" asked Callahn, "Is it gone forever?" "Nope," said Tank, "The lake is already filling again from the river."

Weeks went by and the family worked to start a new farm. Tank was correct in his thinking; the lake filled back up with water. It was the same size as it was before. Because of these things, Callahn and her father did what they loved to do most. They went fishing. They left before daylight and fished various parts of the lake all morning without catching a single fish. Somewhat disappointed, they returned home and helped Grandma Sugarcane prepare dinner.

The whole family ate together that night, and there was a sense of love amongst them all. "So the big storm blew away all of the fish?" asked Grandma Sugarcane. "Yes ma'am," said Callahn, "We did not even see a snake or a turtle." "I am going to stock Catfish Lake," said Grandpa Sugarcane with newfound joy and sturdy authority. "I am going to stock it with blue and yellow catfish, perch, and bass," he said. "Dad, there is really no need for all of that. I know how that is going to cost you," said Walter. "I have an old friend that owns and operates eight different fish farms," said Grandpa Sugarcane, "He will be happy to help us."

"What does 'stock' mean?" asked Callahn. "That means your grandfather is going to fly little airplanes over Catfish Lake and drop fish eggs all over it," said Heather Sugarcane, Callahn's aunt. Callahn was amazed. She slept soundly that night, dreaming of monstrous catfish, five-pound bass, and perch the size of dinner plates.

Four years flew by and the Sugarcane family toiled tirelessly. Each person worked an average of six days a week, and their farm's success was astounding. Grandpa Sugarcane had stocked the lake two weeks after he said he would, yet no one had really had the time to go fishing. They had all secretly thought about fishing. Callahn almost went crazy keeping her mouth shut. She knew better than to ask to go fishing when there was so much work taking place. Things had settled to a normal pace, though, and Walter finally asked Callahn to go fishing, one day.

      Walter woke up early that day, about an hour before sunrise. He went and woke up Callahn, and they left while Grandma Sugarcane was starting to cook breakfast. She watched them head east with their fishing supplies as she cooked some bacon. As the sun rose, the Sugarcane family woke up one by one and began to walk around getting things done. "Where are Walter and Callahn?" Tank asked Grandma Sugarcane, as he gazed upon a beautiful sunrise. "They left to go fishing before daybreak," said Grandma Sugarcane, "They will be back before lunch time." Tank and his mother decided to play cards on the porch table while they waited. After all, it was Saturday, and they had not played cards in some time.

      Time seemed to creep by that morning, but it did pass. It was almost lunchtime, and Walter and Callahn were on their way back with a monstrous catfish. As they came into view of the porch, Tank looked up and said, "Ma look!" Grandma Sugarcane looked up and saw Walter and Callahn carrying a huge catfish towards the porch. She said, "Everybody come out and see!" Grandpa Sugarcane came outside and said, "Look at that everybody! Walter and Callahn went and caught a big old two hundred pound catfish!"

◆

Once upon a time, there was a young scientist driving through the scenic and winding back roads of the northwest. His name was Francis Featherman. A seemingly intelligent young man, he enjoyed reading, exercise, and botany. Earlier that morning, he read a brief story titled *Francis' Party*. The story appealed to him because it included the name Francis. He did not know, however, that the story was his introduction to the genre of horror.

The story was on Francis' mind. It was about magical Christmas tree ornament elves that came to life annually at midnight on Christmas Eve to take the life of a creature stirring. In the story, two elves tie a small mouse to a log and throw it in the fireplace with a fire blazing.

The road he was driving down was peaceful and calm. Francis enjoyed the crisp and lightly foggy morning air. He somehow greatly appreciated these roads. They winded through the hills as they cut through both woodsy areas and pastures. Francis was driving about 70 mph in his *Beep*. His car was a fine-tuned twenty-year-old vehicle made for off-road driving.

He carried a sample kit for testing water this day. Francis was to gather some samples from a private pond to bring back to the university by request of the pond's property owner. He also carried along other scientific instrumentation. Francis always documented his findings. He published them in scholarly journals from time to time.

As Francis rounded a long and gentle turn, between two hills, he heard a pop in his gearbox. One who had considered paranormal activity before, Francis simply figured the sound was a mechanical problem from below. Little did he know, Francis was deep in the heart of Forest Hollow - a vast forest haunted with mysterious and magical creatures of all sorts. He did not notice that the sun was not visible from his immediate local.

Francis continued to drive, and his engine seemed to be running fine. The trip to the pond was about a six-hour drive. A wonderful break from university life, it was a nice vacation for the young and curious scientist. Francis discounted the sound a ghost made and continued to his destination, as the cool wind seemed to carry him there. An intelligent and happy man, Francis had thousands of things on his mind. For one, he knew he had left early; Francis made it to the remote farm before 11 AM.

He met the farmer's family. They ate biscuits and gravy together, and Francis collected some water samples from their pond. He also collected other samples from the property by approval of the farmer. Before leaving, Francis and the farmer popped up the hood of the Beep to inspect any visible signs of damage or any reasons for a noise. Upon finding no signs of a reason for a noise, Francis left to return to the laboratory in the university he worked with and for.

The Beep was a standard shift vehicle, which means one would need to use the clutch pedal to change gears while driving. Francis pretty much enjoyed driving a standard, especially in the hills, because he could down shift to climb the winding turns in a timely manner.

Francis drove for a while, thinking of the wonderful family he met. It was nice of them to offer biscuits and water samples. He was going to test the samples for tiny creatures, possible unknown diseases, and mainly for irrigation safety. The afternoon's weather was much like the morning's - it was dismal, humid and partially cloudy. Francis had filled up his gas tank not to far from the farm, and he was well on his way for a six-hour drive with very few stops.

Francis did not take the exact same route back. After having driven for a few hours, however, the road he was on brought him deep into the woods. Francis was deep in the woods of Forest Hollow, once again. As he descended from a hill, going about sixty-five mph, he felt his gear shifter move on its own. The clutch pedal moved on its own, too. Frantic, Francis kept his eyes on the road, as he watched the stick shift and pedals move in such a way to down shift the Beep. Something was driving his vehicle; it was a ghost. Francis guessed it may be a ghost, and he decided not to be afraid. The ghost safely parked the Beep on the side of the farm road. Francis watched ahead for oncoming traffic as the engine died.

He did not hear or see any oncoming traffic. Francis noticed the surroundings. This was the precise location of the noise he heard and chose to disregard earlier that morning. Francis was on an old farm road, in the center of Forest Hollow. It was mid-afternoon, and he could hear or see no human. His driver side door made a loud pop and swung open creaking. The screeching noise of the old hinge of Francis' door broke the silence and was only followed by the sounds of distant winds coming forth from the hills far away. Almost too frightened to look to his left, he did so anyway.

Francis did not really see anything. The ghost who opened Francis' door for him must have been close by and doing nothing other than watching Francis. Francis exited the vehicle to inspect the forest. What else was there to do, anyway? Francis closed his door and slowly reached for and obtained a water bottle from his vehicle. It was time to go exploring. The idea that the Beep was going to drive away did occur, but the vehicle did not start up. Francis supposed that the ghost must have been inviting him into the woods.

Francis walked perpendicular from the farm road through the roadside ditch, as the crackling leaves beneath his feet turned his fears into terror. Thoughts of breaking bones went through his mind for no known reason. Francis could still since a presence moving with him, and gathered what courage he could to carry on. He peered into the forest, now, able to see into it from the brink of its boundary. The now visible boundary was parallel with the farm road. Francis took one last look over his shoulder to see his vehicle, looked ahead once more, and entered Forest Hollow.

Once past the brink of the forest, Francis could see further. Wind carried rolling waves of fog down the hills. Tall and slender trees where scattered throughout. The landscape was magnificent, somehow. The wind carried a distant and musical sound. It resembled the singing echoes of spirits from the past. Francis decided to jog down the hill to further himself into the woods; the forest was like a huge playground to him, now. Francis began to run more swiftly through the hills. He lost track of time and worry, only to realize that he was moving swiftly in a beautiful existence. So swiftly, in fact, that Francis had joined with other forms of phenomenon, and he no longer had a physical body.

As the landscape's ground was smooth and empty, the wind seemed to carry the playful spirits in all of their continuous dancing manners through the trees in a very expedient manner. This went on for some time. He enjoyed flying around with the spirits. As the fog moved like a frightful form of the aurora, Francis seemed to wonder where his vehicle was. The spirits flew throughout the woods together, and Francis thought for sure he was flying back to the Beep. Everything slowed down, and Francis materialized as he came to a brisk walk on the ground. As Francis trekked toward a familiar hill, he noticed the gravestones beneath his feet. The cemetery startled him some, but he walked on. Having guessed accurately, after walking up a long hill, Francis found his Beep.

He turned to the forest to wave good-bye, and supposed the presence was okay with his departure. Francis started the Beep and drove away. Who would he tell about these occurrences? Francis decided not to tell anyone anytime soon. The drive back was much like his brief experience with the spiritual realm; time flew by as he had fun.

Once Francis made it back to his university, he processed the water samples properly. Francis found and reported a special new alga to his community of scholars. He completed his master's degree and interviewed with various companies.

Interested mainly in learning and people that wanted to, Francis took a job as a professor for his university to take classes and teach. He still went to the graveyard once every few years or so. He enjoyed paying the spirits of Forest Hollow a visit. Francis lived happily ever after.

♦

"Break yourself, fool!" said Angel, as she jumped up on the sofa with her feet in socks and a hair dryer in her hands. Her little brother, Devon, threw his hands in the air. The year was 1972, now, as midnight had just passed minutes before. Their parents were attending a New Year's Eve party with the boss of their father's company and others.

"I have done nothing wrong," said Devon, "I come in peace." "At ease," said Angel. "I think that was one of my favorite things to see on television since I was little," said Devon. "Little? You are still little currently," said Angel, "What are you talking about, anyway?" "The ball dropping in New York," said Devon, "I like to watch it."

"Oh," said Angel, "I think you should watch something else." "What is that?" asked Devon. "Yourself in the mirror brushing your teeth!" said Angel, "Now hurry up and go get ready for bed. Mom and Dad will be here any moment. I will read a story to you." Devon hurried himself to go get ready for bed. His older sister meant business, and when Mom and Dad were gone, she was quite the knowledgeable furor.

Devon brushed his teeth and got ready for bed. Angel also got ready for bed. She read Devon a story from a brilliantly painted children's book with large pictures of animals in a zoo. The story was about a small family who went to the zoo on a Saturday and had a good time.

Devon fell asleep, and Angel went off to bed once her parents came in to retire. Before turning in, she reported Devon's good behavior. She said he enjoyed watching the ball drop every year, and he went straight to sleep after one good story. They gave Angel her ten dollars for babysitting, and they all went off to bed.

Time went by, and Christmas break was over. Angel went back to school - high school, where the culture was what it was. She and her friends were all about the clothes, the dancing, and the music. Angel's favorite shirt was *metallic-dandelion* (gold) in color and had large cuffs and a big triangular collar. She then sported a *fro* the size of a basketball and enjoyed wearing sunglasses. Bell-bottom pants were in, and Angel was in a funk band. Their musical group's name was The Groove Machine, and she was the drummer. Their group included a bass guitarist, Todd, and a lyricist, Justin, who incorporated the use of a tambourine. They spoke out against worldwide violence and hunger. The Groove Machine really liked to get down and boogie.

The Groove Machine met after school two or three times a week for a while and even released a funky dance record with a local label. One time, their agent landed them an after party gig at a golf course, and they brought their joyous sound of dancing rhythm to those who liked to move their feet - even in golf cleats. The golfers enjoyed getting down with the Groove Machine, and Angel went and got some clothes and groceries for her family once she was paid.

Playing with the Groove Machine was fun, but Angel also liked watching police movies and shows with Devon from time to time. Once she was sixteen, her mother encouraged Angel to get a job. Angel wanted to become a police officer. She still had over a year left in high school. Her mother told Angel that her friend was a firefighter who worked for the city. The fire fighter said that police academy in the nearby city was about three thousand dollars to attend, and lasted for nine months. Once eighteen and graduated from high school, Angel could go and qualify.

Angel considered these things, and she planned for a brighter future. Early one Sunday morning, she said, "Break yourself!" She was aiming the Sunday paper at Devon who was sleeping. He woke up and threw his hands in the air saying, "Please! I like church!" They both laughed, and Angel went through the classified ads before attending her family's nondenominational gathering.

She found a job as a security officer's assistant working on Friday and Saturday nights. It was seemingly similar to police work. The security guards she worked with carried items such as guns, pepper-spray, clubs, and handcuffs. The company she worked for had private "peace stations" all over the city for organizations and businesses.

Angel's dad took out a loan to help her get some wheels. They bought a white 1968 model 2-door v6 car with neon green seats and a tan interior.

Angel agreed to pay fifty percent of the note with her finances from working as a security guard assistant.

All went well with the car. Angel took Devon to the mall sometimes, and she and her father paid the car off in two years. They kept it up well with proper maintenance. All went well with Angel's new job, too. She was always there in a timely fashion, always presentable, and very helpful with being good in observation. She enjoyed listening to pop, funk, disco and soul. Angel's aunt, Maurine, once appeared on a dance show called Groove Time.

More time went by. Plenty of Angel's friends went off to college to study various subjects. For some reason, however, she was wholeheartedly devoted to becoming a peace officer. "Why do you want to become an officer of the law?" asked Devon, one day. Angel said, "I think it is my calling," and she did not say, "Break yourself," because she really did want to go catch the bad people. Angel thought there were plenty of criminals on the loose, and that she would one day enjoy police work.

Time passed. Angel became a ranked security guard. While working, she carried items like handcuffs, pepper spray, a baton, and a radio. She manned small security guard stations with other guards. Sometimes, Angel had to call the local police. Once Angel turned eighteen, she began saving money for the police academy. The firefighter friend of Angel's mom came over to speak with her one day. His name was Chuck, and Angel knew him, too.

Angel said, "Chuck! I am so happy to see you. Before you even say or ask me anything, I want you to come and see something out in the backyard." The firefighter happily followed her out there without really putting much thought into it. When he walked out of the backdoor she said, "Break yourself!" aiming a water-hose at him. He threw his hands in the air smiling and said, "I am unarmed." Angel felt like a youngster again, knowing that she was growing up very fast.

Chuck came to bring her good news. The fire department started a donation fund and raised enough money to pay for seventy-five percent of her police academy tuition. She tried to tell her mother without crying and found it impossible. Angel was so happy. She had been saving, and it just had not been adding up quick enough.

Angel graduated from high school, worked all summer as a security guard, and attended police academy in the fall. All went well. She scored an average of ninety-seven percent on her police qualification tests. These final tests took nine months to prepare for and included written exams, driving tests, verbal interviews and firearm qualifications including maintenance, general knowledge and actual operation.

Angel still drove her car; she kept it well maintained. Her parents, Devon, and some of her friends were there to see her sworn in the day she became a police officer. All cried. She finally got what she was after.

Angel and two other officers underwent real-time team training together. She made twelve dollars an hour to catch the bad-guys and patrol traffic. She stayed in training for a year. She was making almost as much her trainers, so she could not really complain. She rented out a flat and brought her parents groceries from time to time.

Eventually, she gained much experience. By the time she was twenty-two, she was driving a sports utility vehicle and had two people on her mini-squad team. They called themselves the Peace Trio and handled matters all over the city. Angel practiced and became quite proficient with her Glock; it was Austrian in manufacture and issued to her via the department. She averaged over ninety-eight percent accuracy at the shooting range.

The Peace Trio went around the city serving warrants and bringing in the wanted, mostly. Usually, they did not have to use any weapons. Once they knew their rights, people came in without too much of a problem - especially once they were in handcuffs. Angel's subordinate officer names were Officer Williams and Officer Clark. Officer Williams was a nice thirty-nine year-old woman, and Officer Clark was a twenty-eight year old man who firmly believed in the law.

One morning, the Peace Trio was patrolling an area. They got a call that a house was being broken into, and that the burglars were armed. The Trio knew exactly where the address was located. "You are a big girl, now," Angel thought to herself. The address was to a large old mini-mansion museum owned and operated by an old woman and her son. He was not in town. The burglars came for the safe and the jewels.

The Trio sped over there in their s. u. v. Officer Williams was driving and confirmed a request for backup on the radio. They would get to the museum before the other officers, because the Peace Trio was closer.

Upon the Trio's arriving, the two burglars had just entered the museum. The front door was swinging open in the wind showing signs of forced entry. The three officers went in the front door in search of the criminals. "Put your hands on your head and get on your knees!" exclaimed a male whose voice was coming from a distant room. The old woman did so, and the Trio spread out to find the burglars. The two lawbreakers both had a nine mm handgun. Officer Clark found one of them going through an old metal oval-like fridge that was a pale-green color. "Place your weapon on the floor," whispered Officer Clark, showing the burglar his badge and his Glock at the same time.

The bad-guy put his gun on the ground slowly and put his hands behind his head. Officer Clark handcuffed the criminal and kicked the gun to the side. He told the criminal to lie face down on the ground with his legs spread out. The criminal did so, and Officer Clark distanced himself from the kitchen in search of the other criminal and officers, keeping an eye on the one on the floor.

Angel and Officer Williams had searched all of the rooms on the first floor of the museum by that time, and no one was there. They found a stairway and heard sounds of struggle upstairs. Tried as they could to get up the stairs without making a sound, the other burglar heard them make it to the second floor.

There were only two floors in the old house. The second floor consisted of two main hallways, two bathrooms, and eight bedrooms positioned in a rectangular fashion. Officer Clark stayed with his criminal, while the other two officers searched for the second burglar. There would be no escape for the fridge robber.

Officer Williams and Angel decided to split up to find the bad-guy. Officer Williams found him and the curator in a room connected to another room with an open door. The criminal knew they were coming and was going to try to escape by taking the curator hostage. "Put your weapon down," said Officer Williams. The burglar said, "Drop yours or she gets it," while holding his nine mm to the curator's head.

Just then, Angel crept in from the side unbeknownst to the armed robber. She took a few silent steps towards him and said, "Break yourself!" with her Glock aimed towards his right temporal gland one inch away. She said, "Place your weapon on the ground." The criminal slowly put his gun on the ground, and Angel handcuffed him. No one shot a gun that day. The Peace Trio brought the bad-guys into custody.

These occurrences were in the news the next day. The museum curator was very thankful and told the Peace Trio how much she appreciated them. Angel remained a peace officer for many years to come, and they all lived happily ever after.

♦

Hubba's Joyous Journey

Once upon a time, there was a young and handsome man named
Hubba. He was twenty. Comfortable in his demeanor, everyone loved Hubba.
He was in business school at the time, studying computer system development
and human resource analysis. His schooling was not too difficult; he had a part
time job as a printer technician for eighteen hours a week.

He and four other students shared an old house they were remodeling.
The rent-house was the cheapest they could find; they would have it looking
nice one day. The five men all worked part time and went to the same college.
Sometimes they smoked. Sometimes they did not smoke at all.

One night, they put together some funds to order pizza. The pizza
man got there in a short while. "Our jobs do not pay what we need," said
Hubba. The other four agreed as they ate their pizza. "What do you propose
we do?" joyfully asked his only housemate with a car. Tom's car was a four-
cylinder Toyota from 1998. His uncle gave it to him to go study biology. "We
could start a computer repair business," said Hubba. "That is a good idea,"
said Erns, who worked in a small sandwich deli only open for lunch, "All of
our schedules conflict." "What if we always take Thursday off?" said Jobe,
who worked for a math professor. "That is a good idea," said Fred, the
Sociology major, "It costs sixty dollars to put a four week ad in the town
classifieds." Fred worked for a newspaper in town as the nighttime janitor.

The five managed to all get Thursdays off. It took them six and a half weeks to save up for their business add, but they did it. They named their business "Line-Co." This was from the idea of running networking lines and the operation becoming a company one day. Their newspaper ad included a line about repairing computers and installing software: "Line-Co, computer networking, software installation, and trouble shooting."

The very first Monday that their ad was in the paper they received a dozen calls or so. One call was from an old woman eight hours away. Tom called her back humorously trying to explain that they were too far away to help her out. She promised to pay for the gas, and what they would request honestly for labor. Tom said that a company representative would return her call within a day or two, that they would need to discuss and decide. It sounded like a fun trip.

Hubba called her on a Wednesday to see what she was after. He explained that they only work on Thursdays, and that they could not solve all problems - just most. Ms. Palmisser was the nice woman's name. She explained that her son bought her a computer with a light fixture timing software package and lights. She said that all this stuff was still in a lot of boxes. She agreed to pay them twenty dollars an hour to hook everything up, as it did not look like it would take too long. Hubba agreed to the journey, agreeing to keep the gasoline receipts so she could pay them honestly. The five had successfully spoken with their bosses to have Thursdays off. They left

Wednesday night at three am, after each drank about half of a gallon of cold coffee. They arrived at Ms. Palmisser's place before noon on Thursday.

Ms. Palmisser welcomed the guys and showed them around her place. Her swamp-house was an old four bedroom log cabin with a large din, a dining room and a sofa room. The sofa room was full of various kinds of slain swamp varmints and critters mounted on walls as trophies. She said the dead animals came from men in her family. The men in her family were her sons and her deceased husband, mainly. The room of animals would have been nothing other than a ferocious nightmare during the night.

The students found boxes of lights and the computer. Ms. Palmisser was not too particular about where to install everything - she just wanted it to all work properly. The men worked for about an hour and where almost done. Ms. Palmisser asked them to take a break to try her lemonade and tacos she made them for lunch.

It was then that the five men saw the gators. They followed Ms. Palmisser to her back porch to eat the tacos and share the lemonade. Lunch was fine. The porch overlooked a large pond-like part of the swamp that connected loosely to a dredged ditch. The old dredged ditch connected to a large river. The river could not be seen from the porch, and the water there would not be something other than dangerous for a swimming human.

The guys watched the gators swim around while they ate their tacos. Jobe almost asked why there were not a lot of ducks in the water, but he just ate his tacos instead. "Those gators must live mostly off of algae and fish," he thought.

"The 'gators' with the wider heads are the older crocodiles," said Ms. Palmisser, "And the more slender ones are the younger alligators. I throw them a frozen chicken, sometimes, even though people tell me not to. It is fun." "What is that above your mantle there?" asked Jobe. Fred could see it through the glass doors. "That is Betsy, my *shotgun-rifle*," said Ms. Palmisser, "I shoot and clean her once a month. I keep her loaded."

The five guys finished their beef tacos and thanked Ms. Palmisser. In about an hour the men had the computer working with the software installed properly. They also had the lighting installed and networked properly with the computer. Tom went over the software with Ms. Palmisser, and she said she would read the help file for fun. She seemed to understand well how to use her machine. She impressively scheduled when she wanted her various lights to come on and off. It surprised Erns - she was rather computer savvy.

Ms. Palmisser discussed with them what she owed to write them a check. They gave her the gas receipts, multiplied that by two, and charged her forty dollars for the approximate two hours of labor. She wrote them a check for two hundred and forty one dollars and thirty two cents. They thanked her and went out to the Toyota to wave goodbye and go home. They happily piled themselves into the car.

"Let me check out our first check!" said Hubba happily. Tom handed

Hubba the check as he was putting his seat belt on to drive. "Ms. Palmisser did not endorse this check," said Hubba. It was an honest mistake. "Go get her to sign it," said Erns. "We will wait for you here," said Fred.

Hubba trusted his guys just enough to go back in there. "Ms. Palmisser?" Hubba called out. She came from the other room. "Long time no see," he said smiling and showing her the check. "I am sorry," he said, "You forgot to sign this check." "Oh dear," said Ms. Palmisser, "I am very sorry. Wait on the back porch and I will go get the same pen I wrote the check with." Hubba walked out to the porch to watch and admire the gators.

He noticed they seemed to be swimming to the side of the pond-like water structure. There was no real bank to the pond. Its perimeter boundary consisted of water and old trees. Suddenly, a huge twelve-foot crocodile emerged completely into the air! It must have really been swimming hard from the depths below. It landed on its two foot wide belly on the railing of the porch with its wide head in the air. Stuck on there, its mouth was open and biting repeatedly as a rabid dog's would be barking towards an intruder. The crocodile was trying to eat Hubba!

"Ms. Palmisser!" screamed Hubba, and she came running with her *shotgun-rifle*. She handed Betsy to Hubba and said, "Shoot that monster!" Hubba aimed the gun at the large croc's head and pulled the trigger. "Boom!" went the gun, and it echoed in the peaceful distance. Ms. Palmisser went to inspect the bleeding croc; Hubba had blown a huge hole in the reptile's head.

Ms. Palmisser signed the check and gave it to Hubba. He in return gave her the gun back. He thanked her once more, and she thanked him. She said, "I am going to cook that croc and eat it like a chicken." Ms. Palmisser finally had her own trophy to clean. She was thankful for the lights working nicely, too. Later that evening she would put her lights on the rotating, fading, and dimming cycle.   Hubba returned to his fellows with the properly endorsed check and told them what had happened. They all got out of the car to go see the crocodile. They were impressed. "Good shot!" said Fred. "That is the largest crocodile I have ever seen!" said Erns. "You sure got you one!" said Jobe. "I bet that weighs over two hundred and forty pounds," said Tom.

The students helped Ms. Palmisser get pull the croc onto the porch. "We must go," said Fred. They waved goodbye to Ms. Palmisser thanking her happily and drove home safely. The students had a wonderful time, and Hubba would never forget their joyous journey.

♦

Lady-geddon

"Did you bring your eight back-up rounds?" asked Ms. Orchid. "Yes I did - eight rounds, just as we decided," replied Ms. Dandelion. The two nice women, both over sixty-five, were having a casual brunch at precisely 9:30 AM on the balcony of a familiar deli. Three stories up, the upscale deli overlooked the streets below. Their server arrived to their table with toast and fried-egg chicken soup, a favorite of both patrons.

Ms. Dandelion and Ms. Orchid were from differing occupations. Both could still get from one place to another rather quickly and well. Ms. Orchid was a librarian making one dollar an hour more than minimum wage and worked about thirty hours a week. Ms. Dandelion worked three to five mornings a week at a small fabrics store. Both of their schedules changed weekly - many times their schedules did not change for weeks in a row.

One way or another, the two acquaintances knew each other rather well. Ms. Orchid and Ms. Dandelion met in the library. Ms. Dandelion and her husband had retired to a larger city - he passed away. Ms. Dandelion frequented the library. They both became avid readers. Ms. Dandelion became acquainted with Ms. Orchid from speaking with her and checking out books to read. Ms. Orchid usually read the books Ms. Dandelion turned in.

Ms. Orchid's husband was also deceased. Both men were ex-military and died of illness before the age of sixty. The two women loved to read novels. Ms. Dandelion always brought her books back within ten days or so. Ms. Orchid read every single book her new confident read. What great discussions they did have! The two read books on prose composition, romance, fantasy, and even science fiction and horror.

Some of their favorite novels involved long and peaceful tales of plantations in the southern states. They enjoyed classical literature. Recently, they read a murder mystery collection of nine novels by a new and upcoming talented paralegal given to writing.

One day, the two shared a questionable conversation. Before their current brunch, they were discussing the many books they read over lunch in another deli. The two spoke on murder.

"Anytime someone kills, they either have a reason, or they do not," said Ms. Dandelion. "Of course," said Ms. Orchid, "Having a decent and sane motif can mean capital punishment when found guilty in this country." "I have lived this long, and I have never done anything wrong," said Ms. Dandelion. "You have never received a ticket for speeding or shoplifting?" asked Ms. Orchid. "No," said Ms. Dandelion, "I tithe on Sundays."

"I understand you, somehow," said Ms. Orchid, "I have never done anything wrong, either." "Before I die, I want to do something naughty," said Ms. Dandelion, "I am no sole culprit." "Oh no," said Ms. Orchid, "I knew we were thinking of it - we will be dead in a couple of decades, anyhow. What can we leave behind? Do you have any important novels to write in the world of fiction or scholarly scientific study?" "I hear you," said Ms. Dandelion, "I have a back-up motivator."

"Is it money?" asked Ms. Orchid. "Not really," said Ms. Dandelion, "We are both poor, though. We can let money be an excuse. We are after a kill." "Who and how?" asked Ms. Orchid. "Your question has an easy answer," said Ms. Dandelion, "What do you know of the worker from the restaurant on Forty-Second?" "He leaves every Wednesday to get to the bank with a weekly cash deposit," said Ms. Orchid.

"I know the restaurant is on the fourth floor of the building. He uses the stairway on the side to get to his vehicle. We can easily catch him in the stairway. We can shoot him, drive his car a few blocks, and leave on foot. We will then change and burn our clothes," said Ms. Dandelion, "We will also need to take hot showers and scrub well with soap." "What about our weapons?" asked Ms. Orchid. Both women carried a twenty-two caliber pistol. Their small derringers housed two rounds apiece.

"We will need to dispose of the guns completely for legal reasons," said Ms. Dandelion. "I will simply go and get a different weapon before our attack," said Ms. Orchid, and so did Ms. Dandelion. They both still wanted to own a gun. "How do you think we should get rid of the used weapons?" asked Ms. Orchid. "A grinder," said Ms. Dandelion, "The old workbench my husband used to play with has a grinder with a spinning wheel."

"It will take some time," said Ms. Orchid. "I will grind our guns down to a dust. I will then thoroughly clean the area with soap and hot water. The authorities will not come for us, anyhow. They will have no chance of finding the real murder weapons. We will grow older and die with some extra cash," said Ms. Dandelion. "Splendid," said Ms. Orchid, "Are you sure you want to do this?" "We only live once," said Ms. Dandelion.

"You present a compelling argument," said Ms. Orchid. The duo finished their soup and toast. They departed from their lunch. A week or two went by and they had the time to plan. Now was the time to leave from their brunch on the balcony. As they washed their meal down with some warm green tea, their server returned with their check. They paid and left after tipping. It was 9:45 AM. "You also have your twenty-two ready with its back-up rounds?" asked Ms. Dandelion.

"Sure thing," said Ms. Orchid. They both checked their purses to make sure. "How are we going to shoot him?" asked Ms. Orchid. "We can both put a bullet in his head and one in his chest. We will have to watch him die and check his pulse," said Ms. Dandelion. "Otherwise he could live, and we might be identified," agreed Ms. Orchid. The restaurant they were leaving was on Fortieth Street. The duo traveled to Forty-Second. Minutes pressing, they left to find the stairway.

Having eaten there a few times, before, the two knew precisely where to go. They walked quickly. Ms. Orchid and Ms. Dandelion found the entryway to the restaurant and took the stairs. They went unnoticed - the people standing around were paying no attention to pedestrians. They walked quietly up two flights of stairs and waited in the stairway. Within only a moment, the worker ran through the door above and jogged down the stairs.

The two had their guns out, cocked, and readied for fire. He saw them in their shades and hats with speckled fabric veils covering their faces, as they aimed their guns. He was already halfway down the flight of stairs, however. The worker could not have easily escaped. Ms. Orchid and Ms. Dandelion both accurately shot him once in the head and once in the chest. Only the worker and the two women heard gunfire. The worker fell, and blood began to trickle from his body down the stairs.

Ms. Orchid got his money pouch while Ms. Dandelion found his weakening pulse on his neck. The surprised worker died. Ms. Dandelion reached into the man's pocket and found his car keys. The duo ran down the stairway and made exodus through the side door the worker normally used. Ms. Orchid and Ms. Dandelion easily found the remodeled burnt-orange 1988 model v6 2-door of the worker. They drove his car to an alley and parked on the side.

The two split up the money quickly and got out of the car. They jogged in a relaxed manner from the shades of the alley to the sidewalk. The duo walked a few blocks and took a cab to Ms. Dandelion's place of residence. They had close to two thousand dollars a piece to save or play with. Ms. Orchid took the guns with her and changed into one of Ms. Dandelion's outfits.

"I will burn these clothes once I take a nice hot shower," said Ms. Dandelion.

"I will shower and do the same with this outfit," said Ms. Orchid, "I will then grind these small *toys* into a cleanable form of dust. Would you like to have lunch, tomorrow?" "Sure," said Ms. Dandelion, "How about the deli on twelfth at noon?" "Okay," said Ms. Orchid. Ms. Orchid left Ms. Dandelion's and went home. They both slept well. They woke up early for work and made it to the deli on twelfth by noon.

"Are you okay?" asked Ms Orchid. "Sure," said Ms. Dandelion, "I burned our clothes and sprayed the ashes away with a water hose." "Are the guns gone?" asked Ms Dandelion. "They are gone," said Ms. Orchid, "In two hours I ground them into a dust and cleaned the area well." A server came. The two requested a deli-sub, and the subs were fine. Their crime went unsolved - the duo lived happily ever after, reading and discussing collections of prose.

♦

Orc Escape

"Ferocious creatures we are, no doubt!" said Heinlan, speaking to the male orcs at a nighttime meeting. Heinlan, Thorndor's assistant, gave a brief speech to the other orcs. His speech was as follows:

Are we underlings? Our hunger and fierceness lead us into temptation – the humans know nothing of actual action upon malevolent temptations. How could they possibly criminalize our efforts regarding survival? Can we not read and write? Do we not make love, converse in these great fields, and serve our masters with undue dedication? We are used and abused as slaves against our will, and we know it. There is no reason for us to stoop to these slanderous accusations of our ignorant king - long live him, nonetheless. We live; we eat from the castle. We do not consume the flesh of humans. Can we not hunt animals on our own? We hunt and bring game to the castle – there are more animals further away. We all back Thorndor's thoughts. It is time we start our own village. We have spoken of it for some time - the mountain pass is not too far away. Thorndor will lead us this next full moon, ten nights from tonight. Prepare with tents and traveling equipment. Get your rest. Let us journey over the river to Flowerside Mountain Range's eastern side, and trek deep into the Far

Forest. We will co-exist with the animals and supernatural inhabitants as necessary. We will hunt and gather to live. The time has come.

Heinlan was Thorndor's scribe and historian. Heinlan kept numerous journals. He addressed the heads of households during this nighttime meeting via Thorndor's request and decision.

Thorndor was the leader amongst the orcs of Grim Castle, who conversed with the heads of households of orc families in secret meetings on occasion. He was, by far, *the fiercest orc to have ever existed*, according to lore and current understanding. Thorndor was taller and stronger than the other orcs - he was surprisingly very good with making decisions and problem resolution.

Grim Castle housed many tradesmen: blacksmiths, farmers, soldiers, knights, religious leaders, instructors, hunters, and various artists. The king, King Don, was a twelfth generation monarch, the first-born of his family, and king of Grim Castle and its areas. Grim Castle operated large fields of wheat and vast orchards with many kinds of fruit trees - mainly peaches, oranges, apples, pears and plums. Like some castles, Grim Castle also maintained a large population of farm animals.

Supposedly, the orcs came from a traveling group of comedians seven hundred years before our current tale's occurrence. The comedians were all men, and they secretly made love for years with the female hogs of Grim

Castle. The comedians were caught raising small magical "pig-people". Grim

Castle's king banished them from the castle and its lands. Kept in the castle,

the orcs evolved as a genealogical group in such a manner. Families of orcs

existed as slaves for a documented twenty generations before the young yet

knowing Thorndor made the decision to attempt a safe and successful group

exodus.

The political rulers of Grim Castle enslaved the orcs. King Don kept

them alive with leftovers from castle feasts and dinners. He used them as his

fathers did for generations to help maintain and process the annual work efforts

of the wheat fields and orchards. King Don had an army of soldiers and highly

skilled knights. Some of his soldiers kept the orcs in line via whips, horses,

and verbal commands.

The orcs kept some large wolves as pets and could ride them like

horses. One large wolf's name was Warg. Depending on the family and their

history, the orcs of Grim castle endured either burgundy, forest-green, or dark-

gray skin. The males could move in camouflaged packs when hunting wild

game or helping in war - they were hard to see in the forests. Orcs rarely spoke

with humans for historical reasons relating to inaccurate accusations and

dungeon oriented death, torture, and reprimand. The wolves could speak, too,

but they did so minimally. There were over a dozen families of orcs, and they

could ride their talking wolves around for fun in the night. The wolves would

serve as very useful in helping the younger orcs keep up with the adults during their departure.

Thorndor himself was quite the dedicated worker and thinker. His philosophy was to do an excellent job and to keep his plans secret. The political leaders beneath King Don considered Thorndor to be the sole leader of the orcs. Thorndor himself knew he made influential decisions, yet he saw the men of the various Orchinean households to be more or less his group enthusiasts or equals. One way or the other, for years and years they performed a large amount of work for Grim Castle. Peasants could work the fields; the orcs had various pains from slavery. It was time to go.

The orcs did as they planned. They slaved away obediently for nine days, trying to appreciate the nostalgia of Grim Castle's territories. They rested and ate well during those days. Their good behavior went unnoticed, and they were ready to leave.

The element of secrecy was a necessity, and no orc spoke of their planned rebellion. Kept in the dungeons, there was one main door to the orc families' chambers. The dungeon master locked the main door with a large key, nightly. Thorndor and Heinlan simply planned to capture the dungeon master as he was locking the door, and fight their way as a group out of the castle to flee to the mountains. The time available for escape depended largely on how long it took other residents of the large castle to recognize that the head dungeon master was missing. If they made proper haste, the king's army would not have the time to assemble properly, and the orcs would be free.

The night of the full moon came, and the orcs had eaten. The males were ready with hidden shields, hand-fashioned swords, and secret weapons for defense only. The females and younger orcs were ready, too, with their various wolf-pets, tents, and packed belongings. The dungeon master's assistants made it up the hallway, leaving him behind to lock the big door, as always. Thorndor quickly gagged the attendant as Heinlan bound him. They tied the master to a dungeon cell's door and time passed before humans found him.

"Time passed" consisted of moments lasting just long enough for the twelve main Orchinean families as well as the other orcs to escape from the dungeon. Once out of the dungeon, they would jog to flee the castle, swim the moat, cross a bridge, and continue on to the mountains as quickly as possible in the moonlit night. All of the orcs, over ninety in number, escaped Grim Castle unnoticed. Once out of the dungeon, they all ran out of the castle in an organized single-filed line. As the orcs were crossing the moat, soldiers in Grim Castle found the dungeon master. Half of the orcs had crossed the murky waters. Various knights and soldiers of King Don saw the last few. They could only yell and had little time to organize. By the time King Don heard of the orcs' rebellion, the orcs had made it to the rear bridge and used it to cross the river in their entirety.

As the king's men attempted to chase the orcs by leaving the castle in a traditional manner, the orcs continued in their efforts and made haste to the mountains. The soldiers took too long in preparation and did not find a single orc during the night. By morning time, the fleeing Orcs had made good distance into Grim Castle's neighboring Flowerside Mountains. The sun rose, and they continued to travel.

Some of the king's men attempted to track the orcs for two days and returned to Grim Castle. Thorndor felt as though his venture had been one of success, and sent Heinlan and two others back to scout the area in chance of trailing soldiers, scouts, or knights of the king. The three did so and caught back up with the community of orcs within two days. No one saw any of King Don's men. There were no known search parties from the castle.

Thorndor was happily satisfied. The orc families had been sleeping in tents and living off salty dried game, fruit, and water. Upon Heinlan's return, Thorndor was impressed with his ability and happy with his party's news – happy enough to reward Heinlan with a hand-fashioned silver snake-pendant necklace. The pendant contained three snakes in a circle with tiny golden fangs and magically glowing red ruby and green emerald eyes. The eyes of the pendant could glow for various reasons – mostly if its holder was nearing any danger or sought destination. Thorndor was quite the jeweler, and the nomadic orcs carried all of their books and possessions with themselves while traveling. These items were efficient in number. Heinlan accepted the medallion in celebration of a successful escape. He was speechless to behold it and mostly kept it secret. It was sure to have its own form of magical power.

The sun rose that day, and the orcs could travel with less haste. They carried on. Only stopping hours after sundown for sleep, the families hiked continuously. No orc wanted one of King Don's possible search parties to place them in *re-confinement*. The orcs would only be safely able to begin the construction of their village once deep into the Far Forest. With any luck, the king's men would suppose the orcs turned wild or learned to survive in or past the hills. As the hills were a land vast in distance, they were hard and discouraging to explore by even the rare few who tried.

Time went by and Thorndor led his families well. They survived the mountains hunting animals, living off streams, and gathering edible berries. In a fortnight, they traversed north through the Flowerside Mountains, and came upon Moon Lake, as Heinlan happily named the large water structure. Heavy rains and seasonal melting snow streaming from the summits of various mountains formed the lake. The orcs went south around the river. They found the tall slender trees of the Far Forest and entered, clearing paths some distance from the edge of the thick collection of shadows. The orcs were not trying to leave a trail - that was for sure.

Making their own trails, the orcs ventured far into the forest to set up temporary camps. They slept in tents for some time, though the orcs eventually constructed a suitable village upon finding a medium sized river winding deep into the forest. They had traveled another two weeks before coming upon the crisp sounds of the new river. The adolescent orcs called it the "magical river of life." The orcs drank a great deal of water, as they learned to hunt with more proficiency.

A human found the orcs one time during that year. A bird hunter came upon them accidentally as he was inscribing his hunting maps. Thorndor and his fellow male orcs spoke with the hunter, and the thin man was released to freedom upon giving his word that he would keep their location secret from Grim Castle. Otherwise, a small territorial war would ensue and lives would be lost. The orcs were free. They perfected farming, hunting and blacksmith working in under five years. The orcs named their village Orc-Rest, and it thrived in secrecy for many generations to come.

◆

Steam

Once time, two people knew each other rather well. They had coffee together once every seven weeks or so, in the same restaurant. Sometimes they ordered food; sometimes they did not. People rarely heard their conversations. Their words were important, however, even if what they had to say was only important to them.

Their ideas affected others - that is why they were so important. When they spoke, the existence and occurrences of the universe of others changed or did not - especially if it involved pancakes, people, or money. Goodhearted people they were, many people appreciated these two individuals.

"How are you today?" asked Beth, as she sat behind a familiar and properly cleaned table. "I am getting older," said the gentleman, Ron. He sat with her, on her right. He was no senior citizen, yet he was a large and tall man, over forty, and rather handsome according to some.

Both had their back to a wall housing a nice window; they could view various incidences within the shades and lighting of the restaurant. Their relationship was indeed strictly professional, yet how and why is not disclosed in this happy tale.

"May I bring you guys some coffee?" asked the nice young waitress. Their waitress Julia was pretty. She carried the semblance of a young woman who often waited on tables in a road diner. Not too endowed, she was cleanly and politely presentable according to company dress code.

"Sure," the two sitting both said. The two patrons relaxed and watched her walk away. She came back with two canisters of coffee and two mugs. "Would you like to place an order?" asked Julia, trying to be as polite as possible. The two looked at each other. The man shook his head, "No," and the woman said, "No thank you, not right now." Julia left them to work on her side duties.

The two enjoyed their coffee. "So, how are things?" he asked. "Things are fine," she said, "How are you?" "I am well," he said, "I have had a second cup of coffee and I am *ready to go*." A waitress from the kitchen, Bella, walked across the floor with five plates, three on one arm and one in each hand. She sat the plates down with learned skill, and the customers were happy.

Many of the customers there were newcomers. Maybe one in a hundred people was not a new patron. These customers were on their way to a theme park; they looked as though they traveled prepared. Then, they were the happy people eating. Their orders were impressively accurate.

There were other things occurring in different parts of the restaurant, too. An exciting bus of sports players was on the other side, eating pancakes and trying fruit blend drinks. A few couples were scattered about in the middle tables. Servers were doing their side work; the hostesses were enduring normal things that happen there. The two hostesses that day were Marg and Phuan.

Marg was an octogenarian with eighty-two years under her belt. People were impressed to see her walk from place to place.

Phuan was a beautiful, young, and pale Asian with nice black hair. Her friends always asked her, "Do you have a *fwan*, Phuan?" because her name reminded them of the word *fan*. Phuan usually carried a real fan, and she could darn near cause people to laugh to death with it. She was naturally funny. If ever asked, "Do you have a fan?" She could say, "I have one here," and show them her fan.

One time, a young man forgot Phuan's name after they had been dating for a while. She caught him unknowing and said in front of others, "What is my name?" He did not know. She took her fan out, opened it right in front of his eyes, and said, "*Fwon!* My name is Phuan!" He meant well, nevertheless. She thought he was near mindless and apologized. The first time they went out, all he could think of to ask her was if her father worked for a camera company. Her father sold disposable cameras at a gas station forty hours a week, and people thought it was funny. Phuan's exultant and jovial Asian family went to Florida every other summer.

The hostesses did a fine job. The restaurant always ran properly. The chefs all worked in shifts, and they shared what love they could amongst each other. They were good with cooking pancakes, eggs, and steaks. The chefs also performed routine cleaning and possessed well-rounded people skills. They were a sort of happy family, too.

The two continued in conversation. They spoke of the weather and the restaurant. Then, Beth and Ron were out of easy topics. "I am hungry," she said. "I cannot really remember the last time I have eaten," said Ron. Their waitress would have been staring right at them if she had not forgotten what she was doing. While enduring this tentative confusion, Julia realized her whereabouts. Her small dilemma ended after all.

Beth looked right at the waitress. This did nothing. Ron looked over to her and gave her the nod. She saw them. Julia went directly to Ron and Beth and said, "I am sorry, I lost track of what I was thinking - I did not know if you wanted anything. What can I bring to you?" "Do you think the menu has changed recently?" Ron asked Beth. Beth said, "I think the menus are new, however we can still order anything we used to get." Ron thought about this for a moment and Beth said, "I know what I would like." Julia said, "Okay." She readied her pen for a quick inscription of what might look like *curled abbreviation language*.

Beth then said, "I will have three pancakes, two sausages, and an over-easy egg with a hash brown. I would also like a side of honeydew melon wedges - I have not had any of those in a while." "Okay," said Julia, "May I bring you a coke?" "Sure," said Beth, who looked over to Ron who agreed to one, too. Julia finished writing these things down in close to no time at all and tried to decide whether Ron needed a second more. "May I have one of those double-patty super-monster cheese burgers that were so popular for a while?"

asked Ron. "Would you like bacon, grilled jalapenos, or onions on it?" asked Julia. "Yes," said Ron, "Yes I would - all three."

Julia knew the whole order and had only twenty paces to the terminal to punch it in. She scribbled out a quick cartoon of Ron instead of writing down his big hamburger. Julia then went over and rang their orders up properly; all was well. Beth and Ron watched the workers and patrons as they sat, walked, ate and conversed. Things were fine. Beth and Ron needed a coffee refill - Julia saw to it that it happened before they actually ran out all of the way. She did well.

Ron and Beth sat conversing. Julia brought their cokes to them and their food was ready. Julia carried all of their food to them on plates in one trip, and everything was perfect. Beth and Ron ate it all and thanked Julia. She had done a good job. Ron was about to leave, and Beth would be leaving soon, too.

Ron reached into his pocket and produced a billfold. Beth happened to have a very small purse on her person. They spoke with each other. When Julia got back to their table, she was hesitant; she did not know if they wanted desert. Ron and Beth both gave Julia a five. "How nice," said Julia on accident, and then recovered nicely with a careful, "Thank you." She asked if they had finished, and they both said, "Yes." Julia gave them their ticket so they could take care of it up front. She thanked them again and left them to go finish her side work.

"I think she did a fine job," said Ron. "Me too," said Beth. The two were going to have to move at some point. They began to muster the encouragement to do such a thing. Suddenly, there was a creaking and breaking noise, and a man fell through the ceiling. He landed on an empty table right in front of the Ron and Beth.

It was an air-conditioner repair man named Juan. Dressed for his profession, Juan's shirt and pants matched in army-green with his name embroidered on his uniform. The air conditioning system needed maintenance from time to time - its vents were not in the part of the ceiling he fell through. Beth noticed these things, and figured out that the curious little man must have been trying to listen in on her and Ron.

"A-C okay?" she asked him. "Yes Ma'am," said Juan, and he left. Ron thought it was somewhat funny, and so did Beth. The two took care of their ticket properly and said their goodbyes. It was nice to eat well for a change; they would sleep well that night. The A-C person was funny, too. People came and fixed the ceiling later that day. All was well. The coffee would steam for a long time to come.

◆

Sports Class

This is an odd story on the mysteries of what makes us human, and how we as humans are what we are. Some of us are brilliant. Some people are *average*. The best of us try hard and harder to do what we can for what we think is important, somehow. We all have a religion or do not. We all have preferences sexually or prefer to stay alone. Sometimes among the laughter of immaturity, one thing or another is found awkward and somewhat unforgettable - despite a failing memory. This is the account of a young football player - a running back who also played as tight end.

One fine morning on a Monday, it was fourth period in high school - *Sports* period. All of the male students went and dressed out. This means they wore thin gym shorts of cotton and short sleeve shirts of cotton, too. This day was a special day. Usually, in Sports there was a time where the coach told everyone what was going to happen that day. The students would then work out, run exercise drills, or *dress out* for close to an hour of football practice. They would do something physical for about forty-five minutes and then shower for class.

The football coach currently used Monday for observational purposes. The football players had just played a game on Friday night, and the coach had the game on a v. h. s. movie. This was very useful to the team; they could watch plays and figure what was most effective for scoring touchdowns and utilizing proper defense strategies. Highlights of touchdowns scored were fun to see by the players who were on the field, and so on.

Junior Varsity was the younger team. The coach led JV into a large sciences room. The players all walked into the room and made themselves at home legitimately. The first athletes through the door sat in the front, and the rest sat down behind them as they all packed into the room like sardines in a can. The running back sat on the second row, the second seat from the left. There were four rows behind him, about seven athletes per row, and some stood in the back.

The coach did a head count and all were present. "This was a great game, Friday night," said the coach. "We won, 52-6," he said, "We are going over the whole game by play selection in the next forty minutes. I am going to point out how they scored, and we will get to see that interception we accomplished when they tried to pass the ball at the goal line. I have mostly highlights of plays we ran properly, and I have some new plays to draw up here on the chalkboard. The plays are simply variations. There are two or three plays we could have run better; we will see those, too."

The coach put the tape in and pressed *play*. Two receivers fell asleep immediately. The coach woke them up by saying, "Fire drill! False alarm." Play after play was enjoyed by all. Anytime there was a key player running the ball or a person making a touchdown, that athlete pointed to the screen and all gave him *high-fives* or pats on the back.   The best play, by popular opinion, was a quarterback reverse. The quarterback handed the ball to a running back and continued to run to the sideline as if he had the ball. The quarterback then acted as if he was going to throw the ball, and the opposing team's defense was on him like flies on sticky-paper. The running back with the ball flanked in the opposite direction, and threw the ball twenty-six yards to a receiver. He ran twelve more yards and scored a touchdown.

The team was impressed with their favorite play. The coach showed the athletes the rest of the highlights, and then drew some variations of offensive and defensive team positions on the chalkboard. All men faced forward as if in a private school of grammar instruction. Suddenly, there was a sound. Quiet at first, a few students heard it. The repetitive bumping sound went, "bump-bump-bump-bump-bump."

The running back could hear it. He paid it no mind and continued in consideration of the new plays on the board. He would get either the ball or block; that was his avenue of criticism. "Bump-bump-bump-bump-bump," went the sound again. The running back heard it for sure this time. It was coming from behind him. The coach had his eyes on the running back *100 percent*; the athlete could not inspect the sound.

The coach drew the next play on the board. All was quiet behind the running back; the athletes were not even so much as whispering. For all he knew, they were beat red in attempted poker faces, trying not to laugh in front of a coach that was no fool. What could be so amusing or funny?

He heard the sound one last time, "Bump-bump-bump-bump-bump." The coach turned to draw an arced arrow of directional travel on the chalkboard, and the running back turned quickly to see what was behind him. Four Caucasian athletes might as well have been Native Americans, as their face was red from trying not to laugh. In the middle of them sat a more aggressive player, a defensive tight end well known for trouble. He had an erection, raised it, and let it *donk* on the wooden desk in front of him repeatedly, making the bumping sound.

The running back immediately felt regret. He just looked down. "What a Neanderthal," thought the mentally scarred running back. The coach speaking concluded his speech on the game. He congratulated the key players on a job well done. The tight end that played with himself got away with it. The coach released the athletes to go and shower for class. Nothing else happened out of the ordinary, and no one ever spoke of these occurrences aloud.

◆

Take Me Out to the Ball Game

One time, there was a young boy named Timothy. His father was a factory worker, and his mother was an Editor's Assistant. Attending school and behaving well in his every manner, he lived the normal life of a first grader. Tim received a small tape player radio for Christmas one year. It could play tapes continuously. He listened to it even whilst he did his homework. His parents were both hard workers, and took him to various places. His mother brought him to the grocery store and various other common places. She worked a normal forty-hour workweek, while his father worked as much as possible. They were a happy family attempting to live the *American Dream.*

The boy enjoyed listening to his new radio, as previously mentioned. One day, he listened to a whole ball game - a baseball game. It was between their city's team and a rival from another state. The game was an *away* game, but the boy enjoyed imagining the stadium, the fans, and the various runs made. He did not take notes on the stats or anything, but he did complete his homework. His loving and hard working father came home that day about an hour before dusk, as always. The boy asked if they could go outside and play catch while his mom was finishing dinner. "Of course, Tim," said his father, and they went out and played catch with an old ball.

That night, over dinner, the boy's parents discussed work and things seemed to be going fine. "I may get a promotion to section manager towards the end of the month," said the father. "That is nice," said the mother, and they all turned in for the night.

A few weeks later, the boy and his mother went to the supermarket, as they commonly did. "I think I am going to get some steaks for us," said the mother. The boy was excited. Steaks meant less frustration at the dinner table, though there was never really any poverty-induced stress in the family. The butcher broke into conversation with the boy about baseball. "Heard we won on the radio, did you?" asked the butcher. "Yes sir," replied the obedient boy. "What a game!" said the boy, noticing the large and perfectly sharp shiny knife well within reach of him. The mother and the boy eventually went home to cook dinner.

The steaks came out perfect. The father was happy, saying it was perfect timing for his new promotion. Everyone was happy. "Does our city have a baseball stadium?" the boy asked his father. "Sure it does," said the father, "It is on the other side of town from where I work." "Can we go there sometime?" asked the boy. "There are three home games left this season for our team," the boy said, trying to sound intelligent for his father. "Sure, Tim," said the father. "The home games are always on Saturdays." The boy glanced towards his mother and could tell she did not mind. "I sometimes work on Saturdays," said the father, "However I'm sure I can take one off to catch a game with you." "Alright!" exclaimed the boy. Then they all got ready for bed and had a good night's sleep.

A week or so went by, and the boy heard on the radio that the first of the last three games was on the coming Saturday. That night, over dinner, Tim asked his father if they could go to the ballgame on Saturday. "Not this time, Tim," replied the father, "Maybe next home game; I have a lot of work that has got to be done that day." The boy was not upset or disappointed. "At least," he thought, "We may go to the next one." They went off to bed that evening, as usual.

A few weeks went by, and the mother and the boy went to the supermarket. This time they spoke with the butcher, but did not get steaks. "Mommy," asked the boy, "Why would we talk with the butcher, but get no steaks?" "That is simply because we are having lobster tonight, Tim," replied the mother. "Wow," thought the boy "We have never even had lobster. I bet dad will be impressed." Sure enough, the father was impressed that night. The lobster was great. He even spoke about baseball before young Timothy had the time to think about it, promising to take him to the oncoming home game. As one might have guessed, they all went off to bed in their marry manners.

Timothy continued to do well in school. His father was increasing profits at work, and his mother even received a small raise herself. The Friday before the home game came. The city's baseball team had only lost one game the whole season, and it was a preseason scrimmage. The boy was excited that evening, he just knew his father was going to have tickets for the game in the morning. Sure enough, he watched his dad get out of his work truck with baseball tickets in his hand! The boy ran outside and hugged his father's leg saying, "You got the tickets for the game on tomorrow!" "No, Tim," said the father, "I was going to tell you in a minute. These tickets are for the last game of the season. I have no way of taking tomorrow off, and we both know that if they win tomorrow they will be one game away from going to the World Series." "No worries," thought the boy, "We will see a live game soon." They all ate dinner and went to bed happily, as always.

About a week or so later, the boy and the mother went to the supermarket. The city's baseball team had won the previous game. They only needed one more win to go to the playoffs. Upon entering the store, the mother asked the boy, "Timothy, what do you think would be a good idea for dinner tonight? We can get anything you like." "Okay if we ask the butcher?" asked Timothy. "Sure," said the mother. They made their way through the store gathering various things. Anything from the butcher would require various other helpings, of course. The two purchased these items upon leaving the grocery store. When they got to the butcher, he was sharpening his knife collection. "That is a neat set of knives," said the boy. "Thanks," replied the butcher before noticing his small acquaintance. "Hey, Tim!" said the butcher, "We just keep winning, do we not?" "They cannot stop us," said Tim, "We are going to the play-offs!" "What can I do for you today?" the butcher asked the young boy's mother. "I'm going to let Tim decide, today," she said.

The butcher turned to Tim and said, "Well?" "What is your most tasty dinner idea?" asked Tim politely. "Our super heavy cut steak and oyster special cannot be beat," replied the butcher. "Is that what you want, ma'am?" the butcher asked. "That will be fine," replied the mother saying, "I will lightly fry the oysters." She knew how excited Tim was to hear of fried oysters - he never tried them before. The butcher cut the thickest steaks available in the city and then said, "I have to go to the cooler for the oysters; I will return shortly."

The mother browsed through the various items in the freezer display while the butcher was gone. Upon his return, the butcher handed the steaks and the oysters to the mother. After having done so, he looked at his knife collection that he was previously sharpening. "I could have sworn I just laid down my largest butcher knife here," he said. After a brief moment of contemplation, he said, "Well, I must have left it in the back. Have a nice day." The mother thanked the butcher. He and Tim waved good-bye to each other, and the mom and the boy traveled home safely. Not even the boy's mother saw him put the large and recently sharpened butcher knife under his jacket.

Dinner that night was incredible. The father returned home from work at normal time. Things were going well on both sides of the table, as far as Tim could see. He had never tried pan-fried oysters or *thick* steaks either one. The meal was to die for. The father was thoroughly impressed with the mother's culinary skill - she included a tossed salad and buttered bake potatoes with fixings for dinner. "Are you looking forward to the big game?" asked the young boy's father. "Absolutely," said Timothy. They then all went off to bed merrily, as always.

The Friday before the big game came about eventually, and the family had dinner and went off to bed happily. Visions of the huge stadium and magnificent crowds danced in young Timothy's head as he slept away. They would be waking up early on Saturday in order to get to the game on time. Late that night, hours before sunrise, the father's work called. He went off to work and took care of his obligations. Upon returning home, he heard on the radio that the city's team had won the game. They were going to the World Series. "Damn it!" said the father, realizing that he went to work without remembering the big ballgame. He and his son were not going to a home game that season.

A huge and heavy feeling came over the father. He almost could not drive properly. He made it to the house, instinctively worried about Tim. He walked through the front door and past the kitchen. The man's wife was cooking dinner as she normally would be. Weakened, the man kept on to Tim's room. Upon flinging open the door, he saw young Timothy sitting on his bed Indian style, with a large butcher knife inserted into his head upwards. Timothy was dead; he had committed suicide. In the background, a tape was playing. It was playing "Take Me Out to the Ball Game".

◆

The Bistro

Once time, in a city of over 500,000 people, there existed four men. These men were of varied occupation, yet they possessed various similar traits. Mainly, they took serious pride in hard work. Their work ethic was of the form of a type of suicidal ballet - they always kept moving. Reincarnation must have remained a kind of insurance in their subconscious minds; they would simply be okay with working themselves *to death* in order to live happily. Sleep and proper diet were also a part of their *ki*, or way of life in their surrounding existence. The men were dedicated to work in an incredibly healthy manner.

They consisted of a male nurse, a paralegal, an art instructor, and a construction worker. There names were Waldon Hobbes, Emery Stone, Bron Hemington, and Tommy Finn. This story, and many of the other stories that may seem highly similar, is and are, about how these men came to run a restaurant and part of a city.

The four confidants originally met at a large weekly gathering of sorts. There were plenty of people in the nondenominational congregation, yet every week, one way or another, the four agreed and disagreed with certain topics, together. This caused them to become closer with each other than most others in the crowd. One could easily say they inadvertently formed a kind of nonchalant team. After about eight months or so, they did not necessarily attend their gathering anymore, for one reason or another. The four men remained in contact rather often, however. They never chose a leader, yet they did have untold influence in their society. The men also enjoyed a long-lasting and rather profitable business association, together. They died together as a kind of four-headed philosophy team, in there nineties.

Jogging down a sidewalk one day with his pit bull, the male nurse named Waldon Hobbes (his name similar to "dirty jobs") noticed a rent to partially posses sign in front of a building. It was next to an old single-projector cinema. The cinema was in existence only due to the market cost of the building's demolition in its entirety. There were also four other businesses in the building. None of the businesses were too overly interesting by comparison, not this fine beautiful morning, which included a crisply blowing spring breeze.

Waldon wrote down the number off the posted advertisement. He called it later that evening with his cell phone on a break from the hospital. The place was for *rent to posses*. The owner of the building, Mr. Fang, would be more than happy to show it to him in the morning. Waldon and his companions not only could use a meeting place, they *needed* one. This looked like a good idea for a restaurant, as well as a place for conversations that could somehow promote their idea of sobriety-induced serenity.

Waldon wanted to scope the place out before contacting his fellows, however. When he called the number on the sign out front, he spoke with the property owner, directly. As mentioned, Waldon spoke briefly with Mr. Fang. They planned to meet in the morning.

That next morning, Waldon went and met with him. They entered into the old section through the rear door to scope it out. Abandoned for quite some time, the suspended air was dusty and still in the shadows. The place was broken down and dirty. It contained cobwebs, dusty broken boards, and debris all over. It needed cleaning and remodeling; that was for sure. The most interesting aspect of the section of the building was the balcony.

The balcony extended far enough over the sidewalk to one day place tables for smorgasbords and the like. It had a mid area and a back area that was somewhat darker. The place had large front windows. The first floor functioned as a two-sided basement divided by a stairway entrance. The ground floor's space was not easily or readily accessible. The front of the section had a stairwell leading up to the old and damaged front door. The section needed refurbishing. It hinted in only an indistinct manner to its beautiful future.

After a pleasant introductory and minimal polite conversation, Waldon asked Mr. Fang, "What is your request for this exciting and cheery place?" "$650 a month," said the property owner, "It is a portion of commercial property. After three years, the section is yours, rent free, and you will own 19% of the total building and property for understood tax purposes. You can avoid paying monthly if you really want the place, for nineteen thousand." "I might *rent-to-own* it," said Waldon.

"Once you make your first payment, you will have permission to redo the inside totally. I remember you mentioned using the place to run a restaurant, right?" "Sure thing," said Waldon, "I will speak with a few of my peers this evening, and I will call you in the morning." "What are you going to call it?" asked Mr. Fang, almost overly enthralled. "If we go through with the monthly payments, together, I am sure we will be able to call it 'The Bistro'."

Waldon, being the male nurse, went to the hospital that day. Once off, he gave his three main pals a ring, and they talked about the interesting new place. They also called each other. The four of them could not answer their return calls at the same time, so they decided to meet behind the building before 6 AM in the morning. Little did they know, the close friends had started a daily occurrence. A near half hour long conversation every morning would become a convenient and necessary habit that would become a sort of daily form of religion for their sanity.

"What an amazing find!" said the art instructor, Bron Hemington, sometime around 5:55 AM that next morning. "Can we go in to talk?" asked the construction worker, Tommy Finn. "I did not pay for the first month yet," said the nurse, Waldon Hobbes. "I will pick this lock," said Emery Stone, the paralegal. With that, they followed Emery through the back door, as he unlocked it with a small two-part metal device he had conveniently procured on his keychain, years ago.

Bron, Tommy, Waldon, and Emery walked inside not knowing what to think of or to say. "Let us not disregard the dangers of *Notion Theory*, lest our dreams existing as nightmares come true," said Waldon. "What is Notion Theory?" asked Bron. "Waldon's idea," said Tommy saying, "Notion Theory is the idea that if we dwell upon a worry or futuristic possible idea it will come true, be it good, bad, or neither." "Wow," said Emery.

The section was void of motion. It appeared as though no one entered it in many years. The four men went through the section inspecting and analyzing every small detail of structure for any ideas possible. They agreed that "The Bistro" was a good name for a restaurant. They also agreed on various interior design structures and possibilities. The "Front" or middle area reserved for cooking, they would definitely need a beverage bar for entree presentations and the like. The electrical outlets and plumbing needed to be redone.

A very interesting section, indeed, they even discovered a twin pair of floor doors that opened to the ground floor. They were in no hurry for the business to actually profit, as they already had steady work. The four were excited, as they had found what would become a decent place to convene. Time having passed, they left the building prior to 7 AM. The four agreed to pay Mr. Fang one fourth of the monthly payment a piece for the three years and agreed to split any actual profits in fourths.

That afternoon, during a quick break from hospital duties, Waldon called Mr. Fang and agreed to the monthly request for payment to partially posses. "Where are you now?" asked Waldon. "I am at a shopping center looking at a table for my wife," said Mr. Fang, "As soon as you pay me, you can have the keys to the front and back doors." "How far are you from the state university? One of my associates is an art instructor there, and he can pay you today, " said Waldon. "I am not too far from there, does he have a number to coordinate a meeting?" asked Mr. Fang. He seemed to be happy to speak with Waldon. "The Bistro" sounded like an exciting idea to him.

"Yes, Mr. Fang," replied Waldon, happy to be getting things squared away. Waldon gave Mr. Fang the number. Mr. Fang called Bron in the afternoon. Bron met and paid him after he completed a short lecture on lighting perspective with the medium of oil on common canvas - a seemingly cliché topic. Bron was not only a professor, but also a highly skilled artist of rare capability and technique. The four agreed by cell phones to meet again in the morning, behind their newly purchased section, before 6 AM. At least they had keys to the place this time.

The morning came and the four where all behind the building before 7 AM. Bron opened the door and they entered with less trepidation than on the previous day. The four settled all matters immediately, confirming given considerations aloud. Bron got ¾ of $650, or $487.50, from the others, and he confirmed that he would give everyone a copy of both keys by the next morning. Bron did so.

They split up responsibilities for acquiring preliminary and basic tools for cleaning out the place. A push broom and some big plastic garbage cans and bags were definitely necessary. They would need a table with four chairs and other things. During this morning, the four mostly talked softly and began making a pile of loose debris by the rear of the section. They would meet again tomorrow, each happy to be a part of something.

Finally, they could discuss matters in private - be the matters important or simply consoling thoughts. One way or another, they were looking forward to the mornings to come. How exciting was that? It was very exciting.

The four continued their normal jobs. Eventually, after having worked on their new section for some time everyday, it was nice. They opened the doors to the public and ran the business well. People from all over enjoyed fine dining, and the four were able to employee people for restaurant work. Everyone lived happily ever after.

♦

The Biker Gang Story

One time, there was a notorious biker gang. Its roots came from post WWII veterans who believed in freedom and the feel of an adventurous ride. They established their non-AMA rules and were known for years by the ATF as nothing other than an OMG. "OMG" meant that they were a known *outlaw motorcycle gang*. They did not ever try to cause any problems, yet they were known for selling and manufacturing speed, condoning prostitution, selling guns and other forms of involvement with group violence linking to murder and organized crime. You name it - many thought these people were a group of criminals. Their founding leaders set up the organization and ended up either in prison or dead. The newer post-fifties generations never really broke the law very often.

They called themselves the *Death Eagles*, and they were born to ride. Any new member could be fully patched in in only a few months. They had methods for not including narcs, rats, or officers of the law. All members were respected fully by other gangs as well as their own group and the leaders of their various chapters. The Death Eagle's patch was the image of an eagle's skull. In time, the Death Eagles constructed three main meetinghouses - one by Canada, one in southern California, and one in Florida. They expanded to travel the nation. The Death Eagles loved traveling across the nation for any reason.

Our story involves the first fully patched female member of the Death Eagles. She came from the son of one of the original founders of a subsidiary motorcycle gang. He was the president of a chapter operating in Texas. This chapter called themselves *The Claws*, stemming as a part of the Death Eagle's vicious grip into a bleeding society. The Claws loved to ride. They spent their time going to swap meets, pancake restaurants, rock concerts, and historical motorcycle clubhouses all over the nation.

The meetinghouse of The Claws was in a small garage north-east of Houston, TX. They used this garage as a legitimate front for various different things. Any money members made went to the garage, so the gang could buy motorcycle parts, jackets, gasoline, and more. The meeting garage operated a normal and legal business for repairing non-member bikes and fixing various kinds of motorcycles. From time to time, they did cook speed - this is not to say that they made an often habit of such a dangerous and illegal activity. They cooked it to sell at rock concerts and were very careful not to let anyone over-use or get caught.

For the most part, members of The Claws paid their dues. The garage's legitimate side of business kept them out of trouble and able to ride. The president of The Claw's name was Snake-Smoke. Snake-Smoke was an intelligible fellow according to his peers. He thought of himself as a man of effort, understanding, and freedom. His woman was a chapter prostitute. She made money selling her time to a few regular customers and paid her dues accordingly. He constantly tried to keep her out of trouble by letting her sell t-shirts or fix bikes, but she always snuck in a fun customer here and there. The only two things she almost loved more than riding a motorcycle were sex and money.

Every great biker gang goes to an annual meeting of some sort. The Death Eagles had a big meeting every year that always involved a rock concert and a dinner cook-off out in the desert area of north-central Arizona. It was here that Snake-Smoke's woman, Bunny, promised him to give up prostitution. For that, he said he would attempt to father a child and gave her a half-carrot diamond ring. They agreed to keep the youngster from evil, and the two fell in love permanently.

The rock music gathering was called N. A. for North Arizona. These two exciting bikers got it on at N. A., right in front of a large crowd of people. The Claw's gang members were yelling, "Get you some! Get you some!" and he and Bunny *finished* on the *motorcycle running*. She enjoyed revving the engine loudly to shake the ground. They were kicked off the property and willingly left. Snake-Smoke said, "Let us ride!" and The Claws roared their twin engines to shake the ground and travel on. Thirty of them attended N. A. that year.

Things went well for some time. Bunny pretty much became the secretary of the garage and Snake-Smoke and his fellows repaired and sold bikes for and to customers from all over the nation. Bunny and Snake-Smoke got married, and she was pregnant. Their miracle of life was coming, and they both worked hard and responsibly to ensure the well-being of her future.

Part of their dedication to her future involved making motorcycles. They made choppers. Snake-Smoke and his fellows were excellent welders and bike mechanics. They ordered engines from well-trusted motorcycle manufactures and sold choppers with the larger engines - the engines were over 1,500 cc's. Most of the motors were V-twins. They did custom paint jobs and airbrushed the gas tanks for customer satisfaction. Because of these things, The Claws became a relatively wealthy and powerful group of people.

Bunny was eight months pregnant, healthy, and tired of her continuously redundant and routine life. "Do I look fat to you?" she asked Snake-Smoke, one night. Snake-Smoke looked over to her from a chopper he was running a fuel line on and thought, "Maybe I can get me some more..." "No," he said. "Come on, tell me you could float me like a twelve-man balloon on Thanksgiving," said Bunny. "Sweetheart," said Snake-Smoke, "You are the prettiest thing that I ever laid eyes upon, and I want to make love with you." It was a little awkward, but the two got it on in the garage.

When they had finished, Snake-Smoke could tell that she was thinking. "What is on your mind?" asked Snake-Smoke. "I think I have become somewhat uninterested," said Bunny. "We have not taken a day off since N. A.," said Snake-Smoke, "How can you be uninterested?" "I want to ride," said Bunny. "You are due in under thirty days," said Snake-Smoke,

"You are already having contractions, and I want you to have our baby in a hospital in Houston - not on the pebbles somewhere on the great roads of America." "I want to ride," said Bunny, "I need to figure out how."

Snake-Smoke somehow understood this woman. He also saw a sincere desire coming from her not so sane side of thinking. "Look," said Snake-Smoke, "We have a big chopper that needs to be delivered somehow to a chapter of Death Eagles in Canada. The shipping was going to be costly. We could always just break in the bike, and discount the overall cost." "Can I ride the big chopper with you guys to Canada?" asked Bunny. Snake-Smoke was thinking, "Her water breaks and that bike is an immediate donation." He then said, "Sure Bunny, anything you want."

It was only about 9 PM then, and Snake-Smoke called four or five of his guys up and told them to get ready for a long trip up the interstate. They would leave in the morning. Bunny was happy. She and Snake-Smoke made love again and went off to sleep.

They awoke early. The bikers were excited to hit the road. They met at the garage and were ready to go at sun-up. Bunny's amazing bike was a 2000 cc Twin-V chopper. They painted the chopper black and it had a silver eagle's skull airbrushed onto the gas tank with platinum-flake flames. The frame was all chrome and the smooth seat was made of swayed black leather. Her Canada-bound machine was a beautiful and priceless handmade toy. They secured the garage and were ready to go.

"Let us ride!" exclaimed Snake-Smoke, and the six bikers made their way to the interstate. Bunny wore a shirt that said, "Canada or bust." The weather was fine. Bunny's bike ran smooth and clean. It was a perfect ground-shaker.

The route they were taking would take them about five days. They planned to stop and see friends and hotels along the way. Their travels were safe, and Bunny took excellent care of the motorcycle. The small gang had seen the same old hotels before, and it was always a pleasure to surprise friends throughout the nation with their presence. The Claws were always ready for a good ride.

The Canadian chapter of Death Eagles was known as "Death Eagles no. 309," and that is what it said on their clubhouse. The six bikers of The Claws arrived in a timely fashion, and they were welcomed by the Canadian chapter. The Death Eagles were thoroughly impressed with the awesome chopper and paid The Claws what they were asking - eighty-five percent of the original quote.

Bunny's water broke early the next day, and they rushed her to the nearest hospital on the United States side of the Canadian boarder. It was nice. Snake-Smoke stayed with Bunny in the emergency room, and she gave birth to an eight pound and four ounce girl. Bunny and Snake-Smoke were going to name the newborn girl Harlia. They went ahead and named the young girl Canada instead of Harlia though, because that is all Bunny kept saying during the little girl's birth.

The baby was in the hospital for close to a week, and Bunny rode with Canada in a baby carrier backpack on Snake-Smoke's trusted chopper all the way back to the garage in Texas. The members of The Claws included in the journey stayed close by their Death Eagle's chapter president, his wife, and their newborn baby, Canada.

As mentioned, nothing out of the ordinary really ever happened with The Claws - they were not as violent as their original members during the sixties and seventies. Something happened, however. A few months after Canada's birth, Bunny took her grocery shopping. A rival biker gang, a group of real dirty men from south of Houston, The Bashers, saw Bunny and Canada in the produce section. They ran towards Bunny and took Canada.

Bunny chased after them and they got away on their motorcycles. Bunny called Snake-Smoke. Snake-Smoke called ~~some~~ about forty of his confidants. About thirty of them were The Claws, and there were a few volunteers and Death Eagles from other chapters. They dressed fully and met up at the garage. "Let us ride!" exclaimed Snake-Smoke, and they departed in a pack to south of Houston, were The Bashers had an old run-down clubhouse.

When The Claws pulled in, there were various scumbags walking around drinking cheap beer. "Who is your leader?" exclaimed Snake-Smoke, "We have come for the baby." "I am *Frog*, leader of The Bashers," yelled one of The Bashers, "And that baby is ours for good." This is something he should not have said, really. There were only about twenty-five dirty Bashers, and they were mostly drunk. The Claws beat the tar out of every one of them, and Snake-Smoke found Canada sleeping on a pillow in a tent around back of the Basher's shed construction. The Claws were rather brutal to The Bashers and left many of them badly beaten. Snake-Smoke and his men recovered Canada.

The Claws road back to their garage with their baby and went home to bed. Canada grew up with the biker gang; Bunny and Snake-Smoke raised her well. She was very intelligent and could speak in full sentences and run before the age of three. By the age of seven she was convinced that nursing was not for her, that she wanted to be a bike mechanic and cook pancakes when she was a grown up.

The Bashers never really retaliated, and the chopper making business run by The Claws became rather successful. Tried as they did to keep Canada out of trouble, she became highly involved with the Death Eagles 309 chapter in Canada. She helped them deliver small packages all over the country with gang members and sunk large sums of muscle money into their organization.

The Claws functioned well; Canada wanted to be a motorcycle gang member. No woman was aloud to do this. Secret laws of the organization involved prerequisites and exercises. No woman had ever been aloud to even know the three preliminary membership requirements. They were to take a man out, cough up a kilo of pure methamphetamine, and pay a sum of one thousand dollars to the area chapter president.

She did it. Canada paid and gave up a kilo. She found the Basher that kidnapped her as a baby and took him out. He was buried with lime in Canada. She made money fixing bikes and cooked some speed under the instruction of an old Death Eagle friend of her father's without Snake-Smoke's consent. Canada was sworn in and became a real terror to many rival gang members. She organized her own chapter in the panhandle, the Death Eagles Chapter 202.

Canada spent most of her days repairing and selling choppers, just like Snake-Smoke. Her chapter raised funds for needy children and taught motorcycle safety courses. Canada cooked pancakes for her fellows and lived a long and healthy life. The Death Eagles rode on.

♦

The Bistro Part Two, The Ground Floor

One time, four hard working men put aside a percentage of their monthly earnings to run a restaurant. They rented a section of a building from a property owner named Mr. Fang. They intended to remodel their section of the building. The men met early in the morning everyday to discuss both business and personal matters. Their names were Waldon Hobbes, Emery Stone, Bron Hemington, and Tommy Finn. They had only agreed to the purchase of their section a few days before this astonishingly fine morning. Various surprises were sure to be horrific. The sun was not up just yet; it would be rising soon.

"Good morning fellow confidants," said Waldon, the male nurse, "I was able to obtain front and backdoor keys for us." While he handed the other three men their keys, Emery, the paralegal, said, "I purchased the large cans we spoke of, yesterday." "I bought two push brooms, four boxes of can liners, and this large sack of paper towels," said Bron, the art instructor. The three turned to Tommy, the construction worker, who said, "I got enough cleaning chemicals for the whole block." With that, they followed Emery through the back door, and Tommy and Bron checked their keys in the lock.

They began piling any debris and the broken boards in a pile towards the back door. Most of the preparation for cleaning the floor only took about ten minutes. Emery and Bron began sweeping the extremely dirty floor towards the front, as Waldon and Tommy admired the front windows. "We are definitely going to need windows that swing open," said Waldon. "What if we just knock these out?" asked Tommy. "You are the construction worker," said Waldon, "What do you think?" "Just knock them out" they heard from the two in the back who spoke in unison quite commonly. Tommy and Waldon began kicking out the old glass windows onto the balcony area. They were careful, yet it was fun for all.

Just as Tommy and Waldon were done breaking the glass out of the large twin window frames, Emery said, "I am going to go get a crowbar from my truck." "Why?" asked Tommy. "To open these trap doors we found yesterday," said Bron. Waldon watched as the dust and dirt blew into the outside air from the front window frames. Emery had returned in close to no time and handed his crowbar to Tommy. Tommy looked at Emery, and Bron said, "Tommy, you are the construction worker. You are competent." They all smiled as Tommy gladly broke the hinges out of the lock keeping the two trap doors on the floor closed. The other three men managed to open the doors and rest them on the floor.

Peering inside, a musty and old house-like smell rose from the ground floor's deadly darkness. "I see where a rope ladder must have been removed from this side," said Tommy, "Is there a ladder on the other door?" "No," said Emery. "How far down can it be?" asked Waldon, as he heard Bron say "I am going to my buggy to get my 'Magna 5,000'." Bron hurried to get his amazing flashlight from his dune buggy machine he called a *4x4 mudd'n machine*. It resembled a military vehicle but utilized large wide tires that cost about as much as a new 4-cylinder car from Japan.

Waldon crawled into the hole on his side while Tommy and Emery held apprehensive facial expressions. The entryway seemed dark to them. There had been little to no airflow on the ground floor for decades. Waldon hung by both hands to stretch out his height, and released his grip to drop down to the floor of the ground floor. As he had guessed, the drop was only about three feet of free fall. The temporary time in the old and deathlike air still scared him a little. He bent his knees to land as safely as possible. Once on the ground, Waldon looked up. "Bron is coming with his flashlight," said Emery. Tommy then tossed the flashlight down to Waldon as Bron crawled and dropped down the close-by entryway, the same as Waldon had done.

"I cannot get the flashlight on!" said Waldon. "Squeeze the rubber part," said Bron. Tommy and Emery were both peering through the entryway, as Bron and Waldon were in darkness on the ground floor. Waldon turned on the "Magna 5,000". The four gentlemen flushed pale as the light came on. There were fully dressed skeletons on the ground everywhere. Tommy and Emery helped Waldon and Bron back up from the ground floor.

Tommy went and got a hammer and nails from his truck. They quickly put the trap doors back and nailed them to the floor with cover boards. They also sealed up the front windows with large black sacks. The four left to go to work. It was almost 7 AM, and they would figure out what to do the next day.

The four men showed up as normal, shortly before 6 AM, and entered the building. "You know what those could be?" asked Emery, "They could be plastic Halloween decorations." "That is funny," said Bron, as he handed Emery and Tommy both a crowbar. They pried open the trap doors and lowered down a rope to climb down to the ground floor. Each brought a flashlight, as well as other tools. It was a given known, somehow, not to communicate with the authorities. Who could have ever been trusted, anyway? At any rate, they had the time within the previous twenty-four hours to collect their wits, somewhat.

"These guys must have been here for a very long while," said Waldon. "I think so," said Bron. "I see what must be bullet holes in their clothing," said Emery, "These guys were all shot to death." "That is going to be a good guess," said Tommy, "Every single victim has possible bullet holes in their clothing, and I also see led pellets."

The four ascertained that a gunman or gunmen had *hosed down* the dead men a long time ago. The skeletons' flesh had turned to dust, and they all had on suits from what looked like the twenties. They decided to clean out the floor as if nothing had ever happened. Time seemed to be of the essence. They searched the pockets of every victim, about twenty in number. The four men found various items and pocket money from long ago, but no identification on any victim. The bodies must have been gangsters previously. "One bad person must have shot them all, took the ladder, and sealed the twin doors to the floor," thought the four men. The doors must have remained unchanged for a very long time.

The four climbed out of the ground floor, nailed the doors back down with boarding, and left. They all four went to work, as always, and slept better that night than the night before. The next morning came, and they met at the back door again, sometime before 6 AM. Bron opened the back door and they all went inside. "We already have bags to put the skeletons in," said Emery. "What are you thinking of?" said Waldon, "Cremation?" "Sounds like a plan," said Bron. Tommy agreed and they opened the twin trap doors, again. They formed and secured two rope ladders, one for each door.

They climbed down the ladders wearing protective dust masks, and only Tommy stayed up top as a kind of lookout. The back door was secure, and there really was nothing to hide, anyway. "Tommy," said Waldon. Tommy was scared out of his mind. "What," said Tommy. "Hand us down a box for the jewelry items and this old money," said Emery. "Please also hand us down a box of trash bags," said Bron. Tommy handed down a box of trash bags, and the three on the ground floor worked noiselessly and efficiently for about half an hour.

The three on the ground floor managed to consolidate all of the old clothing into two bags and handed them up to Tommy. They also handed him the bag with small items and old coins and notes. They assembled a pile of bones towards the back of the ground floor. They bagged all of them together to be able to decide on a cremation site. The three climbed out of there, and they boarded up the floor again. Tommy had swept, and the place already looked more presentable. They left before 7 AM.

The next morning came. Waldon, Emery, Tommy, and Bron were all present before 6 AM. Tommy opened the back door and they went inside to talk. "A cremation location suggestion?" asked Waldon aloud softly. "Well," said Emery, "We have the bones ready to burn, as well as the clothes. We can save the small items and old money for future discussion or nostalgia, but I cannot decide on a good place to have a 'bonfire'." "No problem," said Tommy, "All I need is a cow." "What?" said Waldon. Tommy then said, "We have left those windows open short the bags we taped up there for days, now. The job I just bid cannot start until tomorrow. I will install the swinging windows we spoke of the other morning, today. I will also go get my barbeque pit and burn the bones on the balcony."

"You have a since of humor, Tom," said Bron apprehensively, "I will go to see my butcher friend here in a few moments and bring you something to cook before my first class begins." "People will smell your cooking for miles," said Emery. "We can call them *Bone Burgers*," said Waldon. "I do not have a problem burning the old clothes in my backyard with some leaves and stuff," said Emery, "I doubt there will be a problem with the smell coming from the balcony."

"Well," said Tommy, "Twenty skeletons or so will take some time. That is also a certain amount of smoke. I have a big sack of charcoal. People will be able to see me from the street, too." "What if we put a grand opening sign up for the first of the month?" asked Bron, "That way people will have a chance to think the cooking is really for them, and they can come eat what they smelled then." "That is a good idea," said Waldon, "I will have a sign here before my shift begins, today."

With that, the four had minimal conversations about loved ones, old gangsters, and sociology. They all left before 7 AM, as usual, and Tommy returned with a trailer full of stuff before 8 AM. He moved the huge swinging windows to the front of the section with a dolly alone, and placed his large barbeque pit on the balcony. Waldon came, put up a grand opening sign, and left. Bron came back happy as a lark and let himself in with four large sacks. By the time Bron came, Tommy had his barbeque pit figured out. He already burned close to a fourth of the bones.

"What is all of that?" asked Tommy, as Bron sat down the four large butcher sacks by the barbeque pit. "Well," said Bron, "Four lambs. I still have over half an hour before my class begins." "Okay," said Tommy, "Do you have time to go to my trailer and bring up my ice chest?" "Sure," said Bron. Bron brought Tommy the huge ice chest that contained six bags of ice and went to the university. Tommy burned the rest of the bones by mid-afternoon cooking all four of the lambs. During his cooking, he also installed the swinging windows properly.

Only one person asked about the cookout that day. "What is going on up there?" hollered a curious pedestrian. The young male seemed to be on his way to somewhere and also said, "I see the sign; you guys opening a place to eat?" "Sure thing," said Tommy, "We will have barbequed lamb, salad, and toast on our opening day there on the banner." "I might come check it out," said the man, and he walked away. No one else from the street asked any questions.

Tommy placed all of the ashes in a large sack. Emery came some time before 5 PM and helped Tommy get the barbeque pit back to the trailer. They locked up the back of the building, and Tommy let Emery take the cooked lambs home to his deep freezer. Tommy himself took the bag of ashes to the river and poured them out. The four slept better than usual that night - the skeletons were gone.

They met as usual before 6 AM the following day. Bron let them in the back door, and Waldon removed the grand opening sign. "I brought a box for the small items and old money," said Bron. "That is a nice box," said Tommy. "I have enough barbequed lamb to sell fifty dinners," said Emery. "You burned the clothes?" asked Waldon. "Yes," said Emery, "They are gone." The four conversed a while and left the building before 7 AM.

Waldon, Emery, Bron, and Tommy met every morning behind The

Bistro to discuss their wives, occupations, and town happenings. The four were humbly proud of their sobriety. Time flew by, and each of the four restaurant owners maintained an easier life than before. They usually employed a restaurant manager with bar tending experience, a janitor, and an average of six servers. The business was a success.

The four maintained the business properly. The Bistro sold out of barbeque lamb burgers not too long after opening and ended up selling mostly steak, soups, fried chicken, salads, and baked potatoes. The employees did well, and The Bistro caused its owners to find success in their lives. The restaurant made money for over twenty years; The Bistro carried on.

◆

The Circus Freaks

One time, there were five male workers. One of them was their leader, and they called him Mr. S. He rented a large room with a half-kitchen and a bathroom. It was one of five rooms in a large rent house close to a police station. The other four men lived with their families. All four men were heads of their household. One lived with a younger cousin, one with an aunt, and the other two with their financially struggling and or handicapped mothers.

They had real names, yet they went by code names for both fun and expediency. Mr. Wacky, Mr. Panda, Mr. Happy, and Mr. Polka-dots were their names. They worked constantly and did nothing wrong, usually. This is to say that they stayed busy, and they always tried to stay out of trouble.

One of their only activities that involved leisure was watching a late night show once a week that involved trapping and blowing away zombies with shotguns. At any rate, they helped keep a small business going that sold twenty-seven kinds of chicken pitas. The pitas were made with fried, baked or steamed chicken, a fluffed-bread tortilla pouch, a cheese, lettuce, and choices of vegetable medleys and dressing preferences.

Sales at the business barely paid for the place, but the owner kept it going to *live the dream*. They usually made a decent profit during the holidays. He and his wife worked other jobs and owned two other businesses. The town they were in consisted of about 500,000 people; the city contained people of all walks of life.

One day the business owner's brother told him that his four year old son was ill. The boy had only one year to live. There was a treatment that could be attempted, however it would cost twenty thousand dollars even though they had medical insurance. More than one doctor said that the treatment was possible, yet it was only effective in one in three patients and barely even worth the try.

None of these people knew how to come up with twenty grand, not then. Mr. S. heard these things and was sad. He thought of one thing first. He would get his guys together and they would go throw this child a get-well-soon happy party and try to figure something out afterward. Mr. S. wanted to meet the boy; he would be sure to figure something out. For his loved ones, Mr. S. would do almost anything.

Mr. S. made the schedule that week to include all four of his guys on one day, a Tuesday. There were other employees that worked at Pita-Time besides the five "clowns" in this story, of course, but the ill boy was a reason for an informal meeting. The clowns were always happy to be dedicated to something.

None of the clowns other than Mr. S. really knew or recognized the schedule that week, but when break came, the four were invited into Mr. S.'s small office. A cashier and two food preparers kept the business running during the meeting. Mr. Polka-dots looked over to Mr. Happy who had not the clue; he did not know why they were all in there. They all knew it was on rare occasion to see the five together at once. Mr. Wacky was admiring the small space, and Mr. Panda stared to the ground. He was possibly the wisest of the five.

Before anyone was too overly confused, Mr. S. closed the door and spoke as follows:

We all know the four-year-old of our owner's brother only has a year to live. I have a plan in the works. We are going to dress up like clowns and go throw him a get-well-soon party with a pizza, a cake, and some cola. We will cheer him up. I have a neighbor with a sewing machine, and she will make us our own clown suits. We will have to get her some fabric for the outfits. Each of you are to bring an old sheet from home your next scheduled work day for your outfit. Anyone with a problem bringing an old sheet must speak with me in a moment. She will make our outfits, and we will go throw the party. Bring all of the Halloween make-up you can find to this office. We will also need wigs; we will figure out the wigs *before* the party. Mr. Panda and Mr. Wacky, you two get some wiener-dog balloons. Mr. Polka-dots and Mr. Happy, you get some honker horns from the party store and bring those hand-pump fire extinguishers I know you still have. Run any other ideas for cheering this boy up by me and we will do a fine job. We will save our outfits and I will try to organize a profitable caper. Now, go make yourselves busy until your shifts are over.

With these things said, all men agreed with Mr. S. and went back to work. They brought their sheets with no problem. They collected enough make-up to *re-teenage* an octogenarian, almost. Time went by. Payday came and was gone, and they set the day of the party on a coming Thursday.

Mr. S.'s neighbor happily made the outfits for five dollars a suit, and Mr. S. happily paid her. He also let her design the wigs, and she sold him five "hyper-crazy wigs," as she called them, for ten dollars. Thursday came and they all five had the day off. They met up at Pita-Time to get their outfits and departed together. Mr. Wacky had just attained a brown four-cylinder van four days ago for six hundred and fifty dollars on a loan. This is how they would travel, and Mr. S. was the driver.

They drove over to Mr. S.'s room and *phone-boothed* (changed clothes) Superman-style coming out of there a motley team of clowns. Armed with horn honkers, wiener-dog balloons, and water squirting fire-extinguisher pumping devices, they sped away.

The young boy's house was on the other side of town, about twelve minutes away. Mr. Polka-dots kept quite in the van, and so did Mr. Happy. They did not say much, even though they would have. The clowns looked as happy as a couple of peeing puppies. They were almost too happy to even think, much less talk about the current ongoing occurrences. Mr. Wacky held the hot pizza Mr. S. bought, and Mr. Panda held the cake he brought from one of his neighbors. They all enjoyed the ride.

The owner's brother knew they were coming. Once the five clowns got there, they jumped out of the van saying surprise and danced around a bit. The young boy was certainly happy to see them and did not know really what to think or say. The clowns sprayed their water pumps on the flowerbeds nearby. The boy asked his dad if it was his birthday party who said it was not, and that the clowns were there just to have a fun time. They sang him a happy not-your-birthday song and gave the boy a cake. Some neighbors and friends had come to the get well soon party, and all involved had a good time. They all had fun making wiener dogs and shapes with the balloons. No one could match Mr. S.'s artistic talent with wiener dog balloons. No one even came close to doing such a thing. The boy's favorite balloon was an airplane Mr. S. made that could really fly.

The clowns drove back and dispersed, and Mr. S. knew he was going to have to think of something. He also knew it would not be easy. Risks would be in any situation. Twenty grand was a lot of money to anyone. A bank robbery, a safe cracking, or the knocking off of a jewelry store was needed. It would never be so easy as to just ask a church for money.

Ten days or so went by and Mr. S. was still trying to decide on the safest choice for a quick caper. He figured he could say that the money came from a church, but he would have to get it to do so. He was in his office deep in thought. Mr. Polka-dots came to see him. Mr. Happy was also working; he stayed with the other employees while the idea was presented.

"We may have a possible idea," said Mr. Polka-dots. "Lay it on me," said Mr. S. He was tired of not coming up with anything seemingly feasible. "We know that on the tenth and the twentieth of every month, for at least the last eight months now, an armored car comes to get money out of the Superstore on 12th and Main. Today is the 17th," said Mr. Polka-dots.

Mr. S. said it would work fine, considering that there would be a driver, a guard, and the five clowns to get the money. They would take the morning off and work the evening of the twentieth. They would just wear their clown suits, as they had been made for at least two reasons, and burn the suits after the caper. The brown van could be claimed as stolen, and the plan was on.

The morning of the twentieth came. For moral and courage, they called themselves "The Circus Freaks". They got dressed and assembled near the police station in Mr. S.'s room. "Here is the plan," said Mr. S. The words he then spoke are as follows:

> We know they will get there at 9 AM. One will stand guard and the other will go in and come out with the money. I am the driver of the

brown van. Mr. Happy and Mr. Polka-dots will man the armored car's driver. Both armored car personnel will have a weapon; they will be unable to use their weapon. They will not be able to, because we will be four on two. We are not doing this to be recognized or to waste time. Mr. Panda and Mr. Wacky will jump the guard with the money bag. Mr. Panda will bring that bag to me as Mr. Wacky disarms the passenger guard. All five of us will be in the van with the money. We will drive, and then we will split up. Mr. Polka-dots, you will hold the wrists of the armored car's driver behind his back. Mr. Happy you will take his weapon and handcuff him so the two of you can escape the scene. We also have two handy black felt head bags so the guards themselves cannot see us once we are on them. There will be a few pedestrians - that is why we are dressed this way. I have already found us a good spot to park and go.

By the time Mr. S. had explained the simple caper, he had driven the brown van to its vantage point half a block from the Superstore. He handed a small pair of binoculars to Mr. Panda and the four passengers planned to sit in the van and wait. There was no waiting, however. The armored car pulled in moments after the brown van had come to a halt.

One guard left the armored car, and the four passenger clowns made exodus from the running van. The van was parked under an overpass structure on a small hill unable to be seen easily by the armored car. The armored car was around the corner and facing the other way.

The four stood behind a large metal piling to watch the armored car. Mr. Panda was looking through his binoculars and said, "I can see the front door of the Superstore from here." Mr. Wacky stood with him for when it was time to move. Mr. Happy and Mr. Polka-dots stood together behind the piling waiting to do things to the driver of the armored car. Mr. Happy and Mr. Wacky both had a black felt bag with a drawstring for tentatively blocking the visibility of the guards. There were not too many pedestrians. There also was no payphone nearby.

Finally, the door to the Superstore opened, and the passenger guard came outside with a bag of money. Mr. Panda waved his arm to indicate motion, and the four ran unseen to the corner of the Superstore. Mr. Happy and Mr. Polka-dots were seen by the passenger guard briefly, and they placed a bag on the head of the driver of the armored car. Mr. Happy handcuffed the driver. Mr. Wacky quickly put a felt bag on the passenger guard's head and pulled the drawstring snug. He removed the passenger guard's weapon from his hip and placed it on the ground, while Mr. Panda handcuffed the guard's wrists behind his back and got the bag of money.

Once Mr. Panda acquired the sack of money, he ran back and got into the brown van. Mr. Polka-dots then blew a honker horn at the driver guard a couple of times. Mr. Happy successfully removed the driver's weapon during the honking sounds. He removed the magazine and left it with the weapon and the armored car. The three clowns followed Mr. Panda in a sprint back to the brown van, and Mr. S. sped away with all of them safely in the van.

Mr. S. drove the van in an abnormal but semi-direct path back to his room and parked. The Circus Freaks ran inside with the money, changed clothes, and departed. Mr. S. stayed behind to secure the money under the sink. He then bagged their clown outfits and the money bag into two liners and brought the bags back to the van with a gallon of paint thinner. He drove the van to a remote hill on the outskirts of town and opened all of its doors. Mr. S. spread the clown outfits around the inside of the van; poured the paint thinner all over the clothes and interior; and threw a lit match to it.

The van went up in flames during the dry heat of the day, and he jogged away unharmed. If nothing else, the clothes would be burned. Once people found the van it may or may not have even ran. Who cared? It would be claimed to have been a stolen and found vehicle. Mr. S. heard the van's gas tank blow from a few blocks away - the van was sure to be totaled.

Mr. S. made it back to his place and showered well. He counted the money and it was twenty eight thousand, so it would be enough to try to save the youngster's life. Mr. S. then left twenty one thousand there for the boy and split up the seven thousand left so the Circus Freaks could have $1400 a piece. He hid his there and brought the guys their money at work. They were all on time that day, and the caper was on the news.

Mr. S. successfully paid his guys and they did not rat each other out. Mr. S. also gave the money needed to help the boy to his father. He said it was a gift from a religious companion who helped people anonymously, sometimes. The man thanked Mr. S., and Mr. S. told him that he was welcome. They wanted what was best for the sick boy.

Time went by and Pita-Time did well for many years. Local regulars and new customers as well happily enjoyed the tasty chicken items. The young boy received his treatment and did not die. In time, he recovered perfectly to normal health. The Circus Freaks invested and saved their money wisely, and all was well.

◆

The Duck Hunt

Once upon a time, there was a young boy named Boomer. Boomer was his real name. He was ten years old. During his summer break from school one year, his parents let him stay with his grandparents for a week.

Boomer's grandfather was a retired manager from the water district. He was a duck hunter. He had been a duck hunter for most of his life. It was not until he retired that the considerate old man really had the time to become more accomplished with the sport. Boomer's grandmother was a retired school teacher, and, like his grandfather, she was one of Boomer's favorite people.

He always enjoyed staying with his grandparents. Once a week, they ate bacon, lettuce, and tomato sandwiches on toast with mayonnaise. Boomer usually ate two whole sandwiches. His grandparents taught him how to play dominoes and chess. These fond memories would probably stay with young Boomer for a lifetime.

This week was an important time for him, though, because he had never actually gone duck hunting with his grandfather. Boomer was curious and wanted to learn. He cared. Boomer played with duck calls on the weekends, sometime, and he even had a few of his own. He was a master with them. Boomer knew to never blow on a duck call with all of his might while an older person was sleeping - such things were for outdoors. His grandfather promised to take him hunting real early on a Monday morning.

Boomer already had a very favorite gun, and it was a twenty gage shotgun. It was Sunday afternoon, and they were getting ready. "So cleaning this gun does not just make it look nicer, it functions properly then?" asked Boomer to his Grandfather. "Yes sir," said his grandfather. "How does it reach the ducks, considering that it is only accurate for about twenty yards?" asked Boomer. He was already ready to blast away any form of waterfowl. "Do they not fly too far above, like the geese?" he asked.

"No," said his grandfather, as he was spraying down plastic ducks with a water hose. "That is what we are cleaning these decoys for. We set the decoys out into the water, and when the ducks fly by, they come and land in the water to swim with what they think are the real ducks. Then, whoom!" "That is when we can bring the ducks back to grandmother?" asked Boomer. "Yes sir, for sausage or any other dish you like," said his grandfather. "My school teacher said that there is a popular dish in France with a duck cooked with oranges," said Boomer. "Sounds good," said his grandfather.

"What about the geese?" asked Boomer. "What about them?" asked his grandfather. "Will the geese come and light with our decoys? I know you have some decoys that are geese," said Boomer. "Those decoys are for hunting the Canadian geese in the winter time far north of where we are headed tomorrow morning." "I saw a flock of about seventeen geese flying far over head just yesterday. They were about twenty minutes from here by car." said Boomer.

"Well, Boomer," explained his grandfather, "Not all geese migrate at specific seasonal times. The geese you saw may or may not have been Canadian, and may not have actually been wild geese. They probably were not wild, though, because most wild geese we see are Canadian after all." "Wow," said Boomer, "I hope to be smart like you someday." "I am sure you will, Boomer," said his grandfather, "I am sure you will."

At that time Boomer's grandmother called them in for dinner. Probably the best dinner of the week, this meal would be a large percentage of the week's leftovers, according to Boomer's educated guesses. Boomer almost dropped the twenty-gage to run inside but instead handed it politely to his grandfather who set it down. They washed their hands in the restroom and went to the dinner table.

"What are we having?" asked Boomer, with his eyes on his grandfather. He knew his grandfather had no idea what was about to be placed in front of him, and so Boomer asked aloud. "We will be having fried chicken alfredo pasta with sautéed red onions and green beans," said Boomer's grandmother, and Boomer was very happy to hear it. It would be a good dinner for all; his grandfather sighed in relief. Anything besides a new recipe would be edible.

At any rate, the three ate and enjoyed polite conversation in turn about their recent experiences. Boomer let them in on some interesting summer-time fun that he had with children in the neighborhood playing touch football. He sometimes spent the weekend with friends or family, so there were small stories to share. Boomer's grandparents had questions to answer about their recent occurrences, too.

His grandfather was involved with various different philanthropy organizations and kept busy that way. "Philanthropy groups and church groups help the needy," he said to Boomer one time. Boomer's grandmother spent most of her time gardening fruit, vegetables, and small rare peppers. What seemed like a simple hobby actually took tedious effort and much time. For many days of the year she spent the evening hours cleaning vegetables to freeze for another time. Boomer was very talkative, though, and he happily spoke of interesting things he learned in school the previous year. He even spoke of what he planned to learn about during the next one.

It was Sunday night and all three people were tired and ready for bed. Boomer and his grandfather quickly got their boat and things to bring along to the hunt ready before bedtime. His grandfather's boat had a twenty horsepower outboard gas engine. With a very small motor, it was an inexpensive way to get somewhere in the swamp. The boat took some while to get to its destination. Anything cheaper might involve a paddle.

Boomer took a bath, while his grandmother took a shower in the other restroom. They put their pajamas on, said their prayers together for the well-being of themselves and others, and went off to bed. Boomer's grandfather watched T. V. for half an hour or so. He then went to get ready for bed and almost fell asleep in the shower. He went off to bed.

All three slept soundly in their nice beds with thick blankets, silky sheets, and big fluffy pillows. Night went by as the moon lit it, and the darkest darkness came long before the sun rose. Boomer woke to see a clock at some point, and it said 5:30 AM. He went back to sleep.

Sometime before 6 AM, Boomer heard his grandfather stirring in the other room and sprang to his feet to change clothes. His grandmother was fast asleep, and he heard his grandfather coming down the hall. His grandfather cracked the door open gently and said, "Hey Boomer, are you awake." "Yes, sir," said Boomer. He was putting on his shoes. Boomer said, "I am putting on my shoes. I will be right out."

The two made their way to the truck. Boomer and his grandfather brought some bologna, a loaf of bread, and a twelve pack of cola. Once outside, they checked the rigging on the trailer, the boat, and the truck. This was to make sure all things were safe and secure. They left. Once in the truck they could talk.

"How long 'till sun-up?" asked Boomer. "Under an hour," said his grandfather. The truck was full of gas and the boat was ready to go, too. "I made a blind out in the swamp a few months ago," said Boomer's grandfather, "I have gone to it every few weeks and it is still there. That is where we are going, today." "Awesome," said Boomer, "What does the blind look like?" "It looks a lot like the surrounding brush and dried grass in the swamp," said his grandfather, "The only difference is that it is a small fort-like wall constructed of dried bamboo-like sticks."

"That sounds pretty neat," said Boomer, "I think it is neat. It should suffice for a small structure to hide with. We cannot let the ducks see us, but we have to stay close to the decoys so we can shoot the real ducks." Boomer had not been hunting with a blind before, yet he knew some things about what his grandfather was talking about. He had seen blinds in hunting magazines. "I cannot wait to see it," said Boomer.

They made it to an old boat launch and got the boat in the water. Boomer's grandfather parked and secured the truck, and they were off. Both had on bright orange life preservers, even though they would not really be going into deep water. They were always safe to follow proper boating guidelines. Even if the water was not deep, parts of the swamp were muddy enough to be dangerous and even deadly to swim in, especially for a fully clothed youngster.

They found the blind just before the sun came up, and to Boomer, it was completely awesome. They tied the boat to the up-river side of the blind to keep from drifting in current from the river the swamp was distantly connected to. As the sun was rising, the dark blue sky was turning into a fade of glowing orange with small purple and gray clouds. It was a very impressive sunrise for Boomer. It was the next best thing to what he gazed upon during the winter. The two hunters put the decoys in the water. The decoys highly resembled real ducks. Both men opened a cola. They then got their guns loaded and ready. It was now a waiting game.

They decided to practice with their duck calls. Boomer made sounds so real his grandfather thought he could look up and see the ducks. Boomer's grandfather made duck calls with noise that carried on by years and years of practice and experience. Some time went by, and they saw nothing. Ducks usually fly by season and climate. This was really not the season for their climate, and they had not seen any migration so far.

Then they were coming. "I see 'em! I hear 'em!" whispered Boomer, as his grandfather looked through his binoculars at a flock of ducks headed directly towards them from far away in the north east. Ducks can see a very long way, as all birds can. Both men readied their aim with their guns as the ducks flew closer. "Do not shoot until I say 'shoot'em,' Boomer," said his grandfather softly, "We want those guys to light and swim with our decoys for a more sure shot." "Okay," said Boomer. Boomer held his gun steady with his site dead on the first duck flying in the flock. He even gave a lead to his aim to time the travel of his ammunition, as he had learned to do practicing with his grandfather's friends. Boomer was an excellent marksman with clay pigeons.

The ducks flew closer and were obviously going to fly by. "Shoot'em!" said Boomer's grandfather, and they both shot at the ducks. It was a hard shot for both of the hunters, because the ducks were far enough above and flying fast enough for the shots to be close to impossible. Neither hunter got a duck, and they both shot three times.

The two watched as the ducks flew away in perfect health. It was the most excitement they had so far that morning. Time went by and no ducks were around to be seen. They made and ate a bologna sandwich and had a cola. Time went by and they played around with different calls and duck call sound techniques. The two had a good time.

At one point there was another flock that could be seen flying, and the two attempted to draw the ducks in closer with their calls, however the ducks just kept flying away. Close to noon, the two were about to head back. Boomer's grandfather secured his rifle and was pulling in the decoys. Boomer kept his gun ready for as long as possible. All of the sudden a flock of geese were headed straight towards the blind.

"Are those geese?" asked Boomer, because he thought the waterfowl were out of migration season during the time. Boomer's grandfather looked through his binoculars and said, "Low and behold, I think that is a whole flock of over a dozen Canadian geese headed right for us!" Boomer aimed at the lead of the flock and waited for them to come closer. Just as they were almost directly overhead, they flew lower, checking out the decoy ducks. Boomer let a round of his shotgun off, and shot the leading goose on the first try.

The goose hit the water, and the rest of the flock rose in altitude and flew away. "Well, you got him," said Boomer's grandfather. They paddled over to the goose and got him in the boat. The two looked him over as if they had never encountered such an animal. "That is a Canadian goose?" asked Boomer. "Yes sir," said Boomer's grandfather, "Notice the gray head, the bill, the white neck, and the two distinctive stripes on his neck. He also has white-spotted wings, and this one has huge yellow webbed feet. It is a full grown adult goose from Canada, alright. He was flying completely out of season. Good shot, Boomer." Boomer was proud of his first trophy goose. For him, it meant something. The goose was almost as long as Boomer was tall.

The two finished getting their things put away and returned to the boat launch safely. They got the boat out of the water, put the goose on a bag of ice, and drove home. As soon as they arrived, Boomer hopped out of the truck and brought the goose to his grandmother. "We got us a goose!" exclaimed Boomer. "A goose?" asked his grandmother looking at Boomer's grandfather, "Are they not out of season?" "They are out of season right now," said Boomer's grandfather, "Boomer here got him one. We were just about to give up, too, and a big flock of these guys almost lit with our decoys. We only saw two flocks of ducks, and one was way too far off. The other one just got darn lucky."

"Well I guess I will cook the goose for us then," said Boomer's grandmother. The three were exhausted and happy, too. She brought the goose to the kitchen and the two hunters went to clean the boat and the decoys before they put away their hunting stuff. They cleaned up for dinner about an hour or two later, and all had roasted goose for dinner that night. Boomer's grandmother cooked the goose in honey with a smoker like one would do with a chicken, and it came out fine.

They played games and enjoyed the rest of Boomer's stay for the week. Boomer usually won one out of three games in chess, and at least half of the domino games. It was a fun time for all. Boomer would remember these wonderful times for all of his life.

◆

Time for Tea

Once upon a time, there were two ladies who decided to have lunch together. They met at a church service years ago. One Sunday, after church let out, they discussed where they might have some tea together. One of their names was Melba Worthenheim, and her acquaintance's name was Lucile Lethenhower. Oh what joyful conversations did the two encounter!

"How about the new place with a patio by the river?" asked Lucile. "I have heard good things about it. I understand it is clean, classy, and a pleasant experience overall," said Melba. "We must certainly go there soon," said Lucile. "How about Tuesday? Can you meet me there at 11 AM?" asked Melba. "Of course," said Lucile, and the meeting was decided upon.

Their conversation took place after church on a Sunday morning. Time went by like the gentle breeze of spring, and the two ladies drove into the parking lot of the restaurant a few minutes before 11 AM on Tuesday. One drove a pearl-white Coupe Deville, and the other one drove a completely refurbished Bentley with a straight ten engine. Both women took pride in their expensive cars, and they agreed that life is somehow short after all.

Lucile stepped out of her Cadillac as Melba locked up her Bentley.

"Your Cadillac sure is a beautiful car," said Melba, as she gazed upon the paint job of Lucile's automobile. It sparkled in the late morning with a pinkish pearl hue. "I imagine your shiny black Bentley has a pretty good top speed," said Lucile. "My mechanic and I got it up to 180 mph last time I had it tuned," said Melba. "Wow," said Lucile, as they found the front door of the restaurant.

The two ladies opened the door and walked up the stairway. "This is a pretty neat place," said Melba. "I agree," said Lucile, and they continued up the stairs, as they noticed various oil paintings on the walls. Once they made it to the top of the stairs, they were greeted by a hostess. "Hello. My name is Amy. Welcome to our restaurant," said a young woman named Amy. "Table for two?" she asked. Melba and Lucile nodded and followed Amy to the balcony. The three acknowledged the bar tender as they passed by and found a table in the front of the structure, outside.

The two women sat down and looked through their menus. Moments later a waiter came over to them. He was nicely dressed and seemed happy to see the two nice ladies. "Good morning. My name is Jeremiah, and I will be your server today. Might I bring you some iced tea or some water while you have a chance to look over our menu?" asked Jeremiah. The two women had already read the lunch menu while he was speaking. "May I try the hot green tea with the ice-water with lemon?" asked Melba. "Sure," said the waiter. "If it is okay, I will try the same," requested Lucile. "Okay. I will return in a moment," said Jeremiah, and he went to get their beverages.

The two looked over the menu gazing upon the various items in which they could order. "I wonder what is in the 'Soup of the Day'?" asked Lucile. "No telling," said Melba, "But the garlic butter bread sticks with spiced olive oil seem interesting." They studied their menus' contents and noticed a variety of nice appetizers, entrées, and deserts. Jeremiah returned with their hot tea and ice-water with lemon. "Any questions?" asked Jeremiah, noticing they read their menus. "Might I ask what is in 'The Soup of the Day'?" asked Lucile.

"Well," said Jeremiah, "Today is Tuesday and we usually do the Snail Soup on Tuesdays. It is a popular choice amongst our regular patrons. The snails are steamed to perfection and added to a delicious broth. The soup happens to be very tasty, from what I gather." "Impressive," said Melba glancing at Lucile who was inspecting her tea-cup. "Oh," said Lucile, "I would like 'The Soup of the Day', then. If it is okay, we will split an order of your bread sticks with spicy olive oil." "Me, too," said Melba. Jeremiah jotted down two soups, an order of bread sticks, and two hot teas. "No problem," said Jeremiah, and he then said, "I will return shortly."

The two ladies sipped their tea. "So, how is your grandson in Afghanistan?" asked Melba. "He is fine," replied Lucile, "I received a nice letter from him last week. He cannot wait to return, because he and his fiancé plan to marry in the fall." "How nice," said Melba, and Jeremiah returned with their soup and bread sticks. "So," asked Melba, "Is this soup considered to be 'escargot'?" "I am not really sure," said Jeremiah, "I imagine that it could be. I do know our snails are a very special species and are farm raised specifically for human consumption." "Very impressive," said Lucile, and the waiter departed appropriately.

The nice ladies enjoyed their soup, bread sticks, and the fresh air. Having never eaten snails before, the new experience was fun for the both of them. They sipped their tea, and Jeremiah returned with their check. "Might I bring you one of our deserts or anything else?" asked Jeremiah, understanding that the ladies seemed to be finished. "No, thank you," they both said. He placed the check on the table, and both ladies produced a ten-dollar bill from their purses. The tea was two dollars, the soup was eight dollars, and the bread sticks were three dollars. "Will both of our tens cover the check with an appropriate tip?" asked Melba. "Yes ma'am," said Jeremiah, "And we hope to see you soon." Jeremiah took the money and the check and walked away happily.

"Jeremiah seemed nice enough," said Lucile. "I thought he was a nice and handsome young man," said Melba who then said, "Nice rump." "We will have to further explore the menu some other time," said Lucile. "I definitely concur," said Melba, and the two arose to depart. On the way out they thanked the bar tender, Jeremiah, and the hostess. Melba and Lucile also enjoyed the various oil paintings, once more. They walked down the stairs and out the front door to the parking lot. "I have had a nice time today," said Melba, "I suppose I will see you in church?" "What a lovely time I have had as well," said Lucile, "I will see you in church on Sunday morning." The two nice ladies got into their expensive cars and drove away.

♦

The Giraffe

Once upon a time, there was a college student named Dawn. She was pretty and frail, and she liked to jog in the mornings. She was studying various different subjects. Dawn studied the sciences, business, and technology. Her sister, Jinh, was younger and planning to return to college, one day. She had an eight year-old-son named Luke.

Jinh was a very hard worker, like Dawn, sort of. Jinh was not in college at the time; she worked for a parcel service and helped organize packages fifty hours a week. Dawn wanted to see her sister and spend time with her family. She organized her plans for the weekend and gave Jinh a call.

"What is happening? I hope I have not called you during a bad time. Are you busy?" asked Dawn. "Oh, not really; I just picked up Luke from t-ball and we are going to go get a frozen pizza. Are you okay? How is school?" "I am fine. I wanted to know if you want to come see me for the weekend. You guys can stay the night here," replied Dawn. "Well, I had some things going on, but I will get back with you," said Jinh, and they hung up.

One thing led to another and they decided to go to the zoo in Dawn's town early in the morning on a Saturday. The drive to see Dawn was about five hours or so. Road trips are always fun when they are taken for leisure or exploration.

Jinh and Luke left on a Friday and made good time. "Four hours and forty two minutes," said Jinh, as she got out of the car. Luke hopped out of the car and took off running towards fast traffic. "Luke!" said Jinh, and he stopped. Dawn greeted them happily with hugs and polite conversation. She included questions about when they departed. The two had made good and safe time. The three carried in luggage, went and ate some fast-food, watched some television, and drank some cool water before going off to bed.

The sun came up, and the day was wonderful. The three woke, showered, and got ready to go to the zoo. It was only about twenty minutes away. Dawn drove Luke and Jinh over there happily, and they were there when it opened. A small crowd of people were also there. They paid and went inside. Some people bought peanuts for the animals that could eat them and some did not.

Dawn, Jinh, and Luke walked around reading small information plaques about peacocks, wild birds, and other animals. There were not really too many different kinds of animals there - this was no big-city zoo. There was a large tortoise that was supposedly over two hundred years old weighing close to two hundred pounds. It escaped the zoo once. They found it giving children rides downtown. It was brought back to the zoo safely. There were some spider-monkeys and some small fruit bats. There were maybe over a dozen different kinds of other animals. The zoo's concrete sidewalks winded around its different areas.

Eventually, they came to a small fork in their path. There was a wooden sign made into the shape of an arrow. It said "Giraffes" on it, and Dawn, Jinh, and Luke went in that direction. They did not have peanuts. They walked through a long curve overhung by trees and found a large wooden structure. The three climbed up the wooden steps to a pretty good sized platform and into the dim sunlight.

A whole family of giraffes came to see them, happily. The male of their family was the tallest giraffe. His ossicones were bald instead of fuzzy. The females' and youngsters' horn-like structures mounted on their heads were more cute and fuzzy with hair on top of their ball-like structures. Luke and Jinh enjoyed seeing the giraffes and tried talking to them. Dawn danced around a little making horns on her head with her index fingers resembling the giraffes' ossicones. The male giraffe was sad and turned to go back to their shelter across the field with the others.

"Wait! Do not go," said Dawn. The last thing she wanted to do was to make the giraffes sad. Try as she did, though, the giraffes all turned and walked away. The three watched them go and made their way around the rest of the zoo. It was fun for them, and the animals were neat.

They drove safely back to Dawn's place, and later that day Jinh and Luke drove home safely. Dawn ended up graduating and going to work for a computer company. Jinh graduated and went to work for a phone company, and Luke went off to college, eventually.

Years after they had gone to the zoo, Dawn was still thinking about those giraffes and how they walked away in melancholy. A she recalled, she could not make them happy; she did not know why. Thanksgiving came, and a gathering of about two dozen people gathered to eat together. These people were all related to Dawn, Jinh, or Luke, somehow. They all ate a turkey dinner and had a nice time. Most of the family enjoyed watching a football game.

Dawn was thinking about the giraffes. Then it dawned on her - the giraffes must have come to see them for peanuts. "Hey Jinh," she said, "I figured it out." Jinh and Luke looked over to her. By then, Luke could drive. "Remember the time we went to the zoo and those giraffes walked off all sad and everything?"

"That was a long time ago," said Jinh, and Luke agreed. "They were sad, because we did not have peanuts for them," said Dawn. "Wow," said Luke, "I did not even think about that." The rest of their family were watching football and did not pay too much attention. The three enjoyed the zoo. "I guess that *shows to go you*," said Dawn, "If you ever have a chance to give a giraffe peanuts at a zoo, do it." All smiled and were well. They lived happily ever after.

◆

The King and the Dancer

Greetings, fellows. The following lines describe a fictional account of a beautiful and entertaining tale. Our current story involves struggle, war, and death. For a long time in history, the human skull has been a symbol of death. Death as a person or a spiritual entity has also long been a consideration. As long as we as humans have thought of death, we have also thought of life. This is how our story begins.

Once upon a time, a young queen named Elizabeth gave birth to a little baby girl. The girl was born about ten years after the queen's first baby. The queen's first baby was a boy. The queen died while she was giving birth to her beautiful little girl. The baby was born in a very large castle that resembled a skull, underneath the warm waters of a polished stone bathing hole. The baby's father, a powerful king of the surrounding lands, named her Princess Gnale, keeping the "G" silent, because he liked nightingale birds. Her mother was given a formal funeral. Their castle was large and domineering. Built into a mountainside, it overlooked the northwestern border of *Old Spain* - a land not mentioned often in history. Like many castles in Europe, this one was of pale gray hues with damp fog blowing throughout its dark shadows. The castle was designed after a human skull; its shadows only grew darker in time.

The castle was huge. It contained not only five main floors with countless passages and stairways, Skull Castle also contained a dungeon system. The castle's water came from a neighboring river. The builders of the castle went to great lengths to irrigate its various latrines. They even engineered a flowing water system throughout its external stone shrubbery beds. The stone troughs resembled small ditches, only waste high. The flowing water was quiet, and its gentle trickling brought about a peaceful loneliness throughout the castle.

The astounding castle was partially designed and entirely funded by a king whose name happened to be Henry. As an honest king, Henry was served well. A man that could stand his ground, he was absolutely feared in battle. Henry took the life of his adversaries by hand, with a sword, and many times, with his opponents' weapons. His own knights kept their distance from him. His soldiers thanked their creator daily that their king was on their side.

Ten years before the beautiful princess was born, her mother gave birth to a son. He was a healthy boy, and he grew strong. The king and queen named their prince Victor, and all the people called him Prince Vic, the Young Terror. Prince Vic had a way about him. He was witty and quick to win when placed in contest. Prince Vic never did anything wrong, and he never turned on the opportunity to use what powers he knew of.

Prince Vic was deeply saddened by his mother's death. For the life of himself, he just could not forgive his sister. The maids of the castle, and even the deadliest warriors governed by his father, King Henry, who many people of the castle thought could speak with Prince Vic, could not convince the young man otherwise. According to Prince Vic, his mother, "Queen Eli," whom he loved dearly, would have lived if his sister Gnale would not have had to exist. Nevertheless, Prince Vic carried on throughout his daily routines, and his baby sister became a healthy young girl within a few years.

Young Prince Vic trained with his father's knights and ate as much as possible. King Henry, upon completing the construction of his monstrous skull-like castle, was attacked by three neighboring armies given to territorial war. King Henry's soldiers would have lost, however their adversaries where not united and lost. King Henry was intelligent and deadly. He separated his army of hundreds of men into three parts. The first two groups were smaller and more intelligent armies. They both consisted of forty people meant for gathering information and killing the known leaders of the attacking families.

The third army was huge and operated largely out of fear of the king. The army was to protect the women and the new castle that was not easy to construct. The three armies took turns on the three attacking enemy armies. It was an orgy of death; fresh blood stained the country side for weeks. The initial attack on an opponent was conducted by getting rid of its military leaders with a smaller army. Once one of the smaller armies had its way with their opposition, the large army took its turn. The other smaller army took out whatever was left and necessary of death. These first three battles were a total slaughter and an overall winning establishment for Scull Castle, King Henry, and the lands nearby. The armies buried all of the bodies in a long *earth-*

trench beneath what became a long grove of sinister looking hardwood trees.

The first battles were won for and by King Henry's forces. While these occurred, and continuing into the years after, Prince Vic became a man given to all kinds of war and games. He liked Chess. Good with the ladies, he also enjoyed times of sport with his buddies and their horses. This is to say that he was a healthy lad during his youth. Time went by and Princess Gnale became a beautiful young teenager. Gentle with her intelligently spoken words, she was admired and loved by all who knew of her. She was only known by a few, however. Gnale was close to her deceased mother's sisters; a few people in the castle; and some people outside of the protection of the castle in a nearby town, Town Village. This was largely due to her time spent alone reading, learning, and gardening. Gnale loved composing poetry. Her compositions were known for the proper use of meter and the eloquent utilization of free-writing.

Gnale would have never been allowed outside of the castle. She secretly left it all of the time to go to Town Village, however. She never planned to get caught doing so. People called the village Town Village, because the small village had no official name for many of its first years. Town Village had various people of multiple walks of life, a local economy with various businesses, and a small chapel which retained religious and nonreligious texts acting as the library of the area.

Gnale visited all of these, yet she really only spoke with a few people.

One of the only people that she could trust with any actual personal commentary outside of Skull Castle was a rather productive blacksmith. He was the first person Gnale met in Town Village as a young girl, when she went exploring alone.

One day, King Henry was speaking with his head knight, Gondor, and his political and religious leader, Priest Paul. Prin~~ce~~ Paul was known by the ^est children as *Mr. P. P.* Mr. P. P. gave a ten minute speech to the children on morals and religion, weekly. "We have a vast land surrounding us," said King Henry to Gondor and Prince Paul, saying the following:

Good peoples of all walks of life live near us and benefit from our protection. We collect minimal taxes, and we support the craftsmen of our lands. We would be living in a world of deceitful dreams, however, if we did not acknowledge the castles built recently in distant areas. We know many details and numbers from our hunters and traveling tradesmen of the other lands; we will not ignore these growing powers. There are five kings that we will have to face - all are just as powerful as we are and maybe even more deadly. As their numbers grow, our chances of survival lessen. We will conquer them. We have no choice. One by one, I will have the heads of these five kings, and we will expand our families to live in honest and well governed safety.

With these statements spoken, the three men organized a *topographical attack* on the surrounding areas. Gondor gave a speech to the warriors, and by order of his king, organized a group of head knights to give the army split forms of efficiency. Nine knights had two assistant warriors, and these hierarchies commanded the huge army as a deadly triangle that could attack in various methods and surprise techniques. With only a few months of preparation and training, the King's army was ready for battle and thirsty for blood.

At dawn on the first day of spring, King Henry's forces were awake and prepared to watch the sun peep up over the horizon. He pointed his sword to the sun and powerfully declared, "Attack!" Hundreds of horses and thousands of men traveled east from the mountain of the castle to the nearest surrounding land. The first set of battles was a slaughter. In only a few weeks, King Henry had the first head of a king of five. Upon returning to Skull Castle, they were happy to be home. King Henry said to Gondor, "This is one of five heads, Gondor. We only have four left to attain." King Henry threw the head into the water flowing below the castle to degrade and decompose what was left of the fallen king in nature.

Time went by. King Henry and his armies where both feared by their enemies and admired by the people they governed. The new lands he conquered where not accustomed to a healthy and properly governed economy.

King Henry was appreciated. War after war was won during a three year period. Prince Vic had become a mighty man, by then. He had even proven himself to be more deadly than his father. Often times acting like a maniac on the battlefield, his slayings where known to brink the unnecessary.

Four of the five perceived threats mapped out by King Henry where conquered, and only one was left. His armies encompassed their adversaries like an organism in the form of a wave. King Henry wanted the last king badly. He wanted this bloodshed to come to an end. King Henry longed for a peaceful and safe land to govern over. Prince Vic followed his father, as King Henry figured out how to find the last King. One thing led to another. King Henry found the last king and was slain by his adversary. Shortly thereafter, Prince Vic found the fifth king standing over his father with a bloody sword.

Prince Vic lost his sanity, could not hold his sword, leaped from his horse, and forcefully decapitated the final king by hand. The fifth and final king sought after was dead, as was King Henry. Prince Victor would now be the new king, and no one in the land and surrounding territories would have any opposition to the matter, whatsoever.

Upon the vast army's travel back to Skull Castle, all of the soldiers, knights and various sects of the army sang songs praising and acknowledging their new king. "All hale the king!" they sang, "All hale King Victor, the Victorious! May our lands forever exist in peace and harmony! He is no bogus trick; all hale our mighty King Vic!"

During the years that followed the conquering of the territories and extended territories of Skull Castle, King Victor ruled with relative ease. Farmers farmed, workers worked, and women made babies. His father, King Henry, was who figured out how and why specific attacks on threatening communities were necessary. King Henry also caused no harm to innocent villages and passed by those communities peacefully. His choices were by far the most proper and profitable choices of action. The political and strategic figuring of power was complete, and King Vic remembered his father's brilliance, achievement, and goals of honest ruling. He often answered questions and gave commands according to what he thought his father would have said. King Henry was known for his unquestioned and powerful good judgment.

Time passed. King Vic did so well with his ruling that his life became easier and easier. His lands existed in natural harmony. Hunters found enough game, and the rains often came. Farmers produced large crops of many sorts for locals and other lands. Skull Castle became extremely wealthy and powerful.

Gnale had grown, too. At the perfect age of seventeen, she was absolutely gorgeous in any way perceivable. Tall, slender, and properly endowed, any man would have died to be with her. The maidens of the castle loved her. Many of the women in the castle happened to be her mother's sisters. There were strict rules enforced by her brother in Skull Castle. Women associated with family or rule where allowed strict behaviors only. They were to act properly. After all, there was a representation of reputation for the wealthy to keep. Many of these rules and opinions where known without them being spoken of. No one really ever even risked upsetting King Vic's authority. Who would? After all, there was little to complain of with so much wealth and satisfactory diet.

Gnale was secretive in her delights, though. She enjoyed playing the role of a beautiful princess, yet she also had a life outside of the castle. Only rarely did she leave, yet she did get out from time to time. Gnale got to know her blacksmith rather well over the years, and she enjoyed making small items with him once or twice a year. No one ever knew who was behind her crazed form of tomfoolery, yet she, from time to time, gave golden envelope openers and other items to the literate and the uniquely faceted characters of Skull Castle.

One year, just before harvest season, Gnale decided to meet more people. She thought to herself, "I rarely speak with the harvesters. Maybe I can blend in and make some money." So she left the castle during late hours every other day or so, and fashioned a scythe with the blacksmith. Gnale was paid in shiny silver coins from time to time by some people of Skull Castle. They paid to hear her read her writing of poetry and prose. She saved a whole bucket full of these pieces of silver. Gnale took her rare coins to the blacksmith, and together they fashioned a very special scythe with many of the coins and an added alloy. Once it was done, she paid him well and thanked him properly, saving her last two coins. Gnale could only keep her beautiful scythe secret by sleeping with it, so that is what she did.

One morning, Gnale arose very early and clothed herself in peasantry garments to go and work with the harvesters. She made it from Skull Castle to the fields before daylight and offered to help them out, saying that she had come from Town Village. No one knew her or recognized her being of the monarchy, so they allowed her to work. Her plan went well that day. During the harvest, Gnale became rather talented with going to clear wheat once a week or so. She saved a legitimate portion of funds. Gnale eventually, however, was caught.

Gnale worked out a proper deal with one of the farmers for a descent amount of pay once a week. She sliced the wheat she could, and returned to Skull Castle. Her only mistake, however, was her scythe. The beautiful and glistening tool went unnoticed for some time - Gnale kept it wrapped in a cloth once she sharpened and polished it well, weekly. Her farmer's assistant noticed the scythe one day, however, and he told on her. The harvesters thought she was an intruder and bound her to her scythe with ropes.

Bound safely, the harvesters brought Gnale to Skull Castle immediately. The guards humorously brought her to the king. The guards knew her, however King Vic ruined their fun intentions. He honestly hated his beautiful sister because of his eternal attachment to his lost mother. "Would you gaze upon the attire of this woman?" asked a clergyman to King Vic. "No I will not," said King Vic, after taking one look towards the various influential inhabitants of Skull Castle near him. "Take this wretch to a dungeon for good, for no sister of mine sports such threads. No one permitted her to leave these premises. The wealth of this castle does not slave for the heathens of our fields." King Vic had never been able to forgive his sister for her mother's death. He had continued to miss his mom. King Vic spoke of her and remembered her as Queen Eli. For the most part, he was never really able to even see Gnale without becoming upset, despite how pretty she was.

Gnale was brought to a dungeon. The dungeon was somewhat spacious with a leaking corner due to the river that brushed Skull Castle's northern side of the mountain. In time, she carved this leak into a larger amount of flowing water. The top of the dungeon had a tiny window which seeped in a very minimal amount of sunlight once a morning. One of her aunts knew that Gnale had been permanently ostracized to a dungeon. She brought Gnale food during late hours for years. This was no easy accomplishment, as scheduled dining times had been established in the castle.

One year, Gnale's aunt brought her a big pumpkin, and Gnale kept the seeds. Gnale ate the pumpkin with her secret golden envelope opener. She still slept with her silver scythe nightly, as it had been used to aid bringing her to the dungeon all those years ago. Some nights, she danced with her scythe as she thought of her poetry and sang her heavenly songs. She had to untie herself alone once in the dungeon, long ago.

Gnale's life had a peaceful side, yet it was gloomy down in the dungeons. She may have been able to escape, though she was always very deep in thought. The dungeon was dark and peaceful. She may have gone there for long lengths of time to be alone and write, anyway, had the idea ever crossed her mind. Gnale placed some of her pumpkin seeds in the small stream of water, and they grew. She grew a small pumpkin patch. It was amazing to her - the dimly lit light still provided for the most beautiful yellow-orange flowers.

Years went by and Gnale's secret aunt brought her food two to three times a week. No man would ever know of Gnale's true beauty. Gnale's pumpkins never went without water, and she supervised them constantly. The pumpkins were plump and healthy. She lived mostly off her pumpkins and water for a nice while. The princess also made dolls to pass the time.

Nothing too exciting was to last forever, albeit. Gnale's aunt caught a natural sickness during the coldest part of that year. Her sickness was contagious, and Gnale became deathly ill herself. Gnale's aunt did not survive. Gnale had become her aunt's closest loved one. Gnale's caring aunt died in front of her, sitting outside of the dungeon's large wooden door on the cold stone floor. Gnale died during a peaceful winter slumber a few days later.

Upon Gnale's death, her spirit floated from her body. She placed more of her pumpkin seeds in the path of her "water trickle," and she watched them grow for a week or two. Gnale was surprised that she was able to move physical objects, because she realized she was a ghost. She also gazed upon her own flesh in the week sunlight every day. Time passed, and her flesh turned to dust. Her bones where left for her to see and consider. "I should not stay in this dungeon forever," thought Gnale, eventually, "After all, I can fly around." She discovered that floating around her dungeon was not all that she could do. She went to bed one night, and Gnale housed her spirit into her bones. "Now I can walk and dance again," thought Gnale to herself happily, and she played and danced with her hand-fashioned dolls as a skeleton for some time.

Gnale sewed together a black dress with a hood from her bed sheets. Her aunt had brought them a while back, along with some books and some other small items. Still sleeping with her scythe, nightly, Gnale came to enjoy her new existence. A few nights went by, and Gnale realized that she was Death. Gnail was the Grim Reaper. She could have walked as a skeleton, yet she enjoyed flying more. She picked the lock of the thick wooden door to her dungeon, and decided to pay a few people a visit.

First and foremost were the people she remembered during the time of her dungeon sentencing. They were older by now, however they were still alive. She visited their various quarters throughout the castle. She decapitated them one by one. She wanted them to know what it was like to be her. They should have never incarcerated someone that was of such a beautiful presentation to the attempted world of goodness and genius. They bled to death, each and every one of them she knew of. They were nine in total. She slept well during those nights, somehow to her surprise, back in her dungeon. Gnale thought about it and decided not to take life for a while. No one ever went to the dungeon, and no one figured out who was murdering people.

She was forgotten by the people of the castle. The bodies were buried, and the people thought they had been attacked from an external intruder or one of themselves. The wealthy rulers where given formal funerals in the graveyard west of Skull Castle. Gnale visited their graves during the middle of the night, wondering if their spirits slept in their coffins.

More time went by. King Vic had gained weight. He drank wine off and on during the previous course of his life, yet he drank more often as time went by. He eventually planned a celebration once year for the old date of the 5th king's death and the loss of his father. King Henry died on or around the 31st of October.

One year, King Vic had been drinking daily and drank himself into a terrible stupor during his annual celebration. Gnale had been sleeping in her old and forgotten dungeon as a cloaked skeleton for some time. Where else would anyone come to find an unknown and forgotten person? King Vic was overly intoxicated from boiled wine that evening, and his consumption had not yet fully entered his blood stream entirely.

He was paying little attention to his efforts. He must have been trying to find his bed quarters. He was in no way trying to find a person. The boiled wine that he had been given to was known to cause peoples' vision to be blurred. The stronger the wine, the more likely an individual was to go blind. It would have rendered him completely blind, eventually. It would have.

It was October 31st, and November was only moments away. "This path must lead to my bed," spoke King Vic, as he stumbled down an old stairway thinking it was a hall. There were many paths to many dungeon rooms in Skull Castle. During the years past, the dungeons had been used for prisoners of war, interrogation, and secret political executions. King Vic's thoughts were twisted and blurred in many ways - he needed to lie down. The huge wooden door might as well have been what approached him, as he slammed into it drunken, causing himself to stand straight up and stare at it. "A tree," he said loudly, as he pointed at the door. "Tree," he said, "Get out of my way," and Gnale opened the door for him in polite surprise. She had not even locked it in months.

"A beautiful maiden," said Prince Vic to Gnale, who was somewhat surprised that the man was looking right at her without noticing that she was nothing other than bones floating in a black cloak. "Might I have this dance?" asked King Vic, holding out his hand. Gnale could have said, "Sure, brother," yet instead she lovingly held out her hand and caught his in it. She guided him into the dungeon, and caught his lower back in a spinning motion to keep him from falling. "My you are an agile maiden," he said, as they danced in spins and circles. King Vic spoke to her aloud singing his drunken songs and rambling on about things he thought he knew of.

While the two danced, and they did so for a while, the night grew darker. King Vic fell asleep in her arms from intoxication. They were nearby the roots to her pumpkin patch. She gently laid him in the running water. She laid him down gently enough to have him in the most perfect position for a nice clean beheading. And with one nice swoosh of her scythe, that is what she gave him. King Vic's lifeless head fell over to lie on his right ear's side.

The morning would come, she knew, and all of the people in Skull Castle would most surely notice that their king was gone. Gnale decided to clean house. She flew through every hall, beheading every guard in his sleep, and even those walking awake. She really scared one guard who actually saw her, and he fell to the ground dead with no decapitation. She breached the doorways of every bedroom and all of the sleeping quarters. Everyone in the castle was dead; she killed them all. She returned to her dungeon and slept before the sun rose for November 1st.

Of course, the dead bodies freed many spirits throughout the entire castle. They assembled as a large congregation of ghosts in the chapel. Gnale buried their physical bodies in a long eight foot deep ditch she dug the next day. She dug all day long, and the labor was seemingly impossible to complete. Gnale did finish the long grave in a few weeks, however. She was tired from the work, but gave them a large stone table top for a tombstone. She sang a prayer to them the next day and even spent some time carving a farewell poem to them on the stone that said, "Farewell my peoples, for your time was done. Farewell to you, may you have your fun." The ghosts did not leave the chapel. They watched the sun come up behind the huge stained glass windows and fade away everyday. They never left the chapel, for fear the Grim Reaper may catch them.

Skull castle had been forgotten by people in the surrounding territories during the years of King Vic's lackadaisicalness, and vines and molds partially covered the revealing areas of its structure. Gnale was there, though. She left the castle from time to time, to fly in the night. She maintained her pumpkin patch. She decided to release the spirits of people randomly, starting with the harvesters. She flew around and took the life of her victims from time to time. Throughout the remainder of the history of the Earth, the Grim Reaper always returned to her dungeon in Skull Castle for slumber.

♦

The Masago Monsters

Once upon a time, there were four tiny monsters. They called themselves the Masago Monsters. Close to an inch tall, they lived under the attentive protection of a sushi chef named Charlie. They stayed in more than one place, yet they endured travel times in a miniature air-cooled box with amenities. Colored brilliantly, one was fluorescent orange, one iridescent violet, one effervescent green, and the fourth one fluorescent yellow-green. Their names were Moses, Rose, Farmer, and Howry, respectively. They enjoyed masago as their favorite food, and they enjoyed eating it along with other healthy foods. Rose, for instance, liked diced blueberries.

The masago monsters were into proper exercise and good work ethic. They learned various culinary and life skills from their sensei, the sushi chef. They commonly went on exciting adventures. They always stayed in contact with their sensei, the master sushi chef, because he kept them and protected them from the dangers of nature. As a team of four, they were considered unstoppable.

The Masago Monsters loved to wake up before sunrise. One day, they woke up a few minutes before dawn. The four each turned and stretched their muscles slowly as they awoke. "Who wants to match me in push-ups?" asked Howry. "We all will," said Rose in common retort. The four monsters usually exercised about the same, as they functioned best as an equally balanced kind of team. Their group effort was near the idea of a separate and powerful small organism in the universe. They were happily satisfied with the power only they could know of. They all got out of bed and kept good pace matching Howry's every pushup. They did thirty, slowly, to tear their muscle tissue for future cell rejuvenation and strength.

After working out early, they usually enjoyed a shower and breakfast, somehow. They showered in the bathroom and ate in the kitchen before going to work. Living in secrecy, the chef kept good care of them and sometimes brought them with him to the sushi bar he worked for. Today, they woke up moments before sunlight. They had plenty of time to check out the weather on television. The monsters also watched some of their favorite programming. A cooking show was on with a favorite celebrity chef.

Time went by. Their sensei woke up and got ready for work. They prepared to tag along. "You guys want to come with me, today?" asked Charlie. The four nodded happily in approval. The monsters quickly got into their carrying device like trained professionals, and the five were off.

Once they made it to the prestigious restaurant, they hurried inside early. Some chefs and other employees were there. A stranger was their, too.

Charlie washed his hands and hid his monsters. He asked the stranger if he could be of service. "I do not know if I can help you, but I do not think we are open for another hour," said Charlie. He secretly wondered if the strange and well-dressed businessperson had any sense of humor, whatsoever.

"I was asked to be here at this precise time to speak with the Purchases Operator. My name is Shawn, and I am a distributor of fine wines and aged cheese," said the businessperson. The person he was waiting for came around the corner, and the two went to have a chat in a dimly lit booth section.

While they were having their discussion, the four monsters decided to play *Ninja Tag* - a game they came up with due to their necessity of secrecy. They knew to go and see the chef by secret commands of silent action and spoken word. They played their game by hiding and finding - a surprising find of another monster was always a scored point.

As all of these things were taking place in the restaurant, a huge modified school bus traveling about forty mph slammed into the front door of the establishment. It turned out the bus driver was in a hurry and had incurred natural health issues causing the accident. Over a dozen people flocked to the scene in under ten minutes, and the restaurant was overly busy that morning. Many people wanted to see the bus, look at the door, and eat a sushi roll.

Paramedics came and took the bus driver away, and workers removed the bus. They repaired the front door within an hour. Customers spoke of the surprising accident all throughout lunchtime. The other sushi chef did not make it to work; he must have stayed in bed that day. Charlie rolled sushi constantly for hours. People considered him to be magnificent. The monsters had some trouble playing Ninja Tag, because they were not used to so many people in the restaurant. They loosely tied one person's shoe to a chair;

nothing too bad really happened. The patron discovered their shoelace upon rising to exit - no one was around to accuse of tomfoolery.

The four decided to play it on the safe side, and they hung out in the hidden areas of Charles' usual domain - the sushi bar. Without much to do, and knowing better than to distract the chef, the four monsters created an edible snowman out of sushi rice. The center of the snowman contained a few slices of a rare Alaskan fish from the deep ocean. Various ingredients adorned the outside of the snowman, and the four were impressed with their artwork.

The Masago Monsters sealed the snowman in plastic wrap and put him in a hidden part of the cooler beside the sushi bar. This way, as Charles completed his closing duties, he would find the snowman. He did so, and noticed the four mischievous monsters grinning from around the corner of their carrying case. They traveled in style. Charles was impressed with the snowman, indeed, and he gave it to a new chef in the kitchen on the way out. The new chef did not really know what to make of it; he ate it anyway. He enjoyed the nice surprise.

The five journeyed home safely that day, wondering what adventures would come in the future. It was a fun workday for Charlie; he made decent money working alone. The masago monsters had the rest of the afternoon to play around at home before bedtime. They all lived happily ever after.

◆

The "Man, Those Guys are Good" Story

Once upon a time there were two police partners. One of them was a man, and the other one was a woman. They were on the force for about two years or so. They worked in a city with a population of about 400,000. They operated as normal police for a while. The two finished the academy together, were sworn into the police force together, and finally patrolled the city together as partners for about two years. Our story begins during their third Christmas season together, not too long after Thanksgiving.

Much like common police partners, they handled everyday police tasks. None of their assignments were abnormal. Traffic tickets, drunken pedestrians, and other ordinary police duties were routine for them. Blessed from the Lord above somehow, the two partners never had to deal with any hard cases involving murders or gruesome horrors. The police force they were a part of contained many different facets of *societal activity protection*. They were normal police officers. They maintained routine jurisdictions and normal shifts.

On the morning of December 1st, Officer Harmon and Officer Ruby awoke early and met each other at a known breakfast café before going to report to head quarters. A normal for the two, they ate breakfast together before their shift two or three times a week. They had done so for the previous two years of their partnership. Breakfast was a good thing for them, because they were able to discuss what was needed to be spoken of before work. This day they went to a pancake restaurant; it was one of their favorite morning ideas for breakfast.

"I like this place," said Harmon. "Me too," said Ruby with a gleefully dreamy look in her eyes, "What do you think you will be having?" "I normally get the three pancakes, two sausages, an egg, and a large juice deal. I will probably have that," said Harmon. "You do not get tired of that deal?" asked Ruby. "Not as long as they have it," said Harmon. "Good point," said Ruby, "I am going to go with what I always get here, too." "Is that to say you are going with the blueberry surprise desert pancake with extra whipped cream and a cherry?" asked Harmon.

"Yes," said Ruby, "Yes I am, and I am sure it will make me happy. It always does." The two officers grinned at each other as their waiter returned to their table to take their order. The day was off to a good start. Upon having a nice breakfast, they paid and went to their headquarters to begin patrolling in their routine jurisdiction.

Upon entering the huge office space full of all different kinds of police, the two checked in with their chief as normal. "Morning chief," they said in unison. They usually walked by with a nod, and their chief gave them a nod, and then they proceeded to a patrol car. This morning was different, however. "Officer Harmon and Officer Ruby, please, step into my office," said their chief, Officer Grunt. He spoke with an authoritative tone almost accidentally. The two had no idea what the conversation was going to be about. Having worked together long enough to know each other rather well, they followed behind their chief to his office. While they were behind him, the two subordinate officers glanced at each other to figure out who was going to speak first. Officer Ruby gave a look of slight confusion to Officer Harmon, and he decided to give her a confident nod. This indicated that he would speak first. He would figure this ordeal. Officer Harmon was now the man in charge of problem solving, and they both knew.

The three entered Officer Grunt's office together. He was an efficient man and dedicated to his cause in police work. He kept his force in proper order and his office clean. Everyone loved him, and he loved them all. Officer Harmon and Officer Ruby still did not know what this was all about, so Officer Harmon spoke. "Good morning, Chief Officer Grunt," said Officer Harmon politely, "Is everything okay?" "Yes, of course," said Officer Grunt, "You guys have a seat for a minute. There are going to be some changes for you two, starting today. Good things only, so relax and hear what this is all about." The two subordinate officers were definitely interested. They sat in relief, ready to figure this out.

"You have been on the police force for two years, now, my force in certain ways," began Officer Grunt, "You two have been a phenomenal duo on this team. I have plenty of you guys - duos that do well out there. I think of you to myself sometimes, and I think, 'Man, those guys are good'." Officer

Harmon and Officer Ruby remained silent, waiting to hear what else their chief had to say.

"I am putting you guys on a case. It is only twenty days old, but I need some brains to catch these bad guys, and I think you two have what I am after. There is no longer any need for you to dress in uniform or not. You can keep your badges and weapons as desired or not. Your only requirement is to see me sometime in between 8 AM and 9 AM Monday through Friday or as needed. We all know I work almost everyday, so I am here for you. You are used to the seven different jurisdictions in this city you commonly patrol; you can now go to any area desired. We are trying hard to catch some active criminals. I want them brought to justice."

Chief Officer Grunt continued saying, "We know that in the last twenty days, there has been some form of crime committed once within a twenty four hour period by what we think is a dynamic pair of offenders. We know the crimes are linked. Whether it is a stolen and returned vehicle, a burglary, a defilement, or some other mischievous act, the bad guys always leave one of these." He placed a plastic sack of wooden coins onto the table. Officer Grunt took in a deep breath and exhaled.

"There are twenty wooden coins in that sack," continued Officer Grunt, "Each one found at the scene of the crime committed during these last twenty days. Not one of these crimes were reported, and we have no suspects. The bad guys break the law once a day, and I want you two to arrest these criminals. Upon doing so you can obtain a small financial reward as well as your old duties back. You were both up for your annual salary increase in January - you can have it a month early this year. I want these guys bad. They are wasting valuable time, every day."

"Wow," said Officer Harmon, "This means we can wear whatever we want and have open jurisdiction throughout the entire city?" "Yes," said Officer Grunt. "Not only that," he continued, "We seized a car yesterday that was a part of the cartel our force took down last week. It is a silver sedan and is yours to drive instead of one of the patrol cars you guys normally get around in. I will now mention the log. I want you to keep a daily log of your activities. It does not need to be long, and you can type it up and email it to me with your police cells daily. I want these guys caught. They only operate in this city, but they do their crimes in various areas everyday. They blend in with normal public figures and have got to be intelligent, in some regard, for we have not yet caught them. Here is a folder full of copies," said Officer Grunt placing a folder containing thirty pages or so on his desk.

"These documents contain information on the location, time and some form of possible reason for each of the daily occurrences you are now going to attempt to put a stop to," said Officer Grunt. "I am supposing that the two of you will gladly accept this newfound form of responsibility?" asked the officer, making sure that they were making the conscious decision to put forth some form of effort to solving this problem. "Yes sir," said the two officers in unison. "You have me to help you think if you need it, and you can always call for back up," said Officer Grunt. With that, he seemed to be done with his initial presentation of information. "Do you have any questions?" asked Officer Grunt.

Officer Ruby and Officer Harmon looked at each other, then back to their chief. Officer Harmon said, "We are dedicated to this force. We are going to catch these guys in an efficient and timely manner to put an end to the foolish things that they have been doing. Where can we start?" Officer Ruby looked to the ground. She was glad that it was Officer Harmon that had done the talking this time, and she was somewhat impressed with how well he had spoken with their chief.

"Your verbal instructions on a possible way of solving this case are as follows," said Officer Grunt. "When you do not have much to go on, get to a library. It is a good way of almost guessing where the crimes will occur, and libraries are a good place to decide on action. There are four in town and one, as you know, on the floor above us. You may want to go upstairs and read the file this morning. As soon as we know something, we will direct any calls to you that are possibly related to the bad guys you are after. I also have here a map of the city. I have two, actually. One of them has not been written on, and the other one has some notes on it from other officers who were trying to catch these criminals. You will see what you are up against. Hopefully, you will catch them very soon. Good luck to you, and God bless you. Call me if you need me; you are free to go catch those bad guys!" said Officer Grunt, hoping that there would be some chance that the pair could actually do such a thing.

Officer Harmon and Officer Ruby thanked their captain trying not to thank him too profusely; they both did appreciate the assignment. They figured many other dynamic duos in the department would have been able to tackle the assignment, and they were thankful for their chief's decision. They walked up to the library floor happy and proud of their new rolls in the force. The library floor was a quiet place full of nostalgia and dusty shadows. Like any library, this one possessed normal amenities. The floor consisted of a hallway and two large doorways to the vast collection of books. The two officers entered, spoke with the attendant, Officer Booker and entered the room. Booker was not the man's real name, however he was called Officer Booker for over twenty years. Some people simply called him Booker. Officer Harmon and Officer Ruby found a large table and opened the new file.

"Wow," said Officer Ruby, "I was impressed with your talking back there." "I think it went well," said Officer Harmon, "I will take that as a complement." "Why do you think he chose us instead of any of the other pairs?" asked Officer Ruby. "He sees how we all act and handle different things," said Officer Harmon, "It sounds to me like the bad guys we are after fit what we can catch. I mean that there are those duos we are on the force with that move quicker and handle more serious cases than we do, and they are also more qualified for those more serious cases. We must fit the job description best."

"What is in the folder?" asked Officer Harmon, sliding it to Officer Ruby. She opened it and they began to read. They looked through the crimes one by one as well as the wooden coins. Each coin had a small picture on it, resembling some form of crime. Obviously, the small pictures matched the crime of the day. They spread the reports out and figured out what the pictures on the coins resembled for each crime. "I notice that these crimes occurred give or take minutes of 9 AM everyday," said Officer Ruby. "They sure do," said Officer Harmon, "In fact, they could have occurred at precisely 9 AM, everyday." They then laid out each report to compare the occurrences. "There are seven jurisdictions in this city," said Officer Harmon. "I see what you are saying," said officer Ruby. Each crime had occurred in a new jurisdiction everyday. This meant that the criminals had some knowledge of the jurisdictions of the city. Not only that, the crimes were possibly occurring in some form of order or pattern.

"They are going to commit their crime in jurisdiction seven today," the officers said in unison. The jurisdiction included various different places for crimes of these natures to occur. "In order to catch these bad guys, it may help to predict where they will strike," said Officer Ruby. "Not an easy task," said Officer Harmon, "What time is it?" "It is almost eight thirty," said Officer Ruby, "Where are they going to strike and what are they going to do?" she asked herself and Officer Harmon, as she was thinking aloud. "I see crimes number seven and number fourteen are petty theft, involving a victim. The first one is a pick-pocket, and the next one involved a man's briefcase and two assailants," said Officer Ruby, "Though no one was injured, both acts of theft went unsolved." "I think we should go watch the mall," said Officer Harmon. "Okay," said Officer Ruby, "No better place to try our luck that I can think of."

With that, they left the library and drove to a lookout to see seventy percent of the local mall's territory. They arrived at 8:51 AM in a car that was *new to them*. "Ya know this is a look out, huh sweetheart?" said Officer Ruby, playing around. "That is funny, and you almost caught me off guard," said Officer Harmon, as he dug through the items in the center console. "There are all kinds of things in here," said Officer Harmon from the passenger seat. "May I see those binoculars?" asked Officer Ruby, and he handed her the binoculars. She could see five different parking lots.

As luck had it, at 8:59 AM, she saw two men in a dead sprint forty feet or so behind an old lady. Speechless she quickly gave the binoculars to Officer Harmon and put the sedan in drive. She floored it and they were upon the bad guys within seconds. The two officers pursued the two bad guys on foot and captured them. They placed them in handcuffs. "Here is your purse, ma'am," said Officer Ruby. "Will you come with us downtown to help file this report?" asked Officer Harmon. "Sure," said the woman, as Officer Ruby was walking one of the arrested suspects to the sedan. The officers read the bad guys their rights, and drove to the holding cell at their headquarters.

They successfully typed a detailed report of what happened and also found a wooden coin in one of the suspect's pockets. "This must be their symbol for theft," said Officer Ruby. "Or must *have* been," said Officer Harmon with a grin. The officers were under the impression that they had caught the criminals behind the crimes on their very first day. Time had gone by and 5 PM was approaching quicker than they imagined it would. Sometime around 3 PM, their chief called them into his office.

"Good work officers. I read the report. You display nice usage of our language. I guess you took my advice and used the library as a *think tank*," said Officer Grunt. "Again, good work. You guys can keep the sedan for your patrolling for the week, or until we get rid of it. Report in the morning as normal; I knew you guys could do it. We questioned the suspects, and they said nothing without their lawyer. They will be charged with all twenty one of these crimes with no deal for remaining silent. Something seems fishy to me, but for now this case is closed. Good work officers. I will see you in the morning." Their chief was done speaking, and the two arose and made exodus.

"What do you think seemed 'fishy'?" asked Officer Ruby. "I do not know," said Officer Harmon, "The chief must have had a long day. We caught two robbers and one had a wooden coin. It is not complicated; we got the bad guys." With that the two officers returned home and went to bed.

They awoke before dawn the next day. It was beautiful. They called each other by phone and met at a donut parlor which opened at 5 AM. They discussed the strange nature of the previous day's events over coffee and donuts. "What do you think seemed so fishy?" asked Officer Harmon. "I really do not know," said Officer Ruby, "For one, though, it was a convenient and lucky ordeal that we caught those guys." "They did not say anything," said Officer Harmon, "Maybe they were not the only bad guys." "That probably is not so," said Officer Ruby, "We are just thinking it was a little too easy to catch them, that is all." "I see," said Officer Harmon, "I hope you are right, so we can go back to our normal jobs." "I hear you," said Officer Ruby, "This caper was fun, but it is solved, now. Our job was to catch the bad guys, and we did."

The two officers reported that morning as always, and they departed to patrol the city in their sedan. The two bad guys were to remain in custody for a minimum of three days by order of the court. Once in the car, Officer Harmon asked, "Where would you like to go?" "Fishy is fishy," said Officer Ruby, "What do you think about jurisdiction one?" "No better area," said Officer Harmon, "If you will, check the reports folder once more. I would like to know if we can predict the nature of the crime according to our twenty-one day history, as well as the jurisdiction." "No can do," said Officer Ruby, "The second crime does not mach the eighth or the fifteenth crime. They are different, and though the crime of today that we hopefully put a stop to is in a predictable area, jurisdiction one, it is not really easy to say what crime we would be trying to prevent."

"Okay," said Officer Harmon, and their phones *exploded*. "My phone has an address on it from the chief," they both said to each other. It was a location to get to; another crime had been committed. The address was in jurisdiction one, just as they had guessed.

The officers made it to the address just minutes after the act had occurred. An elderly woman was crying on the bench with a young woman trying to console her. The old woman was bald, and her wig had been glued to a stop sign. The report included a man and a woman taking the lady's wig and gluing it to where it was. The glue had not even had time to set before the officers found it. Upon gently removing the wig after having taken digital pictures with their new phones, they found a wooden coin on the ground.

This coin was nearly identical to some of the others, and the design matched one of the patterns the officers would have guessed. Officer Harmon and Officer Ruby wrote a detailed report on the occurrence and even went to a library to brainstorm that afternoon. Three hours went by like five minutes would have, and they still did not really figure out any form of possible solution that could lead to serenity or solving the case either one. Both agreed that there were more than two or four criminals involved, and that there was either a ring leader or a leadership counsel of some sort behind the planning. They turned in their report, and called it a day.

In the days to come various things occurred. The crimes continued like clockwork, always sometime around 9 AM, and always in a predictable area of the city. Over the next few years nothing really changed. Officer Harmon and Officer Ruby apprehended two suspects every three months or so, by chance and planning, and maintained a vast collection of wooden coins. They figured things out like ink origins. They analyzed the various types of wood used for the coins and found hobby shops, too. The coins, though always true to design, were usually hand carved and branded with a hot wire.

At any rate, our current tale ends for now. The two officers caught lots of bad guys over the years, and they never really found the supposed organizer of events or solid reasons for the mischievous acts. Members of what the two officers called the "Wooden Coin Gang" remained silent upon getting caught and usually received incarceration due to notorious misdemeanor acts related to conspiracy. Why was there so much organization for so little payoff? No one knew. Officer Ruby and Officer Harmon continued to do their job. They remained confident that they would one day put an end to the childish games. When they found a wooden coin, one of them usually said, "Man, those guys are good."

♦

The Optometrist

Once upon a time, an owner of multiple large housing complexes decided to refurbish one of his buildings. The property owner, Mr. Fong, spoke of this before. "This should not be too difficult," said Mr. Fong to his employees. They were in a meeting in an office on the ground floor of an old eight-story building. "No sir, it should not," said one of his employees, Walton.

Walton was an avid tennis player. He was the kind of a man who people thought probably drank various teas. "We have searched the directory of the city, and 'Remodelco' appears to have an interesting advertisement," another employee said. "We have already contacted them," said a third employee, "They give free estimates upon evaluation of the job site." "When can I have them do that?" asked Mr. Fong. "We can have them here first thing in the morning," said Walton. "Okay then. If it is possible, please, let me have the estimate by noon tomorrow," requested Mr. Fong. "No problem," said Walton, and this concluded their meeting. The employees spoke together, and Walton contacted Remodelco that afternoon.

The next day, two representatives from Remodelco, Ron and Rustin, came and surveyed all eight floors of the old building. They thought the building looked as though it was from a Japanese horror film. The Remodelco representatives decided upon a lump sum estimate for the building's renovation project. They calculated the $13,000 estimate. It included both materials and labor. The number was an honest price and would increase the overall value of the building. They walked to the office on the ground floor to speak with Walton.

"We have decided on a figure to refurbish the interior of this building," said Ron. "How have you come up with a figure?" asked Walton. "We counted eight floors," began Rustin, "Each floor will need about $1,000 worth of paint, wood, trimmings, and more. We think a six-man crew should be the most cost effective. All eight floors should take a six-man crew two weeks to complete. We do not mess around. We get the job done."

Ron nodded to agree and continued by saying, "Crew members make twelve dollars an hour. Working fifty hours a week, fifty times six times twelve is $3600 for labor. $8000 worth of materials added to this number totals $11600. We add a profit cost to this number to stay in business; the market percentage now is 12%. Twelve percent of $11600 is $1392. This together is $12992. Our estimate that we are offering to you today, which will over double the value of the building, is only $13,000. For this amount, we will fix this place up to be very nice, and it might no longer remind people of a building from a Japanese horror film!" "Wow," said Walton. "But that is not all!" said Rustin joyfully, "Tell the man about the percentage discount policy!" Ron happily said, "Our percentage discount policy states that if we finish a job for a customer before we say it is going to be done, we refund the customer a percentage of the total cost in order to get to the next job. Our goal is to be done in thirteen days - a day shy of a fortnight." "How much will the discount be?" asked Walton. "The discount will be $1/14^{th}$, or about 7%," said Rustin. "I think that is about 929 dollars," said Ron.

"Wow," said Walton, "Who gave you guys the impressive discount idea?" The two Remodelco representatives looked at each other, then back at Walton and said in unison, "The sisters." "The sisters?" asked Walton. "Yes," said Ron, "They own and operate our company, Remodelco." "Wow," said Walton, a third time, "I have a meeting with Mr. Fong at 12:00 PM, today, and I am going to tell him thirteen thousand. I want you to do a good job with this site; this is not the only property we own. I am also going to let him know about the discount idea. If you finish this a day early, and it is presentable, I assure you that we will have more work for you." "Okay," said Remodelco's Ron and Rustin, and the parties disbursed.

"Well?" asked the Mr Fong, as he entered the ground floor office of the *Japanese horror building* at precisely 11:59 AM. "Thirteen thousand for all eight floors," said Walton, "Your other employees were not present this morning. I spoke with Ron and Rustin of Remodelco. They said that once completed, the building will be worth twice as much. It will also no longer highly resemble a building from a 'Japanese horror film'." "Very funny," said the Mr. Fong, "I think the building will still have that kind of look – just better. Why are you so happy? What else do you have to tell me?" he asked. "If they finish a day early, they will give us back a calculated percentage discount of 7%! They plan to have the renovation done in thirteen days," said Walton. "How about we just use these guys," said the Mr. Fong, "Did you mention the other properties?" "Yes," said Walton "I was impressed with their enthusiasm. I imagine they usually finish their jobs early." "Okay," said Mr. Fong, "Do you think they will be done in two weeks?" "Yes," said Walton. "Wow," said the Mr. Fong. "That is what I said," said Walton. "Here is a blank check," said Mr. Fong, "Write the check to you and have the building redone. Keep whatever is left over for your Christmas bonus." "Thank you," said Walton, as he accepted the check and watched Mr. Fong leave the office. Walton cried a little in appreciation.

Walton called Remodelco after ordering a pizza to the office with his prepaid credit card. "Hi," said Walton, "This is Walton, from the Japanese horror building, may I speak to Ron or Rustin?" Remodelco's secretary, Eva, was who answered the phone. She said, "Ron and Rustin are out bidding a job, currently. Are you the guys with the eight-story building that we gave an estimate to this morning?" "Yes ma'am," said Walton, finally, "I am calling you from the Japanese horror building; we accept your offer. How may I pay you for the services we discussed?" "We can have the six-man crew there to start in the morning. How can you pay?" asked Eva. "What if I bring you a certified check?" asked Walton. "That will be fine," said Eva. "I will have it to your office within an hour," said Walton, having full knowledge of the location of Remodelco's office, though he had never been inside. "Okay," said Eva, "Thank you," and they both hung up.

Walton was so excited that he forgot about the pizza. He wondered what a woman with such a beautiful voice looked like in person. He drove to the bank. He deposited the check into his account for fifteen thousand dollars, and purchased a certified check for $13,000. He then brought the check to Remodelco's office and handed it to Eva. "We will have a crew there in the morning," said Eva. "Thank you," said Walton. He grinned upon his exodus. It was hard not to do in front of such a beautifully pale-skinned woman. Her long and flowing black hair glistened with hues of metallic blue in the afternoon shadows.

The next morning, a six-man crew from Remodelco began stripping the building for refinement from top to bottom. Ron and Rustin were on the crew. The sisters had placed them on the crew as a reward for doing such a wonderful job with landing the bid. The four had a conversation the day before about the job and Walton's liking the percentage discount idea. "We will have to make sure this job gets done at least a day early," the sisters agreed on.

During the next few days, the crew worked hard. They were dead on schedule, working fifty hours a week each, with only one and a half floors left to go before completing the job. They continued to work, keeping in mind that they were trying to finish a day early. The crew worked up until the end of the thirteenth day. "We were almost done," said Ron to the crew. "All we have left to accomplish are the doorknobs on the top floor," said Rustin, "Our time has run out, however." "I will call the sisters," said Ron, and he did. "You guys go on home," said Barci, one of the sisters, "Joan and I will come and install the doorknobs this evening. That way we can give Walton and Mr. Fong their discount. We want those other bids." "Okay," said Ron, and the six man crew went home exhausted.

Joan and Barci arrived at the eight story building at dusk. Joan was taller and a year or two older than Barci with longer, light-brunette hair. Barci was shorter and possessed a more jovial attitude with slightly darker hair. Both women were loved by those they encountered. Walton was home fast asleep, dreaming of Eva. The two of them fell in love that next year and married. On this night, however, the sisters had a job to do. Joan and Barci walked every floor, one by one, admiring how well the building's interior was refurbished. The work accomplished was exquisite. The painting and carpeting were without flaw. The trimming was divine, and the sisters were impressed, indeed. "We trained our employees, well," said Joan. "They have done a wonderful job, here," agreed Barci. The sisters climbed the stairs to the top floor. Once on the eighth floor, they found a box of doorknobs Ron and Rustin's crew left behind. They installed the doorknobs, one by one, excluding the final doorknob, in under an hour.

Joan and Barci had been a playful pair of sisters since they were born. Happy to be so near absolute completion of the Japanese horror-building job, the sisters began to play peek-a-boo through the last door's open doorknob hole. The two had also had some *coffee with their sugar* on the way to the building, so they were not only naturally hyperactive, they were wired physically and full of excitement. "What might Mr. Fong and his tea drinking Walton's discount be tomorrow?" asked Joan laughing as she ducked down from view of Barci through the open hole.

"Oh, I do not know," said Barci, as she removed an unsharpened pencil from her pocket to playfully yet harmlessly poke through the opening saying, "Something like nine hundred and twenty-eight dollars and fifty-eight cents?" Barci ducked down as Joan quickly rose to peep and retort at the same time. Joan ducked back down instead, saying, "I see I am not the only one who can calculate one fourteenth of thirteen thousand." The sisters had coincidentally figured out the percentage discount separately days before this night. They were both hysterical. While continuing to peep and duck back down, Barci stuck the eraser end of the pencil through the doorknob opening. She did so only to scare Joan away from the hole, not to harm her in any way. Joan was Barci's *world*, so to speak, and nothing less.

The eraser's end went into one of Joan's eye sockets without rupturing her actual eyeball. She instinctively backed away and tried to see through the hole to see Barci with the other eye. Barci, without really thinking, tried to scare Joan, again, and performed the same exact action a second time with Joan's other eye socket. Barci did not know what happened.

"Ah! You poked me in both of my eyes!" Joan bellowed, as she quickly retreated from the door. "What?" asked Barci, as she ran to Joan in fright and confusion. "It was just the eye socket on both sides," said Joan, "I should be fine." "Thank heavens," said Barci, "Joan, I am very sorry." Their laughter having ended, they installed the last doorknob and walked to the stairway. They could now justify letting Eva cut Walton and the Mr. Fong a check for $928.58 in the morning.

By the time they had traversed to the second floor of the building, Barci had developed a deep and horrible feeling about her sister. "Are your eyes okay?" asked Barci to Joan. "I guess," said Joan, "I can see fine, but they seem slightly warm and itchy." They continued down the stairs. Upon descending the final flight of stairs, Joan said, "I am having trouble seeing, and not only is my eyesight fuzzy, I feel a little dizzy." "Show me your eyes," said Barci. Joan looked Barci in the eyes. Joan's eyes were bloodshot. Barci exclaimed, "Joan, your eyes are filling full of blood, we have got to get you to the emergency room!"

Joan was dizzy and Barci carried her out to their recently purchased black four-door Mercedes. The two sisters ran Remodelco in a successful way. Barci drove Joan to the nearest hospital's emergency room and sent a text message to Walton while in transit, saying that Eva would cut them a percentage discount check for $928.58 in the morning. Eva would have it ready for them at the Remodelco office, or she would mail it to them.

Upon arriving at the emergency room, Joan was unable to walk. Barci carried her sister through the electronically moving doors and locked up the car with the remote. Barci concluded that Joan's vertigo must have been induced from the bleeding in her eyes, somehow. The head of the emergency room, Dr. Hallsworth, was a very busy doctor, indeed. He was tending to nine patients at the time. Dr. Hallsworth somehow had the inclination to leave the emergency room to check on a nurse in the waiting area. While in transit, he saw Barci carrying Joan towards the nurse's station.

Dr. Hallsworth took Joan into is arms and brought her to a vacant bed in the emergency room. He asked Barci politely to stay in the waiting area. She had briefly and honestly explained what had happened. The doctor examined Joan's eyes. As Barci sat in the waiting area, she glanced down to a table. She saw older magazines with beautiful and peaceful landscapes on their covers. They were constant tortures to Barci's mind, as she wondered of Joan's blindness and the idea of its permanence. "Would Joan ever be able to see beautiful landscapes again?" wondered Barci. She felt absolutely horrible for what she had done. It was an accident; Barci could not forgive herself for it.

Meanwhile, Dr. Hallsworth stabilized Joan comfortably in a hospital bed. The doctor examined her eyes properly and asked her to remain calm in the bed while he went to speak with Barci and other patients. "Is my sister alright?" asked Barci impatiently, upon seeing Dr. Hallsworth. "Barci, your sister, Joan, will be fine," said the doctor, attempting to provide some form of serenity to the obviously frantic young woman. "Can Joan see?" asked Barci, after inhaling and exhaling, slowly, in order to calm down.

"No," said the doctor, "Even when the blood fully drains from her eyes, she will be permanently blind. She will live, however. I almost lost her due to internal bleeding. The nerves on the back of both of her eyes are damaged. Again, she will live, though she will never see again."

Crushed, tears instantly poured from Barci's eyes. "What have I done?" Barci asked herself. Joan was not just Barci's sister. According to Barci, Joan was Barci's *complete and entire world.* Nothing mattered more to Barci than Joan, not even Barci, herself. Joan was taken to a normal hospital room in under three hours. She was released from the care of the hospital to Barci's supervision two days later. The sisters had no living relatives in their current state of residence. They moved to a "big city" to run a business, not to be close to family. Time passed by gently, and Joan and Barci healed, to some extent, psychologically.

Remodelco's employees now numbered close to three dozen. Joan road to work with Barci for about a week or so, sporting stylish sunglasses and enjoying their Mercedes as much as possible. Joan's blindness made Eva feel uncomfortable - the truth hurting as it did. Joan wanted to learn more braille at the house, anyway. "I can tell you are tired of coming with me to work," said Barci one day, on the way home. "You know," said Barci, "I have no problem keeping Eva and the rest of our employees in proper order from day-to-day, if you would rather stay home for those nine hours." Joan listened, patiently. "Our business is doing well," continued Barci, "If we keep getting bids like this, I will hire at least five more workers into training this quarter." "As much as I enjoy helping out with the phones," began Joan, "I have already grown tired of doing so. Besides, I have become obsessed with braille, and I simply learn to use it better at the house."

"Obsessed?" asked Barci, wondering subconsciously about laws, ethics, and temporary insanity. "Yes," answered Joan, "Believe it or not, braille has helped me tremendously with my spelling." The two had purchased a software package and some manuals and books for learning braille the day after Joan's release from the hospital. "Eva's workload has increased these past few weeks," said Joan, "What if we hire an assistant for her and I stay home for a while? I could play around with braille more, and maybe even write some books. I could become a novelist." "Okay," said Barci, in absolute love of her sister, "You know how sorry I still am, Joan. You know I will do anything you say. You know I never meant to blind you." "I know, Barci," said Joan, "I know how you love me, and you know I love you, too." They returned home happily.

Joan and Barci lived in a three bedroom, two-bath house. It was a quick find during their first job in their new state of residence, about a year ago. They were happy to be in a larger city. The house was a rent to own opportunity they found via a Sunday newspaper. Their property owner, Ms.

Parks, lived next door. That night over dinner, Barci began to speak. "You are going to stay here, alone, whilst I keep 'our people' in line?" asked Barci. "I suppose," said Joan, "I do not know why I might need anyone here while I am learning more braille." "I bet Ms. Parks will be somewhat nosy, anyway" thought Barci aloud, almost by accident. "I doubt I will mind her checking on me during the day," said Joan. After finishing diner, the two hugged each other and went off to bed.

Usually, Barci was a little more hyperactive than Joan was. On this night, however, Joan lie awake thinking, and Barci went straight to bed and fell fast asleep. Joan was wondering of what she might like to write. She decided to attempt to write books that readers would enjoy like never before. Joan was almost too excited to go to sleep. She felt it on the inside; she was about to embark on a new role in life, somehow.

As always, the sun came up. Barci hurried to work early to help with a demolition team, downtown. Joan stayed home with her walking cane and her braille. Ms. Parks was next door. That morning while Joan was practicing braille, she wrote a nice short story. She even dictated the story to text on her computer. The story was about an old woman who made magical dolls. Ms. Parks came by around 11 AM, helped Joan sell the story to a periodical online. Joan would receive a small percentage of the sales from the periodical as compensation for submitting the story.

That afternoon Ms. Parks and Joan went to the pharmacy together to get Joan's antibiotics and other medicine. Ms. Parks drove an older pastel colored metallic green Mustang car from the sixties. She kept her car in good condition - it ran well. Joan was still thinking from the night before. She knew Ms. Parks had to be "cool" on some level, because Ms. Parks had spoken of the casual use of herb, before. Joan went ahead with her thinking aloud, on the way home. "So how often do you puff herb?" asked Joan to Ms. Parks. "Not very often," said Ms. Parks, "It helps me with the pains that come from growing somewhat older and with stress, but I really only puff it once every few weeks or so. I do not really see it as harmful, but it is illegal. I get a small bag from my boy down the street every now and then. I find him about once a month or so."

"Why?" asked Ms. Parks. "Oh, no reason," said Joan. Joan drank chamomile tea in the evening from time to time, but she did not trouble herself with the hassle of finding herb. "I can get anything imaginable prescribed to me, now," said Joan. "My boy down the street sells pills, sometimes," said Ms. Parks, "It would not be too risky to let him sell some for us. It would not be legal, of course, but it would be a way to make some money." "Precisely," said Joan, and the two made it back home before Barci returned home from work that day.

Money was what the two sisters were making a lot of, anyway. For the next few weeks, Barci ran Remodelco with invigorating fervor. Joan continued to write stories every other day or so and rode around town with Ms.

Parks all of the time. They split the cost of gasoline and became closer to one another.

One night, Barci was unable to sleep. She remained in a half asleep, half awake state of mind tossing and turning for most of the night. Barci was wondering if Joan would ever be able to see again. Before morning came, Barci decided that she was going to do something about Joan's blindness. Barci decided to attempt to grow her sister, Joan, a new pair of eyeballs. Barci would need medical literature, of course, and was afraid to access certain topics online. She thought topics such as organ manufacture were probably somewhat shady to research without a medical degree of some sort. Barci would have to keep her scholarly journals and textbooks hidden and secret from Joan. This would not be an easy task, because both of them loved to admit to and take pride in their accomplishments.

Barci and Joan had an early breakfast one morning. "Business is doing well," said Barci, "I moved Ron and Rustin up to managerial positions. I let Eva hire two new workers last week, and she and that Walton man are seeing each other. He looks like he is in a dream world every time he sees her." Barci paused for a moment; they were eating pancakes. Barci continued, "I think I want to go buy a truck today. The Mercedes is nice and expedient. It just cannot haul material as a big truck could. I am guessing that you want to keep the Mercedes, but I do not think we can afford to have two vehicles just yet. We need more purchasing power."

"Why do you not go and purchase a Hyperduty?" asked Joan, "I will pay off the Mercedes this afternoon with money that I have been making from selling my obviously delightful stories online." "Surely you have not already made enough money to pay off the car," said Barci, "Have you really already made that much?" "Already," said Joan, "I most certainly have. The periodical that I now write for has obtained national acclaim, and its worldwide sales have increased phenomenally. They publish weekly, and I submit a new '5,000' word story to an editor every five days." "Wow," said Barci. "You sound like Walton," said Joan, and they both shared a heart-warming grin.

Barci drove to work, and Joan paid off the Mercedes that morning. That afternoon, after ensuring jobs were going as planned for Remodelco, Barci went and purchased a new, fully loaded limo-black Hyperduty. It was the largest and toughest work truck in the history of humankind. The amazing "4x4" had a new g. p. s. system and even had Barci's favorite feature - cruise control. The sales representative mentioned a special racing chip for this model on the down low, and Barci decided to make that known to Joan at another time.

Getting the truck to the house was fun in itself. Barci drove the car to Remodelco, picked Ron up, and drove to the dealership. He drove the car and she drove the truck to Remodelco. Then Barci drove her huge new expensive truck home. Ron followed her home in the black four-door Mercedes, while Rustin followed him there in Ron's old work truck. They highly resembled a small traveling circus.

The sisters had both of their vehicles at their house. Ron and Rustin drove back to Remodelco and then went home. Joan walked around the massively impressive truck and felt the treads on the tires. Barci spoke of the new vehicle's main features and answered all of Joan's questions. They were both impressed and enjoyed playing with the nice stock radio for a while.

For the next few weeks, Barci continued to run Remodelco successfully, and Joan and Ms. Park's road around together in the Mercedes from time to time. Barci kept her optometry studies to herself. For these weeks, Barci had made time to collect various medical books and scholarly journals on eyeballs. She put forth as much effort as possible.

As much as she read about the human eyeball and its various components, however, Barci was unable to successfully find enough information on how to grow or synthetically form a human eyeball. Exhausted in her thinking, Barci considered speaking with Dr. Hallsworth. She knew somehow that it would be a risky endeavor. If he could have helped Joan see again, he probably would have mentioned some solution to her blindness the night of their accidental catastrophie.

During the weeks Barci continued conducting research, Joan and Ms. Parks had become *tight* with one another. Joan was prescribed a minimal number of prescriptions. She refrained from taking most of her medicine. Ms. Parks moved all of the pills via her "boy" down the street named Zay.

One morning, as she often did, Ms. Parks knocked on Joan and Barci's side door around 11 AM. "Good morning Ms. Parks!" said Joan as she opened the door, "How are you today?" Joan was drinking some coffee that morning. "I am fine," said Ms. Parks, happily, "How are you, Joan?" "I suppose that I am happily fine, as well," said Joan, "I just uploaded my 9th story. I think I might expand this one into a novella, sometime."

"That is nice, Joan," said Ms. Parks, "I just got back from seeing my 'boy' down the street. Here is that note that I owe you." Ms. Parks handed Joan a hundred dollar bill. The money was for some pills Joan had given Ms. Parks for sale and recreational use. "Got to love that Benjamin Franklin," Joan said laughing, and then asked Ms. Parks, "Have you been puffing any herb today? You sound like you need to talk." "Sure thing," said Ms. Parks, "We smoked on some kind of a newly developed purple indica strain. It was some rare medical stuff, from what I hear. It was a nice and smooth aid to my attempt with stress-free contemplation. However, that is not really what has aroused my interests."

"What, may I ask, has aroused your interests?" asked Joan, as they finally sat at Joan's worktable. "My boy has a new pill connect," said Ms. Parks, "He must be an impressive individual. He only deals with m. d. m. a. - no prescriptions." "I know what you are talking about," said Joan, "We have all eaten 'rolls' here and there, have we not?" "Sure we have," said Ms. Parks, "I happen to have about a hundred of them in a bottle in my pocket, right now.

Do you want any?" Of course Joan might try one; she and Ms. Parks enjoyed a wonderful conversation that afternoon. Ms. Parks and Joan listened to an album from the seventies. It was peaceful, and they enjoyed the nice warm buzz from the pill they took for some while.

What eventually happened did not really take too much time. Joan was making an average of about ten grand a week selling her stories, and she was not running out of ideas anytime soon. Fans worldwide were reading her work and giving her mostly positive criticism. Authors everywhere were fans of Joan largely due to her overnight claim to fame.

Meanwhile, Barci was doing a good job running Remodelco, as always. She continued to read about eyes, too. Barci had obtained plenty of information on optometry from various sources, such as university bookstores, libraries, and elsewhere. Despite her efforts to add water to matter and manufacture a pair of human eyes, Barci was unable to do so. She just could not imagine that such a feat would be impossible. She decided, finally, to somehow speak with Dr. Hallsworth.

Barci kept in mind that she was possibly temporarily insane, and tried to come up with various methods of speaking with the doctor without having to kidnap the fellow. Barci had full knowledge of how busy Dr. Hallsworth must have been. She imagined that busy emergency room doctors like Dr. Hallsworth probably worked a minimum of seventy hours a week. She also took into account the well-being of patients that often need emergency care in order to keep from death.

One day, after some thought on the matter, Barci called Dr. Hallsworth. She phoned the hospital on a lunch break, and asked to speak with Dr. Hallsworth. Barci was desperate, but remained honest enough to admit that the call was not an emergency. She spoke with a nurse who took Barci's cell phone number and promised to pass it to Dr. Hallsworth. "What a long shot," thought Barci. The doctor called Barci that afternoon. "Is this urgent?" asked Dr. Hallsworth. "No sir," said Barci, "I just have a few questions to ask you concerning optometry. May I buy you lunch sometime to answer them?" "Sure," said the caring doctor, "How about tomorrow at noon?" "Okay. Thank you, Dr. Hallsworth" said Barci, "I will pick you up from the emergency room at noon in my Hyperduty. Is that okay? Will you be there?" "Yes," said Dr. Hallsworth, "I will be there," and they ended their conversation politely.

That next day Barci took Dr. Hallsworth to the nicest restaurant in the city. Barci ordered a specialty deep-fried sushi roll, and she ordered Dr. Hallsworth a special chicken cordon blue entrée. They discussed eyes and how well Joan had been doing with her blindness and writing. Barci finally admitted to her endeavors by saying, "I just simply want to know if I can grow or make a synthetic pair of working eyes for Joan, somehow."

"No," said Dr. Hallsworth, "It is impossible to do such a thing as that, currently. Money, science, and research go hand in hand these days; it is the world we live in. To my understanding, you will not be able to grow Joan a new pair of eyes. You also cannot mix up some chemicals and somehow make synthetic eyes that work properly. Waiting lists do exist for various human organs - you were accurate with that assumption. However, I do not think it is possible, currently, to manufacture fully functional human eyes. I am sorry, Barci, your sister, as I said before, is permanently blind. Please, let it go."

Barci was somewhat disappointed, but she was not very surprised. She figured it was a long shot, anyway. They concluded their conversation with minimal discussion on eye surgeries and lasers. Barci brought Dr. Hallsworth back to the emergency room of the hospital and thanked him before bidding him farewell.

During that same day, Ms. Parks and Zay went to Barci and Joan's house to see Joan. Joan had not met Zay; he felt it to be safer to let her meet his connect. No one wanted to get caught breaking the law. Joan heard Ms. Parks knock on the door and let her and her *boy* come inside. Ms. Parks said, "Hi Joan. This is Zay, from down the street."

"Well, Zay," said Joan, "It is nice to meet you." Joan closed the door, and they all went and sat down at Joan's worktable. Not really knowing what to say, Zay said, "So, Joan, is it true that you are legally blind?" "Yes," said Joan, "Might I feel your face? I will know you better that way." Zay agreed to it, having heard of blind people meeting others that way. The three had a pleasant conversation. They did not smoke any herb that day, but Joan agreed to the purchase of a k-pack of m. d. m. a. A *k-pack* is a small bag of one thousand pills - a supposed choice quantity for some people who commonly take and sell pills.

Zay and Ms. Parks both knew people to sell to, and these people commonly sold to other people. Joan had the money to back multiple purchases of this size, especially considering the profit that would come from each purchase. This meeting adjourned, and over the course of a few weeks, things almost got out of hand. People all over the city were eating "rolls" often. So often that Zay asked Ms. Parks if Joan would like to meet his connect; Zay did not want to live too risky of a life. He simply did not like the risk of handling large amounts of money, and Joan thought it was fun.

Ms. Parks happily drove Joan to meet Zay's connection, one day. The connect was an impressive individual. He had men that worked for him 100% of the time; he was the owner of a restaurant. It surprised Joan to find out that Zay's connect was a huge fan of hers. He mentioned that he was a subscriber to the online periodical that she was writing for, and that he enjoyed everything he ever read by her.

Within only a few weeks, Mr. Doughertry, the connect, had provided Joan with her own personal driver. Joan's newfound influence prevailed throughout the entire city. She had become the most powerful ruler of the underworld known. Things happened this way, in part, due to Joan's blindness. People trusted Joan; she was honest and she was of no threat to anyone. People sold pills to others for her. Those sold to many users.

Barci knew nothing of Joan's secret lifestyle or of the people that were buying and selling pills. All Barci really knew was that Joan had a trusted driver named Mr. Leni who was a companion of Ms. Parks.

One night, Barci had been losing sleep due to thoughts of eye surgery. She woke up early to make breakfast for Joan and herself, as usual. She put on a pot of coffee, and something occurred to her that she had not thought of before. Barci remembered someone asking whether she would like to donate her body to science the last time she had renewed her driver's license. Weeks had gone by, but she had figured a possible way to get a pair of eyes for Joan - by acquiring them from a donation to science.

Barci had been watching the news every morning and reading the newspapers, as well. She wondered if car accidents were anything to hope for and almost felt regret just for thinking of such of a thing. One day, however, Barci saw on the morning news that there was a horrible accident on the freeway involving three casualties.

A horrendously sad story, a mother and her neighbor were driving the mother's son to school. They were t-boned by an eighteen-wheeler. The truck was hauling reinforced concrete culverts. The culverts were a dozen feet in diameter.

Barci did not really know what she wanted to do. She jotted down the license plate number of the totaled vehicle on the news. She drove to work in her Hyperduty, as always, and carried out operations as normal. During her drive home to see Joan, that day, after having done minimal research on the topic of cadavers, Barci found a special research morgue with her smart-phone. She figured out that the woman donated her body to science by looking up her license plate number.

That afternoon, when Barci made it home, Joan was fast asleep on their huge and fluffy white sofa. Barci decided that it was best to take a nap, also. She set her alarm for 2 AM, showered, and went to sleep. Upon waking, she noticed that Joan was gone. Barci called Joan on her cell phone. Joan said that she had trouble sleeping and asked Mr. Leni to drive her out for some pancakes. They were on their way back home. Of course, Joan was not yet ready to admit to her involvement with crime. "I am awake, as well," said Barci, "I am going for a drive to get some fresh air and maybe some tacos. I will be back in a little while." They ended their conversation, and Barci casually drove to the morgue.

Barci parked behind a hardware store close to the morgue and walked to its rear door. She carried a small bag including various items she thought may be pertinent to her goal. She kept it under her jacket. As the CEO of a construction company, Barci had little problem picking a large lock to enter the morgue. She found the female cadaver in a special capsule set aside for scientific experimentation and preservation. "What luck," thought Barci, as she also found a jar and some formaldehyde.

The mother's skull had suffered a compound fracture, but her eyes were in perfect condition. Barci carefully performed what she thought of as an "optechtemy". Once she had the eyes secure in the jar, Barci left the morgue carefully. She did not want to leave any evidence of forced entry. She left no visible damage to anything. One would have to re-examine the body of the mother to notice any foul play.

Barci drove through a drive-through to obtain a large sack of tacos on the way home. Upon Barci's arrival, Joan was fast asleep. Barci had already prepared more than one plan weeks ago. She had considered holding Dr. Hallsworth to gunpoint, or performing the surgery herself. "One way or the other," thought Barci, "Joan is going to see again." This was Barci's decision. Barci had obtained a nine mm gun with a silencer, a *Taser*, a canister of anesthesia, and various other items. She just needed to think things through, and this was Barci's way of doing so. She thought about things and read all sorts of literature during the past weeks on eyes and nerve endings. Kidnapping the doctor would take too much time and have its consequences, though exercising the muscle to do so was rather tempting. She did care for the doctor. Barci decided to perform the surgery on her own.

Joan was asleep, and Barci made sure that she was deep asleep via anesthesia and an injection, too. Joan's life was not at risk; that was what Barci was counting on. Joan would see again, soon. Procedure manuals open and instrumentation sanitized, Barci performed the eye surgery on her sister, Joan.

The procedure was much less difficult than Barci had guessed, even though she read and studied the information many times before. Barci gave countless hours of study to optometry the past few weeks. She had completed the procedure before 5 AM. By 6 AM, Barci had successfully disposed of her instrumentation and any evidence that an eye surgery had taken place. The sun was coming up, and it was no surprise that Joan was still fast asleep. Barci made a breakfast including eggs, sausage, pancakes, orange juice and milk, and she ate some cold tacos.

Joan was not awakened from the smell of her cooking, so Barci decided to wake her up. She poured some ammonia onto a dishtowel and wafted an awakening scent under Joan's nose. In the dim shadows of daybreak, Joan woke up and stared dead into the eyes of Barci. "I can see," said Joan. "Awesome!" said Barci giggling in happiness, "I gave you optometry surgery while you were sleeping." Joan was confused and thought she was having a wild dream. She walked into the bathroom and looked in the mirror. "Are you okay?" asked Barci, "Are you experiencing any discomfort of any sort, physically?" "No," said Joan, remaining as honest as possible, "I can see fine and I feel perfectly normal." The two had conversation over breakfast.

Joan wanted to ask her sister how she received new eyes, however she decided not to. She was mildly unsettled, yet Joan was somehow thankful for her caring sister, Barci. Joan's new eyes were pale and hazel in hue. The sisters had a nice morning and went to work.

For years, Joan continued to work in both construction and writing. She usually worked until lunch time and went home to write. Joan did not have an infection from her eyes. Barci ran their business well, and Joan became a well-known author and a millionaire. After a decade, they sold forty percent of their construction company to a group of investors. Barci went to college to one day attend a medical school. The sisters considered various topics, and they lived happily ever after.

◆

The Portal

"I have it!" thought Dr. Rabrarian aloud, "I will make a portal." Dr. Rabrarian was the head doctor of the emergency room unit of his hospital. There were five large hospitals in the city he lived in. He was over a team of younger doctors, and Dr. Rabrarian was sixty.

Dr. Rabrarian worked a schedule of a minimal of thirty hours a week - Monday through Saturday from 8 AM until 1 PM. He was always on call, despite the valiant competency of his various subordinate team members. His team handled incidences involving things from car accident victims to gunshot people. His team sometimes needed his expertise immediately. The hospital team called him in about one hundred times a year.

He was both an humble and a wealthy man. Dr. Rabrarian paid for his schooling with private funds and scholarships. He was not in the medical field for financial reasons. The doctor thought of himself as a helper and a scientist.

During his golden years, which is the part of his life this tale takes place in, he spent his leisure time in scientific study and research. He considered many things. Genetics, space travel, geography, anatomy, sociology, and various sports were among his favorite thought realms.

Dr. Rabrarian's current dilemma had him thinking all afternoon. He needed a way to get to his emergency room faster. A giant tower with a pulley as seen in a cartoon humorously crossed his mind. The previous night, they called him for a car accident patient who was in need of a blood transfusion. His team was unable to identify a proper blood match, and they were short handed.

They reluctantly called in Dr. Rabrarian, who found a matching rare blood type and saved the man. He did so in only moments, though. The doctor thought the victim was a lucky individual. The patient was split seconds away from death.

The next day, Dr. Rabrarian thought of a better way to get there. He normally zipped over there in his v6 turbo automatic two-seater. The race car was a generic orange-pink handmade sports car from Italy that cost him 75 thousand dollars. It came with no a-c and white-gray leather seats with 14 inch wide wheels. Dr. Rabrarian installed a nice in-dash car stereo with in-door and back-hatch speakers. His car was like an organism - it was fun and would be hard to beat in a race. He timed it; the car completed one-fourth of a mile in under eleven seconds from a non-moving start.

His new idea would bring him to the emergency room even faster. "I can design this thing on a tablet," thought Dr. Rabrarian to himself, and that is what he did. His portal operated with software that could draw a life-size rectangle. He designed an application that used two g. p. s. locals - a door to walk into and a door to walk out of. He tried it out; it worked.

Dr. Rabrarian's first attempt with his portal was rather fun for him. He drew a rectangle by his front door and one in front of the "drop off" or entry door to the emergency room. He set the doors to be active for five seconds and walked into one and out of the other.

People saw the Dr. standing in front of the emergency room. They thought that he had magically appeared or that they were seeing things. He waved to them and walked half across town to his home in conclusion of his Sunday afternoon. The portal worked fine. Hopefully, Dr. Rabrarian would never have a pressing need to use his new portal application. He turned in early for a normal day to come.

Monday did come, and Dr. Rabrarian awoke with the sun seeping through his bedroom window at about 6:30 AM. The week was passing by. The doctor oversaw an emergency heart transplant after hours on Thursday night. He was not a necessity that time, however his team wanted him there in case they actually needed him. He just drove. The surgery went well.

Sunday afternoon came and the doctor could not stop thinking about his portal application. He knew better than to let his secret out. The doctor knew of the possible consequences of using something meant for legitimate purposes only for fun or anything other than actual emergency medical need. He was tempted, however. Dr. Rabrarian did not use the portal that day. He read a few articles from *The Modern Scientist*, a periodical he subscribed to for pleasure reading, and went to bed early.

Weeks went by and he only had one call-out. He drove. Dr. Rabrarian saved another life, and thoughts of the portal were almost driving him crazy. "It has so many possible avenues for use," he thought. His view on health was to *let it go*. "It" being whatever caused worry. Dr. Rabrarian's thought, once he let things go, was to ponder upon what could be more important. He often asked himself, "What else is there? What else can I do?"

Being the head of the emergency room was no small form of responsibility in the hospital. Dr. Rabrarian was used to checking on about six patients an hour. The doctor could come and go here and there, and he had access to most of the computers in the hospital. He wanted a more thorough understanding of his satellite access, though, so he went shopping.

At the time, Dr. Rabrarian only had his tablet and an old PC that was out of date and limited in ability internet-access wise. He bought a fifty-inch wide-screen and a PC with a large hard drive, Wi-Fi and a router. This meant that he could then access locations anywhere in the world via satellite video capture and the web.

Dr. Rabrarian justified all of this fun and expenditure for the ability to monitor the surroundings of the hospital and walk through the portal at just the right secretive moment in time. He never wanted to be seen appearing from nowhere again. Dr. Rabrarian did not want to be known of as the incredible appearing doctor that could appear with no known effort.

More time went by. The doctor had his computer-T. V. system up and running properly, and he could g. p. s. video-capture specific locals all over the world. Would he use his portal to go somewhere? No, he would not - not without it being an absolute needed occurrence due to an emergency. This secret was important and could mean the difference in the life or death of a person.

He had some entertaining fun viewing various different parts of the world with his new television. He observed mountains, sidewalk traffic, and peaceful ocean shores. As time went by, however, he fine-tuned his satellite connection to monitor the hospital only.

The emergency room's number one failure with saving lives other than heart problems was due to drug overdoses in the area. The youngsters would bring each other to the emergency room and leave the drug abusers. Sometimes the doctors and nurses had time to save them with anti-reaction medications and or techniques. This was perceived to be the case the next time Dr. Rabrarian used his portal mechanism.

Some people dropped off a young man who Dr. Rabrarian watched try to crawl to the emergency room door. The man collapsed. Dr. Rabrarian did not want to lose this patient. He set up the portal to last for four seconds and hopped through the shining window-like portal entry door. As planned, he arrived directly in front of the emergency room door by the patient. The nurses were there immediately and helped the doctor get the patient inside. According to blood work, the patient consumed a poison. They gave the patient medicine that saved his life. The man might have made it without the use of the portal, however Dr. Rabrarian did not think he would have.

Dr. Rabrarian had no trouble keeping his secret unknown with the nurses and his subordinate doctors. His problem was with the mob. The patient the doctor recently brought back to health happened to be a part of a crime family. He had eaten a poisonous leftover sandwich from a meetinghouse, and the men he was with saw Dr. Rabrarian appear from nowhere.

Dr. Rabrarian knew none of this. Two weeks later, however he saw a four-door black car pull up by his sports car as he was leaving the hospital around 1:10 PM. Two men that he had never seen before were upon him in an instant. One of them had a black felt bag with a drawstring, and the other had a rope that was four feet long.

The man with the bag put the bag on Dr. Rabrarian's head. The man with the rope tied the rope loosely around the doctor's wrists as if the doctor was under arrest. "Do not worry," said a man, "We are taking you to a quiet place to speak with you." They walked the doctor to their black four-door and helped him in the back seat. "You guys want the radio on?" asked the driver. "Sure," said someone. The passenger must have turned the radio on. There must have been four men other than Dr. Rabrarian in the car.

The car sped, slowed, turned, and stopped repeatedly for about twenty minutes. The doctor knew not to care too much about trying to figure out their whereabouts. The car went down and up, slowly. Dr. Rabrarian figured they were pulling into a lock-up garage. He was accurate in his thinking.

The four men got out and walked the doctor through a short hallway and into a room. They sat him in a chair and tied his ankles and hands to the chair. "Thank you for your cooperation, Doc," said the voice of a man that then said, "Remove the bag."

Dr. Rabrarian closed his eyes, and they removed the bag carefully. The doctor slowly opened his eyes to a squint and looked down to see the floor. There were two men behind him and two in front of him. There were actually three men in front of him, counting the man behind the small wooden desk. The doctor reluctantly looked up just long enough to see the man behind the desk, who happened to be the intelligible person speaking. Dr. Rabrarian then looked back to the floor guessing that the time was nearing 2 PM.

The man behind the desk was the patient that he saved a few weeks back. "Thank you for saving my life," said the patient. "No problem," said the doctor, "I think you were somewhat lucky." "What was in the anecdote shot?" asked the man behind the desk. "That was a simple antibiotics concoction-medley. I have designed one of those under pressure once before for someone that was sick from improperly cooked oysters. There is a theory that nine out of ten forms of food poisoning will never occur in humans and therefore will not cause death."

"I guessed right about the serum," said the boss. He went on to say, "I could have sent you a simple thank you card after I cleaned up. My boys said you appeared, though. They said you were not there. Then, you appeared suddenly, like an 'angelic mo-fo' or something. They did not know what to think. We brought you here." "I am a scientist," said Dr. Rabrarian. "Most doctors are," said the boss. "I designed a portal transfer application to help save lives," said Dr. Rabrarian. These people were the last ones the doctor would ever want to have the portal.

"How does the portal work?" asked the boss. "I cannot explain that fully," said the doctor, "I use an application and the web to do it." "I want that application," said the boss. "I am sorry, sir, I cannot not give it to you," said Dr. Rabrarian, trying to figure out how to keep the portal from them. "Put that bat down," said the boss. A man behind the doctor wanted to make him talk with a bat. "This is a very important doctor," said the boss, "This doctor saved my life, and we will work this out. I do not suppose you want a sandwich?" The doctor would have laughed, yet he was a little scared for his well-being. "No thank you," said Dr. Rabrarian.

"What will it take for you to give me that application?" asked the boss "I will send you a thank you note and a fruit basket for helping me live." Dr. Rabrarian was out of ideas. He had to give them what they were after. "Can you put it on a disk?" asked the patient, who happened to be the boss, as the doctor knew by now. "Sure," said the doctor. "My boys will bring you to your car. Have that disk with you tomorrow, and we will meet you there at about 1:15 PM. Then, you can give us that disk and we will not bother you. That is unless somebody eats a sandwich," said the boss with a grin. The patient was thankful, and he was no-one's fool. "Take our companion here back to his car," said the boss leaning back in his chair.

Dr. Rabrarian felt the black felt bag drop over his head once more, and they pulled the drawstring snug again. The men untied him from the chair and tied his hands behind his back again. They then walked Dr. Rabrarian back to their car safely. They drove the doctor to his car, untied him, and drove off with the bag still on his head. The doctor removed the bag almost as easily as a motorcyclist would take off his familiar helmet. The afternoon was cloudy; the doctor was somehow thankful to see it.

Dr. Rabrarian did not really know what to think of in regards to these things. He did not really know what the men wanted with the portal, but the doctor guessed it would be of nothing good. He also knew it was probably best to let them have it, considering his own welfare and that of others. He decided to give it to them and keep it a secret. That evening he put the portal application onto a disk and the disk into an envelope. He then went off to bed.

The next day he performed his normal duties at the hospital; no one even noticed that he had some things on his mind. He simply left the envelope under the seat in his car by the felt bag and cracked a window open. Dr. Rabrarian went out to it after 1 PM. The package was fine. As guessed, the clean black car pulled up nearby and a back window rolled down a few inches. The doctor slid the envelope into the felt bag and into the window of the car. The car drove away. Dr. Rabrarian drove home and played around with his satellite television for a while, did some reading, ate, and went to bed.

The next day came and Dr. Rabrarian thought about the mob all day. He guessed it was real. This was mainly due to movies. He thought real life inspired movies. He thought about how the mob was similar to a second form of government and hated by some. He thought about image and peoples' perceptions of each other. He wondered if criminals really "did" people or not. The mob certainly had some form of activity, he thought, because those men had a clandestine place to convene.

During all of the things that were going on in the doctor's mind, he helped one patient after another. He also oversaw his subordinate team member doctors, as always. "Things are what they are," he thought to himself, and he let it all go. He would not have even thought of it again, maybe, and around noon, a delivery girl came to the emergency room door and gave a large basket to a nurse. It was the promised fruit basket; the card on it said, "Thank you, Dr. Rabrarian, for your services; live long and prosper."

Dr. Rabrarian accepted the fruit basket and said that it came from a patient. He continued his tasks for the day and went home. Throughout the years to come, he helped people as he was able to do so. Dr. Rabrarian never heard from the men in the car again, and he eventually retired. The doctor only used the portal device once or twice a year while he was still working for the emergency room. His finely maintained car sufficed for most of his call-outs. The doctor had his car refurbished once a decade. He never knew what the mob wanted the portal for, nor did he know how well it served their purposes.

◆

"Hey there my little poppet," said the businessperson as he walked through the door. His name was Miguel Throne. "Do you have your things all together?" he asked, as his adorable young daughter ran up to give his leg a hug. "Yes, sir," said Amy. She had packed her belongings and was ready for a small journey.

The two left the Mr. Throne's city-flat and made it to the subway. They made their way to the townhouse of Amy's aunt on the other side of town. Amy was to stay there for the weekend. This was so her father could go and close a business deal in another city. Amy's aunt, her mother's sister, was an interesting woman. Amy stayed with her from time to time and learned how to be a more polite young girl.

Amy and Mr. Throne arrived on time and spoke with her aunt. They called her Ms. Jone. He left. "Come and unpack your things, Amy," said Ms. Jone, and Amy did so. Amy was sometimes a bit energetic. She often found some form of maturity and acted more like an innocent angel with proper posture around Ms. Jone. "We are going next door for dinner tonight," said Ms. Jone. Amy asked, "Which side?" The townhouse was in a row of six houses. "The Bobbingtons are on our entryway left side," said Ms. Jone, "They are cooking hamburgers."

Amy sat politely on one of two of Ms. Jone's small couches, as Ms.

Jone was tidying up her kitchen. "What does Mr. Bobbington do for work?" asked Amy, loving Ms. Jone. She realized how happy she was to be able to attain some information. For Amy, any dialogue with Ms. Jone was a language lesson greatly appreciated. "Mr. Bobbington is a magazine editor for a financial studies periodical. The company he works for analyzes Fortune 500 Companies for stock brokers and anyone who wants to read about big computer companies, airplane manufactures, and others."

"Wow," said Amy, "Do you think he went to college?" "Of course," said Ms. Jone, "I think he received a degree in finance with a minor in business writing. He worked for a few years and let his company send him back to college to obtain a masters degree in business. That was when he met Mrs. Bobbington." "Does Mrs. Bobbington still substitute teach?" asked Amy. "Yes, sweetheart," replied Ms. Jone, "She also plans to be a nurse one day." "Do you think they will ever have a baby?" asked Amy. Amy was trying to figure these people out.

"I do not know," said Ms. Jone, "I think they are waiting a while on that one. They will probably consider that once she becomes a nurse." "Oh," said Amy. "Last time I saw Mr. Bobbington, he seemed to be under stress, somehow," commented Amy. "Yes, Amy," agreed Ms. Jone, "Some people operate best with a little stress. I have always thought that Mr. Bobbington creates his own gravity in order to get things accomplished. He is an educated fellow. I think he will be less stressed when Mrs. Bobbington is more satisfied, career wise." "I see," said Amy.

With these things said, Ms. Jone had finished getting ready to go next door. Amy and Ms. Jone washed their hands before leaving. She held Amy's hand, and they walked over there. Amy always thought that the townhouses were stacked together like a small collection of shelf books. Once inside one of them, it was always an entirely new world.

The Bobbington's place was nice and well kept. Mrs. Bobbington welcomed Amy and Ms. Jone in happily, and they smelled smoke from a barbeque pit as she opened the door. "Perfect timing!" said Mrs. Bobbington, "Gideon is just bringing in the burgers." Mr. Bobbington's name was Gideon. The four ate and had a wonderful time. Gideon was impressed to hear that Amy could read well even though she was only five. She read a part of an article from one of his periodicals one time. Amy was impressed with her aunt's ability to speak of fine art and current artists. Ms. Jone worked for the art museum. As Ms. Jone spoke of art to guests and her peers. She usually did not voice her own honest opinion. However, she could do so outside of the museum on certain occasion, such as tonight. Ms. Jone's favorite painter was Monet, because she liked to see brush strokes and enjoyed pastels.

Amy was done with her burger while the others were still conversing. She excused herself to go to the restroom and wash her hands. Upon doing so, she found a small piece of Gideon's hair. She also found a longer piece of hair that belonged to Mrs. Bobbington. Amy decided to keep both pieces of hair and said nothing of it to her aunt. Amy put the hair in her pocket. She washed her hands well before returning to the adults.

Once dinner and conversation were over, Amy and Ms. Jone returned home. Ms. Jone read Amy a nice bedtime story about a young girl with a porcelain doll collection, and they slept soundly. The next day Ms. Jone took Amy to the art museum, and Amy was completely amazed. She saw oil paintings that resembled actual photographs of people and the countryside, as well as an entire display of an artist's paintings of florescent geometrical figures. Amy did not spend too much time with the paintings of peoples' faces, because they seemed a little too real to her.

Amy had a wonderful time with her aunt, and her father came to get her on Sunday night. They both always enjoyed the subway. Amy always asked about the interesting traveling pedestrians after she had seen them. Mr. Throne was always attentive and helpful to explain various different peoples' probable occupations.

They made it back to the city-flat of Amy's father somewhat exhausted. He read some to her, and they went off to bed. Amy's father was exhausted, and she could hear him sleeping in his room within only a few minutes. She wanted to play. She made a doll of Mr. Bobbington and one of Mrs. Bobbington including the strands of their hair she kept. Amy used paper, glue, and sock cuttings to make the dolls. She had some scissors and a small sewing kit, so the construction of the small poppets went rather easily.

Amy was somewhat impressed with the outcome of the dolls. She played with them a few minutes, and hid them in a shoebox before turning in. She prayed that all good and healthy things would come to the Bobbington's for being a blessing in her life. She slept soundly.

During the next few weeks, all good things did come their way. The Bobbington's were on their way to success in life. Mr. Bobbington was doing well at work. Mrs. Bobbington planned to attend classes at the community college across town. She wanted to study nursing in the fall. Her applications for financial aid were accepted, and she attained a partial monetary scholarship for books.

Amy spent her "business days" with her sitter reading, watching television, and napping. She played with her dolls every night after dinner. She gave them new clothes one time. Within the week, the Bobbingtons sported new attire they went and purchased. She fixed up a small rectangular box made of two of her shoeboxes. Amy lined the inside with paper normally meant for writing letters and installed a small night light that could cast a shadow for her dolls. She became quite the puppeteer.

Once a night, for an hour or less, she played with her poppet box. Amy's skits and routines came with dialogue. Mr. Bobbington would come home from work, and Mrs. Bobbington would converse with him about large companies and business over dinner. The box had a lining Amy placed in the back of it. The lining was a simple watercolor painting resembling the inside of the Bobbington's townhouse. Mr. and Mrs. Bobbington enjoyed a wonderful relationship together during those times.

One night, Amy replaced the background of her box to resemble the sidewalk of a city street. "Here comes Mrs. Bobbington," whispered Amy, and she walked the doll down the street in the box. The background included an old streetlight like the ones near downtown. "Suddenly a special wind came," said Amy, "And Mrs. Bobbington floated in the air for four whole minutes. Pedestrians saw her floating there, at least five feet in the air, and wondered, 'Why is that woman floating in the air? How are we standing here, while she is up there?'" Amy set down her doll and walked Mrs. Bobbington off the box stage safely. She said her bedtime prayers a second time and went to sleep.

The next day was a good day for Mrs. Bobbington to go and get some groceries. She went all the way to the other side of town to get to the nicer grocery store. The store was smaller, yet it always had a fresh produce section. Mrs. Bobbington was especially impressed with her selections this day. She decided to make a turkey dinner with rare steamed vegetables. She traveled with her groceries on foot towards home.

Mrs. Bobbington could have taken the transit bus, however she decided to walk. About half way there, she noticed an old street light. "Those street lights remind me of those a person might see in an old black and white film," Mrs. Bobbington said to herself. To her surprise, she suddenly floated up into the air!

Somewhat confused, Mrs. Bobbington exclaimed, "Will you kindly let me down?" Nothing happened. She remained suspended in the air. A youngster on the sidewalk tugged on his mother's coat and pointed towards Mrs. Bobbington. Pedestrians gazed in awe and wonder. About five feet in the air, Mrs. Bobbington could move her legs, but did not know why she was floating.

Three minutes and fifty seconds had gone by and people had begun to gather around her. She descended slowly and felt her feet touch the ground safely. Mrs. Bobbington then walked home wondering what could have caused such a phenomenon. She supposed that it probably was some odd occurrence of atmospheric pressure.

Amy would have never known what had happened. She also did not know of the powers she toyed with. A few days had gone by, and she lost interest in her poppet box. She was reading books before slumber. Her father received a phone call on a Thursday. It was Ms. Jone.

"I am going to cook a nice cuisine tomorrow night for the neighbors and I wanted to invite Amy," said Ms. Jone, "You are also welcome to come along. They said she is a nice young girl." "Amy would love to join you," said her father, "If you would like, I will pay you to keep her for the weekend." "Okay," said Ms. Jone, and Mr. Throne wondered what he would do with his time. He was sure he could find something on cable. He liked science, history and car races.

Ms. Jone was a highly skilled *chef-artist* in the kitchen. This weekend she cooked a rare dish involving glazed lintels and a chicken salad with buttered garlic toast. Amy was all excited. She and her father took the subway, and he returned to his flat for some rest and relaxation.

"Hurry on in to wash you hands," said Ms. Jones, "My salad presentation is already ready, and the Bobbingtons will be here any minute." Amy went and washed her hands. The Bobbingtons came over and they all gave thanks before dinner. The chicken salad was nice. Cracked pepper on lemon-steamed chicken tasted divine.

The four ate. Amy cleaned her plate in its entirety. They spoke of things like the big companies in Mr. Bobbington's business periodical and Amy's books. Mrs. Bobbington was happy to speak of her plans to become a nurse, and they almost ran out of conversation.

Mrs. Bobbington figured she could save them all from the looming doom of pure boredom silence would surely bring. She said, "On the way back from the store across town the other day, the strangest thing happened to me." Amy blushed and looked down. She did not even want to know. Ms. Jone saw her and did not say anything. Amy did not say anything, either, not really knowing what Mrs. Bobbington was going to say. Mr. Bobbington was curious and wanted to hear the story.

"I was walking home with some groceries and I noticed this neat looking old street light," said Mrs. Bobbington, "Suddenly, I floated up into the air." Amy's face turned red and she tried not to laugh by looking even further down to the ground to avoid any attention. She did not want to be rude to these people. As a *giggly-girl*, Amy could not give up her reasons for laughter in this company. Ms. Jones saw her. "I was there for a while," continued Mrs. Bobbington, "I must have been at least five feet above the ground, and people were looking at me in wonder. I held on to my groceries as time went by, and then somehow descended safely to the ground. I think it was possibly a natural form of atmospheric pressure. What do you think Gideon?"

The three looked to Gideon, and Amy gave him the best poker face she could muster, somehow managing to breathe. "Well things of this nature can happen," said Gideon, "It probably was an occurrence of the sort you are guessing involving some wave of gravitational energy." With that, the dinner ended, and Amy did not have to say anything about her secret poppet box. The neighbors expressed their gratitude and said their goodbyes. Amy thanked them for the nice conversation and said it was a pleasure to see them. They all slept well.

The next day Ms. Jone took Amy to see the new art exhibit. It was just as exciting for Amy this time as it had been a few weeks ago. Amy kept in her mind the occurrence of Mrs. Bobbington, and she decided to ask for good things only to happen with and for other people. Amy knew to keep her secrets. The weekend ended, and her father came to bring her home.

"Hi honey," said Amy's father. "Daddy!" she exclaimed and ran to give him a hug. He paid Ms. Jone well. Ms. Jone said that it was nice, as

always, to have Amy around. Ms. Jone said, "It was nice to bring Amy to the

museum. There are more exhibits coming during the year." Amy and Mr.

Throne thanked Ms. Jone, and he paid her. They left and made it to the

subway. The two had normal conversation and walked home. Amy went to

bed early that night; she decided to play with her box some other time. Her

father turned in early, too. He had dreams of spacecrafts, lions, and race cars.

♦

The Representative

Hello, comrade. What you are reading is a brief tale of a young man and his perils one day. His name was Randal Sin. During the beginning of the story, Mr. Sin explains his life to a stranger in front of a street-side Chinese chicken stand.

"I see you are waiting on a chicken," said a well dressed man to Randal. "That I am," replied Ran, "Nice outfit." "I am a lawyer," said the stranger named Norman Sides, "Looking nice is part of my job. My name is Norman Sides." "I see," said Ran, "I know some about you." Just then a little Chinese man waddled around the corner to hand Ran a honey-glazed, wood-smoked chicken.

"I will give you five dollars for that chicken," requested Norm. Ran glanced to the Chinese man, Wok Foe, in wonder if there was another chicken. Mr. Foe nodded in assurance, and Ran said, "Sure." Mr. Foe handed the chicken to Mr. Sides, who in turn gave Ran a five dollar bill. Ran gave the five to Wok, and Mr. Foe went back inside to cook another chicken.

"Would you care to join me?" asked Mr. Sides. "Are you not in a hurry?" asked Ran. "Not today," said Norm, "I won a long and difficult case this morning, and I am off for the day. Why? Are you in a hurry?" "No," said Mr. Sin, "I plan to enjoy a whole chicken and turn in for slumber early today." He somehow remained thankful. The two sat down at one of vacant tables. It was still very early in the afternoon.

As they sat down, Mr. Sides noticed Mr. Sin's new looking street attire. "Mid-sleeve casual shirt not tucked in with loose casual khaki pants and nice new running shoes" commented Mr. Sides, "What do you do for work?" "I am the founding leader of the Church of Satan," said Ran, "Here in New York, NY." "I do not think you are telling me the truth," said the lawyer.

"No lie," said Ran, "I, along with eight other people, two of them fornicating nuns, founded the Church of Lucifer three years ago. Since then we have changed the name to the church of Satan, in appreciation of Anton Szandor LaVey's attempts in understanding his personal disagreements with people who believe in Christianity. We use silver in our practices instead of gold due to his documented considerations. Silver also relates to common societal perception. Money has played at least a partial role in our efforts, so far. We accept funds daily. Our bleeding of resources has only just begun, and we invest in many markets, legally."

"I have personally contributed to your organization, annually," said Mr. Sides, "Do you know anything about that?" "Sure," said Ran, "We got the design for the bird on your card off a Ruger 1911." "Why the bird?" asked Mr. Sides. "Well," said Ran, "Because, a gun to humans can be a symbol of a life taking mechanism, as Our Dark Lord can be thought of. I can be seen as something that enjoys taking life without hypocrisy. I formally house the devil as a human."

"I see you are holding down some laughter," noted Norm verbally, "What is the most enjoyable thing you can think of, in regards to being the devil?" "Well," said Ran, "That is what I was thinking about. Here lately, it has been allowing magical force to flow through the brightly lit shining eyes of the sparrows due to the problem with birds down on 9th Street." "That is amazing," said Mr. Sides. "They are used for fertilizer," said Ran.

"So you are the leading founder of the Church of Satan, after all?" asked Norm one last time. "Yes," said Ran. "I am the only true representation of the devil on this planet, currently, and I have gained quite an honest following. There are many leaders amongst our disciples. I embody the same angel the Creator watched leap carelessly from heaven long ago. Via communication with legions of spirits late last night, I know that today is a special day in my life." "Wow," said Mr. Sides.

Just then Mr. Foe came around the corner with ice water, a coke, and another chicken. Ran gave him a crisp new twenty dollar bill to cover for the dinner. As he was an old friend, he also handed him a unique gold coin with a bird engraved on it.

"So," began Norm, as they devoured their chicken (they were both hungry), "How is today a special day for you?" "Well," said Ran, "For one, I was reincarnated yesterday." "What happened?" asked Norm. "I was shot," said Ran, "After being found not guilty for murder and accusations related to abuse." "You could have easily read about that in the paper," said Mr. Sides.

"Sure I could have," said Ran, "If I would have picked one up." The two laughed and continued to dine.

"Tell me more about your life," asked Norm. "My life has been a journey in effort, childlike curiosity, and action," said Ran. "I obtained a bachelor's degree in business. I was an exterminator while in college. I majored in finance and minored in sociological studies. I went to work for the corporate offices of New Cola about ten years ago. While working those years for New Cola, I considered various different forms of religion. I thought of Christianity, Asian religions, occult practices of varied sorts, and finally, Satanism. I eventually, along with others, helped form the Church of Lucifer."

Still interested, Mr. Sides asked another question. "What are your major functions in the Church of Satan?" asked Norm. "Fund raising and musical praise," replied Ran with a smile. "It must not be to overly complicated," said Norm. "Not all of the time," said Ran.

"My spouse and I organize grottoes all over the world. Her name is Chrochina. She stays busy; I rarely see her. Groups send in their information, and we grant, deny, or help organize smaller gatherings to aid in raising money for the praise and worship of Our Dark Lord," said Ran. He then continued by saying, "I, or someone we approve of as a group, give a speech on Sunday morning. We usually compare what we think to other groups and religions. I take it you have not come to a gathering?" "No," said Norm, "I usually am too busy." "I see," said Ran, "Practicing the law must require some amount of energy from time to time. I also perform wedding ceremonies; teach classes on rituals and occult practice; and I edit and maintain our free biweekly journal for fun."

"How do you get paid?" asked Norm. "In blood," said Ran, joking. "No," he said, "I get paid a percentage of our documented donations, annually," assured Ran. "I work hard for a modest annual income, and I enjoy helping souls decide upon our consideration of *enlightenment*. In the last few years, I successfully, yet not entirely directly, disobeyed all Ten Commandments from Exodus in God's Holy Word. This is not a requirement in the various aversive recommendations of our faith. I enjoy crafting small figurines and creating art. One of my favorite activities, as I do not consume alcohol, is playing my black-opal twelve stringed Ovation guitar in the church auditorium downtown. A recovered alcoholic, I partake in hobbies as opposed to drinking. I am an honest individual."

"That sounds like a neat guitar," said Norm. "It is," said Ran, "I use an electronic pickup and nine different distortion pedals. I have it restrung and tuned by a professional musician before 8 AM on Sundays. The guitar brings rock and roll to our praise, and it sometimes reminds me of electronic-acoustic style *medieval* music. We all carry different forms of musical talent. There are a few drummers in our organization, so we keep a large drum set with three bass drums and a second chair. We often use the *simple* set with symbols to play with at the church along with the fine guitar." "*Simple* drums?" asked

Norm. "It is all we really need," said Ran, "We play our music live-feed style on the internet. It is good fun, and more people join the gathering all the time."

"And you have the time to paint?" asked Norm. "Sure," said Ran, "I donated my last painting to our church, and it sold for over one million in an internet auction." "I actually saw that," said Norm. "Oh?" said Ran. "Yes," said Norm, "It was painted with the blood of a goat on an authentic cashmere canvas. It appeared to depict the Grim Reaper decapitating a large cow over an empty drinking trough." "I guess you saw it, after all," said Ran. "Some members of our clergy wove the canvas with goat hair from the Himalayas, and I obtained the blood and some instructions on sanitary practice from an Irish butcher. It was supposedly sold to an indoor farmer." "You have somehow amazed me, today," said Norm. "We enjoy adding creativity to our carnal desires as we can," replied Ran with a simple grin.

A sudden and final test to see if Ran was a devote devil worshiping disciple occurred to Norm. "This chicken was delicious," said Norm, and held his fist up to Ran. Ran made a tight fist and bumped Norm's knuckles. Norm's testing was over. Mr. Sides knew for sure that Ran was a die-hard believer of the faith. Norm had been a follower for months.

The men had finished their chicken, and Mr. Foe came around the corner with white cake topped with vanilla icing and "squiggled" with light corn syrup. "Thank you," said his two customers. They began to eat their cake, and Norm decided to reveal a few final inquiries.

"So," began Norm, "Why do you think today is going to be a special day for you?" "Well," said Ran, "I am planning to pass my supreme powers to someone else, today. I will still help maintain the clergy, living off residual income and playing my fashionable guitar. I will help guide the new actual devil in spirit sometimes, as well. Someone's eyes can shine brightly, today, as they embody the devil on Earth. It will not be me - not anymore."

"How did you decide to worship the devil, and embody him on Earth?" asked Norm. "Well," said Mr. Sin, "My decisions where based on what I call 'dark faith'. This is the idea. When we perish we are no longer in life; we are in the afterlife. We are still where we were, however. Be us in hell due to the absence of God; or in Heaven as the opposite; or in some form of purgatory or non-existence; we are still in the same place, somehow. So, why not do as you want? Why not stand up for physical strength, honesty, and the fulfillment of ritualistic desires? After having proven this to be true through a surprising reincarnation, I want to pass my powers to someone else, even though my dark faith turned to fact for me. Who could turn down that much magical ability, sexual fulfillment, and money?"

"No one, I do not suppose," replied Norm. The two had nearly finished their cake. It was no easy task. Being rather overly rich in sweetness, many of Mr. Foe's customers usually ate about half of one of his desert servings.

"So," asked Norm in honest and re-establishing curiosity, "You intend to disembody the devil from your body into someone else, so that they may carry and continue his power and influence about the planet as a human?"

"That is correct," replied Ran, while pointing to a small insect on the pavement. The insect popped, and a small flame arose and vanished. Ran smiled as he said, "I think you may enjoy being the devil, yourself."

"Who, me?" asked Norm. He had been so caught up in figuring out the motivations of Ran that his own selfish desires had been compromised. "You will have infinite knowledge and supreme command over forces of evil that you cannot possibly currently comprehend," said Ran. "What kind of Creator makes all of these beings and leaves us with no leadership other than our own form of *anarchical* guessing and observance of irresponsible atrocities to the ignorant and the innocent, anyway?" asked Ran. He was still trying to explain that he had, at some point, given these simple decisions *some* form of thought. "This is a creator that can honestly be questioned in the realm of belief and logical power," said Ran, remembering that he was speaking with a lawyer.

"I have experienced realms of understanding that living men often never know. I have played with magic and power. I have simplified ritualistic actions and governed the leaders of this planet. I have bled fattened beasts and fed starving souls. I have watched the golden edges of darkness drip and fall into the shining darkness of the wicked night. I have seen all with my blind diamond eyes open. I am moving on," said Ran to Norm. "So," asked Norm with courage, "How exactly would you give such a *fun* time to a man like me? What would be your plan? To walk me down to the dark shades of the old trees in the park, hold your fist up to me, and say, 'By the Satanic powers of Beelzebub, I cast thee into Norm?'" "Close," said Ran.

"I have already seen it, Norm," said Ran, "I have a magical black opal crystal ball in my house donated to me from a witch doctor from India. It is the size of a basketball. Its viewing clarity *far* surpasses that of a television with four million pixels. At any rate, I watched it under a spell I cast at midnight this morning. You and I met here, ate chicken, walked to the park, and I let you become the devil." "Wow," said Norm.

Ran was more confident with the future. He said, "I will perish during the transmission of power into your body, and I will physically reincarnate shortly there after. The night will then be yours, and I will go home and go to bed."

Wok Foe then came around the corner. He wondered why the two men were still there. "Thank you for the dinner, Mr. Foe," said Ran, "His name is Norman Sides. Norman, this is Wok Foe." "It is nice to meet you," said Norm, as he and Ran rose carefully. Norm tipped Mr. Foe with a hundred dollar bill. Wok bowed respectfully thanking the two gentlemen. Ran and Norm left, walking in the direction of the park.

"It is just getting dark," said Norm, as they made their way to the park. "Yes," said Ran, "The spirits of goblins and various other creatures are spiraling around us in confused excitement." They made it to the park. Ran chose a dark path to a small clearing underneath the huge trees timeless in age. There was minimal light, but the two could see clearly, somehow. Spirits of every sort gathered forming an invisible dome around the two.

They stood face to face in the clearing. Norm did not really know what Ran was going to say or do. Ran, holding his fist up to Mr. Sides then said, "Do you, Norman Sides, take on the eternal powers of Lucifer, the absolute leader of legions of angels and demons in the spirit world, the bringer of death to life in this universe, the ruler of beings on planet Earth, the almighty power of the devil himself?" Norman thought to himself, "I am going to be the devil." Then he said, "Yes, Ran, I do," and Norm met his fist with the fist of Ran.

During this exact moment in time, the eyes of both men shown millions of lumens of light as their heads where cast back and their bodies were pressed to the ground. The bright light lit the park up like a magical explosion and could be seen from all around. The light faded in more time than it took to occur. Norm stood slowly, as he was now the devil. He understood so much, now. He saw Ran's spirit float up from his lifeless body and take four steps from him. Ran began to re-materialize on the fifth step, and was a full-blown walking human by his seventh step away. Norm decided he would take the corpse somewhere and bury it with lime.

"I will be seeing you," said Ran, as he looked over his shoulder and waved to the devil in the dark, smoldering night. Norm waved and said, "Thank you. I will be seeing you." Norm decided to go to his office later to consider the occult and to delve into various considerations of magic. Ran went home, did some cleaning, set his alarm for 7 AM, and went off to bed. Everyone lived happily ever after.

◆

The Roller Coaster

Once upon a time, there were two young lovers. They were out of high school, yet they still lived with their parents for the time being. As many do in America, these youngsters planned to work until they could move out. This pair was no different. The female, Cloudia, answered phones for an insurance company. The male, Braun, worked as a butcher's assistant at a local deli. Their city consisted of about 300,000 people, and they loved nothing more than loving each other.

One night, it was *happy time*. The two were always trying to find somewhere to make out. Both sets of parents' houses were less desirable choices for the two, especially on a nice night like that Friday. The cold sky was crisp and clean, and the stars were sparkling and brilliant in a romantic way.

Braun had an old pickup he was constantly working on. Once he had it fixed up, he maintained it properly. It was a v-6; the cab was rather spacious. The engine made a deep and clean sounding gurgle - only something tuned that well can sound like it did. Their truck was part of their fun on weekend nights.

Braun drove from his house to Cloudia's. She was waiting for him outside. Cloudia said, "Let us go and find a nice make-out spot," as Braun pulled into her driveway. This was always fun, because they had multiple choices in favorite locales for various different reasons. "Nothing like finding a new location," said Braun, and he drove in a random direction. The truck had a large cab, as mentioned, yet Cloudia snuggled up close to Braun, a strapping lad, as they drove around.

Getting lost for these two in this city became close to impossible. Braun drove and drove until he found a road less traveled. "Where does this road go?" asked Cloudia. "I am not exactly sure," replied Braun. He was happy, because she was curious and happy. These things were always good things. The road was dark and winding, and they drove for a while. "Oh," said Braun, "I know where this leads to." "Where might that be?" asked Cloudia, as she watched old trees go by in fare pace in the night. "I think it goes to an old fair ground," replied Braun.

They drove for a while; the road lead to an old fair ground, after all. The grounds closed years ago due to poor sales. There really was no need to get out of the truck. "Let us go and check it out," said Braun. "I do not think that we should," said Cloudia, "It looks and feels spooky here." He took one look at her, and they both new they were going to go check it out. They were far too curious to be scared of anything, and young Braun was quite the ferocious animal, anyway.

He got out with his headlights dimmed and opened an old gate blocking a back entry way. The gate's creaking broke the silence of the crisp, dark night. They drove around the grounds and decided to park and walk a while. The night was nice, and there was no one around. They walked around and spoke of what must have gone on around there while business was still hopping. The owners of the property must have filed bankruptcy and left the grounds alone to disintegrate with the passing of time.

The various booths and stands were unoccupied, yet things appeared to have been frozen in time. They found a booth for tossing rings onto bottles and it still had the big teddy bears in it. Braun looked over to Cloudia who said, "No thank you." The dusty old bears looked nasty and dirty to her.

They walked hand in hand, admiring the nocturnal ghost town of sorts. They found a large wooden structure. They leaned against the structure; gazed into each others eyes; and almost kissed. As they leaned closer, the two wondered what the structure was. "What is this big wooden thing?" asked Braun. "Maybe it is a big windmill or a stage," said Cloudia. They walked around it some. "No," said Braun, "This is an old roller-coaster. Notice the tracks." "Wow," said Cloudia looking up through the structure, "This thing is massive." They tried to see the top of the huge formation. "It must have broken down long ago," said Braun.

The two made out for a while, and then decided to try to climb around on the large wooden coaster. They made it to close to the top of the structure. "There are no cars on this thing" observed Braun. "I do not think that the track is complete," said Cloudia, "Look over there." "That is a good point," said Braun, "There is more than one place where the track does not continue."

"This coaster's construction was never complete," they both said aloud. The dark wind of the night was blowing peacefully. "Hey look," said Cloudia, "I can see your truck from here." "Yeah, I see it," said Braun, still at awe with the massive structure. "It is getting late, now," said Braun. "Yeah, I am about to fall asleep," said Cloudia. It had been a long week for both of them.

They drove home safely and went to bed. Neither one was really ready for actual sex, yet. They decided to save that for marriage. Playing around with minimal heavy petting was good enough for them. During the next week, they both had the roller coaster on their mind. Cloudia's boss said friends of his friends still owned the property, but they were busy with other businesses. They had been for years. Braun asked his boss about it, and his boss said he remembered the fair. He said the coaster was going to be a huge and amazing structure, yet the fair went out of business before it was complete. One time, the butcher sold hickory smoked turkey legs there over the weekend.

Braun could not get the coaster off his mind; neither could Cloudia. They spoke of it so much that Friday that they almost forgot to make out, almost. They both wanted to see the structure built somehow. It was Cloudia that had a grand idea - they could have a punk rock benefit concert. That is what they decided to do.

The fair ground was large enough, but it neighbored a vast field of wild grass. The vast field was on a gradually inclined hill. It would be perfect for a concert. Some of Cloudia's high school friends had formed a punk rock band and even got kicked out of prom for playing music that incited crowd violence. They called their music *death metal* and enjoyed *thrashing hard.* They called themselves Psycho Lohiya, a name they came up with while trying to learn Spanish. Psycho Lohiya liked their name and it stuck due to their psychotic behavior on the stage.

The people got together. The band went to see this amazing structure with Braun and Cloudia, and Cloudia's boss organized a meeting with them and the property owners. Together they organized the concert's specifics, and the two lovebirds decided to put on the show in five weeks. That gave the people time to market the shindig and it also gave the band time to practice. They placed adds on the radio and gave people flyers and the reason that they all were invited to rock hard - to finish the construction of the roller coaster.

The property owners called the original engineer of the structure, and he said that he would be more than delighted to finish the construction. The engineer even gave them an honest estimate on the costs. "It will not be too hard to do," he said.

The time came for the concert, and tickets were sold - sold out, rather. Even with a huge field only ten thousand tickets could be printed, and they were. They made enough money to complete the coaster, and the concert turned into a pounding and deadly mosh pit. All people had a grand time, and the death metal was astounding. Psycho Lohia's most popular song, "Cides", was as follows:

"Thrash it bash it smash your heads,

Thrash it bash it bloody heads!

Floating spirits, deadly deeds,

Smash it bash it bang your heads!

Do you want some *cides?*

We have some *cides!*

Aborti-acari-algi-amici-avicide!

Bacteri-bio-ceti-dei-ecocide!

Elephanti-feli-femi-feti-filaricide!

Feli-formici-fratri-fungi-gametocide!

Do you want more *cides?*

We have more *cides!*

Geno-germi-gyne-herbi-homicide!

Infanti-insecti-larvi-liberti-lupicide!

Macropi-mariti-matri-menti-microbicide!

Mildew-miti-ovi-parasiti-parenticide!

Do you want some *cides?*

We have some *cides!*

Parri-patri-pediculi-pesti-phytocide!

Proli-rati-regi-rodenti-senicide!

Sorori-spermati-sui-tauri-tyrannicide!

Uxori-vati-vermi-vespa-vulpicide!

Thrash it bash it smash your heads,

Thrash it bash it bloody heads!

Floating spirits, deadly deeds,

Smash it bash it bang your heads indeed!"

sang Psycho Lohiya.

With the money to build the coaster, the engineer and a crew finished its construction over the course of a few weeks. He even redesigned the initial drop to being eight stories tall and dug a large tunnel in the ground to add to the fear factor of the *monster*. The initial drop would give the riders the image that they were going to actually hit the ground, yet they would go through a tunnel and rise up to five stories above the ground and enjoy the rest of the winding and hilly ride.

The day of the unveiling of the coaster came. They called the ride "The Coaster", and Braun and Cloudia got to sit in the very first car of the roller coaster. Two celebrities, Jack Nicholson and Henry Rollins, sat behind them. Cloudia and Braun were excited to see the lead singer of Black Flag and the "Joker" sit behind them. The Coaster clicked and clanked as it rose closer and closer to the top of the first big vertical drop.

"So, Henry," asked Jack Nicholson, "What is one of your favorite bands to listen to other than Black Flag?" "A British group called 'The Fall'," said Rollins, "I used to play their music on one of my radio shows all of the time." "What is your favorite movie that you were in Mr. Nicholson?" asked Braun with Cloudia's secret permission. "Probably 'Easy Rider'," said Mr. Nicholson, "The film was fun to make, and I thought the choppers were cool as hell."

Just as he said that, the first cars of the coaster went over the first summit of the track slowly. The passengers were hanging on to a bar in front of them, looking straight down to see nothing besides the ground eight stories below. Then, as the rear end of the coaster approached the summit, the set of cars was set free to gravity, and the cars were off. The passengers could see nothing besides the ground coming towards them in a very fast manner. The cars zoomed through the tunnel and rose up pressuring the passengers into their seats at speeds of over 100 mph.

The engineer happened to be a physics enthusiast, and the weight of the coaster cars was used to accurately predict the ride's maximum speeds. The train of cars rose and slowed and sped up and slowed down over and over until the ride eventually came to a safe ending near its initial vertical drop. The roller coaster functioned safely for years to come. Claudia and Braun bought a lot, got married, built a house, and lived happily every after. Everyone involved had a wonderful time.

♦

The Train

"Here at *THE FICTION HERALD*, the *prose* are written by the *pros*," said Bob Staulkner to Amy Gathalowitz. They both laughed. Amy was his niece with brunette hair. She was eight years old. They ventured to the library together for the submission of an entertaining story to a fiction magazine. The periodical was known for publishing creative stories written with exceptional grammatical style. Bob was an unpublished writer. He was waiting to share his creativity with anyone who might enjoy what he deemed an entertaining and properly well-written story to be. Bob found full-time work at a local hardware superstore after not quite finishing college.

He ran out of scholarship money and decided to pursue a career without a degree. "An exciting and well-written story can be appreciated by an interested audience," Bob thought. He submitted a few stories to fiction publications before - none of his stories were selected from the thousands of other submitted manuscripts. What was Bob after, anyway? Was it fame, recognition, or money? Who knew? He knew. Bob sought a sense of accomplishment. He loved to write, and Bob wanted to properly entertain people for money.

This one, Bob hoped, would be a *first ringer*. Bob's leap into fiction writing was his own idea - a great way to paint a pleasing picture for view in the mind of someone else. He could do it. Creative writing was much easier for him than college curriculum, even though he had made good grades and found most of his classes to be overly easy. Writing could be an easy way for him to give an audience a peaceful escape from the terrors, stresses, and boredom of daily life and effort in America. No one ever had enough of anything. Who cared? Due to a difficulty in having hope, no one cared. Writing was still fun for Bob, somehow, and nothing could keep him from it.

Bob enjoyed the study of various grammar styles and story composition. He found witty sentence examples in all too time-consuming passages of every grammar book he obsessed through to be profound and seemingly impossible to surpass. He tried free-writing, and it was fun. A daily journal of prose was far more intriguing and fun to him than a good old-fashioned diary. It seemed as though only Bob could justify his writing; his niece understood him fully, however. He wrote for the escape - she developed new universes with his every passage in her own young, beautiful mind.

Writing took up most of Bob's time outside of work. Acquiring compensation for his compositions seemed impossible. The hardware superstore kept him living; he sold and remodeled bathrooms. Bob worked overtime hours for other departments from time to time. He watched new training videos about once a month. Amy liked his stories. Bob liked to read them to her before she went off to bed on Friday nights, sometimes. This one was fun for the both of them. They looked up the word *trains* on the internet and saw all kinds of differing and wonderful rail machines and boxcars. Trains have quite a history in the world and America, and the two found this history to be as fun to watch, see, and learn about as cars and trucks in normal everyday life.

Bob submitted their story and printed out a copy of it for both Amy and himself. With three columns per page, both drafts combined cost Bob the undue sacrifice of 168 cents. He gave Amy two dollars to pay the librarian and said Amy could keep the change for her gumball piggy-bank. She saved change to buy books. Every collection of well-written prose she purchased meant a great deal to her. Their story involving The Midnight Pearl was exactly 8,000 words - twenty columns, fifty lines, and an average of 8 words per line. "Well, we had to at least come close to guessing a good number of words this time," said Amy, "I hope they like your story." "They have a high volume of stories, dear. If they do not like it we will simply add it to my collection of stories," said Bob, "It will be available for others one way or another."

"Eight thousand words is lengthy according to some who say three to five thousand is what more commonly enjoyed short stories are," said Bob, "They are not our world-wide published political articles and fiction periodical, however, and it can take seven thousand words to explain a story's properly painted scene and storyline, nevertheless. I am happy to have the extra space. It can mean more detailed explanations and a more creative and brilliant world for the mind of the reader if desired. We can put these exciting ideas down, and the audience can see a magnificent train and wonder what might have really been possible during its dark night of peril."

"Forget the novella - stretch out what you thought was long enough in your short story," said Amy laughing, "Pull that egg noodle before you fry it and it should look nice on the plate." "You sure are bright for an eight-year-old," said Bob. "I love to read," said Amy, as they were nearing the subway hand in hand with their bedtime manuscripts. Amy was with Bob the whole time while he wrote the train story, so he planned to acknowledge this whenever possible. As he developed ideas for a semi-romantic murder story, she helped along the way. The library was on the other side of town from the flat Amy's parents lived in; the subway was a decent way to get there. The subway ride was long but fun. Bob bought them boarding passes, and they entered an underground boxcar for a trek to her parents' flat.

The subway was fun for Amy. She stayed near Bob, because of obvious known possible dangers. What seemed like a long, winding, and speeding electronic serpent slowed to a stop, and its doors made their sounds upon opening. The two boarded a subway car, and Bob fell asleep while Amy read their story. She read it as if she had never even seen it before - it was the best way that she could have appreciated their work of art. Her young mind was vivid and dreamy, and Amy enjoyed watching the story occur as she read it. She was quite the prodigy.

Bob wrote the story as follows:

THE MIDNIGHT PEARL,

by Bob Staulkner and Amy Gatholowitz

One time, there was a passenger train named The Midnight Pearl. It

was to travel north through a dark and gargantuan evergreen forest in the

night. The vast forest consisted of trees tall enough to block out the setting sun

and did so daily on the western side of our great American continent. The

Midnight Pearl departed at 10 PM. It was to arrive at its destination at

precisely 6 AM, as it had many times before. The train made a scheduled trip

once a month. This gave the maintenance crews time for the interior

remodeling of its various vehicles.

The locomotive consisted of twenty cars. Both the exciting

innovations of current technology and the nostalgia of classical forms of transportation were kept in mind upon the engineering of the train. The train consisted of eighteen classy passenger cars, a leading engine, and an upscale spacious caboose for romantically involved patrons. People who reserved time slots in the caboose boarded the train with special passes. There were only six forty-five minute time-slots for the first come first serve romantic caboose goers.

Caboose time-slots numbered 11-5, because they started on the hour. The quarter hour *transition break* gave patrons time to come and go. 10 PM to 11 PM was open for cleaning and preparation by the caboose crew. Car 13 was the kitchen. Cars 2-12 were set aside for the more expensive seating and catering. People thought the other cars were nice, too. Cars 2-12 each came with a unique theme.

The massive train was impressive to all. Only a certified mechanic could describe the huge engine. Its overall horsepower was not even rated. This was because the engine's combustion chambers handling explosions were over a foot thick with a specially designed metal. The engine was powerful

enough to safely haul the twenty vehicles at speeds exceeding 100 mph. The

Midnight Pearl's exterior was sleek and reflecting in black hue; only a rare few

saw the white lights below its cars travel by. The twenty rectangular cars had

rounded exterior edges. The vehicles showed glossy. The Midnight Pearl was

an astounding marvel to all who beheld her magnificence.

The Midnight Pearl carried many passengers that dark night. She

totaled 120 exciting people with many seats vacant. Theme cars were

purchased by groups of patrons, not individuals, so there was plenty of room

aboard the train. It contained seventeen workers; two operated the front

engine vehicle, Car 1. They were the Conductor, Captain Frank, and the

Conductor's Assistant, Mr. Barnes. The kitchen's chef was named Mickey.

Mickey could cook absolutely anything. Not too many people really knew

much about him. He, in his lifetime, made a cautious study of human

consumption and culinary practice. Mickey thought of himself as a scientific cooking genius and an humble student.

All of The Midnight Pearl's workers were a proud part of their train's services. The caboose crew consisted of three servers. The other dozen employees thought of themselves as servers, waiters, waitresses, or train attendants. Barb was the train's head waitress. Barb had spent most of her life serving others; she was possibly the only server with the brains able to keep up with the rest of them. Barb helped organize breaks among the train's other servers. The employees were thankful for the opportunity to serve The Midnight Pearl. Captain Frank was an older white-haired man who still looked meaty and strong. Mr. Barnes assisted him with boarding passes and the general observation of the entire train. The conductor stayed in Car 1 nearest to the engine, and Mr. Barnes made it to the caboose twice a trip, on average, making sure all was well.

The passengers could not see the full and shining winter-crisped moon. Each car had a differing seating arrangement. Most vehicles contained four tables and complementing privacy curtains. All enjoyed the nice vehicles.

It would be a trek to remember for the satisfied passengers. People of many

occupations looked forward to their journey through the night. A small family

of people consisted of four important characters on the train. Donovan and

Autumn were two adult acquaintances *deciding*, and their children were Sean

and Lucille. Lucille went by *Lucy* and was Autumn's little girl. Sean was

Donovan's son. They were a happy family. Donovan and Autumn had the

second to last time slot reserved to spend their time together in the caboose.

What would they be thinking? The four of them would travel with four others

in Car 18, close to the back of the train. Like many other vehicles of the train,

Car 18 contained four sections. Four two-man tables, two perpendicular

separation walls and four exquisite privacy curtains provided privacy for two

passengers a time in *18*.

The two adults knew each other well, yet they did not know if they

wanted to be more than close friends. In Car 18, the other four characters were two senior citizen couples. The two couples remained seated for most of the ride playing cards, reading, and sleeping. They were the Marshalls and the Oedinheimers. The parents did not really know what they wanted in regards to their relationship. Before the train ride, both parents said they could be happy either way - as they were or with physical benefits. The two adults knew that if they became involved physically, their relationship would not be the same. The ride and the caboose would be a possible way to help decide. It would be a happy journey either way.

Upon boarding The Midnight Pearl, the four acknowledged her overall amazing beauty. "This train is completely and totally awesome," said Sean. One train attendant's name was Tom. He said, "Hi. I am Tom," and he hole-punched their tickets. The holes punched made seven-point stars. Lucy was the last of the four to board the train. She said, "Thanks, 'Tom'," upon boarding with a small giggle. The four entered the train and made their way to their car for the ride each with their compact carry-on bags. It was only about

9:30 PM, and many of the passengers had not arrived to line up, yet. A dark and dangerous night was waiting. The four made their way through the middle of the train to Car 18.

The Midnight Pearl had two passenger entryways on its left side. The train's interior smelt of finely remodeled swayed leather upholstery, like the front foyer of a new hotel. It was luxurious. The Marshalls and the Oedinheimers were already counting out their playing cards and readying their scorecards. Donovan and Autumn sat across from each other, as did Sean and Lucy. Sean was ten. Lucy was nine. The four made themselves comfortable. A train attendee came to check on them. All guests were fine.

"Is everyone okay tonight?" asked their waitress named Ana. Ana was pretty. She had blonde highlights in her brunette hair, and a deep look of understanding behind the marvelous lavender irises of her eyes. Ana was twenty-nine. She was able to bring the last three cars of the train what they needed and tended a dozen tables every train ride. "Can I bring anyone a glass of water or a snack?" she asked. "Sure," said Donovan, "Please, bring us all a glass of water." She brought them their glasses of water within only a few moments. They thanked her; Donovan gave her a ten dollar bill.

The four got comfortable in their chairs; they brought things to do during their train ride. Each had something to write with, something to write on, and a book. The adults both brought their scheduling planners and journals, and the children brought small notebooks for writing, drawing, and coloring. The children brought a deck of cards, too. As far as books were concerned, each of the family of four had their own. Donovan was reading an old western novel including a gunfight over a woman. Autumn was reading a thriller involving a stocking lawyer trying to kill his ex-wife because of outrageous alimony charges and unemployment. Sean was reading a factional novel on the Wright brothers, their bicycles, and their airplanes. Lucy was reading a story about magical stuffed animals that came to life on the twentieth of each month at 12 AM to bake muffins. The four loved to read and ponder upon their tales.

The Midnight Pearl had small circular windows - there was nothing to see in the fast moving external night. The small sealed windows were stylish. The train's lighting was an impressive trade for the *black holes*. The fixtures curled like vines in their glowing metallic frames. The bulbs showed like hollowed drops of pearls the size of Christmas tree lights. Their seats were made of smooth white leather. The smooth, thin tables were made of polished black marble.

As nice and impressive as the back half of the train was, the front vehicles were even more extravagant and almost overly gaudy. "This is actually a pretty nice train," said Autumn, and the other three agreed. The adults dove into conversation about their careers, and the children began a card game of *Battle*. It was the longest card game the children could think of to play. There were hours to go before the end of the ride.

Like the adults, the children were close friends. Sean and Lucy had met at the food market when their parents randomly saw each other one time. They became close friends who cracked each other up. The children never really understood the adults; they always enjoyed playing games with each other, staying out of trouble. Captain Frank came on the unseen speakers moments before 10 PM and said, "All aboard. Welcome to The Midnight Pearl. We are embarking on an exciting journey tonight; the weather outside is nice." He spoke some more words, and the train began moving at precisely 10 PM. The train departed with the smooth and gradual inertia of a magnificently giant organism in pristine perfection. The Midnight Pearl's engine was massive and powerful. The train used a unique array of modern electronics to control its handling of the track, turns, and speed. The train's track was a new form of technology involving wheels with long-hanging edges made for higher speeds and better handling than normal and traditional modern passenger trains. The Midnight Pearl used a new and innovative track design known as S. T. T. - Safe Tracking Technology.

All passengers called the conductor *Captain Frank*. Together, he and Mr. Barnes provided for an enjoyable journey through the night. The intelligible crew working shared a great deal of love for one another - almost entirely. The massive collection of twenty cars was moving well. Its passengers felt close to no inertia whatsoever, as the train easily climbed to its normal average speed of one hundred miles per hour in less than ninety seconds. Lucy and Sean played their game of battle; Donovan and Autumn continued to share in conversation. No one even bothered with the flat screen on his or her side. Players divide a deck of cards in half for two-player battle. Each player plays a card until one of the players wins the entire deck. Aces win the game. Lucy had three aces to begin with; won Sean's only ace in a "battle"; and won the whole deck. Lucy won.

The kitchen made all kinds of food. Ana reminded her patrons of these things. Autumn requested two orders of chips and salsa, and the four enjoyed the nice snack. Time went by. The children slept a while, even though sleep was not necessarily part of their planned activities of the journey.

Sometime around 3 AM Donovan ordered a pizza, and it was great. The large pizza was thin, nicely prepared, and delicious for all. The couples who had reserved a scheduled time in the caboose had to walk through Car 18 to get there. Car 19 had no scheduled time in the caboose. Its passengers saw the couples that did, however. The passengers of Car 19 also saw what the caboose couples looked like coming out of there. One or two couples came out somewhat disheveled - they tried to act as though nothing really happened. They must have thought that there was the chance no one else would notice.

4 AM came. It was Autumn and Donovan's time to see the caboose and share sparkling water together. The adults would return before 5 AM. The children had absolutely nothing to do whatsoever. "I am very bored," said Lucy. "Would you like to play the alphabet game?" asked Sean, as he noticed the shiny brass vent. "Why are you staring at the ceiling?" asked Lucy, because Sean looked like he just went off into another realm of understanding. "I am

wondering about that vent," said Sean. "I see," said Lucy, "It has air coming out of it." She thought it was the best he could figure. Little did she know, though, they could crawl through it.

Sean and Lucy climbed up onto their table in socks and could almost reach the vent's shining brass grate. He let her get on his shoulders. She easily opened the latches of their newfound passageway and crawled inside. It was actually somewhat spacious. She took him by his hands and helped him into the vent. Sean easily closed the vent from the inside, and he and Lucy crawled carefully towards the front of the train. Car by car, they made their way towards the kitchen vehicle, Car 13. They wanted to try to see out of the front of the train. The children did not know if such a thing was possible.

Most of the passengers on the train were of no surprise in appearance to Sean and Lucy. All characters were nicely dressed and unique in style. Car by car, the children could peer through the vents and see the many colorful patrons. The women wore nice jewelry; the men were dressed properly. The attendants of The Midnight Pearl wore clothes that resembled old western films. They were all dressed nicely. The train attendants sported white shirts with ruffles and black vests with a small red rose. Their pressed black slacks were always impressive. The little roses symbolized that they knew enough about the train and its policies to serve its patrons properly. The employees were all proud to have attained their small roses.

As Lucy and Sean crawled through the vent, they analyzed various patrons. Many passengers were sleeping or reading. The various different people were obviously from different lifestyles. Once the children made it to the kitchen, their corridor-like vent opened up wider and was more spacious. The servers of the train were seen the most coming in and out of the kitchen. They brought fine beverages and cuisines to their assigned tables. The delicacies seemed fit for the curious, not the hungry. Sean and Lucy thought the dinners they saw were overly exquisite. The cost of food was included with the payment of the patrons' boarding passes. One plate Lucy thought looked amazing was a twelve-point star of Chinese style aged egg wedges. The wedges were turned blue and adorned with slivers of oranges and kale with purple stripes.

The two continued to crawl carefully past the kitchen and towards the front. They stopped for some time to listen to two executives talking. The businesspersons were both stockbrokers who shared information that might as well have been secret. Certain businesses in technology would be advancing; others would not be. They seemed to be able to agree and disagree on why. They even exchanged more than one handwritten check, purchasing shares in advance from each other. "Should not that take place at the 'Exchange'?" whispered Lucy trying not to crack up. Sean turned beat red trying not to laugh aloud and just shrugged his shoulders indicating that he did not really know. Well-dressed men of that looking caliber might as well have been breaking rules unknown to others, anyhow.

Sean and Lucy crawled for a while and got their breathing in proper order. They went through the rest of the nicest cars in the train admiring the luxurious customized handmade curtains and carpeting. Car 9 was one of the cars with a "Thematic Interior" - "The Sixties". Sean and Lucy knew that because they read about it in the train's brochure: "The Midnight Pearl Tour of Available Custom Vehicle Choices". Any of the theme cars could be custom made for a single train ride. There were over a hundred themes to choose from in the brochure, and there were ten most often chosen ideas. The hypnotic aura of The Sixties theme was enjoyed by intrigued passengers almost every train ride.

This particular car was interesting, indeed. The patrons had its black light on with its disco ball spinning slow enough for the car to resemble a roller skating rink. The numerous white ovals of light traveling round and round resembled the spinning coat of a leopard. Sean and Lucy saw that the passengers had their privacy curtains half open and were leaning back in their seats, watching the ceiling. The lighting's motion and blinking disguised the children from the passengers below. Somewhat dizzy, the two carried on.

Their parents told Sean and Lucy the "Cartoon" theme car was too expensive, just as all of the other theme cars. The two begged and begged, anyway. The only other car the two had a tough time hearing "No" to, due to cost, was the "Thema Americana" car, Car 4. Sean and Lucy tried hard with that one, because they thought they had a chance.

"The adults might like it," they both thought. Money was the factoring issue, however. The other cars towards the front used differing themes - "Western", "Ballroom", "The South", "The Gaud of Gold", and others. The "Thema Americana" was an often chosen vehicle. It contained red, white, and blue interior attributes, like the flag of the United States. The privacy curtains had firework displays, and the seats were smooth white leather with read and blue stars. There was a nice projector in this car for viewing documentaries on the history of America. A show, "The Way the West was Won", a factional documentary and dual murder story, was on. Sean and Lucy continued crawling. The two children were nearing the front of the train. Two

things occurred. One made them want to drop out of the vent, and the other

event caused one of them to try to get them both back to their boxcar as

quickly as possible. Both events involved death.

Sean and Lucy were trying to see the conductor and his trusted

assistant, Mr. Barnes. Maybe they would even be able to see out of the front

windshield of the train. Eventually, they made it to Car 2. Sean and Lucy saw

a man dressed in smooth black leather. He had on a sleek dark hat and dark

sunglasses. This patron was a shady character, indeed. They watched as he

opened his security compartment and removed a small carry-on bag. The

children thought at first that he was playing with medical tools. The highly

questionable individual was playing with no such instrumentation, however -

they watched him assemble a nine mm handgun with a machine-threaded

silencer. He loosely placed the readied weapon back in its case and back into

the security compartment above his table.

The children wanted that *toy* badly, yet they had no real reason to have it. They went to see the front of The Midnight Pearl. It was magnificent. The children felt the deep and muffled roaring of the extremely powerful train. Captain Frank had his eyes on the track lit, and Mr. Barnes was in conversation with him. The Midnight Pearl's magnificent and huge singular front light brightly lit up the tracks below in the pitch-blackness. The children could actually see through the front of the train to see the track flying by underneath them. Lucy and Sean were impressed.

The sophisticated control panels of Car 1 shown with small red, yellow, and lime-green blinking lights. They indicated different pressure levels of the mechanics of the train, traction feedback, and various levels of engine function. Though the train could nearly drive itself entirely on its own, the conductor kept his eyes on the track with only one break during his shift. Captain Frank usually spent his break in a fun way - drinking a coffee and keeping his eyes on the track as usual. Sean and Lucy were ready to go back to

Car 18. "I am sleepy," whispered Sean, "The control panel is probably the most awesome thing I have seen, though." "It is fascinating," said Lucy, thinking of Christmas tree lighting and wondering how many lumens the front light of the train probably produced.

During that time, the two were about to go back, having seen most of the vehicles. A waitress named Matilda came through the door of Car 1, however, slowly. The two watched, because she looked like she was up to something. She was not their waitress from Car 18. This women was older and had a purple feather in her hat. Lucy saw the server's face. The two watched as Matilda slowed her tray of two beverages and opened up a small ring on a finger of her right hand. She poured an amount of a white powder into what looked like a small glass of tea and quietly snapped her ring back together with her thumb. She then made herself known by softly dragging one of her high heels on the nice white carpeting of Car 1, the engine vehicle.

Mr. Barnes and the conductor acknowledged her presence. The two men did not pay too much attention to her. Matilda handed the *doctored* tea to Mr. Barnes and the normal tea to Captain Frank. The conductor never saw which server came into the car. The children did. Before Lucy or Sean could have even thought and said something about the tea, Mr. Barnes downed his like a fast shot of liquor. His body stiffened immediately straight and Mr. Barnes fell to the ground hemorrhaging. The conductor called for help and a waiter named Thomas came in immediately to see the victim's feet pointing down straight in line with his legs. "Cyanide," said Thomas. "Mr. Barnes must have consumed it. There would not have been time to save him even if we had a doctor nearby. Mr. Barnes is deceased," said Thomas sadly. He closed the man's rolled back eyes for him. Tears of confused sadness trickled down Tom's cheeks. Thomas left Car 1; Matilda escaped. The children crawled back towards 18.

Thomas found Barb to figure out who had the poison. Barb demanded a head count and full-body article search. The children saw them in

Car 13 from the vent. Matilda rinsed her ring after using it. It was a nineteen carrot gold luxury item with silver snake-like linings. The pastel purple polished stone flower on the top of the ring hid the small compartment used for hiding poison. The ring matched Matilda's feather in her hat. Her feather was what she commonly used to write with, in a unique indigo colored ink.

Lucy knew no person or group entity would have any proof of what she and Sean saw. She would have no proof, herself, and the murderer would get away with ease. These things drove Lucy insane, and she could barely think in her madness. The two would have loved to see what else went on in the kitchen, grown-up conversation wise, but they crawled back towards Car 18 instead. Their conversing parents would be out of the caboose soon, and trouble could be providing of unknown and unplanned punishable merit.

While in the caboose, Autumn and Donovan conversed. Much conversation already had time to occur while the children were crawling through the vent. "So that is it?" asked Donovan. "I suppose so, now that we have so thoroughly gone through these things," said Autumn agreeing, "If we just are not ready for the physical side of a monogamous relationship, then we are not. We both agree that things would be different for us with kissing or after including sex with what we share. We enjoy our intelligible conversations, and our time goes buy happily. What more could we want? We will satisfy each other when we both want to."

Donovan wanted to please Autumn. It was his way of defining his love for her; he thought her to be frail and pretty. He would have only acted upon his own carnal desires upon her request. He was happy either way. She would probably want something physical eventually - he would not be the one to complain. Autumn was pretty in a delicate way, with smooth flowing hair and a gentle manner of innocence, and she thought Donovan was a handsome, hardworking man.

"Speaking of time," said Donovan, "We still have about twenty minutes in here." "Okay," said Autumn, "What do you think of that flat screen?" Donovan looked over to his left and saw an eighty-inch flat screen plasma television. "That is a cheap one," said Donovan, "Those cost more when they are waterproof." "How do you know that?" asked Autumn. "Well," said Donovan, "This one really is a very nice and highly expensive television." He turned it on and its picture quality was amazing. It was set to a sports channel; a football game was playing. "I know about expensive televisions, because I saw a magazine ad one time for really nice high-end televisions. I have never owner one myself, however."

"Oh," said Autumn, as she watched a defensive football player catch an interception pass and make a run for it. "Waterproof televisions cost more?" she asked. "As far as I know," said Donovan, "They also usually are not as large as this one, and their picture quality can be questioned. I saw a waterproof television advertised for eight thousand dollars in 2010." "Wow," said Autumn. They watched football for the last part of their caboose experience. They were both happy to put things of no concern to either of them off for a while.

Donovan and Autumn sat rather close, that was all. While their parents were watching football, Sean and Lucy were crawling back to Car 18. Lucy was thinking. It was not always a good idea for her to think, not always. Thinking usually tempted Lucille to break a rule or partake in evil, somehow. Sean said, "I am tired," and he almost fell asleep on top of Car 14. They kept on, and Sean fell asleep on top of Car 17. Having at least fourteen minutes left, Lucy decided to go back.

She crawled as quickly as possible to the front of the train. The vent was rather secure; no one heard her as she scurried in a hurry. Once in Car 2, she saw Mr. Gucciani. He was sleeping like a baby. She opened his vent and acquired his gun from the carry-on compartment. She closed the compartment and the vent quietly. Once with the gun, she checked it. It had four rounds - one was ready. Lucille carefully left the safety off. Lucy crawled car by car to find the waitress with the purple-feathered hat. She found Matilda in Car 11 - the "Air Conditioner Theme" car. Engineers kept the history of cooling in mind when designing the theme car, and it was actually one of the neatest

vehicles on the train, according to some.

There were four thermostats in Car 11 that controlled the real-time

heating and cooling of the entire train. The flat screen in this car contained

over forty hours of videos and movies all having to do with air conditioning

systems. There was a ninety-seven minute black and white comedy about how

to install window units in sky-scrapers. In the comedy, the units sometimes fell

to the streets below to cause confusion or car damage.

Lucy had made up her mind. She flung open the brass grate to knock

the hat off the murderer. Lucy needed to identify Matilda - it was her. Lucy

shot the waitress in her left temple from the shadows of the vent. It was a

precise hit, and Lucy was almost proud of the perfect shot. The whispering

noise of the nine mm went unheard. Matilda fell loosely to the ground and

began to bleed from her head wound. Lucy closed the grate and kept the gun

with her. She crawled back to Car 2 and returned it to its previous location.

Lucy then crawled all the way back to Sean, who was still sleeping soundly. The humorous idea of leaving him there did not even occur to her. Lucy would have been exhausted, except that her adrenaline was pumping. She knew she was pressed for time.

She closed her eyes as she carefully crawled over the complicated conversations occurring in Car 11. Thomas and Barb were conversing over Matilda's body. They asked and answered questions of each other. Lucy made it to Sean. She woke him up and said, "We need to hurry. They will not be in the caboose forever." Autumn and Donovan finished their time-slot and successfully turned off the impressive television set. They thanked the waitress, Charlotte, at the door, and they made their way back to 18. Sean and Lucy climbed out of their vent; put it back; and sat down to wipe off their table with the privacy curtain reaching conveniently. They did so, and Autumn and Donovan entered 18 as soon as the children returned their curtain to normal.

The two children were safe. Sean played possum and fell asleep, nonetheless. Lucy arranged a game of solitaire after shuffling, and their parents then peered in their privacy curtain to see Lucy. They did not notice that she was half freaked out. She played it cool by placing a card, and the parents went to get comfortable in their own section. Sean was asleep, and the parents sat at their table. Lucy relaxed. The parents were fine. The ride was almost over, and Matilda was dead. It was not an easy decision for young Lucy; it was then or never, however. She decided to forget that these things ever happened. Never would Lucy be able to fabricate a justifiable reason for Matilda to have poisoned and killed Mr. Barnes. Such a nice man; he only did his job. Be spite or envy Matilda's motivation, in Lucy's young mind, Matilda got what she deserved.

It was about 5 AM, and the train ride would last for at least forty-five minutes. "I, for one, have had an enjoyable time this evening," said Autumn. "Me, too," said Donovan. They gazed into each others eyes and then looked away. Maybe one day they would actually fall in love - it just was not happening this night. The train traveled on into the darkness. Its destination was nearing. Donovan and Autumn kept a journal of daily prose. They participated in free-writing as a hobby. Of differing actual professions, they found their writings fun to compare. Rarely did they disagree on style; they were often times the happy grammarians conversing. At this time, they jotted sentences about their fun train ride and the caboose in their journals. Their descriptions of the train were a source of entertainment for them.

As they were writing, actual concern and panic was occurring in other cars of the train. Terrified and confused, the people did not know what to do. Of two dead bodies, one left a small pool of blood. The other body was also a mystery; no one knew of Mr. Barnes' poisoning. Matilda placed her cleaned ring with a few other small belongings in her purse. Because of these occurrences, the leaders of the train decided on actions. The head server, Barb, and the conductor, Captain Frank, decided to take pictures of the bodies. They also left the woman who was shot were she was for the soon to be available detectives. Captain Frank and the head Waitress shared in conversation.

"Who ever shot her has a gun on this train," said Barb, trying to think logically. "That is a good and obvious statement," said Captain Frank, "We will arrive in half an hour." "There is no crazy person running car to car shooting people," said Barb, "This means that they are here, and that they are possibly hiding and planning to go unnoticed, somehow." "These things will not happen," said Captain Frank, "We will find the gun, for sure. I can only hope we find the person. We will find the weapon, because we will search every person upon their exodus. I have contacted the authorities for when we disembark. If we find the gun on a person, we will probably find the primary suspect of the authorities."

"So what do you want me to do?" asked Barb. She always tried to do her best. "Do you think we are in any danger?" she asked. "I do not think we are in danger, because all of our passengers are either seated or sleeping, for one. No one has any hostages, and our ride is almost over. We will find the underlying cause of this. Please, listen to what I want you to do..." said

Captain Frank. He knew the ride would be over soon, and people would have

these things all figured out.

He then said, "Take a deep breath and exhale. Go and gather your

attendants in the kitchen. Keep your words brief, we only have a few minutes.

Tell them to keep watch over every car. The authorities will search us all upon

exodus. Stay in close communication. You, Barb, stay with Chef Mickey to

hear others. Let anyone that is worried know that we have this situation under

control. There is nothing to worry about."

Motivated, Barb went to the kitchen and formed a quick employee

meeting. The attendants cooperated. No one acted crazy. There were no more

murders. The servers never witnessed anything else mysterious. The ride was

almost over. The sleeping man in black leather woke to the faint alarm on his

wristwatch at 5:50 AM.

The man secured his weapon. Mr. Gucciani did have malevolent intentions. His motivations were for plans once he was off the train. He checked his gun. The man noticed that someone shot the gun. Mr. Gucciani was unsettled. No one had walked to the compartment of the gun. Mr. Gucciani did not realize that he slept so soundly. "There must be some kind of a magician on this train," he thought. Mr. Gucciani placed his licensed weapon in its carry case and into his long coat; he planned to leave the train and carry on with his previous plans, too. Lucy actually won her card game of solitaire, and the train slowed down to a gentle and safe stationary position. The authorities waited to allow people off the train. They quickly and politely checked out the passengers upon disembarking. The law found the gun on the mysteriously powerful-looking man - Mr. Gucciani politely agreed to go with them downtown. Once he was in cuffs, people nearby and the authorities were less frightened. The authorities gathered information from the train's employees and patrons.

Donovan, Autumn, Sean, and Lucy traveled to their hotel by cab and

Lucy was the first to take a hot and thorough shower. She had been sweating and decided to drink a cool glass of water. Lucy saw a show with gunshot residue included in its plot one time. The authorities took the man in black leather downtown. The forensics team investigated The Midnight Pearl's crime scene for close to sixty hours.

Once downtown, Mr. Gucciani explained that he retained a legal license to carry his gun - he had no intentions of someone shooting it on the train. He said, "Someone must have taken it while I was sleeping, though I do not know how." They checked his clothes and hands for gunshot residue and found none. The authorities believed Mr. Gucciani's story. They kept his weapon temporarily and released him. They would attempt to solve the mystery, somehow. The authorities released the story to the news. The release indicated that a Conductor's Assistant was poisoned and an unknown suspect shot a waitress with a nine mm during The Midnight Pearl's transit through the dark night. People found the investigation confusing.

Of course, the authorities contacted and spoke with every passenger of the train. Lucy's family had no knowledge of anything. She herself did not say anything. The authorities questioned everyone, and no one ever knew anything. The authorities eventually closed the unsolved case. The train continued its services as usual. All was well. This concludes the story of "The Midnight Pearl".

Amy finished reading the story, "*The Midnight Pearl*", as Bob was waking. "This is a nice story," said Amy; she stated her opinion as follows:

Even if it is never even published, I liked it. I liked the big expensive train. I visualized the twenty cars and many of the passengers. I saw theme cars that I designed in my own mind, because they were not all mentioned specifically or described in the story. I felt sorry for Mr. Barnes. I wondered why the waitress poisoned him, and I thought she got what she deserved. I think it would have been hard to catch her; she cleaned and concealed her ring. Even if they were to find the ring and prove it relevant to their case, someone shot her. The gun was with its rightful owner. The shooter could have been anyone on the train. There was no found *extra passenger*. I did enjoy this story,

Bob. I hope they accept it. I cannot wait to read your next one. I like watching your writing style improve. I think you will eventually display a refined, polished, and noticeable writing style of your own. If nothing else, I encourage you to keep adding stories to your anthology.

"Well thank you," said Bob, "It always helps to hear sincere and honest positive feedback. I take it you did not find any spelling or grammatical errors?" "Not really," said Amy, "I do not really know why you combine some sentences with semicolons or dashes, and then you have shorter sentences that are seemingly on their own. It did seem to have its own rhythm, though, and I suppose it was good enough to present to an audience somehow or somewhere. I am glad the girl went unharmed and was not caught."

"That is delightful," said Bob, "And thank you again for your compliments and helping me with what you did, here and there. The lady with the purple-feathered hat, Matilda, she was your idea, right?" "Yes sir" she said, as the subway car came to a halt. "I included you as an author of the story. If it sells we will both make money, and you can buy a bunch of books. We will know within three months," said Bob. "Thank you," said Amy, "I do want more books. I imagine many of the published contributors of the periodical work there as editors. Have you considered starting your own periodical or working as an editor?"

"Of course I have," said Bob, "Becoming an entrepreneur takes time and money. I think it would be a fun idea to do a speculative fiction *zine*. We could write about fantastic beings, spaceships, and the future of science. We can always learn with reading and writing. My fiction magazine would be amazing to many customers - scientists, children, and all other interested readers and writers would find it enjoyable." "Wow," said Amy, "Maybe I can help you, one day. Maybe I can write a story of my own for publication!" "There is nothing stopping you, Amy. You are brilliant. More power to you. I cannot wait to see your prose," said Bob.

"Can I tell you a story one day? While I am telling it to you, you can write it down. Then you can read it back to me and see if I can write the words down with my own presentation of stylish grammar," suggested Amy. "I would be delighted to help you write your first story," said Bob, wondering if the young prodigy knew that she constantly amazed him. She was intelligent - Amy always caught Bob by surprise.

The two made exodus from the subway vehicle and stretched for a nice while. They walked toward their destination hand in hand. Amy's parents lived about seven blocks away. Amy still had the story on her mind. Bob nearly blew his own mind from thinking of possible new story ideas. The number of possible story ideas he thought of everyday was over one hundred.

Keeping his job, Bob drafted and revised a story every week or two. Wizards, dragons, people, spaceships, robots, plots, and happy little elves -

what else was there for him to consider? Would he create multiple new fantasy worlds? He knew little of the origins of the English language, yet Bob was learning. He loved to write well and hoped to one day professionally please an audience. Someday someone would enjoy a world of Bob's creation. Someday he would have an audience, and his audience would be excited and waiting for his every story. This concludes the story of *The Train.*

♦

The Wizard Ship

"Forward!" said Fandrim, and the ship moved to the left. Wondron and Taldrin maneuvered it from the right to the left side, in the middle of space. The wizard, Gongolfen, just looked down while shaking his head. Fandrim was obviously in a good mood, or he would have given the command, "Left." They would have moved forward. They sat for a moment in space. The six characters were happily trying out their new spaceship. They were quite a fun team and known by some as The Hexids.

Their home base was in the epicenter of their home planet, and they were traveling to planet Zars. A real place, they had only once been there. A holy hand of natural occurrence once zapped the six supernatural beings to the epicenter of their home planet from an aquatic microcosm, however that is another story. Wondron, Taldrin, Reldon, Fizl, and Fandrim were the names of the elves traveling with Gongolfen, "The Wise Master of all Known Lore and Magic," as he was sometimes called by Fandrim.

Gongolfen invented his own spells from practice and study, and he used the considerations of many other students of the occult. Gongolfen carried a very powerful magical staff that he could use for various things. With his staff he could form, aim, and utilize a shrink ray, for one. He could also use it for *spell casting* - the action of casting a spell to produce either a traditional spell or some other magical form of being, matter, or existence.

Gongolfen's magical staff resembled a long golf club with a rectangle on the top of it. The mirror-like viewing part of his staff showed lands, spells, and shades of feelings.

The spaceship highly resembled a football chopped off in the back. It was bright and neon salmon in color on the outside with a pale tan interior. The interior also included six white polished animal hide seats. Their spaceship's name was Fireball. Fireball had oval windows coated with a magical *pseudo-iridium perma-glaze*.

The windows reflectively shown as brilliant gold and were used for casting beings of various sorts onto planet surfaces. They did these things for purposes of *actionology* - the study of the behavior of various beings' interactions amongst each other on various planets. The windows were fun for the elves, because Gongolfen could use them to spellcast beings onto the surfaces of planets. Their two favorite sorts of beings to spellcast were sparrows and tyrannosaurs.

In Fireball, Gongolfen manned the front and faced the back of the ship most of the time. Fandrim operated the back, and Wondron and Taldrin manned Fireball's left side when headed forward. Reldon and Fizl operated its right side, and they all had seats and operational panels installed accordingly. Fireball was a sizeable and spaceious space ship. Fandrim was the leader of the other four elves for reasons regarding their crew's efficiency, and Gongolfen was their wise and knowing master.

The Hexids were on their way to Zars. Zars, a planet full of exciting beings and lands, seemed to be calling them. Gongolfen was trying to orient Fireball in such a way to get there with the super-booster. Fireball had seven jet engines and a very powerful magical super-booster designed by The Hexids. The super-booster could allow the ship to travel at the speed of magic - faster than normal electromagnetic radiation/light. Its only challenge occurred with the orientation of the ship.

If The Hexids were going to use the super-booster to its fullest extent, they would have to aim the vessel in a proper vector space. Fireball could travel within close to the same vector space, or a similar straight direction, for great distances while in space. They first had to leave their current galaxy, as they were just far enough from their home planet to see it as a large ellipsoid void of movement or life.

Fandrim purposely gave a misguided directional command for the sake of humor. For this strange and surprising act of the head elf, the wizard decided to relate that he too was indeed in a good mood. Gongolfen turned, raised his staff towards Fandrim and said, "Woodenoden!" zapping Fandrim into a two year old Scandinavian dwarf-baby sitting in a leather seat. The other four elves really wanted to laugh, but they did nothing other than to release a quick giggle and blush partially.

Being zapped by a humorous spell caster recalling historical names was not what anyone wanted. "Do you guys all think this is funny?" asked the dwarf baby. "I do," said Gongolfen, "I really do. I think that particular spell wears off in a while, however." The six of them gazed at the stars for some time. Then Fandrim started jumping up and down saying, "Googoogagading! Googoogagading!" trying to cast a spell on the wise old wizard even though Fandrim knew nothing at all of magic. Afterall, he was a Scandinavian dwarf baby.

Fandrim eventually morphed back into the elf he was before and all was well. Gongolfen and the elves were done with playing around for the time being. They decided to try out the super-booster. The super-booster was the one exciting idea that got the elves motivated to care about common goals like new magic books and Zars. The other jets could actually get Fireball up and going to pretty fast speeds on their own. These jets were, however, only directional devices meant for aiming Fireball into a properly defined vector space for further travel.

The fuel for the super-booster caused it to leave a sparkling trail of glitter-like magical dust in space to shine temporarily and fade away from its silvery sprinklings of indigo and gold. This was largely due to the origins of the fuel. The super-booster's fuel came from Fairy World. Gongolfen made it from dust given to him from a society of girl-fairies from this world, which is yet a whole other story in itself. Gongolfen, priding himself with knowing a great deal of magic, chemistry and alchemy, found he could make a kind of magical rocket fuel. He did so by mixing a spirits potion with the magical dust given to him from fairies who practiced their own tiny form of special magic.

Gongolfen fused this fuel with electrical force resembling white lightening. He was usualy able to make four barrels of it at a time in the epicenter of their planet. Fireball could endure one hundred magical super-booster bursts with a full tank. It carried about four fifths of a barrel of fairy fuel. The six installed the fuel tank in the bottom of Fireball. It was covered from sight; Fireball resembled a solid piece of pink-orange and gold glowing metal.

"I am going to aim my staff to between two stars, and you can aim the ship in that direction. We will let the super-booster have its first magical firing shot," said Gongolfen to Fandrim, who was rather excited. Gongolfen aimed his staff to between two stars, and Fandrim could see the approximate route of travel. The Super-booster's first shot would propel Fireball out of their current galaxy and far away from the ten closest galaxies. It would take more than a single magical burst to get to Zars.

"Taldrin, fire your rocket," said Fandrim, and Taldrin did so. Fireball oriented in an exact opposite manner of the proper direction, and all was fine. "Reldon, fire your rocket," said Fandrim. Reldon fired his rocket, and Fireball oriented very close to the appropriate angle for burst direction. "Wondron, fire your rocket minimally," said Fandrim. Gongolfen held his direction with his staff; they were getting closer. Wondron did so, and Fireball was properly aligned.

"May I use the first burst of our super-booster?" asked Fandrim. Gongolfen said, "We are dead on target for departure. Fire away!" With that, Fandrim charged the super-booster. It made a small high-pitched tone, and he pressed the magical firing button. All six of The Hexids were safely compressed in the capsule and propelled in a seemingly instantaneous great speed and mighty *sending* very far away - far outside of any galaxy known to any common being.

Fireball eventually decreased in speed, and The Hexids were in what they called *Black-Space*. Deep outer space to them was anything outside of the dozen or so closest galaxies to their own, or rather, Black-Space. Fireball's speed lessened even more to what seemed to be a halt, however the spaceship was still moving in space. "Where are we now?" asked Taldrin. Reldon, Fizl and Wondron looked to him and said, "Black-Space, Taldrin." Fandrim came to from the blast and looked up to see Gongolfen playing around with his staff.

"I will figure out our location," said Gongolfen, "I think my guesses will be accurate." He used his staff to materialize his spell book. It was his life's work and contained anything from common recipes for cooking to advanced magical spells. Only a life-long and learned practitioner of occult magical practice could even begin to comprehend such a collection of ideas. He could use his book to do almost anything. These magical feats included time travel and certain displays of special rarity.

The wizard searched through maps in his floating book of magic, and the five elves still gazed upon it in wonder. Gongolfen had the book floating in the air as if it were levitated by the very white light that emanated from its presence. He turned a few pages by the waft of his hand and said, "Sure thing, we are in the middle of nowhere." The elves just looked down. Gongolfen aimed his staff at an angle and closed his book, which vanished in thin air. He then said, "We are on track, close enough. We are headed to an intermediary galaxy, before we trek to Zars itself."

This was good news to the elves. Intermediary galaxies were nothing more than a glowing ball of fun in regards to space exploration and travel. Gongolfen's words also meant that they were not actually lost in space, just out in the middle of Black-Space, drifting very slowly with only slight and minimal carry-over inertia. Gongolfen aimed his staff in a certain direction and asked if all were ready for another super-booster blast. "I certainly enjoyed our first one," said Wondron. "So did I," said Taldrin. "I agree," said Reldon. "I too, once more," said Fizl. "I thought it was a lot of fun," said Fandrim. "Okay then," said Gongolfen, "Fandrim, line us up with the angle of my staff."

Gongolfen's staff shined a very thin, bright white light resembling a lazer in a certain direction. It was a second vector space command. "Please, Fizl, give us a small blast," said Fandrim, and Fizl did so. Fireball oriented accordingly. Fandrim was almost confused. He was very close to being right on. "You figure this out and I will give you an elven king scepter that magically appears when you say, W*azurqer*!" said Gongolfen. He had to think

for a second, yet Fandrim figured it out and said, "Taldrin, open your blaster to

idle and Reldon, please, give us a tiny burst." The elves did so and Fireball

aligned perfectly with the direction of Gongolfen's staff.

Wondron, Taldrin, Reldon, Fizl and Fandrim were relieved. "It is

peaceful out here," said Gongolfen, waiting a moment to endure another

exciting and less experimental blast. The wondering elves looked to Fandrim.

Fandrim said, "Wazurqer!" and raised in his hand his mighty scepter as if it

were not the first time anything with life had ever seen such a thing. "Be

seated," said Fandrim happily, and the elves sat down on their nice seats.

"Ready the super-booster, Fandrim," said Gongolfen. Fandrim readied the

super-booster, and a high-pitched tone occurred. "Fire away," said Gongolfen.

The elves held on to their seats. Gongolfen readied his stance with his

staff like a soldier with a flagpole in the wind. Fandrim aimed his scepter

forward, and he pressed the magical button. The super-booster blasted them

very far away, once more. The long trail of sparkling dust once again shown

like millions of tiny stars in the sky, and Fireball's inertia carried them all the

way to the enchanting galaxy of *Spin Swirl*. Spin Swirl looked like small

spinning swirls of stars in a larger structure of a spinning swirl.

Deep in the heart of the galaxy, Fireball was moving at enormously

fast speeds, yet still slowing steadily, somehow. "We are much closer," said

Gongolfen, "I think the planet I am trying to find is not far from here." He projected a map with light from his magical staff like a geometrical plane in the air. The elves looked up to the map that resembled a bunch of spinning and sparkling stars in a spiral with a small orange-pink sphere and a small sphere of shining gold.

"We are the neon sphere," said Gongolfen, "And we are trying to get to the golden one." Fandrim gave the elves commands and they blasted away quickly with their smaller jets. Eventually, they neared the golden sphere and could see the planet. It was a large sphere-like space object with dunes, mountains, and valleys.

The newfound planet was void of water. "Which planet is this one?" asked Reldon. "It does not really have a name," said Gongolfen, "And we can now call it planet *Resdune*, because it has dunes and we can rest or at least recover from the last blast to ready ourselves for the next one. We will eventually make it to Zars, too."

"It has Dunes and we can rest?" asked Fandrim. "You are amazingly accurate," said Gongolfen, taking the rare opportunity to sit in his seat. Gongolfen never really liked to sit down. Fandrim sat, too. The elves watched; The Hexids neared the huge planet's atmosphere. "We are not going to try to land, are we?" asked Fandrim. "No way," said Gongolfen, "We will arc-drift in the planetary pull of our newfound Resdune, however." "Can we window-cast?" asked Taldrin, almost too excited to speak. "Once we are a little closer, we may give it a try," said Gongolfen, "I am not even sure if it will work."

"I think it will," said Wondron. "Of course it will," said Fizl, saving Wondron from saying something similar to, "Considering the things we have seen happen to Fandrim." "What kind of beings can we cast?" asked Reldon. "I think Gongolfen can cast any of them," said Fandrim, hoping the wizard would not do something too terribly horrible to him. Gongolfen said, "I am sure we can have some fun, now. We are going to definitely do things to this spheroid." "How will the beings survive?" asked Fizl. "That is a good question," said Gongolfen, "And I have a good answer." He caused his gargantuan spell book to appear and waved many pages by without touching the floating book.

"We are in orbit of the planet, now," said Gongolfen, "We are going to cast a change-wave spell. This is a very powerful spell, because it changes large amounts of matter from what they are into the same thing or into other things completely. For instance, this planet is mostly quartz, and our spell will change a percentage of the sand into other things like water and vegetation. We will also gain a large amount of the sand for magical energy by storing its previous 'existence presence' in our glazed windows' abilities."

"Wow," said Fandrim. The Hexids acted as a group unit on occasion. "Let us all raise our hands to our windows and say the word *Wavshangorkor!*" said Gongolfen. They said it. A sphere of light encompassed Fireball and shot a huge beam of light wide in diameter directly towards Resdune. The light circled Resdune making what highly resembled a large brilliant vertical ring. The huge ring spun 180° and faded away. During its spinning, the spell changed most of the mid-portion of the planet into a very large lake that resembled a wavy oval. There were various forests, fields, hills, mountains, plateaus, and even an exciting cave system. Four rivers could now be seen on planet Resdune. They consisted of two rivers from the mid-lake going to Resdune's top and two going to its bottom. The rivers were spread apart from each other rather evenly.

The spell made Resdune an impressive planet. Upon the request of Gongolfen, Fandrim saw to it that Fireball traveled closer to the surface of the planet in order to spellcast beings and occurrences. The Hexids were inside of Fireball. They were very close in orbit to Resdune's surface yet still far enough away to see a large enough area for plenty of beings. The Hexids could have viewed a whole heard of running wildebeests from this distance.

"So, what are we after here?" asked Gongolfen, with his book ready to recall spellcasts for various beings. He then said, "Our windows are fully charged from the sand transformations." "I have one!" said Wondron, "What if we do a whole heard of flying marsupials?" "I will look up kangaroos and condors," said Gongolfen, as he waved through his pages of his gigantic magical book. He seemed to find an old familiar page and searched for another one. The elves gazed upon the terrain of Resdune as they moved at a perceived to be slow pace around the horizontal circumference of the ellipsoid.

"I have it," said Gongolfen, as they came closer to a vast prairie field with loosely blowing lime-green grass. Fireball's idling engines caused the spaceship traveling at fast speeds over the terrain. Gongolfen was using two different spells to create a whole new being. The elves thought these were going to be harder to do than other beings they already knew of. Gongolfen raised his hands to Reldon's window and said, "Kangadoiken!" and a bright ball of white light with many tiny shining spheres of lavender swirling around formed in between his hands.

He threw this ball of light through a window of Fireball and the window's glaze transformed the magical ball into a golden light beam. This beam struck the surface of a large prairie field on Resdune. Close to one hundred kangaroos with condor wings fitting in size suddenly appeared.

The flying kangaroos were of both genders and all ages. There was a mother "condoroo," as Fizl liked to call them, who took flight with her baby way up into the air and soared around in a hanging glide. The condoroos were lavender. The new beings were healthy and seemed to be having a good time. "I have an idea," said Fandrim. "What is it?" asked Gongolfen. "I think Resdune could use some wuzinques." "And what, dare I ask, is your definition of a 'wuzinque'?" asked Gongolfen. Fandrim said, "I imagined them to be like prairie-dogs but with only black mink hair and tiny yellow magical glowing eyes to see in the dark."

Gongolfen did not even need to look this spell up, however he did think for a moment. As Fireball's rear window aimed towards the surface of Resdune, Gongolfen raised his hands in the air. He pulled them apart from each other slowly, creating a black ball of spinning magical light with small and glowing golden balls. "Wuzinqer!" said Gongolfen.

A black magical beam of light beamed from the ball through Fandrim's window to the bottom of a hilly area on Resdune. The light magically penetrated and sewed itself in curls repeatedly throughout a small area of ground, giving the new adorable tiny beings an existence playground for them to run around in. The small fuzzy creatures resembled miniature black squirrel families and behaved like prairie dogs with glowing yellow eyes as expected.

"That was fun," said Reldon. The Hexids were trying to decide on what animals or beings to put on Resdune. The little fuzzy black things were fun enough to watch, but The Hexids wanted to carry on to their more important matters and reasons for travel regarding Zars. "Why do we not just cast a whole group of safari animals?" asked Taldrin. Gongolfen held his left hand up to Fizl's window and said, "Safaricana!" A twisting multiple-colored beam of light came from Gongolfen's hand and passed through Taldrin's window to the surface of Resdune. All kinds of safari animals immediately existed in a huge stampede. A large dust cloud trailed the movement of the many animals.

"Those animals are amazing," said Fizl, and Reldon agreed. "This has been fun, however I for one would like to get on to Zars," said Fandrim. "I agree," said Wondron. "I want a new book on how to make magical elf toys from Zars," said Taldrin. "I want to see one more being," said Wondron. "Me too," said Fandrim, "Will you come up with one, Gongolfen?" "Alright," said Gongolfen, "How about a family of two-headed swimming snake-monsters that feed off aquatic life?" The other five laughed in approval.

The snake-monsters would be a good addition to Resdune's gigantic lake. Gongolfen raised his right hand to Wondron's window and said, "Snamonstriker!" Then a powerful green magical beam came from Gongolfen's hand, passed through Wondron's window, and struck the huge lake of Resdune. The spell came along with fish-like creatures and various other forms of aquatic life. Even diving birds that liked to spear small swimming forms of prey were there. The two-headed snake monsters were a lot of fun to watch, as they broke the surface of the water hunting for food and talking amongst each other.

"I think I am ready to go to Zars," said Fandrim. "We will make it," said Gongolfen, "We will then blast our way back home." Gongolfen magically materialized his large spell book and waved through its pages. He closed his book and caused it to vanish, now knowing how to get to Zars. He aimed the beam of his staff away from Resdune. Fandrim fired one of his two small rockets to better orient Fireball. "Reldon, please, fire your rocket minimally," said Fandrim. Reldon did so to properly align Fireball in the right direction, once again. The Hexids heard a high pitched tone as Fandrim charged the super-booster. Gongolfen said, "Fandrim, press the magical button." All steadied themselves, and Fandrim did so.

Many of the creatures of Resdune looked up in the night to see what looked like a shooting star blast away with a shimmering trail of magical dust shining the colors of a rainbow into the abyss. The Hexids were well on their way to Zars. An average sized star shined brightly on Resdune's opposing side.

Fireball's super-booster blasted The Hexids into Zar's atmosphere perfectly. Zars itself existed as a very large planet inhabiting natural and supernatural beings of many kinds; having all sorts of plentiful mountainous areas and jungle-like lands; and many other legitimately imaginable forms of terrain. The Hexids wanted to visit Zars for more than one reason; they were happy to be there. The third blast was tiring for them, and they fell fast asleep in their comfortable seats. Fireball orbited in the atmosphere of Zars.

Some time went by and the elves and the wizard awoke. "Now that we are here, what do we want to do?" asked Taldrin. "I know what you guys are after," said Gongolfen, "And I myself just wanted to see the planet, mostly. Taldrin, I know you want a book - Caprakam!" A magical book appeared glowing right before Taldrin's eyes. The book descended and Taldrin beheld it. It was above average in size and contained three titles. "I combined the best three books on making magical elven toys from Zars and put them into one book," said Gongolfen. Taldron was impressed and said, "Thank you. I still want to fly through the forest." "That is the whole reason I wanted to come here," said Reldon. "I just want to go have fun," said Wondron. "Myself ~~Even~~ even more," said Fizl. "Wazurqer!" exclaimed Fandrim, and he held his magical scepter up in the air for no apparent reason.

"Down to the forest!" exclaimed Gongolfen; he saw the edge of the Great Forest nearing. Fandrim gave commands to fire all five blasters full throttle. Fireball dove and increased to great speeds as it came closer to the surface of Zars. The Hexids were familiar with the Great Forest, and that was their destination. Once there, Fireball flew and winded along the tree line speeding along at an overly rapid pace. The elves were having the time of their lives flying through the forest for some time. Night was nearing, however, and they decided to slow down and maybe even land.

"I will find a clearing for us," said Gongolfen. He cast a map of the forest with his wand and found a clearing. He aimed his staff, and Fandrim gave commands to get to the clearing. They were tired. They found the clearing and landed. The Hexids went back to sleep by the light of a distant moon.

Morning came and The Hexids arose to the mothering star of Zars, Gilmara, as the nocturnal shadows crept back receding slowly into the Great Forest. There would not have been much harm that could have come to The Hexids while sleeping in Fireball, especially not without waking them up. As they arose, however, they decided to exit their spaceship's protection to walk around some and prepare for the trip home. Little did they know, many creatures of the forest had spent the night gazing upon the spaceship and wondering what it was.

They were greeted by a large community of elves. They were forest elves from Zars. These elves were commonly hospitable, as well as potentially dangerous. The Hexids spent some time with the local elves. They played with the youngsters and explored the trails of the Great Forest, minimally. Zars was a huge planet. It contained mountains, natural catacombs, rivers, and close to any other form of terrain imaginable. There was even the dark sea, with depths deeper than most known oceanic trenches. The dark sea had many forms of life. One of these communities known of was the *merdwarves*. They were male and female magical swimming dwarf-beings with tail fins, gills, and lungs.

The elves of the Great Forest had an elf king. He was very old, yet he looked like an adolescent. This was because of magical spells and experimental potions. The five elves played around with the other elves. Fandrim found out that his new magical scepter could do all sorts of things.

Gongolfen and the elf king, Seaunale, ("so - nail") had conversations regarding Zars, its communities, and its terrains. Seaunale gave Gongolfen a map of the entire planet of Zars. Gongolfen asked what he wanted in return, and Seaunale said he wished he knew more of spellcasting. Gongolfen materialized a small spell book for him that contained two hundred pages - each page contained a spell any elf would want to know.

The Hexids spent the day playing with the elves of the Great Forest of Zars, and returned happily to Fireball. They said their goodbyes and departed. Once in the spaceship's fuselage, Gongolfen said, "Please, get us out of the atmosphere of this planet." Fandrim gave the commands to do so, and they were off. Once in the outer atmosphere of Zars, Gongolfen aimed his staff with a shining beam of light towards Resdune. Fandrim gave commands to the elves and they aligned Fireball in its proper direction.

The Hexids had gotten better with navigating their new space ship. The elves had a lot of fun learning to operate Fireball. "Power up that super-booster," said Gongolfen, and Fandrim did so. The elves heard the high-pitched tone. "Press that button," said Gongolfen. Fandrim pressed the magical button and away they blasted, leaving behind a sparkling trail of magical dust for the many beings on Zars to behold.

They arrived perfectly inside of the atmosphere of Resdune, able to see its life existing naturally. "Are we ready for another blast?" asked Gongolfen. All agreed to another blast, and the wizard aimed a beam of magical light out into the infinite. Fandrim and the others lined up Fireball to the light, and charged the super-booster. "Press the button," said Gongolfen, and they blasted all the way back to Black-Space.

The Hexids were exhausted. Gongolfen rested comfortably in his seat. The others rested in their seats, too. The five had brought sacks of small magical items back with them from Zars and played with their new magical toys for a little while. Deep within the shadows of the Great Forest, Fandrim somehow obtained a reproduction of an in-depth book on the history of elven lore, magical practice, and war. Various beings fought wars in the Great Forest, and Fandrim's book of 1,000 pages was a mere attempt to summarize these occurrences and their various causes. He skipped through it for a while, admiring a few of the drawings that separated its properly composed chapters.

Once they all rested, Gongolfen conjured his map to find home. He aimed his staff one last time to complete their journey. Fandrim and his crew aligned Fireball. He powered the super-booster, and away they blasted. With a successful expedition home, The Hexids slept well that evening. As you may have guessed, The Hexids lived happily ever after.

◆

The Zombie Scarabs

Once upon a time, there was a young biology student studying genetics. He and his girlfriend, Mathrildya, enjoyed considering consideration together. Their relationship was physical when it needed to be, yet they usually enjoyed conversation more than sexual fulfillment. His name was Tom, and his friends sometimes called him Buffalo. Math, which is what his girlfriend went by, called him Buffy.

These two people made a beautiful couple. This story is about what they made in a laboratory, one day. It was a Saturday afternoon, and the two went on a walk together. "What is on your mind?" asked Math, because she knew Buffy was thinking. She saw him walking, watching the ground go by underneath him, and contemplating something deeply all the while. "Beetles," said Tom.

"Awesome!" said Math, "Like the band?" "No, Babe," said Tom, "Like the real bugs themselves." "Oh," said Math, "Why?" "Various reasons," said Tom, "I saw the same species of beetle more than one day in a row and figured out that it was a darkling beetle. They are the black ones and are longer than the average beetle found around here. I read that there are over 250,000 species of beetles in the world. I also read that scarab beetles were thought to be sacred by the ancient Egyptians. I think the little guys made the Egyptians special fertilizer balls. Beetles are neat…" Tom lost track of his conversation, because he saw concrete steps instead of grass beneath his feet.

The two went into the genetics laboratory on their campus. It was part of the back of a whole building donated to the school for the study of Biology. The genetics laboratory contained vast resources of information documented and described by the government as well as information discovered by the university. The university's students reported many findings found in the laboratory and elsewhere directly to the government. Tom had unlimited access to project information because of his scholarships. He worked part-time for a professor. The man Tom worked for had a PHD in genetics as well as many other college degrees.

Tom and Math spent the afternoon drawing small pictures of beetles and even got it on in the laboratory. No one else was even around. At one point, they made a big poster with a shining blue scarab on it. They both thought it was a neat picture. They wrote the behavioral characteristics of their unknown species up on the poster.

"What could be so special about this beetle?" asked Math. "What do you mean?" asked Tom, "Special like its rarity or its indigenous origins?" "I mean this scarab could be special for reasons that we could not even fathom as humans," said Math, jokingly and in a loving manner. "I know," said Tom, "Let us say they have a deadening venom. The little creatures fly to humans and bite their skin. Their tiny fangs inject a special local anesthetic, and then they bite a very small piece of flesh from their human victims and fly away.

Then, they use these small bites of flesh to make miniature balls for one reason or another. People will not be hurt when the beetles nibble on their epidermis. Many species of beetles protect a small area of environment if they can; they posses behavior that is able to be studied."

Math was so happy that she could barely see. "Wow," said Math. "Not only that, we can do more. Let us make these things..." said Tom; he paused his words. Tom knew he and Math could not resist the idea. They were going to stay up late genetically designing a new beetle.

"Let us say," continued Tom, "That if a human consumes one of our magically glowing and shining metallic blue scarabs, that the scarab's *anesthesia venom* reacts in the human's bios system to produce what we can call 'specific disintegration neurotoxins'. They chemically deteriorate the very parts of the human brain that make us who we are." "These sins will not be pardoned," said Math with the dreamy look of dedication beaming from her eyes. "Who dares eat such a wonderful little creature?" she playfully asked, "They must have another use... I have it. As time goes by, every other day or so, they grow new wings under their old ones. When they lose their old ones, the old wings turn to dust except for shiny little blue wires made mostly out of platinum. We as humans could use these little wires for making microchips!" "That is awesome," said Tom. "Can they also be like fireflies?" asked Math. "Of course they can," said Tom, "Easily, too, because a firefly is a type of beetle." "I did not know that," said Math, as she dreamt of little scarabs flying around in the night making blue light-tracers, swirls, and squiggle lines.

The two were overly excited and began to activate the computer system to map out a genetics chart for the larvae seeds of the beetle. "I am hungry," said Math. "Why do you not dial up the pizza man on your smart phone?" asked Tom, knowing he was going to pay. "I do not have any money on me," said Math. "I will pay for the pizza," said Tom. She called and got the "buy a large pepperoni pizza and get a second one free with a 2-liter coke" deal. They began doing research as they waited for their pizza.

Designing the scarab was not too difficult. They gave the little insects a hypothetical scientific Latin name: *bitaetius bluiscarabdae*. The larvae would go through growth stages until it turned into a grub worm, and the grub worms would eventually morph into excellent and magical metallic little blue scarabs that could decorate the darkness of the night with bright blue light swirls. The only parts of them that would have the metallic blue color would be their wings and their thorax. Their actual fangs would be tiny and white, and their legs and feelers would be ink black. They would be closer to a circle in shape as opposed to an oval.

As far as mating was concerned the grub worms would make more larvae seeds. All of the grub worms would be female, and then they would develop male genitalia. The grub worms would turn into the male variety at different times, or not at all, so that mating could occur. Once the development stage began to occur to change from a grub worm to a scarab, their gender would remain constant.

This way there would be both male and female flying scarabs. They would be magical, glowing in blue light, and shiny in metallic hue during the noontime sun. They would hide little epidermis balls in the bottom of a tree's roots somewhere. The female scarabs would fly with newly made seeds to find the best tree for inoculation, or seed planting.

The pizza came and the two had already finished designing both the physical scarabs and their behavioral properties. Tom let Math pay and keep the change. She did so and tipped the delivery boy. The two designed the scarabs to faint when in perceived extreme circumstances or terrible danger, so they would appear to be dead to a bird or other predator. The scarabs' brain would send an impulse to one of their four tiny heart chambers to get them moving again minutes later, so long as they consumed water that day. Only one drop of water or so would keep them living all day. They would wake before the sun to swim and survive when possible.

It would be a little bug that could survive. The scarabs would decide to light up or not depending on if they needed to see in darkness. They would also glow for other reasons such as finding each other. They would live off freshly fallen leaves, bark, and water. They would prefer to burro secretly into the bottom of a tree to eventually hollow out ample space for a colony. The beetle grotto would not kill the tree, but the scarabs would secretly feed the tree's roots their tiny dried *trophy-balls*.

As said, the female scarabs would fly to find the best and most suitable tree for a mother tree, taking into consideration the taste of its bark and physical surroundings. The small creatures' instincts would include biting their victims secretly. After all, they would only be trying to survive.

"You know, we could send this design to the bio-chem lab," said Tom. "Oh could we?" asked Math, "Would we not get into trouble for designing a new species?" "No way," said Tom, "We will go and burn the printout, as well as this magnificent poster we made and these sketches we used to think with." She wanted to see it done, so Tom did it. He sent the necessary genetic coding to the other laboratory. They went there and processed the chemicals within a few hours. Both lovers ended up with a test tube half full of distilled water. The water was saturated with magical blue scarab larvae eggs.

Tom secretly stored his sample in a dark and cool place behind a small book in his miniature personal library. Mathrilda was so happy that she was close to crazy. She took hers back to her dormitory. Math did a magical dance with it casting life spells for the future of the creatures so that they could exist as beautiful forms in nature and an aid to botanical life. She slept an hour or two, and arose. The sun would not be up for an hour or so, and she thought and thought about the trees she knew of in the city.

Most of the trees in the city had a location in Math's memory. There were trees that were large and old, and even pretty shrubberies that would probably qualify as trees. She thought about them all. Her favorite tree was an old cherry tree on the shaded west side of the library. The library was a large building the shape of a 135° angle.

It had six floors and two main hallways on each floor. There was a reading garden there, on the west side, with some really old stone tables and various decorative shrubberies and trees. The largest trees were the very tall pecan trees that dropped pecans annually. The pecans always made a "thonk" sound on the library windows with the blowing winds of fall. Math decided to go to the cherry tree. The tree made cherries once a year; no one really ever ate the cherries. Math secretly washed one off and ate it once during her first year of college. As she recalled, it was sour, more like a wild fruit rather than a store-bought black cherry or a common red cherry.

She made it there unseen. Math brought an ice pick with her to break some bark lose from a root on the darkest side of the tree. Any human would have to look closely to see the root, for the markings where not easily visible to the naked eye. She poured the contents of her test tube out onto the root and sprinkled some earth from nearby onto the dampness. Math jogged away unseen; the closest vehicle was an early morning receptacle truck. She made it back to her bed and went off to sleep soundly.

Tom had gone to sleep that night, too. They both slept until about 1 PM that Sunday and met up in the foyer of a dining hall to finish their weekend schoolwork. "What are you going to do with your test tube?" asked Math. "Well," said Tom, "I think I will dispose of it. I thought about keeping it and using the little guys for a study some day. I would not want to chance their escape and risk human consumption, though." "Do you think it would actually make magical scarabs if one poured the tube out outside somewhere?" asked Math. "Oh sure," said Tom, "Their chances of survival would be pretty good - beetles are intelligent little creatures. The larvae could easily develop on most plant material."

"Why Math?" asked Tom. He actually looked up from his biology text, "What would you do with your scarabs if you had not already flushed them down the toilet? Bring them to a third world country so that zombies could consume each other?" "I did not even think of that," said Math, "You got that one right though," she said playing with her boyfriend, "I could not sleep this morning, because I was having nightmares of giant scarabs biting off heads of people. I woke up and flushed the contents of my test tube down the toilet bowl. After that I slept soundly."

Tom almost got a little curious as to the validity of her story, but he let it go and went back to his reading. Days and time went by, and fall was starting to fade into the cooler time of winter. Math and Tom were both tedious students who were interested in their work. They stayed busy and were both known overachievers by many of the professors on campus. This semester, like all of them, took some brainpower on both of their parts to do well during finals. Tom had forgotten all about his and Math's one playful Saturday afternoon. He stored his test tube from the lab with his books and totally forgot about it.

Math forgot about the scarabs, herself. Most of her peers considered her a more feminine young woman, yet she did posses a secret tomboy side. Her scarabs crossed her mind one time. She easily let her notions pass by keeping her mind on her school work - Math did well that semester.

A few weeks before finals, exciting things were happening around the cherry tree. The only human that even went around the tree for weeks and weeks was an old janitor that walked over there to clean a piece of windblown debris from the grounds. Had he slowed to look closer, he would have noticed tiny divots in a root on the west side of the cherry tree.

The seeds hatched. The tiny larvae were alive and ate small holes into the shady sides of the bark of the root of the tree. The sunlight there was indirect and minimized. The larvae turned into burrowing grubs in an decent amount of time. The ground surrounding the cherry tree stayed moist from the leaking pipes of the library. The happily active and perfectly healthy grubs formed this ground into a mating bed and populated the ground well.

As they were designed to do so, the adult grubs burrowed into the bottom of the tree. Ample time went by, and the grubs ate the tree's cavity so that it was large enough for the grubs to gestate in their tiny late fall cocoon-like beetle sacks. The wintertime came, and it was cold. Temperatures dropped to below freezing, but the tree did not freeze solid and lived as always. The ground's freezing did kill off seven percent of the larvae, but the rest survived the cold.

Finals week came and Math and Tom did well. Math got a "B" in speech class, but all of the other grades she received were an "A". She did well in her difficult classes. Their avid and devoted study and work allowed for success in the sciences and upper level mathematics. Tom decided to not go see his family in person that year. He went to cuddle up with Math in her parent's log cabin up north instead.

A few days before Christmas, the magical blue scarabs where ready to hatch inside of the cherry tree. They would fly around like button-sized blue Christmas lights in the nighttime. During the darkest hours of Christmas Eve, nasty winds blew the damp leaves of the city around, and the very first blue scarab broke free from his little cocoon. He crawled out of his sack he made, and he felt his way out of the trunk of the tree. The little creature stretched his wings to dry in the wind on the eastern side of the tree for a few moments. He even attempted to cause himself to glow temporarily. He did it. He then took flight. He could fly! The scarab flew into the wind. He rose and fell as he flapped his wings overly tediously or at times not at all. The scarab became talented with being able to fly in the wind.

He flew all around the grounds of the university. The shining little fellow landed to rest on a parked car, which started up and drove to the subway. The scarab drank some water off the trunk of the car. Here, pedestrians were waiting to board the underground train. The scarab flew to his very first victim.

An older man in a dark green leather trench coat was waiting with a newspaper under his arm. He sported a hat with a small colorful feather. The scarab flew to the grim man's collar and lit for rest. He gently crawled to the man's epidermis and bit his wrinkly old skin. The man did not know. The little creature's anesthesia venom worked properly. The shiny blue scarab flew all the way back to the cherry tree on the winds, with his ball of flesh from the subway. He glowed blue to enter into the tree.

Other scarabs where hatching, as well. They also took flight, and a few dozen flew around the city. They behaved as their DNA suggested, and the cherry tree prospered well.

During Math and Tom's Christmas vacation, only half a dozen of the scarabs that left the new small colony flew to inoculate other trees successfully. The scarabs chose a large pecan tree on university grounds, an old maple tree by the public park, and others. The new colonies developed into full-blown societies of scarabs by spring.

Tom and Math were in the middle of the spring semester by then. No one in their town paid any attention to the rarely seen beetles. Children sometimes found them and thought they were marvelous. The number of children in remedial classes went up two percent by the next year. The small scarabs were shiny, blue, and quite spectacular to anyone that actually saw them. They were good at hiding. Nine times out of ten, their bites went completely unseen.

No problems had occurred during these weeks of development. The small scarabs where at one with nature and were successful at hiding from most other forms of life. One day, a sleeping bum awoke under an overpass to find a shining blue bug crawling away from him. The hungry bum snatched up the shiny metallic blue scarab and swallowed him whole.

This was a big mistake for the bum. He was dazzled with hallucinations within twenty minutes. His whole world of perception swayed into swirls of confusion. His head suffered a *weight* of pain, and then the pain went away. He crawled to his feet and walked instinctively to the nearest place of many people. It was a restaurant known for pancakes and more.

The bum had turned into a zombie. He bit an old woman's head in public, and the authorities incarcerated him. He should not have eaten the shiny scarab. Months went by and no other humans turned into zombies. These things all changed, however.

A private restaurant sold crickets. A chef there cooked them for sale as a crunchy delicacy to go with his various soups. He found a scarab colony in a tree near his restaurant one day and thought they would be a wonderful way to increase sales. They were. He bred them in a terrarium and cooked them for sale as a small decoration beside his soup. People were amazed. Not too many people really saw these dishes; he told them that the beetles were from Australia. He lied to make money. No one turned into a zombie, though, and people still had mild hallucinations. This was because their chef roasted the scarabs to be crispy. This rendered the scarabs, unknown to the chef, to be less poisonous.

He brought his terrarium for private viewing to the restaurant, one day. The terrarium was an eighty-gallon glass tank. It contained hundreds of little metallic blue scarabs living in and off the log of a tree. The chef properly changed its water bowl. People noticed the mild psychoactive properties of the sometimes-glowing shiny blue metallic scarabs and wanted to eat the beetles alive. They did so, and the zombies ate the cook. He would have had a fighting chance, but the zombies had him outnumbered.

Over a hundred people had eaten a living scarab during dinnertime that night, and they dispersed into the streets of the city in hunger for brains. Journalists reported various confusing atrocities all over the city. Zombies were attacking people. People were trapping and shooting zombies. Consumed with their schoolwork, Math and Tom never caught wind of the terror on the news. The authorities caught and incarcerated one zombie after another. One zombie tried to sneak up on a man who was armed. Upon the attempt of the zombie to bite an ear of the man, he pulled out his forty-five caliber handgun and blew the zombie's useless brains onto the pavement.

All of the zombies were either shot or locked up within a few days. Their brains deteriorated beyond Tom's prior perceived guesses, though, and any of the zombies that had eaten a living scarab died from being brain dead within a few weeks after the initial consumption of the scarab. No one had any link in regards to the acts of the private restaurant zombies and the scarabs. All of the living scarabs flew away from the restaurant's terrarium.

Time went by. The shiny and sometimes glowing little blue scarabs continued to live on in their secretive and modest ways. Not too many people consumed any of the magical little creatures for a few years. Tom and Math obtained their bachelors degrees and went on to become scientists in another city. Tom did not even piece together that the zombies on the news were caused from their beetles. Math forgot all about the cherry tree due to her studies; she attended another university to work towards her second degree. Tom kept his test tube in his books for years and years. Math eventually became a professor, and Tom became an archeologist.

Not many in the city ever really noticed the magically shining metallic-blue scarabs. They were there seen as tiny blue lights in the night from time to time, nonetheless. The scarabs continued to make small colonies all over the world. Together with people, they all lived happily ever after.

♦

U. F. O. Granny

One time, there was a group of neighborhood boys. They spent time together hunting and watching television and playing with electronics. They lived on the outskirts of a city of about 300,000 people. Their fathers were of differing occupations: a mechanic, a computer technician, a chemistry lab assistant, and a welder. All of the boys graduated high school in the same class.

Their names were Tom, Luke, Gerald, and Moon. "Moon" was Moon's real name; his mother decided on the name while having him. Moon was a 10 lb and 4 oz baby. He grew up eating well and trying hard. Moon always meant well and became a *big old boy*. Tom, Gerald, and Luke were Moon's good buddies. All four of them participated in some form of learning after high school. Moon went into a construction program and made about twelve dollars an hour for insulation work. Tom, Gerald, and Luke all three went to college and had to return home due to partying. All three could have held almost any occupation.

They still had dreams and aspirations; the three wanted to be scientists. Beer and liquor took up too much of their time, though, so they put school off for a while. Alcohol is never cheap for some. Upon returning, the three men other than Moon found out how frustrating it can be to try to work and live with parentally guiding figures.

They obtained jobs in restaurants and merchandising. Tom worked at the mall folding clothes. Gerald and Luke both worked in fast food but in separate locations. The three tried here and there to help with their parents' bills; they were having problems with their social lives.

Moon lived in a single-wide trailer with a shower, a kitchen, a bed, and a den. He helped install insulation for a company that worked for both residential and commercial entities. Moon paid for proper plumbing. No one wants to try to sleep and wake up for work itching, so his shower was important. Not all of the insulation he helped install could cause an itch, however.

Tom, Gerald, and Luke went to go see Moon on Friday nights and usually pitched in for pizza or Chinese food. The three young men other than Moon did not really ask Moon to pitch in, because it was his place. All four were somehow grateful.

"This pizza is great," said Moon one night, "Are you guys sure you do not want a few dollars?" "No," said the three. They ate their pizza while watching a car race. Moon was thinking. "I am cramped," said Moon. "Do you want us to go?" asked Luke. "No," said Moon, "I mean we need more space. Tom, please bring me that paper from the fridge." Tom had his hands full with a coke and a tricky slice of pizza, so he said, "Gerald, will you get that for Moon." Gerald was in some dream world and came back. He walked to the fridge and got the paper for Moon. Moon said, "Thank you."

"I am looking in the ads for a place for us four to live. That is if you guys want to split a place together," said Moon. Tom said, "I am down." Gerald and Luke agreed, so long as the cost was not too high. The four of them looked through the classifieds and found a house for rent for five hundred a month including water and electric.

The four agreed to get together and check it out in the morning, and they did so. The property owner said she lived next door, and her name was Ms. Daugherty. The house was rather huge. It had a large den, a dining room, a large kitchen, four bedrooms, two baths, a work closet, a storage room, a two-car garage, and a three-car patio in the back with a half-wall. The back, side, and front yards were unattended and overgrown. Age cracked the framing of the house, and the roof was at least thirty years old in appearance.

"No one has been in there in over two years," said Ms. Daugherty. The four looked at each other and then back to her. "I was going to sell it when my aunt passed," she said, "She left it to me. I did not get along with three different realty companies, because the house did not sell. I decided to rent it out." She walked them inside.

"What do you think of the interior of the house?" asked Ms Daugherty. "It is overly rundown and very dirty," said Luke and Moon in unison. "It looks like no one has been in here for over a decade," said Tom. It had broken cabinets, torn furniture and walls, and a possible rodent problem. The guys were all excited and wanted to clean the place to make it look like new. "What do you guys think?" asked Gerald. "I like it," said Luke. "Me, too," said Moon. "I like it, as well," said Tom.

"If you guys are planning on cleaning the place, I can take money off of the rent and all. Keep your receipts, and show me what you have done," said Ms. Daugherty, "I can give you up to a hundred off a month for cleaning supplies and all for a month or two."

The four signed a document to split the rent of the house for half a year. Moon and the other three worked on the place and got most of it cleaned out in about four days. It only took them two weeks to move in. In five weeks, they had the place looking much better.

They worked and paid their way. Ms. Daugherty was a nice person, and Moon enjoyed bringing their payments to her. She usually gave them brownies when he came to pay the rent. Weeks went by and they maintained a nice and proper living space. Eventually, though, things became mundane.

The four were watching a show on outer space one day, and Gerald said, "How hard do you think it would be to build a space ship?" "Impossible," said Luke. "It cannot be too impossible," said Tom, "The space program builds ships that really go into outer space with astronauts all of the time." "We could build a dune buggy and sell it easier than we could build a spaceship," said Moon. "Space travel would be fantastic, though," said Gerald.

"I have had an idea for a spaceship since I was eight years old," said Luke, "It would have a *jet-hole* in the center and propel itself upwards in a slight angle." He sketched his idea on a napkin. "That is not really that bad of an idea," said Tom, as he checked out Luke's quick sketch. "I saw a diagram one time in a science magazine," said Moon, "It explained how a nuclear jet engine would operate. I still have the periodical." "Wow," said Gerald, whose father was a chemist.

"Since when do you have a science magazine?" Tom asked Moon, saying, "No offense." "Ms. Daugherty gave it to me a few weeks ago," said Moon, "She said she thought I might like it and she thanked me for always bringing her the rent money on time." The other three just looked down.

They were happy to live there. "I think we should try to build this ship," said Luke. Moon was looking at the ship's sketch and said, "It looks too little for me." "We will make it large enough for the four of us," said Gerald, "We are going to need a very powerful fuel." "How will we land?" asked Tom. "We will figure that out as well," said Moon, thinking about how space capsules commonly land in water near a shore line.

The four discussed the ship while they were watching a car race. Tom sketched out a new sketch, and it looked fine. Within a few weeks, Gerald enriched a by-product chemical with Luke. "What can we call this stuff?" asked Gerald, "Its reactivity is off the charts." Luke said, "Why do we not call it 'quazonium'?" "Quazonium it is," said Gerald, "I think it would work with the same kind of engine in Moon's diagram." Moon and Tom had perfected the design of the ship while Gerald and Luke formulated a new fuel.

"We have the rocket fuel," said Gerald. "I see what you are saying," said Moon, "We still need the materials for the hull of the ship and the engine." "We could easily order these things if we had the money," said Luke. "What is this outer layer, here?" he asked as he was looking over Moon and Tom's diagram. "Carbon fiber" said Tom. The four had tired some of the idea - they went off to bed.

Time for paying came, and Moon brought the rent to Ms. Daugherty, as usual. "So, what have you guys been up to?" asked Ms. Daugherty, "Work?" "Oh sure," said Moon, "We just got a new house to put insulation in the other day where I work, and the other guys are keeping up with their schedules. We even designed a real life space ship and Gerald and Luke formulated new nuclear fuel for it."

"Are you guys going to build it?" asked Ms. Daugherty. "No," said Moon. The four had already put together the materials and their actual prices from ordering catalogues. "We priced the materials for the construction of the engine, the fuselage, and the exterior. All necessary materials would cost close to seven thousand dollars."

"What if I gave you guys seven grand?" asked Ms. Daugherty, "Do you think it would fly?" "Of course it would," said Moon, "Tom even has a calendar with a map on it. We could time when we left the atmosphere and land in the ocean on New Years. We could give you pictures of earth from outer space," said Moon. Moon thought the old woman was crazy. She may have been. She was a nice and presentable senior citizen, and Moon secretly thought her long frail hair was pretty.

The afternoon's shadows were creeping into the front of the windows of Ms. Daugherty's house. Moon had already paid the rent for the month and they spoke on the rocket ship. Ms. Daugherty did not have a whole lot of family. He was about to leave, as always, and she said, "Moon, the doctors told me last week that I am terminally ill; I will be gone in under a year. I am dying." Moon did not know what to say other than that he was sorry. "I am sorry," said Moon.

He departed, and Moon told the guys about her later. They continued to work and pay rent. Ms. Daugherty's medicine may have been able to keep her living a little longer than what the doctors said the worst case scenario was, so the guys were not too unhappy. They considered death to be a part of life, as we all do, sometimes. December came and Ms. Daugherty *over-nighted* the materials for their spaceship to her front doorstep. Tom, Gerald, Luke, and Moon did not even know what to say. It was all they could do to pay her for their rent. They could never repay her for these things.

The four accepted the materials. They draped their back patio with plastic to make temporary walls. The four had the engine as well as the four-man fuselage constructed before December 20. The spaceship was a fine machine. The middle of the ship contained a nuclear jet engine mounted in an angle. The carbon-fiber coating caused the outside to have a very clean look and feel. The fuel would only be enough to burst the four out of the atmosphere and into orbit. After some time, the ship would fall back towards the planet and break into the atmosphere in a fireball to land in the ocean and float.

The four decided to blast away on New Years Eve, and requested off. On December 20, Ms. Daugherty was cleaning out her pantry while she was watching a Christmas film. She found an old bottle of scotch, and an unopened bottle of vodka. She normally did not consume alcohol, however she did a few shots of both kinds of liquor and decided to dress up like Santa Claus.

The guys were watching the animal channel and doing nothing. Their front door burst open suddenly, and Ms. Daugherty came in overly intoxicated. She was still dressed up like Santa Claus. She had a jar of purified petroleum jelly in one hand and a half drunk fifth in the other. She took a good swig of scotch and pointed directly to Moon and said, "Moon, I want you to do me!" The guys did not know how to react; they just looked to Ms. Daugherty. Tom was guessing that she was about seventy. Moon said, "I will go and tuck in our nice old friend."

Moon walked her home safely, returned, and they all went off to bed. Christmas came, and the five exchanged stocking-stuffers around a Christmas tree singing carols. They also spent what time they could with their biological families. New Years Eve came, and they rolled their spaceship out into the backyard. Moon was in the front of the four-part vessel. Tom, Luke, and

Gerald operated the other three sections. Ms. Daugherty was there to watch them blast away. The plan was to get into orbit, take some pictures of the planet, and land in the ocean upon return. One of Ms. Daugherty's daughters had a husband. His brother would drive out to them and bring them back in his full-size Blazer. The four thought The Coast Guard would find them if they did not drift to shore. That was their plan.

Luke, Tom, Gerald, and Moon manned their spaceship. They turned its lights on, and Moon readied the engine for activation. He sat comfortably in the front. Tom spoke a countdown while watching a wristwatch, and Gerald was able to press the ignition button at the stroke of midnight. Luke guided the small directional fins as they blasted away.

The ship powerfully soared through the sky and away from the planet leaving a sparkling dust cloud of radioactive material. It passed through the atmosphere, and drifted in space as if it had stopped its motion altogether. The ship was spinning slowly, so all four passengers could see the planet for some time out of their windows. They all had a disposable camera; they took turns taking pictures.

Moon, Luke, Tom, and Gerald remained in orbit for a few hours. The ship began to return in gravitational pull. It gained speed and continued to do so until it passed into the atmosphere with a fierce amount of friction giving off the glow of a brilliant ball of fire. This perceived ball of fire fell and fell until it struck the surface of the ocean only a hundred yards from the shoreline. The four men lived through the immense impact without harm. The guys drifted ashore during a lazy sunny afternoon, and Moon phoned the man with the blazer with his cell.

The man with the blazer's name was Mack. Mack drove to the guys with a trailer and picked them and the spaceship up to bring them back to their house. The five had an enjoyable trip back and returned safely. The four space-travelers developed their pictures within a few weeks. Ms. Daugherty certainly enjoyed Moon's pictures the most. "He definitely has the best picture with this shot here," said Tom, as they were looking at the pictures. They all agreed. Moon had taken one good picture of the continent of Australia.

Time went by and the four continued to work and work more. The trip burned the exterior of the ship as theorized. Maybe one day they would rebuild it and do the same thing again.

Ms. Daugherty's health was failing. Her medicine worked well for a few months, and then it did not work at all. She was in pain and passed. Her family conducted a funeral and about fifty people decided to attend. Moon, Tom, Luke, and Gerald dressed up nicely and attended. Their rent would go to Ms. Daugherty's heirs, now.

During the funeral, all who knew and loved her missed Ms. Daugherty. They watched solemnly. The funeral home employees lowered Ms. Daugherty into the ground. Her spirit remained inside of her coffin. Moon had a grim stare behind his dark shades that went unnoticed. All returned to their home and life went on as always.

Weeks went by, and all was well. One morning the paper came and there was a gruesome story on the front page. Someone or group dug up and re-buried Ms Daugherty. Tom found the article in the morning paper and was shocked. He showed it to Luke who showed it to Gerald who brought the paper to Moon's bedroom.

Moon was fast asleep, and there was a pair of dirty shoes by his bed. The mud on the shoes highly resembled the dirt on Ms. Ms. Daugherty's grave, and the three called the authorities. "We believe you did not do this," said Tom, Luke, and Gerald. The authorities came and arrested Moon, anyway, who cleaned his shoes and the floor well before they got there. He also had the time to check various areas of the property for obvious items of possible accusation.

Moon had to wait two nights in the county jail before going to court. His lawyer told him that the judge was going to ask him one simple question, and to say, "No Contest," - nothing more. Moon would be free to go.

These things happened, and Moon attained no punishment. Luke, Tom, Gerald, and Moon were watching a show that night, and Luke asked Moon a question. "Did you dig up our old neighbor, and have you had sex with her before? We are just curious," said Luke. Moon saw that the other three were not upset; they just wanted to know. "I did it with her while she had been drinking during the holidays," said Moon, "But now she is gone and not forgotten; I dug her up and done her rotten."

♦

Zoom Ring

In the year 2010, the government denied a subsidiary contract organization funds necessary for a project involving outer space. Unqualified scientists sometimes receive funding. Proven scholarly theory and scientific fact involving physics does not change due to its finders' previously proven knowledge. The members of the contract company did not care too much about having no actual four-year diploma. One of the seven of them had a one-year certificate in nursing; the rest of them were avid readers and researchers of many subjects.

The seven scientists contributed books to their collection. Even with no four-year *papers to frame*, they still provided newly developed scientific innovations and presented profitable programs to their government. Space programs, military endeavors, education, and biological research all gained from the scientists' findings. What originally brought the team of seven together was a sci-fi forum on the internet. Trying to compose believable tales led to their meeting each other. The seven scientists moved to the same city and started a writing guild. They proved theories regarding space and conducted scientific research together. They sold a newly designed ceramic plating technology for rockets to an unnamed government space organization towards the end of 2009. The ceramic plating deal a success, the seven scientists had money to save and use for future research. Their newfound direction was a less stressful and optimistic climb to more success with projects to sell to purchasing entities.

"What of time?" asked one of the seven, Ann, as she finished the latter half of a large cup of cooled coffee. There were seven science students: Ann, Nolan, Al, Lucy, Max, Cith, and Pat. The former nurse was Al. The scientists varied in ages ranging from twenty-three to twenty-nine. Pat looked like a woman, was really a dominant man. People commonly found his name fitting. Pat said, "What do you mean, 'What of time?' Are you purposely trying to blow my mind this morning?"

"No," said Ann. "What are you talking about?" asked Nolan. "I spoke with her earlier," said Max, "To her, simple or complex ideas that no one has ever fathomed are easy and already there." "I will take that as a complement to my intelligence," said Ann. "What are you guys talking about?" asked Lucy, "Am I the only one who has not endured the possible ideas presented along with a question like 'What of time?' to a group of scientists this morning?"

"No," said Cith, "Those guys went to get coffee together on the way here. Supposedly, Ann already *blew their mind,* today." "Do not look at me," said Al, "I am waiting to hear what she has to say again." Al had driven Ann and Max to get coffee on the way to the lab that morning. The *lab* was a whole floor of an old rundown building the seven people paid for collectively once a month. They used the lab to conduct experiments and figure ways to request government funding for scientific advancement projects.

Their lab had running water, a marble waste-high counter with a sink, plenty of glassware for chemicals, and a shower. Space and found results dictated the time the scientists kept their physics research machines and equipment before disposing of used material. As a collective team and a guild, they normally sat around their large oval table on a couch. The couch was a comfortably spacious white leather couch with three sections. They met once a morning at 9 AM, Monday through Friday, and took seven holidays off annually. The team read, took notes, gave each other ideas, and presented information. Information sources included libraries, schools, and the web. They decided on projects and worked to complete them before goal times and requests of their purchasing companies.

Having all walked in the door just moments before 9 AM, they started talking long before they sat down to think. This was largely due to Ann - it was usually against their unwritten rules to speak with each other about professional ideas without the other scientists present. There were reasons for this rule. Everyone wanted to be included in any conversation, and their ideas were more profound when they thought about science as a team. This time, Ann simply could not wait to share her idea. She would not risk forgetting such an obviously worthwhile possibility.

"Well Ann, what is your *idea?*" asked Lucy. Ann's answer in regards to her space station time machine idea was as follows:

The government usually denies our funds for one reason - our nation is in a great deal of debt to China. Scientific principles that promote or define fact are not always easily proven on paper. Funds support our ways of testing material and its moving reactions. As economists, we do not really know enough about borrowing and spending nationally to be able to recommend economic policy to presidential programs in the past - we will. With proper spending on science, this nation would have never been in debt. Airplanes and computers make our government money, so can other concepts originating from scientific research. As scientists, however, we can easily make a time machine. We could travel back in time and present a profound economics proposal for government investing. We will use a more financially stable government to subsidize our actual efforts as far as the team is concerned. What are we after? We all have our individual interests. As a group, we have learned what we could be further interested in, yet we are too poor to fund these endeavors. Al's rocket-ship robot-toy idea utilizing a simple walking robot to collect matter for study from the surface of other planets is one example. How hard can it be? Even better, Max's dream of floating magnetic cars safely traveling in packs over one hundred miles an hour can be a reality. We could not even get certain known ideas funded through our actual *government contract mother company*. What would the chances have ever been for our really interesting and expensive ideas? These projects are able to promote the research of abstract phenomenon and worthwhile complexities. I ask, 'What do we need?' I answer this question with the name of a money-enabling project: *Zoom Ring*. What we need is a large donut-like space station with a vehicle inside that can travel extremely fast due to magnetic force and anti-gravity. The vehicle's rate of travel could cause a change in time, as defined in my recent studies in abstract physics and particle collision theory. I will prove and define the usefulness of my 'C. A. C.' concept. Some space stations that have been designed and either used or not in secrecy have highly resembled a donut, a bottle, or other common container. Even the fake space stations we see in movies are interesting and close to possible ideas. Solar panels more powerful than the panels currently used for real space stations will be necessary for the outer shell of Zoom Ring. Small reflective mirrors will allow for a newer, more powerful kind of solar panel. We will need a great deal of electricity for the magnets. A hollow donut design with a central circular tube has its architectural benefits. For us, however, we will need what I thought of as a 'time ring' inside of our cliché space donut. The time ring will have its *vehicle* inside its magnetic ring. The enclosed vehicle should resemble an aerodynamic cylinder. Zoom Ring will contain waste-height counters and research boxes for anti and controlled gravitational studies all around its lower walkway. Its walkway will be directly below the inner vehicle's magnet tube. We can use this *gravity-void*, magnetic floating vehicle to attain the necessary speed required to defy time as the laws of physics tell us we can do. Once we have traveled fast enough inside of Zoom Ring, we will travel forward or backwards into time. We can present our government proposals to politicians or their assistants to attain research money necessary for our endeavors. My dreams and our efforts can be a newfound form of fact. We knowingly think alike in the realm of scientific discovery from time to time. We can use time travel to further science, to satisfy our intellectual needs. We will use technology to provide for a better life on planet Earth.

"I believe it is possible, and my mind is blown," said Pat, "Just when I thought it was going to be blown due to a new discovery or the *now known unknown*, I realize my mind is actually blown from the whole idea that in the history of our world no scientist or team has ever done this before. Having studied the written proofs of all of the researchers in history, one could say that no one person or team of scientists has ever successfully proven time travel in any way, shape, or form before."

"I hear you," said Max, "It is like I already knew about it. I just do not have evidence of the idea to be a fact. Ann encouraged me to think of it instead of other things, however. I think it is possible. A powerful magnetic floating monorail-car in a ring out in the vast area of space **cannot** be that terribly impossible. Thank you for your thoughts, Ann." "My pleasure," said Ann, trying to consider why Russia or China had not proven time travel. The *space travelers* made it to the moon, and Ann could not really figure why governments had not built a space station out there for time traveling. "Government in America contradicts itself sometimes, and things do not really get done as they could," reasoned Ann.

Cith looked at her watch. "It is exactly 10 AM," she said, "We will need a blueprint for Zoom Ring and its physics proofs as soon as possible. One thing, though. What, may I ask, is 'C. A. C.'?" " 'C. A. C.' stands for 'Controlled Active Collision'," said Ann, "It is an idea I was considering while studying particle bombardment and collision as opposed to atom splitting. Controlling specific molecules and how, or timing when and with what known or decided rate of speed, can possibly provide for new forms of energy and new substances. Particle bombardment theories are often used and proven - we do not really use much unseen force for controlling bombardment currently, however." "Oh," said Cith.

"I think the idea of Zoom Ring is dreamy and tempting. Time travel has always been a phenomenon scientists have chased with no known proven results," said Al, "I think we can do it, nonetheless. You seem deep in thought,

Lucy; do you think Zoom Ring is a good direction for the endeavors of this team?" Lucy said, "This team has been bouncing from one attempt of approving one rehashed scientific idea to another. Zoom Ring is a very powerful and expensive ordeal. We live in a real world, and a project of its magnitude will change the life of anything on the planet upon its success. The few small projects that may bring us in money to survive can still be completed. I think we should put forth ninety percent of our scientific efforts into the construction of Zoom Ring."

"I am absolutely excited about this project," said Nolan, "It includes physics, electricity, space, and time travel. We will have trouble with the funding; the design, construction, and physics proofs will be of no *overly exciting* task. Once completed, we will need to be careful with whom we talk with and what we say. We will change the world to provide for a better chance with wanting to live life. Does anyone here have any problem with us, as a team of seven, going through with project Zoom Ring?" Max looked around to the other scientists and said, "No."

They all nodded in approval, and silence came due to their thinking. Pat re-introduced vibrations into conversation by saying, "I know how we can keep part of our efforts secret. The vehicle at lower speeds can contain chemical concoctions - Zoom Ring can be an anti-gravity centrifuge of unique size. It will not need to be **only** a time machine. This way, mentioning time travel to investors or the government is not immediately necessary. Anti-gravity research for new substances and medicines will also be conducted on shelves outside of the vehicle's magnetic tube. Study tables and boxes will be included all around the lower walkway below the central tube. Not mentioning time travel may be a good idea for our actual efforts. Our inability to gain adequate funds will no longer exist."

Cith said, "I agree with Pat. We all know anti-gravity research is currently conducted in space stations; they are not only used for movie-bound Utopian dream ideas. I think we should draw out Zoom Ring and go get blueprints."

With those things said, Zoom Ring's idea was born. The team drew out an impressive donut-like space station, leaving a forth of the ring sectioned to see the various interior aspects of the massive centrifuge/time machine. The inside included all they mentioned and more. The space station's setup was simple enough. Zoom Ring contained a vehicle large enough for eight people; programmable magnets around the vehicle's outer tube and a lower walkway; widened waste-high research shelves and see-through box-like enclosures; capacitors to store energy from the solar panels and an external access; and an operations panel for overseeing the vehicle's speed and controlling the other inner functions of Zoom Ring.

Max said, "We should go to the hobby store. A real blueprint is fine, however a nicely constructed toy-like model will increase our chances of success with an investor." "I agree," said Ann. All seven scientists were always excited to go to the hobby store. They usually went there as a group or with a *nominated* individual bringing a list. They did not often go their alone, because art products were expensive to them. They also purchased their laboratory equipment together. If any one scientist had a good enough idea, the team agreed on it.

The team of seven refined their paper sketch and put their physics proofs on hold. They went to the hobby store as well as a specialty store open for the sell of custom plastic models. Manufacturers often bought plastics from the specialty company for cars and planes.

They brought their design to an architecture contracting company, and an engineer promised to have a real blueprint drawn out by the end of the week. Once back at the lab, they ordered pizza and 2-liter cokes. The scientists finished the construction of the plastic model as well as their physics theories. Their theories included the weight of the vehicle with eight people; the strength of the magnets; and the actual speed of the capsule's travel to provide for time travel.

It was late by the time the team came to a good stopping point. They went home, slept, and returned in the morning full of excitement. "Who are we going to tell sell this to?" asked Nolan, "I think we should ask BLAST to fund its making." *BLAST* was the only current direct government entity able to fund space travel, galaxy research, and satellite traffic. The acronym stood for beings, laboratories, and space travel. "That is an obvious and reasonable first attempt," said Max. "I will call and make an appointment," said Lucy. "One of us should go alone to ask for money," said Cith. "Okay," said Ann. "I will go," said Pat. "Okay," said three of the seven. The team did not like to argue. They enjoyed efficiency.

Pat scheduled an appointment with BLAST for 9 AM Tuesday morning the next week. He made an impressive and professional appearance and presentation of project Zoom Ring. BLAST's investment team admitted to being impressed with the project. They would need time to decide and would get back with the team. BLAST got back with them towards the end of the week and said that the funding would not be possible.

These things taken into consideration, the team decided to endure other ideas to fund Zoom Ring's construction. They continued with their ongoing projects; Al and Max both had an idea ready to present for patent by the end of the week. Monday came and all researchers made it to the lab for conversation before 9 AM.

"What now?" asked Ann. "BLAST would have been too easy," said Lucy, "We are going to have to find another entity to fund our endeavors concerning Zoom Ring." "My thoughts exactly," said Al, "We all know how many are out there." "Sure, sure," said Max, "And as always, we just need the money for parts and labor." "Of the investors out there, we may better our chances with a pharmaceuticals company. An anti-gravity centrifuge would have to be important to them for making new medicines," said Nolan.

"That is actually a profound idea," said Pat, "Though BLAST decided not to back Zoom Ring, a medicine company will want the technology for research. Also remember that if it takes Zoom Ring to discover a better medicine, Zoom Ring will be needed for its continued manufacture." "That is a pretty good point," said Cith, "We can somehow benefit financially from its use after the construction is complete." "What if it works?" asked Ann. "We will then time travel," said Al, and all seven scientists went deep into thought.

While all of these things were being thought about, Max decided to look up pharmaceutical companies on his phone. "One of the top ten largest manufacturers of medicine in the country is in Cooksville," said Max. Cooksville was a neighboring city. "I forgot about that," said Lucy, "Can I go this time?" "I do not see why not," said Pat, "I have the project ready to be presented again. I hope the best for you." Lucy was excited, because she wanted to go.

Max scheduled an appointment for Lucy on Thursday of the same week with the medicine manufacturer. Armco was the name of the large medicine company she was going to speak with. Time went by. Cith and Lucy partook in a mock interview on Wednesday, and they had a nice time. While the other scientists were continuing their work, Lucy was sure to find success.

Thursday morning came and she did so. Armco backed the project entirely, including a sciences construction firm for specialized space materials. Unknown to Lucy, Armco was already conducting competitive anti-gravity research with above ground chambers. The expansion would be necessary to become the new world leader in medicine sales. The team would receive a percentage of sales upon the completion of the project for their own research, and the representatives of Armco were impressed with Zoom Ring. Armco's scientists were intrigued with the idea of an anti-gravity centrifuge - they did not speak of or even notice the possibility of time travel. Armco also agreed to allow access to Zoom Ring for particle collision studies conducted by the team. "This way," thought Lucy, "The seven of us can time travel."

Things went well, and Armco stayed in communication with the seven scientists for weeks. Armco used a subcontractor for getting Zoom Ring's newly designed materials into outer space with private space shuttles. Astronauts constructed the space station in its entirety. Astronauts assembled the beautiful donut-like structure far away from planet Earth, past the moon. Armco obtained funding from the government in order for Zoom Ring to operate constantly. Its solar panels took close to seven days to charge its storage capacitors and batteries.

Zoom Ring being complete, it was up and running perfectly. Scientists from Armco journeyed to Zoom Ring for medicinal research. The team scheduled a trip for travel into outer space. "Oh what fun we will have!" thought Al.

The seven were happily thrilled to travel into outer space, regardless of their notion of time travel. During the weeks Armco spent constructing

Zoom Ring, the team of seven researched politicians and documented government decisions. Armco patented 237 new medicinal substance combinations and manufactured four newly designed prescription medications for sale. Doctors would make new medicines for a wide variety of purposes ranging from heart medicine to psychiatry.

Armco's investment in Zoom Ring was sure to pay off, and the team received 1.2% of Armco's profits coming from Zoom Ring. The team was well on their way to finding success with their original thinking. Ann had the time to put together a wonderful particle bombardment experiment; she planned to send her results to a private physics research firm for analysis.

The seven traveled to Zoom Ring as scheduled. Astronauts constructed the space station from the scientists' original design so physics proofs could still hold true for time travel. Getting to and from Zoom Ring alone was a lot of fun. Scientists and psychiatrists from Armco utilized miniature shuttles with extremely highly volatile rocket fuel. The shuttles resembled Zoom Ring's inner vehicle and sat up to eight people.

It was the day before the team's first scheduled departure. The scientists made it to the lab before 9 AM. Al had something to get off his chest and decided to begin conversation immediately. He said, "I know we are all excited about going to Zoom Ring tomorrow. It is the most amazing contribution to science we have ever known of. I just want us as a group to consider the drawbacks of time travel. We know of its benefits. That is why we needed it in the first place. We wanted to go back in time and restructure the government's economic future with a well drawn out investment and borrowing proposal. Can someone give me at least one single drawback?"

"I cannot think of one," said Ann, after the group was silent for some time. "I do not think we are doing anything wrong," said Lucy. "I cannot figure a flaw," said Max. "I think Al is right," said Nolan, "There are consequences for playing with nature. Anytime something changes nature, results are displayed. We are after a good result, however, and I do not think we have anything to worry about." "I agree with Nolan," said Cith, "Pat?" "I want to go back in time," said Pat, "This ethics discussion is not even necessary. If there are consequences for these risks we are going to take, we will face them when they come."

The scientists did their work for the day and went to bed early that night. The seven people had accomplished various arduous tasks. Cith and Pat helped Ann with her particle project. Al, Max, and Lucy did most of the work on the economics proposal. The team planned to travel to November of 1999 and present the proposal to a young senator.

All went well. The team used one of Armco's mini-shuttles to get to Zoom Ring and dock. "Earth is so far away," said Max, as he saw planet Earth upon entering Zoom Ring. The space station was huge and built to design perfectly. The walkway was wide enough for four average-sized people to walk abreast. Its circumference totaled five hundred meters. Any one of the scientists could jog the entire walkway one time without too much of an impossible dilemma.

The team toured the space station's various study chambers admiring various species of medicinal plants and small experimental projects. Pat found an experiment with living effervescent algae. The algae appeared to be glowing puddles of *neon jelly* to him. As they new, six of the scientists could enter the inner vehicle. One scientist would have to stay out to operate the control panel. "Who stays for the panel?" asked Max.

"I have the proposal," said Al. "I want to travel," said Nolan. "I will stay," said Ann. They agreed and all went well. Ann operated the panel. It was an exact replica of the model. She set the controls to show November 12, 1999. The other six scientists entered the inner vehicle. Cith carried Ann's particle bombardment cylinder. The scientists designed the vehicle in such a way to buckle large drums to its interior for centrifugal actions. The scientists buckled themselves to the vehicle under the dim rays of medicine-safe lighting.

Ann sent the date command to the vehicle from the panel via pressing a large rectangular button. The floating vehicle moved slowly through its surrounding magnet tube one full loop to prove it void of malfunction. The vehicle then increased in speed gradually. It went faster and faster. The vehicle achieved precise speed, and the entire space station flashed in a gigantic sphere of white light.

Eventually, the vehicle slowed gradually and came to a safe halt. The six travelers terrified Ann as they came down the walkway. She had not expected the enormous flash. At first, Ann did not know who or what her companions were. The scientists were fine. She turned to them and said, "I think it worked…" Ann checked the screen on the control panel and it said, "November 12, 1999, 12:00 AM." "It worked!" said Ann, and the six made it back to her. "How was it?" she asked. "It was amazingly fun," said Lucy, and the others agreed.

The team entered the mini-shuttle and traveled back to Earth. Al found the young senator and handed him a folder with their economics proposal. The senator passed it on to appropriate politicians, and the government's economy changed for the better. After delivering the proposal, the team returned to Zoom Ring to travel back to their previous time. They made it; it was as if nothing had ever happened. Ann was happy that it worked. Upon the scientists' return, politicians in the news reported a healthy economy. All was well.

It was 9 AM the next day. "Well, we should not have too much of a problem backing our research, now," said Max. "No," said Al, "I am going to design a new enzyme that consumes black mold." "Wow," said Nolan. "I think we should do something fun with it," said Cith. "That sounds dangerous," said Ann, speaking up. "What if we bring a famous scientist back in time?" asked Pat, "Would not that be fun? We could meet someone from a textbook."

"I do not see a problem with that," said Lucy, "Who would we bring?" "I have it!" said Al, "Einstein! He said before he died that his proofs were incomplete, that he still had more work to do." "That is a pretty good idea," said Max. "Sure it is," said Cith. Most of the team forgot that she had at one time had sexual fantasies of Einstein.

With these things in mind, the team was motivated to pursue the fun side of scientific exploration. They found all sorts of information on Einstein and his life. They even read about how The United States got him from Germany. They rehashed what they knew of concerning his atom bomb studies and research, and the team found his near whereabouts five years prior to his death.

The scientists traveled and found him. They gave him an information packet along with a biography they quickly composed for him. Einstein was impressed. They let him know about his unfinished work - that he currently had five years to live. The team gave him some of their physics proofs and theorems. They let him gather information he thought he wanted to bring along, and they brought the man back into his youth with his theorems.

Einstein accomplished a vast amount of work, and he humbly asked to travel nine more times. He conducted an approximate total of eight hundred and seventy-two years of research alone to complete his physics theories. He finished them and wrote a six hundred-page book titled, "Comprehensive Physics".

The team was fine and had made enough research money to last them all a lifetime. The scientists used Zoom Ring for time travel eleven times. They did not plan to travel in time any more. Armco's research was healing people worldwide; the company cured various forms of cancer. The seven scientists all possessed exciting and new project ideas. Having become wealthy did not end their research.

Cith was not happy, though. The other scientists were satisfied, and she was not. Cith wanted more. Was conducting research with six other intelligible people on a spacious floor good enough for her? "No," thought Cith, "I want more money. I want a really nice house and private purchasing power. I want endless means." For an avid researcher given to the science of knowledge, Cith had sure become dangerously greedy. At first, she thought it would be impossible.

"How can I travel alone?" Cith asked herself in thought. Weeks went by and she thought about it. An easy answer came to her. She would use Max's robot idea for her own means. "I will make an artificially intelligent robot of my own," thought Cith to herself, "He will be able to operate the control panel, and I can go back in time."

She did it, as far as the robot was concerned. Cith lived about five minutes away from the lab. She built her robot next to her own television. He used an 8-bit operating system much like an older computer. His legs could extend to give him enough height to access the control panel. She built him from research material thrown out of the lab.

Cith's robot seemed to function properly. She named it Panel. She figured out a plan to get him to Zoom Ring. Cith tested various sequences with the robot, and he seemed to be flawless. Panel operated on assembly code. Cith thought of assembly as a computer language that was sometimes hard for humans to predict. Once she traveled back into time, Cith would start an investment firm. The firm would only invest in new companies known of by her to have become financially dominant in her current time. This way, Cith would become a powerful billionaire.

Her planning went fine. She secretly got along well with the other scientists for weeks. She stole a mini-shuttle from Armco one night and flew herself and Panel to Zoom Ring. They docked properly and went inside. Cith gave him a command sequence in order to send her back to January 1, 1982. She entered the vehicle, and Panel operated the control panel. He functioned properly at first, setting up the proper date and readying the vehicle. He set the speed improperly, however, and pressed the large rectangular button.

The vehicle in Zoom Ring could travel even faster than needed in order to defy time. Panel had not given the vehicle a maximum speed to obtain - the vehicle would increase in speed indefinitely. The vehicle traveled at speeds too fast. Cith's physical body burst into a gelatinous bloody mist and was then vaporized entirely. Zoom Ring caused an implosion in space. The entire space station compressed to less than nothing causing a magnetic pull lasting for close to half of a year.

Of course, it would take no team of rocket scientists to figure out what had happened. The other six scientists found Cith's investment and robot plans. The government set aside a booth in the Smithsonian titled "Zoom Ring" with a detailed account of its entire story. The information included possible attempts with time travel and information on the physics behind implosion theories. The six scientists continued their work, and they eventually became physics professors, keeping their efforts in the furthering of science. Short Cith's tragedy, all lived happily ever after.

♦

Epilogue

The purpose of this epilogue is to include some information about the stories in "A Collection of Tales". Each story was inspired from various ideas. This epilogue contains information about what I as the author hope you found to be entertaining. The book is entirely fiction and does not allude to actual people, places, or events, directly. As far as genres go, I have tried to stay mostly with horror, action, some romance, some fantasy and science fiction, and all around good stories. I hope you enjoy the following sentences; I enjoyed writing them.

"A Chess Game in the Park" is a story which vaguely alludes to my grandfather who taught me how to play chess before he passed. I knew him when I was a boy. He fell and harmed his head before he died. He endured no gunshot wound in real life. He lived for some time bedridden. Many of these stories are far more personal than the stories and books I plan to do in the future. The next works I plan to present are more for you as an audience I plan to please. I am sure that I will enjoy these next works, too. I have no actual knowledge of explosives - they worked fine in our first story.

"A Girl Named Nightingale" is a story I wrote for an unnamed co-worker of mine. I wrote a few of these stories in such a manner. My goal was a set of stories for a book; I shared some with people along the way. I shared this story and "The King and the Dancer" with the same person. The two stories have their similarities, as you may have noticed. Death definitely occurs in "A Girl Named Nightingale". The story uses a prehistoric setting raising questions regarding costly methods of untold barbaric survival; how could we now know of the things of those plentiful or trying times?

"A Night on the Floor" is one of my favorite stories. It was the first one I wrote when I decided to write a bunch of stories for a book. It is from a time when I stayed the night with a young friend of mine as a young boy. I did not sleep well that night, and there was a grandfather clock. No one died then, however, and I did not see ghosts.

"Beautiful Amy" was also a rather personal story. I have learned that holding resentments can be an unhealthy practice. This story definitely displays a character who holds a resentment and attempts getting away with a terrible decision. The story ends without her getting caught. In real life, this would probably not be the case.

I wrote "Chemorphosis" for various reasons. I did not intend on advertising costly sex changes with this story. I wrote it mostly for humor and the notion that bio-chemical science is a very powerful and real form of fact. The idea that we have a spirit as humans goes unmentioned in the story. The notion that we are chemical reactions is indicated, however. The story was an idea from the Russian author, Franz Kafka. His book, "Metamorphosis", was supposedly published by his family against his will after he died. It was about people changing into insects. I hope you enjoyed "Chemorphosis", as well as other tales, with minimal thoughts of their author.

"Catfish Lake" was a story I did for a co-employee and myself. A hostess, she had spent part of her childhood fishing on a lake with her family. I love to fish and hunt. I did include some gore with this one - the decapitation of a big fish. This story also reminded me of hurricanes.

"Forest Hollow" is a story that I can almost live in. I attended college about five hours away from loved ones, so I drove through the woods routinely. Many rural farm routes have old cemeteries. I never flew around with dancing spirits in real life. I often revised the story while I listened to horror music from movies or classical piano music.

"Glock Funk" was a story I wrote for a server co-employee of mine. She enjoyed it, and I re-wrote it over three times. I purposely included some element of suspense. I made sure no one was shot; I enjoyed letting the good people win. I also enjoyed the main character's career-oriented success.

"Hubba's Joyous Journey" was a fun story I did for yet another co-employee of mine. I meant for the story to be fun and entertaining. It includes a scary room with animals mounted as trophies. It also includes young men surviving before large corporations hire them. The main character blows away a large crocodile in defense. The man I wrote the story for claimed to enjoy it. The same man was the inspiration behind Mr. Panda in "The Circus Freaks".

"Lady-geddon" was a story I wrote for a writing competition. It was not selected for publication by the contest's judges. The narrative includes conspiracy to commit murder for limited financial gain and the destruction of evidence. It also mentions the bad people getting away. These ideas were for entertainment only. I liked that the women read novels and stuck together. The word "lady" was a difficult decision for me to use, because it can be a reference to narcotics, from what I read.

"Orc Escape" was a delightful first attempt with the fantasy genre. I wanted to write a story with orcs. Fantasy fiction largely leaves orcs out of its stories. Other beings such as elves, wizards, dwarves, dragons, and fairies are more common. A book I plan to write will include most *fantasy beings* we as readers of fantasy fiction know of. I may include beings unknown of so far, too. I like the idea of "Orc Escape", because it presents a setting where creatures avoid a terribly dangerous and gory war. The orcs find a plentiful, safe, and wonderful existence out in nature. They also never slay or eat a human.

"Steam" was a story I wrote while I was a restaurant employee, as were most of these stories. I shared Steam with two people who gave me a job, as well as a few other people. It is a fun and harmless story in my opinion; I hope you enjoyed it. I did.

"Sports Class" was a story I almost did not include. It was an idea I had that raised notions of what people of differing sexual preferences think. It was not a test of my own personal sexuality, nor was it in anyway an attempt to deviate from my beliefs.

"Take Me Out to the Ballgame" was a rather disturbing story I am telling for a second time, in some manner. I first told the story as a speech thinking it was a rather creative idea. It raises questions regarding attention, selfishness, and dedication. The father was dedicated to his family by working hard. He did not purposely miss bringing his son to the amazing stadium. The insane boy who committed suicide could have been a little less selfish; he might have lived. With some thought, one might ascertain that the mother took her son's life. This cannot be possible, because I clearly state that he took his own. I found the tale to be entertaining. I thought of music while composing it. The story certainly had a horrific ending. I looked up the old song the title reminds us of, and it is an interesting piece of history.

"The Bistro" and its second story were both ideas thought of by me as stories that could inspire television shows about the mob. What do we know outside of what we see in the movies? We probably know a minimal amount of information. These two stories were inspired largely from an unnamed series of shows with a mob boss as the central character, as well as a row of real buildings I once saw. One day, as I traveled passed those old businesses, I thought to myself, "If I had the money and the time, I could put a unique restaurant there."

"The Biker Gang Story" was a story I wrote for a person who gave me a job. She was running a restaurant with patrons of all natures. Many of those customers were bikers that lived nearby or that loved to ride. The ladder group came from all over The United States. Interesting enough, I got online to find some of the jargon used in the story. The leader of the Death Eagles was inspired by a manager of mine, and the individual I wrote the story for inspired the daughter he goes to save from the rival biker gang. I hope you enjoyed reading it as much as I enjoyed putting it together.

"The Bistro Part Two, The Ground Floor" was a story put together largely because of my being impressed with its preliminary counterpart. Hemingway's famous story "A Clean and Well Lighted Place" was an inspiration to "The Bistro, Part One", because it begins and ends much like a synopsis. A clearly evident climax is not in the tale, but some readers with vivid imaginations may enjoy the bistro stories more than others.

The second bistro story can seem to be more entertaining than the first - the restaurant owners find a bunch of dead gangsters from long ago. They evade the law and handle things as if it would have been better to do so in such a manner. I wrote these two stories with the idea that they could inspire more stories with the same settings and ideas, one day. I may or may not be more interested in other ideas. I was unaware of how much time an author can spend presenting ideas. A person can never have the time to cover the topics out there during their life.

"The Circus Freaks" is a fun and hopeful attempt to present a story full of action. It was inspired and written for a manager of mine whom I hoped could somehow identify with Mr. "S". The other four characters who rode in the brown van were also inspired by real people, one of those being myself. As intriguing as that sounds, the real people are actually law-abiding citizens that would never risk prison-time for crime. I found the story to be enjoyable; I liked how they achieved their goal of helping someone live.

"The Duck Hunt" is a story that means a lot to me. A boy and his grandfather go duck hunting and come back with a goose. It was fun to do and meant to be a sort of harmless story for the enjoyment of all. My grandfather in real life on one side of my family, as previously mentioned, was a duck hunter and involved with waterfowl conservation.

"Time for Tea" was about the third story I wrote for the collection; I wrote it while I was still unaware of the number of words one can easily put on paper with adequate and costly time. I worked for a restaurant for about a year that sold Japanese steaks; a buddy of mine was highly skilled with sushi and sashimi. This restaurant was a lot of fun. It inspired one of my favorite stories "The Masago Monsters".

I actually wrote "Time for Tea" for a server, however. He was always on time and polite to me when he really had no reason for it. I hope he enjoyed the story. He was the inspiration behind the server in the story who brought the women escargot soup. I imagine a soup of that nature would be a healthy treat. I hunger for a well-concocted broth as I think of it.

"The Giraffe" was a highly personal story I wrote that is the closest thing to factional writing I have in this book. I once went to a zoo with some close relatives; we did not buy peanuts. The giraffes really did look sad, and I really did not figure out why until over ten years later.

"The King and the Dancer" was a story I did for a female acquaintance of mine that deserved more than I could have ever given. No person could ever deserve her company. I highly respected her, and others I knew shared my opinion and loved her, too. We all wanted what she did. She was that magnificent. This story and the previously spoken of "A Girl Named Nightingale" were both stories that I shared with her before she moved away. One thing I can mention about "The King and The Dancer" is that it ties real places in the world with ideas that never occurred. As a youngster, Tolkien's Middle Earth sometimes seemed to be a possible reality to me. I had notions of this nature in mind whenever I mentioned both Spain and a possible theory of the ridiculous notion that there ever was such a character as the real Grim Reaper.

"The Masago Monsters" was a story I did for my sushi chef friend. He has since moved, though he may read it one day. I highly enjoyed the idea of the small muscular people running around and playing their version of Hide-and-Go-Seek. Sticky rice can be fun for all ages. The surprise of the bus crashing through the front door was the climax of the tale. The small characters have brilliant colors to enhance audience pleasure.

"The Man Those Guys are Good Story" was a story I did for a couple of co-employees. They inspired the two officers in the story. The story included minor references or ideas that came from the two movies "Dumb and Dumber" and "Seven". The chief of the police department in the story was inspired from the chief in "Seven". "The Wet Bandits" from the Christmas movie "Home Alone" inspired the petty crime ideas behind the wooden coins. I like to read this story. To me, it is like a Christmas movie. I wrote it during the holiday season of 2012.

"The Optometrist" was inspired by a near terrible childhood occurrence of mine and a relative involving a pencil. No one was actually injured. The idea that someone I loved dearly came close to harm caused me to write the story. The worst-case scenario from real life led to ideas. I put them on paper, and I liked the big truck. I also included someone that was not a doctor who performed a medical feat. I suppose that not everyone becomes a doctor. Many people have thought of it.

"The Portal" involves a doctor. The story was inspired from a time when I saw a doctor in an emergency room. He saved a man after the man was shot five times. One bullet missed his main aorta by one-half of an inch. The gunshot victim would have died if the bullet hit his main aorta. I was there out of ignorance with a small injury. I almost submitted this story to a science fiction writing contest and did not. The car was inspired from a real doctor's car in Houston, TX. The real car was a very impressive vehicle which resembled a miniature Lamborghini. A close relative inspired the dialogue from the mob boss in the story.

"The Poppet Box" was a fun story inspired from my making small dolls out of candy. I used my own, self-taught candy recipes for amateur stop animation I uploaded to the web for the original notion of using *modeling candy* for animation instead of clay. Over five hundred years ago, young women called their magical puppets "poppets," and I used some of their magical history in this story. I also left this story on my blog for a while to have a reason for having a blog. I enjoyed the story; the girl reminds me of the young girl in "The Train" - smart and secretly forced to make decisions.

"The Representative" was a story I wrote as I considered comparing Christianity to anything besides it. Who could ever be tempted to justify the temptation to consider any religion that disagrees with our Creator? Who knows? I think the story can help those with faith keep it.

"The Roller Coaster" had nothing at all to do with a recent movie I never saw. It was for a couple of *lovebirds*. They liked the story. I included two famous people my co-employees I wrote the story for mentioned. They both enjoyed the story – I hope they read and enjoy the entire collection. As far as the song goes, it was inspired from songs by the bands "Slayer" and "Static-X".

"The Train" was a story that I actually submitted to "The New Yorker". It was not published then; it is now in my first book. The actual story is exactly 8,000 words including the story within the story and its title. I liked that the tale includes a story. A company named "Train" makes huge air conditioners. The beautiful co-employee I wrote the story for inspired the story when she mentioned her air conditioner going out next to her trailer. The nice train in the story was a dream I had while awake; I could only imagine how much it would cost to construct. Someone I knew little of inspired the sinister character towards the front of the train.

Many films that included a road trip inspired "The Wizard Ship". I purposely included both science fiction and fantasy genres when writing this story. I shared the story with a co-employee who seemed to enjoy the preliminary draft. In his draft, I named the elves One through Five to write the story in a more efficient amount of time. The same real person who I thought up Mr. Polka dots from inspired the leader elf. Of course, the wizard's name was inspired humorously from Tolkien's more serious wizard Gandalf. I did not have the time to go hit golf balls as I wrote the book, however I briefly described Gongolfen's staff to resemble a golf club. By doing so I dared to include something from our real world in a fantasy tale.

I wrote "The Zombie Scarabs" for the same person I thought up Mr. "S" for. Beetles actually do possess behaviors, as animals think. The person with the dark green trench coat was inspired from the same sinister man in "The Train", as well as "The Man in the Green Hat", from an old Warner Brothers cartoon with Daffy Duck involving a train ride and poison. The college campus in the story was inspired from a college I once attended. I highly enjoyed imagining the winter as well as the small glowing beetles. The zombie idea itself came partially from a popular show on cable television, "The Walking Dead" on A. M. C.; the story did not actually include post apocalyptic settings. I liked the idea that complete extermination did not happen to the scarabs. They were still alive, and there was also an unharmed test tube.

"U. F. O. Granny" was inspired from life as a post-eighteen year-old man seeking a career. The gruesome dialogue towards the end was from a joke I heard years ago that I never forgot. The property owner reminds me of the Matilda character in "The Train", except she is a good person in "U. F. O. Granny". Moon reminds me of more than one real person.

"Zoom Ring" is the last story I finished for the collection. I purposely wrote it for the last story of this book. I wrote it with thoughts of science fiction in mind, and I wanted to include a seemingly justifiable dramatic occurrence close to the end of the book. This way, we as the reading audience have no gruesome thoughts from the second-to-last story. We can wonder what one could see or remember in the real Smithsonian; we can wonder if it is that hard to travel in time after all.

I chose the character names in "Zoom Ring" at random and purposely used mostly shorter names. "Cith" was one of the names in the set that I invented. I mainly made the name from the word "suicide". The letters "c" and "i" being used from the word and "t" and "h" being used from the more common proper noun "Beth". The tragedy that occurs to Cith is not actually a suicide, however the accident is fatal and so seemed to compare.

Thank you for your time and reading my first set of stories. To the few people I wrote the stories amongst, thank you for enduring the time we have spent together working so far. This is the first book I have published. I plan to write a few novels, too. The stories I mention within the stories in this collection were unwritten when I composed this epilogue. I may write them while I write a few novels. I hope you have enjoyed these pages, as I hope you will enjoy my writings in the future even more.

♦♦

The End.

Made in the USA
Charleston, SC
05 September 2014